PRAISE FO…

"[Ash Tuesday] *is a love letter to New Orleans while also being a tale of loss—which, when it comes down to it, is part of what we love about New Orleans, right? We are able to lose ourselves in the city's stories, divorce from the parts of ourselves that no longer fit, become new selves and parade them down the street on Mardi Gras. This novel is a rich tapestry of stories; you'll fall in love again with this special, haunted city.*"

–Becca Ballenger

"*In the eyes of the straight world, the characters in Ariadne Blayde's* Ash Tuesday *are misfits, even freaks. Modern-day witches. Drunk wannabe writers. Tantric vampires. But in this extraordinary first novel, Blayde peels away the flashy exteriors to reveal the fragile workings within that make each character deeply human and endlessly fascinating. This is a novel to savor and a new writer to watch.*"

–Michael Bourne, author of *Blithedale Canyon*

"*Ariadne Blayde's characters jump off the page, as vibrant and imperfect as the city they live in. Through the tales each guide tells on their tour, we find a piece of them that connects to New Orleans, and in turn we find pieces of ourselves. It's a difficult task to capture the joys of festivity existing simultaneously alongside such deep mental, emotional, and spiritual pain, but Blayde does it with finesse, each chapter reading like another bittersweet line in a doomed love letter.*"

–Linnea Gregg

"*A darkly joyful ride, Ariadne Blayde's* Ash Tuesday *is a wonderful debut from a bright new voice. Blayde's prose is lyrical and addictive, brimming with heart and soul.*"

–Louis Maistros, author of *The Sound of Building Coffins*

"[Ash Tuesday] *explores the full range of human experience from the light-hearted to the gut-wrenching. Sometimes you will laugh out loud, and sometimes you will get teary-eyed....[the book] also offers a close-up, insider's view of New Orleans that makes you feel much more connected to the city and its culture and history.... [Blayde] seamlessly weaves together folklore, history, and compelling characters.*"

–Denise Baker

"A supremely engaging character-driven ensemble drama with the great city of New Orleans in a starring role. Blayde's writing, sublimely textured dialogue, and character development feel like a warm hug.... These characters are all so real, you feel very much like you've already met them. Easy five stars!"

–Ian Hoch

ASH TUESDAY

by Ariadne Blayde

edited by Lance Umenhofer
design and illustration by Alethea Hall

APRIL GLOAMING

This book is a work of fiction. Names, characters, places, and incidents are the product of the author's imagination or are used fictitiously. Any resemblance of actual events, locales, or persons, living or dead, is coincidental.

-First Edition

Publisher's Cataloguing-in-Publication Data

Blayde, Ariadne
Ash tuesday / written by Ariadne Blayde / designed by Alethea Hall
ISBN: 9781953932099

1. Fiction - General; Fiction - Occult; Fiction - Ghost I. Title II. Author

Library of Congress Control Number: 2021952597

For Jack
Rest in peace, and be safe out there

and

For Ian
I would spend an eternity in this city with you

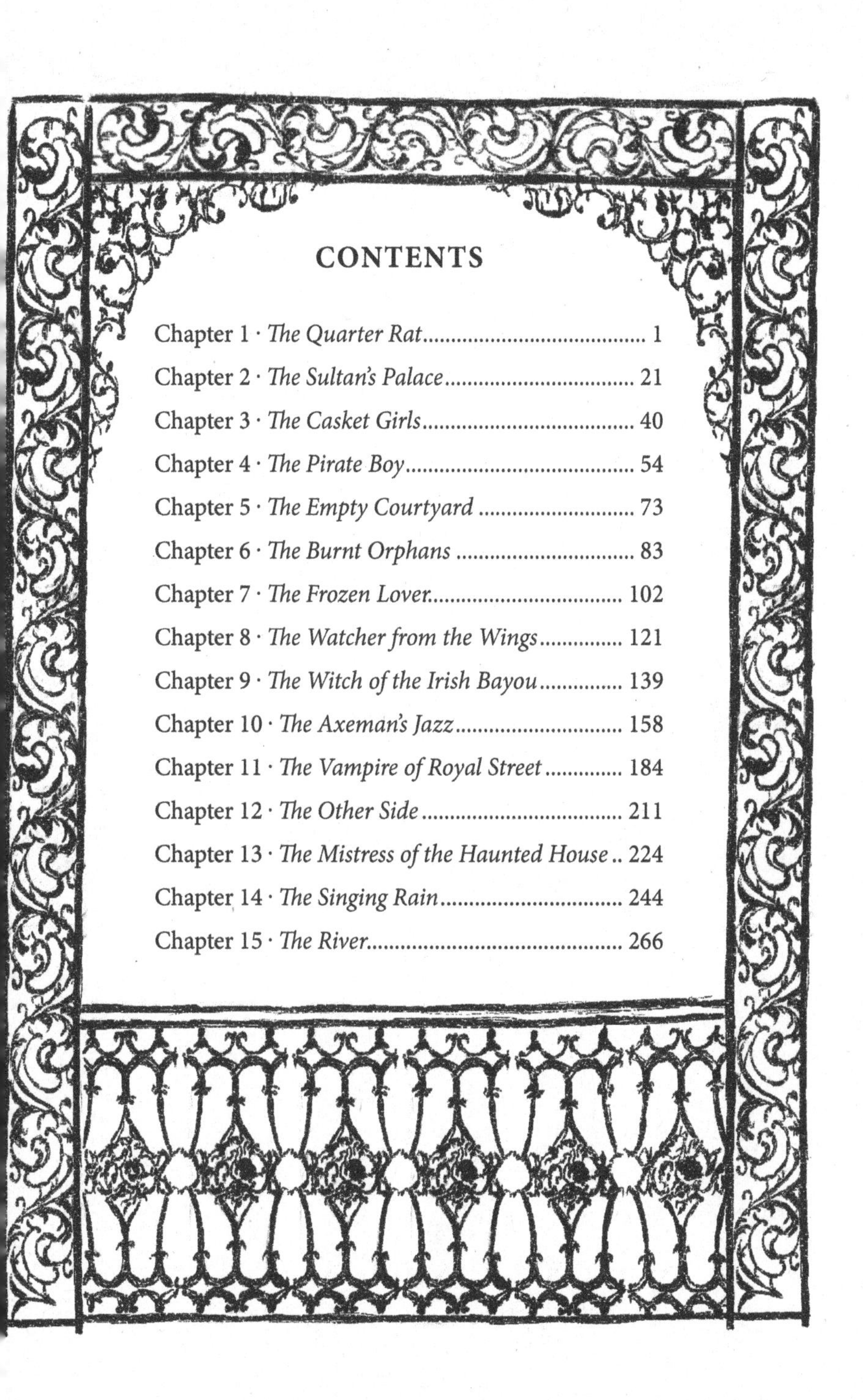

CONTENTS

Chapter 1 · *The Quarter Rat* 1
Chapter 2 · *The Sultan's Palace* 21
Chapter 3 · *The Casket Girls* 40
Chapter 4 · *The Pirate Boy* 54
Chapter 5 · *The Empty Courtyard* 73
Chapter 6 · *The Burnt Orphans* 83
Chapter 7 · *The Frozen Lover* 102
Chapter 8 · *The Watcher from the Wings* 121
Chapter 9 · *The Witch of the Irish Bayou* 139
Chapter 10 · *The Axeman's Jazz* 158
Chapter 11 · *The Vampire of Royal Street* 184
Chapter 12 · *The Other Side* 211
Chapter 13 · *The Mistress of the Haunted House* .. 224
Chapter 14 · *The Singing Rain* 244
Chapter 15 · *The River* 266

CHAPTER 1
The Quarter Rat

It's the same every night: when the ghost tour is over, the guides start drinking. Around ten we all begin to gather in the courtyard of the Quarter Rathskeller to talk over each other and argue and suck down beers and shots, and as the night edges toward midnight, the courtyard starts to feel like the stage of a play, a little tragedy we've all been putting on for years. Tonight is Thursday, and the show is beginning right about now.

Traditionally, I guess, a "rathskeller" is a tavern below street level. In this case, the term is hilariously inaccurate, because in New Orleans, nothing is below street level except briny groundwater saturating the dirt and bringing up the skeletons of old St. Peter Cemetery, which is paved over now but which still shoots up a body or two or thirteen every time someone tries to put a swimming pool behind their condo. That's one of the reasons we started using above-ground tombs in the late 1700s: as soon as it rains heavily, anything below the surface that can float (e.g., a coffin) just pops right back up to the top, like a *Jacques-in-the-box*. That's a joke I make on my tour—pretty stale by now, but the dads always like it. Anyway, I don't know why this bar is called the Quarter Rathskeller when it's very much above ground; normally we refer to it just as the Quarter Rat, which coincidentally is also a term we use to describe ourselves. It's appropriate, I guess. We scurry around in the shadows after dark, darting in and out of our little hole-in-the-wall bars, trying to outsmart the traps but rarely succeeding.

But look, the Rat isn't necessarily a dive. In fact, when you really look around, notice the matching amber pendant lights and the decent tables and stools, none of them wobbly or with rips in the vinyl, you realize it's as nice a bar as any. But most of us don't spend time in the bar itself. The courtyard is where we gather, on stools around the big wooden hi-top tables which are long enough to accommodate however many of us there are at any given moment. It's wedged between the bar's interior and the dimly-lit bathrooms, surrounded by high brick walls that make it feel so enclosed that sometimes you even forget you're outdoors.

I'm sitting in the courtyard over in the corner while Vik shouts at James across one of the hi-top tables. It's not angry shouting; tour guides shout self-righteously, sure, but rarely angrily. You'd think that maybe after hearing the sound of our own voices for hours at a time, we'd relish a little quiet over our post-tour beers, but that's not the case. Vik, in particular, enjoys shouting, and he's shouting now about the beat poets.

"Sociopaths, every one of them!"

"What do you mean, sociopaths?"

Vik lists them off on his fingers. "Kerouac was a raging alcoholic, Ginsberg was a pedophile, William S. Burroughs *killed his wife*—"

"Well, you can't dismiss their work just because they were awful people," James says in his Kentucky drawl.

"But their work sucks too. *Naked Lunch*? Meaningless, pornographic gibberish."

"Maybe you're just not intelligent enough to understand it."

"Don't you conflate intelligence with edginess! Although I've got plenty of both, dammit."

"Yes, dear, you're very smart."

Vik takes a drag on his vape and aggressively blows out a cloud of scented mist. "I'm just saying. Despicable people writing about despicable people, what's the point? Art should be meaningful. Redemptive."

"Life isn't meaningful, why should art be?"

"God, you're such a cynic."

"I just know human nature," James shrugs. "And the beats did too, you can't fault them for that."

Vik grumbles. He's handsome, with thick, messy black hair just barely graying at the temples, high cheekbones, stubble, and intense gray-green eyes. He dresses for the job better than any of us, with his combat boots and black skinny jeans, the leather vests, the earrings. The look is maybe a bit questionable for someone past thirty, but he pulls it off for now. He likes to brag about how all the bachelorettes who take his ghost tour fall in love with him.

He changes the subject. "So, how was your tour?" he asks James, who's peering into his gin and tonic like there's something wrong with it.

"Pretty good. Sixty-five in tips."

"I saw that group, it was all blue-hairs," Vik says, rolling his eyes. "Old people just like your Tennessee Williams shtick."

James smirks. "What can I say, everybody loves a New Orleans queer. Local flavor and all." He takes off his trademark leopard-print trucker hat and runs his hand through his thinning, dirty blond hair. He's stocky, with a proud mustache and surprisingly long-lashed eyes, too pretty for his personality.

"You gonna ask how mine was?" Vik says.

"Your what?"

"My tour, ya feeble-minded faggot."

"Oh. Forgive me. How was your tour?"

"Excellent," Vik says loudly, slamming his hands on the table. "I am a damn good tour guide."

"You're a damn conceited tour guide."

"You should have seen their faces during Axeman. Anyone who thinks what we do isn't art—"

"Art? Hah."

"It *is* art, goddammit! It is *theatre*."

"Oh, please. We tell ghost stories for a living."

"It's folklore."

"May I point out that you're wearing a hoodie covered in pentagrams and a denim vest with a giant applique of—what is that, a maggoty skull?"

"So what?"

"I'm just saying, you're a far cry from Laurence Olivier."

"At least I'm not a hack like you."

"Ex*cuse* me?"

"I heard you the other night, pointing at the Cabildo and telling your group that Napoleon had an affair with Andrew Jackson there."

"Oh," James shrugs. "Yeah. They were wasted, I just wanted to mess with them."

"It's disgraceful. You don't take it seriously."

"It's a *ghost tour*."

Vik growls, and James tries to be a little more polite. "So, how were your tips tonight, Peter O'Toole?" he asks.

"Eh, fine. Fifty."

"People will be tipping okay for another week or so," Poppy says from across the courtyard. There are three hi-top tables back here, and she's alone at one of the others, the rolls of worn-out skin on the underside of her arms jiggling faintly as she lays out a line of tarot cards. "The ones in town now have money to spare, but the ones who just come in just for Lundi Gras and Mardi Gras day will tip shit," she says without looking up. "Same every damn year." Poppy is over fifty, and unlike most of us younger lot, she's been in the Quarter almost all her life. The years have not treated her kindly. She's fat and wrinkly, skin softened and tanned to buttery leather by a lifetime out in the Louisiana sun, and she's missing a tooth. Like most of us, she always wears black. Tonight she's in a worn-out black tank top that says "Beware Pickpockets and Loose Women." She wears that one a lot.

It's 10:15 PM now. City law says tours have to be off the streets by ten, so everybody from Spirits of Yore is finishing up and making their way to the bar. Ruby comes into the courtyard in a huff, tossing a wad of tips onto the table. She's skinny and pretty and usually mad.

"What's wrong, baby?" Vik asks with an exhale from his vape. Something is always wrong in Ruby's world. She had a pretty bad breakup a few months ago, which I don't really know the details of, but you can see that she carries it around. She looks tired all the time now, her eye makeup always smudgy and her skin breaking out.

"This fucking group!" she snarls, tossing back her reddish mass of "white girl dreadlocks," as James calls them. "Eight of them left at the bar break, so I only had like ten people at the end. And half walked off without tipping."

James peers at the bills she is roughly flattening with her red, raw fingers. Ruby picks at her cuticles constantly, leaving scabby gashes from her nailbeds to her knuckles. "Doesn't look like you did too bad," he says. "You got a twenty."

"One twenty and a bunch of singles. I *really* do not have the patience for shitty tours right now."

"Do you ever have the patience for anything?"

Ruby shoots him a look and then turns on her heel to go back in the bar, just as Ralphie comes out.

"Hey, guys! What's up, buddy?" He gives Vik a high five and slaps James on the back.

"Hello, Ralphie," James says with something like disdainful endearment. Ralphie's a human puppy, energetic and friendly and sort of a mess. He's odd-looking, with droopy eyelids, a hook nose, and a lopsided smile, but his eyes are the brightest, most sparkling blue you've ever seen. He often comes to work with his shirt inside out, and it was a big deal when I taught him how to scramble an egg. He was my best friend, once.

"How was ya tour, baby?" Vik asks. Sometimes Vik puts on more of a Yat accent than he needs to. He's not even from here.

"Great. Good group, they loved me, awesome energy. This crazy thing happened at my bar break, though—" Ralphie embarks on his tale, hard to follow because he always talks too fast. He often misses consonants or whole syllables, to the point that I sometimes wonder how his tour groups can even follow what he's saying. When I first met him, I thought his rapid, slurred speech was an indication of unintelligence, but now I'm sure it's the opposite—his mind goes a mile a minute, so fast his mouth can't keep up.

Vik has no patience for it. "Slow down and start over!" he yells.

Ruby comes back from the bar with a drink, interrupting him. "Ugh, that's a little better," she announces, sipping her vodka as she flounces over to the table and sits. "But seriously, does Avery not like me or something? I feel like she always gives me such a light pour."

We all know that the reason the bartenders give Ruby light pours is that she tips shit, but no one says a word. Ruby is louder and angrier than anyone when she wants to be, and none of us feel like feeding that tiger right now.

And then, surprisingly, Angela comes in. She doesn't usually hang out back here after tours. Angela's tall and thick with dyed white-blonde hair, and she dresses immaculately, always wearing elaborate makeup and Victorian clothes. Angela is probably *actually* the best tour guide at our company, with her encyclopedic knowledge of New Orleans history and the occult. No one likes her.

"Heeeey, Angela!" Ralphie says cheerily as she walks through the courtyard on her way to the bathroom. No one likes her except for Ralphie, that is—Ralphie likes everybody. "Nice to see you back here, you gonna have a beer with us? Thursday niiight!"

"Actually, I just dropped in to visit the ladies' room before my walk home. I have rather a lot of errands to run in the morning, and I'd like to get started quite early."

"Oh, darn," Vik mutters.

"—But now that you mention it, it might be nice to rest my feet a bit and enjoy a libation before I begin my journey. Beer has never appealed to me, but perhaps a cocktail or a glass of wine." Yes, she really does talk like this. "Let me take my little sojourn to the ladies' room, and then I'll join you."

She goes into the bathroom, and James glares at Ralphie. "What on God's gay earth did you do that for?" he hisses in a stage whisper.

"C'mon, she's one of us."

"Personally, I was not in the mood to spend the next hour of my life bingeing *The Angela Show*," Vik says.

James makes a face. "And what is that transatlantic accent she does? Like girl, you're from Ohio, why do you sound like Gore Vidal?"

Vik snorts in laughter. And then in comes Sofia, one of the newest and youngest tour guides. She and Ruby exchange a little girly hug, they're friends, and she sits down next to Vik, they're dating. At least in theory, they're dating. They don't really express affection publicly, and most of the time they seem to be arguing. Sofia is mixed race, Cajun and Latina, and very pretty—small and curvy with big doe eyes and jet black hair dyed ombre into teal blue. The only imperfect thing about her appearance is her teeth, which are a crooked mess.

Vik asks how her tour was, and James gets up. "Anybody want anything?" he calls out. Poppy requests a brandy, Ralphie wants another Abita Amber. It's so easy to just sit here all night and drink. The bar gives tour guides a steep discount; you can get completely shitfaced for like fifteen bucks.

But I'm not drinking tonight, not even really making an effort to join in. I feel distant lately, tired of hearing the same conversation over and over. All dialogue at the Quarter Rat is essentially a competition, a series of one-ups about who tells a particular story best or who knows the most obscure bits of New Orleans history or who handled a heckler the most savagely. Vik is telling a story now about how he shushed a loud, drunk woman who disrupted his tour tonight. At least he says it was tonight. I feel like I've heard this story before.

"And she says, 'Are *yew* shushin' me? Ah *know* yer not shushin' *me*, son.' And I said, 'You know, ma'am, I'd show up at your place of work and behave like an inebriated idiot if I could, but that'd probably get me kicked out of Walmart.'"

Everyone laughs except Ruby, whose jaw drops. "That's *my* line."

Vik scoffs. "What? No, it's not."

"Yes, it is, I said that like four fucking months ago to some idiot outside my first stop, and told everybody, and now you're acting like you came up with it? The fuck!"

"Jesus, calm down," he says.

She stands. "Calm down? Fuck you."

"Goodness! What'd I miss?" James says as he returns with everyone's drinks.

"Ruby's throwing a fit for no reason," Vik says.

"He stole my line!"

James' blond eyebrows crawl up his face. "Wow, can we all just simmer down a little, please?" Ruby flips him off and goes into the bar.

"I saw that guy in the Pikachu costume take a piss tonight," Ralphie grins, trying to break the tension. "Right in front of my group, by the LaLaurie Mansion."

"At least it's too cold to smell it," Poppy says drily from the other table.

"I'll take the smell of piss over these God-awful temperatures any day," James says. It's been dipping into the thirties lately, not very pleasant for people who have to work outside at night.

"Agreed," Sofia says with a little shiver. Vik's leather jacket is draped around her shoulders, and she pulls it closer. "I hope it warms up for Mardi Gras."

"Yeah, come on weather, get your act together!" Ralphie hams, shaking a fist at the sky. "You've got ten days!"

"Twelve days," Angela corrects.

"Twelve whole days till Mardi Gras? I don't know how I'll make it," James says with a little sniffle. "Especially in this terrible cold."

"It's good for *Julie*, though," Sofia says.

"Yeah. I only tell that one in the winter," Vik says. *Julie* is a tragic love story about a young free woman of color and her white lover, and it is traditionally set on the coldest night of the year.

"Oh, I prefer to tell *Julie* in the summer," Angela says—she's gotten a glass of white wine from the bar and is now sitting at the table next to Vik, who looks positively miffed about it. "A well-crafted tale about the cold can have a striking mental effect. I believe it actually allows the group to forget the heat."

"You can't 'forget' how hot it is in August in New Orleans," Vik says.

"You haven't heard my Julie, then."

"And what a tragedy that is."

"You're welcome to follow my tour any time," she says brightly. Social cues and Angela aren't terribly compatible.

"I feel weird telling *Julie*," James says. "Isn't it kind of racist?"

"Racist? How?"

"It's all like, oh, free people of color, they're so important in New Orleans and they had so many rights blah blah blah, except the women still had their lives and agency and sexuality totally run by white men? And let's romanticize that? No thanks."

"Well sure, *Plaçage* operated within a system of white privilege," Vik says. "But that doesn't mean none of it was real." Here we go. This usually happens once or twice a night, everybody nitpicking some little historical detail, a competing chorus of former liberal arts majors showing off their useless degrees. I'm glad I'm over here in the corner. They're all just talking over each other, and I'm not feeling very social at all tonight. I'm in a pretty dark mood, and I have this weird pain in my side.

"Just look at some of the tombs," Vik continues, launching into one of his monologues. "For example. In Lafayette Number 1, there are two tombs belonging to the Toledano Family that are side by side, each surrounded by their own little iron fence. Story goes, Christoval Toledano never married, as he had fallen in love with a quadroon girl named Basilice Barbay, and interracial marriage was illegal. Well, alas, Basilice precedes Christoval to the grave by ten years, but as she was a woman of color and obviously not married into the family, mom and pop deny Christoval's request to place her into the family tomb. So, what does he do? Builds a second Toledano tomb right next door, puts her in there, and then himself and the kids too when it comes to be their turn. Why would you do something like that if it's not true love?"

"Well, actually," Angela says. "If you look more closely at the records, there is no indication that Basilice Barbay was a woman of color at all." She continues like this, and everyone sort of pretends to listen for a minute—everybody except Ralphie, who is pacing the courtyard and carrying on a conversation with himself under his breath, which usually starts to happen two or three drinks in. But eventually the last vestiges of politeness wane, and James just straight up interrupts her, screeching "What *is* this?" as he looks up in horror at the speakers on the wall. The song has just changed.

"Seriously, is this like, Blink 182? My God." James pulls out his phone to change it. The bar has a digital jukebox that you can use with an app, and James likes to be in charge of the music. A few seconds later Alanis Morissette is on, singing Ironic.

"We're just gonna continue with the nineties throwback vibe, then," Sofia says.

"Were you even alive in the nineties?" Vik says into his beer as he takes a sip.

Angela is still talking about *Plaçage* even though no one is paying attention to her anymore, and James is smiling and swaying with the music, eyes closed. "I love Alanis," he says. "She helped me through a really difficult time in my life."

"I thought Jesus helped you through a really difficult time in your life," Vik says.

"Him too."

Ralphie stops pacing for a second. "Wait, James, you're religious?"

James opens his eyes. "Oh, hell no, not anymore. But I was a born-again Christian in my late teens."

"No way."

"Oh yeah, just briefly. The great thing I realized about being a Southern Baptist? It doesn't matter what I put up my nose, doesn't matter how many dicks I suck, I'm still going to *heaaaaven*," he says in a singsong voice.

"You motherfucker," says Vik.

"Shut up, you love me."

"I despise you," Vik says, smooshing his lips against James' cheek and peppering him with kisses.

"I was actually raised Catholic," Angela begins. "And Catholicism is of course a very guilt-driven religion. In fact, I was only six years old the first time I was forced to go to confession. Imagine me, just a small child, trying my hardest to come up with some *sin* that I had committed."

James rolls his eyes. "Yes, I'm sure that was just as hard as growing up gay in rural Kentucky."

"So what are y'all doing the rest of the night?" Ruby asks, coming back in from the bar with another vodka. She seems to have calmed down.

"I think I'll probably just go home," Ralphie says. "Unless anyone has any coke?" He looks hopefully at Ruby.

"All I have is weed." Ruby is our resident drug dealer; she's always pulling somebody into the bathroom to exchange eighths of weed and, occasionally, little dime bags of cocaine. I did the same thing in high school. I didn't have a lot of friends, but the fact that I sold drugs certainly increased my social cachet. It's been a while since I've done any drugs though, probably a year since I've even smoked weed. Now I just sit here sober, watching everyone else get fucked up.

"What about Adderall?" Vik asks Ruby.

"Nah, my guy's out of town."

"Goddammit. Mine too, and I'm almost out. Got any other sources?"

"Talk a little louder about your drug deals, by all means," Sofia says.

"Oh, who the fuck cares?" James says.

"Just saying."

"*Like I said*, all I have tonight is weed," Ruby says, getting annoyed.

James is stroking his chin. "I kinda want to go to the Corner Pocket."

"You'll spend all your tips," Ruby says.

"That's true, I will. But I'm kinda drunk, so I kinda don't care… wanna come?" he asks Vik, who is proudly bisexual.

"Yeah, maybe."

Sofia crosses her arms. "*That's* what you wanna do tonight? Go to a male strip club?"

Poppy's metal stool makes a screeching sound on the courtyard's flagstones as she hauls herself to her feet. "Give Julio a good tip for me if you do. He's a sweetheart."

James makes a wicked face. "The cute Mexican? Oh, I'll give him more than the tip…"

"Eww!" Sofia exclaims.

"Oh, grow up, Dora the Explorer."

"Goodnight," Poppy sighs, the tattered edges of her gypsy skirt brushing the ground as she shuffles through the courtyard toward the bar. The skirt covers her ankles, but I know they're so badly swollen that they spill out over the sides of her shoes. Poppy doesn't give too many tours anymore. Her body is failing, and she's almost always in pain.

"Goodnight, Poppy," they chorus.

I watch her leave the courtyard. Before heading out to the street, she stops and chats for a minute with Jeremy, who's sitting there inside the bar, alone. He and Poppy are about the same age, and they've both been giving tours forever. But unlike Poppy, Jeremy doesn't hang out back here, doesn't talk to us younger guides at all. There's something really eerie about him that I can't put my finger on, and it's not the fact that he has vampire fangs. Lots of people in New Orleans tout themselves as "vampires," even the weird little guy Elijah who works in the Curiosity Shop next door; it's a whole subculture here. Jeremy dresses like a character out of an Anne Rice novel, always wearing a red or black shirt with billowy sleeves and tight black pants, and he has long stringy hair. I hear he used to be really sexy a couple decades ago, but these days, he's just creepy. After Poppy goes, I watch him stare into his wine for a few seconds before taking a long drink, and then I guess he feels my eyes on him because he suddenly glances toward my dark corner of the courtyard with an intense but hard-to-read expression.

Vik has noticed Jeremy in the bar too. "Since when does Jeremy hang out at the Rat after tours?" he asks James.

"Oh shit, Jeremy's in there? Eesh."

"Go talk to him. I dare you."

"Me? No way. I do *not* vibe with that gentleman," James says.

"It would be a fun experiment, don't you think? To just talk to him and smile at him and pretend like he's a regular human being? Maybe eventually he'd be nice," Sofia muses.

"Or he'd rip my spine out through my chest and eat it like a shish-kebab. No thanks."

"Oh, come on, he's just a person," Ruby says. Nothing scares Ruby.

"*Vampire*," Ralphie corrects.

"What a loser." Vik rolls his eyes.

"You're just jealous because he gets more good reviews than you," James says.

"Actually," Angela announces, "I have more five-star reviews than anyone at the company. Two hundred and seventy-six, in fact."

"Pretty sure I have over three hundred," Vik says.

James takes a sip of his drink. "People with no other hobbies or ambition do tend to accumulate them."

"What's *that* supposed to mean?" Vik says.

"Oh, hush."

"I have hobbies."

James smirks, and Vik gets mad. "And what's *your* great contribution to society, James Baker? What new frontiers in macaroni art did you explore with the octogenarians today?" James teaches art at a senior center a couple times a week.

"Simmer down, it was just a joke," James says, picking up his phone.

"Personally, I have many hobbies," Angela announces. "I have a blog, I write fan-fic, I cook, I grow my own vegetables..." She goes on like this for a minute, and everyone ignores her. Ruby leans over and watches James messing with his phone.

"Who you texting?" she asks. "Knockoff Alexander?"

Vik snickers. "Good one."

"His *name* is *Landon*," James says. He has a serial fondness for slender twenty-something boys, and the one he's hooking up with now happens to look almost exactly like the last one, a med student named Alexander. "And you know, he asked me to be his boyfriend the other day."

"What did you say?" Sofia asks.

"What do you think?"

Ruby laughs. We all know James and commitment don't mesh. "So I'm guessing you're not doing anything with your boy toy for Valentine's Day?"

"Ugh, is that tomorrow? Don't remind me."

"You're so cruel," Vik says. "All these little chickens fall in love with you, and you just break their hearts."

"Chickens?" Ralphie asks.

"Young fags. Which means James here is what they call a chickenhawk."

James gasps with mock offense. "How *dare* you presume my gay taxonomy, sir! I am a *platypus*, thank you."

"That's not a thing," Vik says.

"Shut up, Mr. 'Bisexual.' You don't get to have an opinion about gay culture."

"Eventually you're gonna have to pick one of these boys, you know," Vik says. "They're not going to be fighting over you forever."

James flicks his eyes toward Sofia. "You're one to talk."

"Hey," she says. "I'm twenty-two."

"Besides," James continues. "I may fuck twenty-one-year-olds, but at least I don't think I *am* one."

"Oh, eat glass," Vik glowers.

"Cute emo hoodie by the way, it really goes with your receding hairline."

"His hairline is fine," Sofia says, and Vik glares at her too.

Angela, oblivious to everything but Angela, stands and announces her departure. "Well, everyone, this has been a lovely evening, but I think it's about time that I began my journey home."

Vik glances up at her. "Oh no, however will we manage without you?"

"I'd be happy to join you all again another night," she says brightly. "Ta ta!"

"Kisses!" James shouts very gayly and very sarcastically. She goes, heels clicking neatly on the flagstones.

"Thank the dark lord Lucifer in hell," Vik exhales as soon as she's gone.

Sofia gives them a scolding look. "What did that poor, awkward lady ever do to any of you?"

"Vik just doesn't like being upstaged. She's the only one of us who's more insufferable than him," James says.

"Do *not* compare me to that awful woman," Vik barks, slamming his hands on the table.

"Alright alright, no need to queen out about it."

"Do you guys have to *fight* all the time?" Ruby says angrily. "Seriously, everybody needs to just chill."

"We're not fighting, we're riffing," James says.

"Speak for yourself," Vik grunts.

"Well, whatever it is, you can keep it to yourselves because I do *not* have time for this kind of fucking negativity in my life right now." She's rooting with annoyance through the tiny purse she carries, bobby pins and credit cards and bits of drug accoutrement spilling out onto the table.

"You don't have time for this kind of 'fucking negativity,' huh?" Ralphie teases.

"What's that supposed to mean?"

"Oh, nothing," he says sheepishly.

Finally, Ruby finds what she's looking for, a chubby little green pipe. James looks over with interest.

"Safety meeting?" he asks.

"Yeah, who's coming?"

"Definitely. It's gotten a bit *stuffy* back here," James says, pursing his lips at Vik.

"I'll go," Ralphie says, wandering over to her side.

"Guys?" Ruby asks Vik and Sofia.

"Nah. I'm just gonna go home," Vik says darkly.

"Bye then," James shrugs.

They go into the bar and out to the street, and I can see Ruby's thin cardigan flutter in the chilly breeze as soon as they step outside. She never seems to get cold, though, even in this weather. They'll walk a couple blocks to the back of the Cathedral, smoke a little weed, come back waxing poetic about something or other. That's how it always goes. They didn't ask me to join, but I don't care. I don't have the energy to go with them. Or the desire.

Sofia turns to Vik. "Go home?" she pouts. "But I want to go out."

"So go out," he says, picking at his black nail polish.

"Without you?"

"I'm telling you, I just want to fucking go home."

"Why are you so cranky all of a sudden?"

"I'm *not*!"

"You—"

They quiet suddenly when someone else enters the courtyard. It's Max, everybody's favorite person at Spirits of Yore, and they both soften when they see him. He's a black guy in his seventies, and he moves slowly, a little hunched over. But despite his age, he's the epitome of cool, always wearing boots and skinny jeans and popping the collars of his jackets. Sometimes he talks about his days in the Peace Corps or his friendship with Malik Rahim, one of New Orleans' O.G. Black Panthers, but mostly Max just asks how you're doing and means it. His wife died last year. None of us really knew her that well, but we all went to the funeral and cried at the eulogy he gave. It was the most moving thing I've ever heard.

"Hey, Max," Vik nods.

"Hey there, kiddo," he says in his tobacco-ravaged baritone. "And Sofia, aren't you a picture." She smiles.

"You're out late," Vik says. Max usually catches the bus home right after work.

"Got caught up talking with a couple who took my tour. Good people."

"You need a ride home or anything?" Vik asks.

"Oh no, my bus is right around the corner. Just came in to get my umbrella, I think I left it back here. Haven't seen it, have you?"

"Can't say that I have," Vik frowns, scanning the courtyard. "Certainly wasn't here when we sat down."

"Ain't that a shame," Max says. "Guess I'll have to locate myself a new one."

"Sorry about that, man."

"Well, a lost umbrella's not so terrible, in the grand scheme of things. See you both tomorrow."

"Have a good night, Max."

"Same to you. Y'all be safe out there." He says those same words to me before my tour every night. *Be safe out there.*

I watch him go, his slow gait a little off-kilter as he makes his way back into the bar and then out into the cold street. I don't like to imagine him under the fluorescent lights of the bus alone, going into his empty house alone, getting into bed alone. At least he has a dog.

Sofia lays a hand on Vik's arm. "Is it because James was being a dick? The thing about…?"

He pulls away. "Jesus, can you just leave it alone? You're so fucking overbearing sometimes."

"If you want to just go home, I'll go with you. We can watch a movie or something."

"Not in the mood," he says, sucking down the last couple gulps of his beer.

"What about tomorrow? Are we doing anything for…you know…"

"What? Oh—Valentine's Day? Christ. You care about that?"

"Well—no, but—"

"I wouldn't expect you to. Buncha made up corporate bullshit."

"I just thought we could hang out."

"Maybe." He stands. "I'll text you."

"So that's it? You're just leaving?"

"Yeah, I'm just leaving." He gestures to the leather jacket still draped over her shoulders. "Can I have that back?"

"Seriously? I have like nothing on."

"So, learn to dress better."

She takes it off and shoves it at him.

"You don't have to be such a jerk, you know."

He turns and leaves the courtyard, pulling on the jacket without even glancing back.

"Wow, really?" she calls after him. When he's gone, she puts her face in her hands. I think she might be crying.

Then a young man enters the courtyard, and Sofia gets up and rushes to the bathroom.

The kid sits and checks his phone. He's probably twenty-one or twenty-two, slender and smooth-skinned with a trendy haircut, buzzed on the sides and floppy on top. His face lights up when he hears James' voice approaching from inside the bar; it sounds like he and the others are back from their "safety meeting."

"Hey!" the boy says, standing in greeting as they come into the courtyard.

James' smile fades slightly when he sees him. "Oh…hey. What are you doing here?"

"We said we were gonna go out."

"Yeah, but…later. I told you I was still at the Rat."

"I thought I'd come meet you," he smiles, reaching out to touch James' back. His hand lingers there for a few moments and then falls away again.

"Cool. Uh…guys, have you met Landon?"

"Do we ever meet any of them?" Ruby says dryly.

"Hey, buddy! I'm Ralphie," Ralphie says, with a friendly wave and a grin that seems to get stuck on his face for too long after the words have left his lips. He's so drunk and stoned that he's forgotten how to manage his facial muscles. I've seen it happen a million times.

"Nice to meet you. Y'all give the haunted tours too?" the boy asks politely.

"Yep," Ruby says.

"What you do, buddy?" Ralphie asks, slurring his words.

"Oh, I wait tables."

"Let's get out of here, yeah?" James says quietly to the boy.

"Whatever you want."

"You're leaving? Where you going?" Ralphie asks.

"We're gonna go to the Corner Pocket and then probably the Phoenix."

"Can I come?

"To the *Phoenix*?" James laughs.

"Why're you laughing? I like to hang out."

"Oh, you sweet summer child."

"What?"

"It's a gay bar, Ralphie. There's orgies and stuff," Ruby says.

"Oh."

"Wait, though," she adds. "Wasn't Vik gonna go with you?"

"Yeah, actually, where'd he go?"

Sofia emerges from the bathroom, red-eyed from crying. "Vik left."

"Why?"

"I dunno. But I'm going home too."

"Goodness," James says. "Trouble in paradise?"

"Are you okay?" Ruby asks Sofia.

"Yeah. See y'all tomorrow," she says, avoiding eye contact with them as she pulls on her little glittery backpack with the bat-wings and leaves. James turns to the others, eyes wide with potential gossip.

"Oh, don't start," Ruby says. "You're so catty."

"I didn't say *a word*. Anyway, we're out of here too. Stay cute." James leaves the courtyard, boy in tow.

"Nice meeting you!" Ralphie slurs after them. The boy turns to smile and wave.

"So much *drama*," Ruby sighs when they're gone, sinking into a chair at one of the shorter tables. There are a couple regular-height tables back here with two chairs each, usually used only when the group has thinned.

"Yeah," Ralphie says, although I'm not sure he's even listening.

"I'm just tired of it, you know?" She's getting angry again. "Like, people need to just shut up and be cool and live their lives, you know?"

She sees it too, the tragedy we put on. We all show up night after night to posture and strut and recite our lines, and no one ever really listens to each other, and no one ever breaks character.

"You wanna shot?" Ralphie asks.

"Sure."

Ralphie goes into the bar and comes back with two over-full shot glasses pinched between wet fingertips and gives one to Ruby. They shoot.

"That's the business," she says, slamming the shot glass down and wiping her mouth.

Ralphie sways on his feet for a moment, blinks slowly twice, and then says slowly, "Do you think we'll ever…"

"Ever...?" Ruby waits for him to finish. "Ever what?"

"Like… *do* something."

"...Define 'something.'"

"You know. With our lives."

There it is, the infamous question. It's like asking somebody's age or weight or how much they pay in rent—kind of private, a little taboo. I assume we all think about it regularly, but we don't bring it up much. I've actually been asking myself this question quite a bit lately. Will I ever make anything of myself, and do I care enough to try? Sometimes I feel like I was doomed from the start. Maybe we all were. Most of us have too many issues—mental, emotional, social, whatever—to contribute to society in any meaningful way. Ghost stories are all we've got to give.

"Hey, speak for yourself. My life is pretty fucking baller," Ruby says.

"So you're doing — doing okay then?" Ralphie hiccups.

"I'm doing great. Kicking ass, taking names, going hard."

"Cool. Cause you seem—"

"What?" she says, an edge in her voice. "I seem what?"

"Nothing," he burps. "Glad you're, glad you're havin' fun. But me, I should go. That last shot... whew," he says, and pulls out his car keys.

"Wait, you drove here?"

"Mmhmm."

"You can't drive home, you're way too drunk."

"I'm fine. I'll sober in the sit — sit in the car. Sit 'n sober up."

"Seriously, Ralphie. Especially after—"

Ralphie holds up a finger, closes his eyes. "Don't fuckin' say it."

"Jesus, wow. Okay."

"I just don't need that right now."

"And you know what? I don't need to sit here and babysit you," she snaps. "So, bye. Try not to get a DUI. Or, y'know, kill anyone."

Ruby stands, gathers her purse, and struts through the bar to the street in her high heeled boots. How the hell she gives tours in those is a mystery.

"So thass how it is, huh?" he shouts after her, but she's already gone.

Ralphie and I are the only ones left now. He's not acknowledging me; we haven't been on good terms for a while. But he's so drunk, I'm not sure he even notices I'm still here. He sits down, puts his head in his hands for a minute, then gets up and staggers out. I'm pretty sure he forgot to close his tab.

And so it looks like tonight's performance is over, to be repeated again tomorrow. The theatre goes dark, and I am here alone.

I guess I should leave too. But I just can't muster the energy to get up. I sit for a minute, maybe five minutes, maybe an hour. Who knows. Who cares.

And then I catch a glimpse of somebody coming into the bar off the street. Somebody wearing bedazzled sneakers, pink harlequin pants, a skin-tight snake-print top, a furry pink coat, and big pink sunglasses, all of it very obviously secondhand. It's Veda–there's nobody else in the world it could be, and she's coming to the courtyard. I realize she's the only other Spirits of Yore tour guide who hasn't been back here yet tonight.

"Hi, Veda."

She looks around for a moment, wondering where the voice came from, before her eyes come to rest on me in the dark. She looks a little surprised to see me.

"Hi," she smiles. Veda is a trans-girl, not that you could tell if you didn't already know. She's very feminine, with messy black hair, tiny inch-long bangs, and pretty caramel skin. She's Native American. "Are you the only one here?" she asks.

"Everybody else just left. Did you give a tour?"

"Yeah," she says. "Kind of a weird one."

"Why weird?"

She takes off the bug-eye sunglasses, which I see now say "Bride" in big curly letters around the side. Her eyes are ringed in heavy red eyeliner and her eyebrows are painted blue.

"There were just a lot of portals open in the French Quarter tonight. I think it's because Mercury is going into retrograde."

"Oh, yeah," I say with fake understanding. Veda is one of these people who does magic rituals and meditates to other dimensions or whatever. A few of the tour guides believe in th

at sort of stuff—Ruby is always burning palo santo back here to cleanse people's auras, and Poppy is a for-profit witch—but Veda takes the cake in terms of full-hearted commitment to weird-ass woo-woo shit. I don't really get it, but I love her anyway. She's an old soul.

"Look at what I just found in the river," she says reverently, pulling something out of her pocket. It's a little pink comb, missing a few teeth at one end, and there's a picture of Big Bird on it. She holds it out to me, cupped in both palms.

"I told my spirit guides I needed an amulet, and this just manifested. And it's pink! Pink is my favorite color."

"I know," I say. "I can tell by your outfit."

"Oh," Veda laughs. "Yeah." She's so young, so sweet and chubby-cheeked, and her clothes are always crazy, all ratty and frilly and dripping with glitter. The boss tried to get Veda to stop wearing such freaky shit to work but gave up after a while.

"Did you want a beer or something?" I ask.

Her eyes widen. "Oh, no. The only alcohol I drink is strawberry champagne."

"I don't think they have that here."

"They don't," she shrugs. "I just wanted to come and see if any of you were still around."

"Just me."

"It's really nice to see you," she says, then frowns a little. "Are you alright?"

"I dunno. I've been feeling a bit weird."

"I can tell."

"Yeah. I don't mean to be antisocial, but..." I look around at the dim, smoky courtyard then out through the bar to a dirty little sliver of French Quarter street. "Everything just feels so pointless lately."

"Well. Maybe it's time for you to move on to bigger things."

"Maybe."

"Is there anything I can do to help?"

"I don't think so."

"You can talk to me anytime," she smiles.

"Thanks."

"Well," she says, looking up at the moon in the slice of murky night sky between the high courtyard walls. "It's getting late. I should probably go home."

"Okay. Goodnight, Veda."

"Goodnight."

I feel a sudden wave of fatigue and close my eyes for a moment. When I open them again, Veda is gone, and I'm still here. I've been here all night.

I am consumed, sometimes, by darkness. Not the darkness of evil, but the darkness of absence. A heavy gray veil that settles over everything, desaturating the colors and dimming the light until everything's the same bland monochrome, so dull that I'd rather just close my eyes. And when the darkness comes, which these days is more often than not, I just can't get fired up about being miserable for another four or five or six decades and then ceasing to exist. Sometimes I get the urge to just duck out early.

The French have a term for this feeling: *l'appel du vide*, the call of the void. It's why you get that startling little urge to jump off the platform in front of the train, why you might itch to yank the steering wheel toward oncoming traffic. Succumb to the inevitable and leave the rest behind. "Morbid curiosity," I guess you could call it. But I have a suspicion that it's something more than that. See, I think that the urge to jump is actually a brief and profound realization of how easily all the drama and pain and mundanity could just—*poof*. Disappear. Frightening, isn't it? To realize how thin the line between life and death is, and how close the end can be, if we want it. Oftentimes, it's no more than a few inches away.

Of course, this momentary realization is entirely pointless. Because very few people ever accept that invitation, the call of the void. In fact, most of us go to great lengths to ignore it. We spend our whole lives sticking our fingers in our ears and humming as we lay brick after brick after brick along that razor-thin line between us and it, trying to build a wall, refusing to acknowledge how easily it could crumble.

I don't totally get why, to be honest. It's not like we're happy here. The fact that everyone's actually pretty fucking miserable most of the time has got to be the worst-kept secret of the human experience. Even here in the courtyard, amid all the joking and negging and drinking and debating, it's undeniable, this deep and restless unhappiness in all of us. It always settles in by the end of the night.

I should quit giving tours. Leave these people, leave this city, move on.

But I don't know how.

CHAPTER 2

The Sultan's Palace

"It's fun to be the big spoon," Landon giggled from between James' shoulders. They had just woken up and were cuddling in bed.

James sat up and groaned at the sudden throbbing in his temples. "Ow."

"Are you hungover?" Landon asked.

"Yeah. You're not?"

Landon shrugged. "Not really. I am a lot younger than you, though."

James shot him a look and rubbed his eyes. "What did we even do last night?"

"We started at The Quarter Rat with your tour guide friends, then went to the Corner Pocket, then the Phoenix. Remember?"

"Oh, right." Images of dancing, drinking, smoking. He let himself fall back onto the pillows next to Landon. "And there was some twink you knew?" James vaguely remembered a young man about Landon's age, an Asian with a blond mohawk, the blurry shapes of the two young men grinding on the dance floor. A little ball of jealousy fluttered into being in his gut.

"Yeah, Jax. I introduced you, remember?"

"*Jax?* God, what kind of name is that?"

"He's just a friend, you don't need to be catty about it."

Catty! The audacity. "I don't care if he's your friend, friend with benefits, hookup, whatever. You do you," he said, sprinkling just a little disdain into his voice. He had told Landon time and time again that they were not monogamous and never would be. Why should they be? Landon was young and attractive enough that he could have whomever he wanted whenever he wanted, and James was generally able to find plenty of interested parties himself. Just last weekend he had hooked up with a big hulk of a man from Grindr. He assumed Landon fooled around with other people too, and he didn't—shouldn't—have a problem with it. Not that he needed to know the details.

"I don't want anybody but you," Landon said, brushing his toes against James' under the covers. Their faces were just a few inches apart, and Landon's eyes were deep, deep brown, like a dairy cow's. James found himself gazing into them for just a little too long. He got out of bed and pulled on his jeans.

"You're not leaving, are you?"

"Well, yeah, I wanted to hit the gym before the Senior Center."

"Not before you open your present!"

He caught sight in the mirror of Landon standing behind him, holding a box wrapped in shimmery paper. "Happy Valentine's Day," the boy smiled.

"Oh…"

"It's okay if you didn't get me anything."

"No—I did. It's in my car."

James had forgotten today was Valentine's Day, wouldn't have spent the night if he'd remembered. Luckily, he did have something for Landon, just a little thing he'd picked up on a whim a couple weeks ago. He went down to get it, pulled the price tag off, stuffed it into an empty paper bag he found in the backseat. Briefly toyed with the idea of just getting into his car and driving away. But his shirt was upstairs.

When James returned, Landon was sitting cross-legged on the bed and patted it for James to join him.

"I hope you like it," he said, handing over the fancy box. James unwrapped it and pulled out a vintage camera. It was a Kodak Duaflex II, a cute little rectangle of a thing with a flip-up viewfinder, a detachable flash, and a neck strap.

"It works," Landon smiled. "And I got you some film too, see?"

Shocked and pleased, James examined the camera. Landon had listened, it seemed, when James had told him photography had been a hobby in college, that he'd loved spending hours in the art department's darkroom listening to Death Cab for Cutie and developing photographs. "This is amazing," James said, forgetting to disguise the sincerity in his voice. "Where did you get it?"

"Ebay. Got into a bidding war," Landon smiled. "I probably paid a little too much, but no way was I gonna let 'eatprayknit22' get her flabby mom-hands on it."

James laughed and leaned forward to kiss him. "This is so cool. Thank you. Really."

"My turn?"

"Oh…sure," James said, handing over the paper bag. He found his cheeks flushing hot as Landon pulled out the plushie sparkle-eyed panda, embarrassed by how stupid and inadequate it was in comparison. What right did Landon have to buy him such a thoughtful present? He'd gotten the stupid stuffed animal at a fucking *Walgreens*, and it made him look like an asshole, or worse, an idiot. He wanted to say something defensive, sarcastic, even mean, as the top of its fluffy head emerged from the bag. But Landon squealed with honest delight and hugged it to his chest as soon as he pulled it out.

"Oh my God, how adorable!"

"It just… I dunno. Reminded me of you," James shrugged self-consciously. But it had. The panda had been so sweet and cute and sparkly that he'd wandered away from the toothpaste aisle to pull it off the shelf, knowing right away that it was for Landon. "You can hug it when I'm not around."

"I will. I love him." Landon picked up the Kodak and held it up to the panda's sparkly eyes. "See? He's a photographer too. Just like you."

"Aww."

"I do, you know."

"Do what?"

"Love him," he said meaningfully.

"You're cute," James laughed, and stood. "I'd better get to the gym. Thanks for the amazing present."

"Don't you want to stay for breakfast? I could make us pancakes."

"Wish I could. I'll text you later, yeah?" He gathered his things and was out the door a few minutes later.

"Bye! Happy Valentine's Day!" Landon blew him a kiss from the top of the stairs.

James could always tell when the boys he dated were about to use the L-word, and he had gotten pretty skilled at shutting it down. Usually, he broke things off a few weeks after the word entered the picture. Landon was sneaky, though, he'd said it in a way that wasn't really saying it at all, which meant that maybe James could let him get away with it—for now, anyway. In a week or two he'd end things, he'd told himself at Christmas. He was still telling himself the same thing nearly two months later. Another two weeks, after Mardi Gras. Well, maybe three weeks. A month. Surely for another month it could be just this, something easy and uncomplicated.

James pulled into the parking lot of his gym. Expensive and exclusive, it had been around since the late 1800s and was something of a New Orleans institution. Everything in it was cutting-edge modern, except the ritzy, old-fashioned decor. Rows of fancy touchscreen ellipticals sat under dim sconces and filigree crown molding like you'd find in some noir-era smoking parlor, and the club's puce green walls were decked in black-and-white pictures from the thirties and forties, portraits of important old men and fading team photos of gymnastics and tennis teams in diaper-like booty shorts. One of the pictures, a portrait of a mustached old man who looked like Warren G. Harding (how James even knew what Warren G. Harding looked like, he wasn't totally sure), hung on the wall directly across from James' favorite treadmill. The man looked vaguely pissed off, and when he'd first joined the gym, James had teased him in his mind as he ran—*What's wrong, Daddy, you mad there's fags and blacks and women in your fancy athletic club? Why don't you come on up to the steam room. Let's see if your balls are as weird and tiny as your spectacles.* Over the years, though, the angry mustached man (whose name, James learned from reading the plaque beneath the photo, was J.J. Gottschmidt), had become a sort of workout buddy, a confidante.

Today, Gottschmidt was giving James shit as he ran on the treadmill. *Why are you so unkind to that boy?* his tiny, frustrated eyes seemed to ask. James did feel bad for blowing Landon off that morning. Would it really have been so bad to have stayed, to have cuddled on the couch and watched an episode of The Golden Girls together over breakfast? They'd been messing around together for how long now, four months? Five? Last week, Landon had asked James to be his boyfriend, and he had almost said yes. He liked him. Very much.

But it's not simple, he told Gottschmidt. *He's so much younger.*

They all are.

So?

You like to keep it that way, don't you? Ever since—

Shut up.

He mopped the sweat off his brow and upped the speed of the treadmill. Hell, if he'd become one of these balding, fat old bears whom all the twinks laugh at behind their backs. Just a few nights ago one of them had practically begged to suck James' dick in the bathroom of a little hole-in-the-wall club in the Quarter, and he'd had to force himself not to laugh in the man's pathetically hopeful face. Terry and Cleve, a couple of pretentious old married queens who owned lots of real estate in the neighborhood, had noticed and started snickering audibly over their Chardonnay about it, and that had annoyed James, annoyed him so much that he almost wanted to take the man by the hand to the bathroom and let him do it, close his eyes and pretend it was Elliot. He tried not to think too much about Elliot, had stopped masturbating about him years ago, but that could be an exception, couldn't it? He wondered who Landon thought about when they fucked. Probably Jax, the blond Asian kid. James' insides knotted in jealousy again, and he nearly laughed aloud of the stupid hypocrisy of it. He recalled his encounter with the Hulk, as he'd been mentally calling the guy from Grindr. Why did he care if Landon hooked up with other sweet, stupid young boys? Let them have their fun. What did any of it matter.

After his workout, he showered, dressed, and drove across town to the Senior Center. None of the supervisors gave a shit what he did, so James had long made it his personal mission to make Arts and Crafts class "lit as fuck," as he described it to Vik and the others. At Halloween time, he'd announced that they'd be "bedazzling Satan's wicked little fingers" and had the old people trace their hands on orange construction paper, adding ghastly veins and long pointed nails and rhinestones, lots and lots of rhinestones. At Christmas, they made "Gay Elven Wonderlands" with piles of glittery cotton-ball snow (nobody blinked an eye at the name). Today they were finishing up their papier-mache Valentine's Day hearts.

"And when we finish, we'll be starting our Mardi Gras Masques of Transgression," he said, holding up the one he'd made. "See, now I'm in disguise. Once you put these on, I won't recognize any of you, which means you can get away with whatever you want, any of the seven deadly sins. Except probably murder, don't murder anybody. I'm looking at you, Irene."

"Murder's not one of the seven deadly sins," Irene groused back. She was a fat and sharp-witted old woman whom no one really liked. Most of the old folks were vacant and cooperative, but he and Irene often heckled each other.

"Maybe not, but that kerchief has got to be," he said, gesturing to her garish orange scarf. It was patterned with purple flowers that looked like puckered assholes.

"Burn," chuckled the woman next to her. Some of them, adorably, had picked up James' millennial slang.

"Well, not too long from now, *he'll* be burning in hell," Irene muttered sourly under her breath.

"I heard that. Not too long from now? What's that supposed to mean?" James said, his hands fluttering to his cheeks. "Do I need a different moisturizer, Irene? Am I wrinkly?"

Blatant homophobia was not something James had to deal with on a daily basis anymore, given the circles he ran in. In situations like this it felt humorous and quaint, creating in him a sort of nostalgia of disgust for his adolescence in rural Kentucky. His parents, not particularly political one way or the other, had accepted his queerness with the same lack of interest they took in his photography and track meets. Of course, there were the same school bullies and dumb jocks that every gay teen has to endure, but James was generally able to shut them up. He had a killer sneer and knew exactly what to say and do to make anyone feel powerless and insecure. It was a skill he prided himself on, and he honed it constantly by keeping a cynical running commentary in his mind, a never-ending inner monologue of condescension toward everyone and everything around him. He had to be careful, especially when drinking, not to let these cruelties slip to the surface and come out of his mouth, to keep his playful negging from crossing the line into real hurtfulness. It did happen, and he knew what it looked like on each of his friend's faces. That momentary flash of shock and hurt, so quickly replaced by a blank smile and minutes, hours, even days of keeping him at arm's length emotionally. *Whatever*, he always told himself. People shouldn't be so sensitive.

"Okay, everybody," he said at the end of the class hour. "Leave your hearts on the rack to dry. Everybody except Irene, whose heart is already as dry as a ten-day-old dog turd."

There it was, that momentary flash of pain and vulnerability across the old woman's face. He didn't care.

Anthony, a sweet old man who James was pretty damn sure was a homo too, took him aside after class as he packed up the supplies.

"You should try to be gentler with Irene," he said. "Her daughter just died, you know."

"Was her daughter a homophobe too?"

"Oh, she doesn't mean those things she says. She just wants attention. You know, she doesn't get any visitors."

James watched Irene as she shuffled over to the rack to put her heart out to dry. "LOVE! LOVE! LOVE!" it said in glittery all-caps. He'd watched her painstakingly letter the words with her shaking hands. She really did work hard on the art projects. Apart from her shitty attitude, she was probably the best student in the class.

He got in his car and drove home in a foul mood. Why had Irene's daughter died, he wondered. Probably overweight like her mother, a victim of high cholesterol or something like that; James didn't understand people who didn't make an effort to stay in shape. But still, to lose a daughter. He'd lost a friend last year, one of the other tour guides, and that shit could get dark. He thought again of Irene and her shaking hands. Her scarf hadn't really been that ugly. At least she made an effort to be different, at least she wore something other than the plain scrubs so many of the residents showed up to class in. If he was in a boring-ass nursing home, he'd probably wear weird shit too. He pictured himself, old and infirm, wearing his by-then-threadbare leopard-print trucker hat just to get attention from the staff who didn't even like him. Irene never had any visitors, Anthony had said. James' anger began to soften, a gloomy knot of sadness blooming in his chest. Surely, when he got old, he'd be alone too, abandoned in some nursing home with no one to visit him. Most of the other residents had spouses who'd died, but he was fairly sure Irene had never had a husband to begin with. She was too much of a cunt to find love. Like him.

In his sudden despair, James allowed his mind to come to rest on Elliot. Just for a moment, he told himself, just until the feeling passed. He pictured Elliot at his desk in Cambridge, surrounded by books and papers and telescopes. Not that a quantum physicist needed telescopes, but it was a nice image. One of his students would be there with him, and Elliot would be animatedly explaining some convoluted mathematical concept, slipping into the lisp that sometimes came out when he was excited. James had loved listening to Elliot talk. They'd spent whole days lying on a blanket on the Loyola quad, drinking cheap beer under the autumn sun while Elliot talked about string theory and James listened, his head in his lap. Elliot was a genius. His hair had been fine and soft like brown cotton candy, an amorphous fuzzy mass upon his head, and his eyes were deep green. He had a nice dick too, but his hands had been what James found most sensual—they were as expressive in gesture, gentle in touch, the nails always neatly trimmed. James and Elliot had dated throughout most of college. Then Elliot had gone away on a graduate scholarship to Harvard.

They'd kept in touch at first. Mostly through letters—Elliot had been such a romantic—but gradually, the letters ceased, and when they did, James was sure Elliot had found someone new, some fellow genius with ambition and drive and talent, who would show him all the devotion and kindness and love he deserved. Surely, they'd be married by now, with two or three beautiful children and tenure-track professorships. Elliot deserved all that and more.

James' basic-bitch roommates were in the living room when he got home from the Senior Center, two young medical students who clearly thought of him as their sassy gay friend. He didn't even like them.

"Oh, hey girl!" one of them called out as he walked in.

"Hi," he sighed. They didn't seem to notice his dejection.

"We're going out tonight!" the other one exclaimed. "Wanna come?"

I'd rather put rocks in my pockets and walk into the river than hang out with your sorry basic asses, he thought, but feigned disappointment. "Darlin', I can't, I have to work."

"Oh right, your little ghost tour thing. Funnn!"

"*So* fun," he spat. "It's *adorable*."

"Well, we'll be thinking of you!"

"You're gonna *kill* it in that outfit. Slay!" Whenever James was feeling particularly hateful toward the girls, he punched up the queerness to comic extremes, just to see if they'd call his bluff, but they never did.

"Thanks, girl! Tonight's gonna be so lit."

"Yas kween! Praise Beyoncé!" he said, and slammed the door of his bedroom.

He checked his phone: a text from Landon, *"How's ur day?"* with three blue hearts and a rainbow. He started typing about his workout at the gym, about the seniors and their crafts and Irene's bad attitude, about his stupid roommates and how sad he was feeling and how much he wanted to take Landon in his arms and hold him and be held by him until everything felt better, and by the time he was finished, he'd written a chunk of text two or three inches long. Annoyed at himself, he parked his thumb on the backspace key and deleted it all.

"Fine," he sent. And then, four minutes later, added:

"U?"

After dinner, he drove to the Quarter, found a parking spot at Dauphine and St. Ann, and walked the few blocks to St. Peter Street, waving hello to a few acquaintances as he passed the gay bars. He wrinkled his nose at the acrid smell of piss on the block of St. Peter approaching Bourbon, where drunk idiots always ducked around the corner to relieve themselves. Sometimes there was shit too, and tonight a new pile of orange vomit had appeared next to somebody's front stoop. James pursed his lips and tried not to inhale as he made his way through the crush of humanity on Bourbon Street. There were packs of drunken, bead-wearing bros hollering at the strippers smoking on the balconies, basic bitches with fresh blowouts and hand grenades trying not to trip in their stilettos, and dumpy middle-aged couples clutching each other's hands, looking simultaneously ecstatic and terrified.

Finally, he reached Madame Livaudais' Curiosity Shop, outside of which the Tour of Lost Souls departed nightly at eight PM. The shop was cluttered and homey, stuffed with charms and Voodoo dolls and incense, and the green paint on the shutters outside was old and peeling in that quaint, authentic way that always made people *ooh* and *aah* over the old-world charm of the three-hundred-year-old city. Sofia and Poppy were already there outside the shop when James rolled up, and Graham, the manager, was sitting on his stool selling tickets. He was an absent-minded lush, a sweet and ordinary guy who always showed up to work with a big smile on his face, hammered. He got fired and rehired over and over.

"Hello," James said as he approached. Sofia glared at him.

"My my, if looks could kill! What's up, Princess?"

"You were kind of an asshole to Vik last night, you know."

James tried to recall the prior evening's events. He remembered that he and Vik had parted ways without saying goodbye but wasn't entirely sure why.

"Was I? Hmm. Not all that unusual."

"That stuff about not having a life or whatever really got to him."

"None of us have a life, what's the big deal?"

"I don't know, but he's been moping all day."

"Oh, for goodness' sake."

"It's not really my business, just thought you should know."

"Well, aren't you a gem."

She rolled her eyes and turned away. Sofia was nice and all, but James couldn't understand why Vik dated her. They'd started hooking up a year ago, and she'd been just another piece of ass then, one of many beautiful boys and girls that Vik enjoyed and released in much the same way James did with his young conquests. But she didn't disappear like the others. At every bar, every event, there was that cute Latina girl with the crooked teeth and blue hair, until she finally started working at Spirits of Yore—and Vik hadn't even put up a fuss about it! Lord. James knew Vik had tried to tell the girl that he didn't want a relationship, that his sexual precociousness simply could not be stifled by monogamy, but somehow—James was sure it involved some mystic spell cast by her vagina, utterly bewildering to a gay man—here they were almost a year later, bickering and reconciling and cuddling up together every night like all the other boring basic couples in the world.

Launch time arrived, and Graham wobbled down the sidewalk to send out the tour guides. He split the gaggle on the sidewalk into two groups, one departing toward Bourbon with Sofia, and one heading in the other direction with James toward the Cathedral.

"This better be cool," he heard the young woman directly behind him say to her boyfriend as he led the group away. They were sort of trashy-looking, with bland spray-tanned faces and matching sports jerseys. The girl was in cheap and uncomfortable looking heels, and the man's pants were sagging stupidly below his ass.

"Are we gonna see ghosts?" the boyfriend said, somewhat aggressively, to the back of James' head.

"Well, you know what they say," he drawled, not in the mood to have to make this joke. "The more spirits you drink, the more spirits you see."

The girl laughed, but the boyfriend was not placated. "What we paid twenty-five bucks for if we're not gonna see any ghosts?"

"Take lots of pictures, you might catch something."

"You heard that?" the man said to another couple behind them, evidently their friends. "He said you might get a ghost in a picture."

"Yeah, whatever," James heard the second man say. "Don't we get free drinks or something?"

James braced himself for a difficult tour and tried to warm them up with small talk. "So, where y'all from?"

"We go to Alabama," the first guy said disinterestedly, and the one in the back yelled *"Roll tide!"* like a dog drooling at Pavlov's bell. James rolled his eyes so hard, it hurt and hoisted his pimp cane higher in the air as they turned the corner onto Royal. He hoped the Alabama bros and their girlfriends would be sucked into the crowd as they crossed the street and vanish from his tour. But such miracles were rare.

In the shadow of the Cathedral, he gathered his group close around him and delivered his introduction. "Good evening, everyone! My name is James, and I'll be your tour guide this evening. But before we get started, just a bit about what to expect. First of all, and I hope you all know this already, this is a walking tour. We'll be strolling around the French Quarter, stopping at several different spots that are all important in New Orleans history and also—you guessed it—haunted." Most of the crowd was nodding along pleasantly.

"Now I'm sure you're wondering, are we going to go into any of these haunted places? I'm afraid the answer is mostly no, but a little bit yes—halfway through the tour, we will be stopping into the city's oldest and most haunted bar."

"Fuck yeah," one of the Alabama bros grunted. The drunk ones always perked up when they heard there'd be a bar.

"Another question I get asked all the time: James, are we going to see any ghosts on this tour?"

"We better!" one of the bros yelled again. James took a deep breath.

"Well, it's certainly possible. Bit of a disclaimer, though, I personally cannot summon ghosts and spirits at will. If I could, I probably would not be a tour guide working for tips on the streets. No, I would be in a very nice haunted mansion, with my own TV show, surrounded by handsome scientists."

The bros snickered and muttered to each other. He ignored them and focused instead on a smart-looking middle-aged lady up front, who had laughed at the joke and was smiling at him. He finished going over the rules—don't stand in the street, don't lean on the buildings, etcetera—and then started the tour.

"Alright, folks. It's the beginning of the tour, which means I'm going to start right at the beginning of New Orleans history. This city is old, y'all; we were founded in 1718. And back then, Louisiana was a colony of France. This spot was chosen as the capital, named La Nouvelle Orleans for the Duke of Orleans, some hot-shot in France at the time, and it was slapped down right here at the mouth of the river because in those days, whoever controlled its mouth controlled the trade. Great idea, right? Not so much. Because back then, this whole area was a big 'ol nasty swamp. Bienville got to work draining it, but even after that, nobody really wanted to live here, because New Orleans was gross. I mean, it kind of still is..." That always got a laugh. "But in those early days, it was absolutely swarming with snakes and alligators, the streets were a dumping ground for raw sewage, and you'd catch an infectious disease if someone within ten feet of you so much as sneezed. If you came down here from somewhere else and you weren't used to this climate, hadn't built up any immunity, oh honey. Any given summer, you would probably just...*die*." The group laughed again. James went on to describe how, in the early 1700s, Bienville had begged King Louis to send settlers to the swampy new colony, and how the King's response had been to open the Bastille, put the heretics, drunks, murderers and crazies on ships, and send them to New Orleans. "Kind of explains a lot, doesn't it?" This type of humor about New Orleans, playing up its debauchery, always went over well with the tourists. It was lowest-common-denominator type stuff, but you had to get them interested somehow.

He talked about the transfer of Louisiana from France to Spain, the French coup, the gruesome display of the rebels' corpses here in the alley, and the ghosts of the French priests who stealthily abducted the bodies during a hurricane in order to give them a proper burial. He was working his magic, reeling them in. The women up front were nodding and smiling kindly, the way middle-aged women sometimes did, and it made him feel surprisingly warm and grateful in some obscure part of his heart.

These women fell into step with James up front as he led them to the next stop, asking how long he'd been a tour guide, where he was from, whether he liked giving tours, and all the other basic questions he answered every night of his life. The Alabama bros and their girlfriends were at the back of the group, and he could hear them shouting dumb nonsense.

"You must get tired of dealing with tomfoolery like that," one of the nice ladies said, leaning toward him confidentially.

"Oh, it's constant," he said. "You learn to manage it."

They crossed Jackson Square, and he stopped at Muriel's, the imposing restaurant on the corner, to let the group peer in the window at the table that was always set for its resident ghost. Then they continued down Chartres, James' favorite street in the Quarter. It was usually quiet on Chartres, and a little darker too. Some blocks were illuminated only by dimly flickering gas lamps, which the tourists always loved. He liked this part of the walk, the entrée to the Lower Quarter, where the streets weren't so bright and smelly and the beautiful old buildings weren't covered in gaudy signs, and you could actually breathe a little, away from the crowds. He could always hear the group murmuring about how pretty it was around this point in the walk, and he usually fielded a few questions about the architecture, the unending row of two- and three-story buildings lining the street, their facades uninterrupted except for gated alleyways to hidden courtyards.

A chilly wind blew up Dumaine Street from the river, and James zipped his jacket. Since when was New Orleans this cold? There were always at least a few nights in December and January when the temperature dipped into the thirties, but this year, winter seemed to really be feeling itself. New Orleans wasn't built for cold, he thought, glancing around at the unhappy tropical plants that hung from the wrought-iron balconies over the street. Someone should have brought them inside.

He told the group briefly about the vampires in the Ursuline Convent then led them up the block to the house where he always told the story of the Swamp Witch. She was a beautiful young girl seduced by a degenerate who broke her heart and betrayed her, but who lived on to develop witchy powers and exact vengeance upon him and everyone he held dear. The women liked it, but he could hear the Alabama bros snickering at the back of the group, making fun of his voice.

"She moves to the Swamp and begins to communicate with the birds and insects—"

"And *butterflies*," one of them whispered with an exaggerated gay sibilance. His friends laughed.

James made meaningful eye contact with the guy as he spoke his next paragraph. This asshole wanted to have a dick-measuring contest? James was happy to oblige.

"And in the swamp, she realizes just how much better off she is without that idiot who laughed at her and cast her aside. From her servant Labasse, Kate learns hoodoo and begins to make gris-gris and potions by hand. In fact, she starts to realize that many things are better when done with her own hands. You see, her former lover's income wasn't the only thing he had that was positively...tiny."

He flicked his eyes downward to the Alabama bro's crotch as he said this, and everybody, Mister Bigshot Bro's friends included, snorted in laughter. The guy tugged self-consciously on his big "A" hat and looked away, his cheeks reddening. His girlfriend was still laughing when James finished the story and led them away.

Later, at the bar break, he took a deep breath of the cool night air as the group dashed into the bar to pee and buy overpriced beers. With groups like this, the break was key to his sanity. Just a few minutes to himself, to chill out and look at his phone and—

One of the Alabama hoes tumbled out of the bar and into James' personal space.

"So, is this all, like, true?" she asked aggressively, puffing out her tits at him like some kind of exotic bird. He took a step away.

"The history is."

"What about the hauntings or whatever?"

"Well, I suppose that depends on whether or not you believe in the paranormal."

"I'm a Christian," she said disdainfully.

"And?" he said.

"It means I think there's certain stuff that God, like... *frowns upon*."

"Like coming to a city full of addicts and queers and sinners to get wasted and have premarital sex and beg every local you encounter for a coke hookup?"

Her mouth flopped open and closed three times before she gave up, glared at him, and wandered away.

Oops. Having directly insulted two of them, James was certain that she and the rest of the Alabama cretins would fail to rejoin the group after the bar break, but he was surprisingly mistaken. All six of them re-appeared, fresh beers in hand, and though Bro #1 and Hoe #3 looked cranky about it, the others seemed excited to continue. He told a story at the Andrew Jackson Hotel, which was haunted by the ghosts of prank-playing orphans then took them down the street to the Bourbon Orleans Hotel, where he described the famed Quadroon Balls of the 1800s.

The last stop on his tour was his favorite: The Sultan's Palace. He pulled up his group in front of the big pink building at the corner of Dauphine and Orleans and began his final story.

"Take a look at this beautiful rose pink building behind me, y'all. This building was the home of a wealthy antebellum plantation owner called Jean Baptiste LaPrete. After the Civil War, though, when slavery was ended," (he half-expected a *boooo* from the Alabama kids, but none came), "LaPrete found himself running out of cash. No longer able to afford this place, he was forced to rent it out. But because it was so large, and because nearly everyone in the South was hurting financially after the war, he had a hard time finding a renter for it.

"But finally, in 1872, LaPrete was in a bar bitching and moaning about his unhappy situation to anybody who would listen when a handsome, dark man in a turban introduced himself. Think Arjun Rampal—" he said, looking around at the blank faces. "—What, no Bollywood fans? Guess all those hours I spent watching shirtless Indian guys dance around for research were a waste of time–darn." That got a laugh. "Anyway, this man claimed to be Prince Suleyman, a Turkish Sultan, and told LaPrete that he was looking for a place to stay with his large family. LaPrete didn't know whether this guy was legit or not, but he agreed to rent the house to him on the condition that he pay two full years' rent up front. Believe it or not, the man presented the money the very next day, and LaPrete skipped off to spend it.

"So, Prince Suleyman moved into the mansion with his 'family.' But it becomes evident pretty quickly that they're not family at all. They're friends. Special friends. In fact, what we have here is Prince Suleyman's *harem*, dozens and dozens of beautiful, sexy, young people, both women and men."

One of the hoes wrinkled her nose and went *"Ew."* James ignored her.

"And then he began to party. The Prince's household feasted, drank, and enjoyed a never-ending supply of opium and hashish, twenty-four hours a day. This party just never ended. Now, I don't know about y'all, but uh...where's my invitation?" Most of them chuckled.

"It went on like this for a month. Then another month, then six months, then a year. This house becomes a whole world unto itself, a world where pleasure is the only pursuit. The Sultan has everything he could possibly want. He's surrounded by beauty, sex, and every drug known to man at that time. You think New Orleans is a haven for pleasure and debauchery? What goes on in this house makes the rest of the city look like a convent. It's never-ending ecstasy, or never-ending sin; I guess it depends how you feel about that sort of thing. But it's a moot point anyway, because no one from around town is invited to join the Prince in his revelry. He keeps bodyguards around the perimeter and stays locked up inside his mansion, alone with his harem.

"This goes on for eighteen months straight. The Prince and his household remain shrouded in mystery until one day in 1873, when a young lady walking by the house feels a drop of something wet on her shoulder."

"Blood!" one of the middle-aged ladies whispered, and James nodded.

"Looking up, she realizes in horror that there is a steady drip-drip-drip of hot, wet blood coming from the gallery above. She also notices a thick pool of blood oozing out from under the door, spilling down the stairs.

"When the police arrive and enter the house, they find a nightmarish scene unparalleled in New Orleans history. The floor is covered in a layer of blood so thick they can't walk without slipping in it and have to hold onto banisters and mantelpieces to help them move through the house. There are arms, legs, and heads strewn all over, and quickly it becomes clear that every person in the mansion has been brutally murdered, dismembered and decapitated. In fact, the police have to do a 'head count' to assess the number of victims, and I mean that literally: they're actually picking up severed heads off the floor and putting them in a row. But after all their counting, one person seems to be missing.

"The Sultan!" Bro #2 exclaimed.

"The Sultan. They don't find him until they go out to the courtyard and notice a stiff hand reaching up from below the ground, as if trying to claw its way out. Some digging reveals the body of the Prince himself, his face covered in horrible disfiguring cuts and his throat so crammed with dirt that it's clear he was buried alive.

"The massacre at the Sultan's palace is the largest mass murder in New Orleans history. Nearly seventy people were killed here. Now, at the time, people around town suspected it was the work of pirates. But today, we have a different theory. It turns out that in the nineteenth century, middle eastern countries had a rather gruesome custom. Whenever a new Sultan rose to power, he would send assassins to kill all of his male relatives, to ensure that no one except his direct descendants could ever ascend the throne. We think that Prince Suleyman was not actually the Sultan, but the *brother* of the Sultan, who had fled to New Orleans when his brother assumed the throne. But alas, he didn't run far enough. His brother sent emissaries to track him down, and of course when they found him here, he and his entire household were murdered in cold blood.

"Today, the Sultan's Palace has been broken up into six smaller apartments. Are the tenants here aware of what happened in 1873? You bet. Many report hearing strange sounds in the night—the sound of fleshy thuds, like body parts hitting the floors. And every so often, someone will report seeing a pool of fresh blood in the foyer, only to vanish an instant later.

"And if you live here, you might someday turn the corner from one room into another and see before you, clear as day, the entire massacre, just as it looked that fateful day in 1873. Blood sprayed across the walls, piles of arms and legs, and a few disembodied heads gaping at you, their mouths twisted in screams of agony. Because here in New Orleans, history always rises to the surface eventually. You can try to be like the Sultan's brother—run from your past, conquer your fear with debauchery—but it always catches up with you eventually, doesn't it? And it'll bury you alive, if you're not careful."

He took a dramatic pause. "And that's the end of the tour."

There was a smattering of applause: mostly from the middle-aged ladies, who immediately stepped forward to tip.

"Hey," one of the now-very-drunk Alabama bros said after the ladies had departed, staggering toward him with his chest puffed up. He made a sudden threatening movement toward James but then clasped him by the arm all the way up to the elbow.

"That was awesome, dude. You're cool." He handed James a ten.

"Bless your heart," James said. Ten bucks wasn't great for a group of four, but he hadn't expected anything at all from them. "Now run along," he said, shooing them away like a mother dismissing her toddlers. "Go have fun on Bourbon Street! Alcohol, mmm."

When they were gone, James shoved his tips into his pocket and went back to the bar, like he always did after tours, ready to bitch to Vik about the night's bullshit. But the only other people there in the courtyard were Ralphie, Angela, and Ruby. Ruby he liked okay—she was a bit of a drama queen but also a bit of a bitch, and he respected that in a person. Ralphie was just Ralphie, so ridiculous you couldn't help but love him, as annoying as he sometimes was. But Angela… no one liked Angela. She was already in the middle of some pompous lecture.

"The important thing to remember about goth culture is that there's no one *defining* characteristic. True, Karl Lagerfeld's instruction on his invitations to the Soirée Moratoire Noir party, *'tenue tragique noire absolument obligatoire'*—black tragic dress absolutely required—could be said to be a guiding tenet, however there are simply too many different subcultures to—"

"Excuse my interruption of this *fascinating* conversation," James said, sliding onto a stool next to Ruby, "but have y'all seen Vik?"

"He went to one of the parades with Sofia," Ruby said. "Cleopatra or something."

"It's still going? It's after ten."

"She thought they could still catch some of it. You know how she is about parades."

"That's true, she's a total hoe for them…ugh. Vik could have at least told me."

"I think it's like, a date," Ralphie said. "You know, where two people who like each other romantically hang out and do cute stuff together without their friends tagging along."

"Not that you would know," James said, and a look of hurt sprung to Ralphie's face. *Too much?* James wondered. But it was true, Ralphie was eternally single. Maybe if he'd learn to wear his clothes right side out, he'd have better luck with girls…he was getting up, now, going into the bar.

Ruby tried to say something, but Angela was talking over everyone again. "I generally don't go to many of the uptown parades, but I'm looking forward to Chewbacchus tomorrow; it's always been one of my favorites. I've actually marched with the Delorean Royalty sub krewe on one or two occasions, but I took issue with the way the responsibilities were delegated, particularly regarding—"

"As deeply compelling as this topic continues to be, I need a refreshment," James said, going into the bar after Ralphie. Angela didn't pause.

"God, does that woman ever shut up?" he said, sitting on a barstool next to Ralphie and gesturing to Avery for his usual, a G&T. "Why is she even here? She never comes to the Rat."

"Yeah… I think that may be my fault."

"What? Why?"

"Last night, when she was here, I told her she should hang out with us more."

"Dear God, Ralphie, why!"

"Hey, come on, she's not that bad."

"Have you *met* her?"

"I respect Angela. She's a strong, independent woman."

"She's also got literally zero self-awareness and an ego the size of Russia, my God."

"I just don't want anyone to feel left out."

"Well thanks, Saint Ralphie. Now I can't even enjoy a drink after my shitty tour."

"Jeez. Sorry," Ralphie said, looking hurt again.

"No, it's not you. I'm already in a pissy mood."

"Why?"

"I told you, bad tour."

"What happened?"

"Just a bunch of ignorant rednecks making my life difficult."

"I'm sorry."

"It's whatever. Well, I'm gonna head out."

"Gonna go find Vik and Sofia?"

"No...you're right, they're probably being all gross and couple-y. Wouldn't want to intrude."

"Don't you have a boyfriend? Couldn't you go be all gross and couple-y too?

It's still Valentine's Day."

"He's *not* my boyfriend."

"Oh. But he was here last night, I saw you kiss him—"

"You sweet, old fashioned thing. A kiss does not a boyfriend make."

"Is that Shakespeare?" Ralphie grinned.

"Yeah, *The Two Faggots of Verona*."

"Oh right, his most famous gay romp. Or would that be Coriol-*anus*? Heyyy-o!"

James laughed and rolled his eyes. Ralphie was surprisingly clever sometimes; James was always a bit taken aback when he was reminded of how smart the dope really was.

He finished his drink, said goodnight to Ralphie, and went back to his car. Settling into the front seat, he pulled the wad of tips out of his pocket and counted them. Sixty bucks: not terrible for such a weird tour. He wanted to be proud for bringing the Alabama group around, for shutting down their bullshit and earning their affection, but he couldn't muster anything but apathy. Fuck those people, honestly. Fuck straight privilege, fuck ignorance and plain-old stupidity, fuck everyone who came to New Orleans to get wasted and trash their Airbnbs and piss in the street. Yes, he'd force-fed them some substance and history, but only by beating them into submission with shame and derision. Thinking about it made James feel deeply lonely. If he could just talk to Vik about it, laugh at the sad state of humanity, at least have someone to feel superior *with*...he wanted to text him and apologize for being an asshole the other night, but that wasn't the sort of thing James did.

He stuffed his tips into his wallet and pulled out his phone. A text from Landon: *"Hey! I miss u, wanna get into some trouble?"* Yes, he thought, yes, I do want to get into some trouble. I want drugs and I want alcohol and I want to forget; I want to fuck off and forget about all of this, everything.

But not with Landon. Landon wasn't trouble. Landon was something else entirely, James thought, the boy's big dairy-cow eyes swimming in his mind.

He leaned back in his seat and gazed out through the windshield at the gay bar across the street. There were a few people outside drinking and laughing, their breath little puffs of white in the cold night air. He closed his eyes.

A minute or two later, his phone buzzed in his hand. It was a notification from Grindr. A DM.

"Hey." The DM was from someone named Troy. Peering at the picture, James realized that it was the Hulk, last week's fling, the big muscly brute he didn't think he'd ever hear from again. Another message came a second later.

"I'm free tn if you want to hook up again."

The first time James had been to New Orleans was with his parents and sister on a family vacation, decades ago. And although they'd spent most of their time wandering up and down Bourbon Street with the other bland out-of-towners, twelve-year-old James had gotten enough glimpses at the weirdos and queers on the side streets that he'd understood what kind of place the French Quarter really was—understood that it wasn't really *for* people like his parents, but for people like him. And he'd dreamed of living in the Quarter, a place where whole blocks flew rainbow flags, a place where he could be safe and happy and surrounded by all the other gay misfits of the world who had been drawn to this magical place of belonging like moths to a flame. And of course, in the fantasy he had a boyfriend, a soulmate, a person to share it all with. On a Friday night like this, they'd go to a bar like the one across the street, socialize for a few hours, and then walk back home to their perfect decrepit little apartment hand in hand, laughing and tipsy and in love.

He looked at his phone again. *"I'm free tn if you want to hook up again."*

James knew where he lived. He remembered the way.

"I'll be right over."

CHAPTER 3
The Casket Girls

The brie-and-cranberry croquettes were browning nicely in the oven and th carrot-ginger soup would need to simmer for just another minute or tw Angela thought as she tasted a bit of it on the end of a wooden spoon. Wer the lemon tarts plated properly? Yes, they looked picture-perfect there on he grandmother's china. It was mid-century Wedgwood with a blue-and-pink flc ral pattern; perhaps too formal for such an event, but what was the point of hav ing nice things if they were never used? She'd enjoy telling her guests the stor of the china, of its journey from England when her forebears had immigrate from the Old Country and her grandmother's insistence that Angela be the on to inherit it, based on her appreciation of the finer things in life. "I'm a bit of a Anglophile," she'd laugh, and tell them about her childhood obsession with th Queen and English tea-time rituals.

Angela had been meaning to host a little get-together like this for som months but could never seem to find the time. She had to admit, she kept s busy with her tours and her reading and blogging that there never seemed tim to socialize. But it was important, wasn't it, the act of spending time with othe people, particularly those with shared experiences and interests? She took th croquettes out of the oven, perfectly browned and deliciously fragrant, look ing forward to the opportunity to share her favorite dishes with friends. Wa "friends" the right word? Perhaps not—Jennifer was more of an acquaintanc and Sofia was a coworker. But there was the *potential* for friendship, and surel a pleasant lunch together would help move things in that direction.

She went into the living room of her apartment to make sure everythin was just-so. Her favorite sage-currant candle filled the room with a soft an pleasant aroma, and she'd already set the table with linen napkins, utensils, an a glass pitcher of homemade raspberry tea. She smoothed the couch cover an fluffed the throw pillows. Everything was tidy and stylish, and her friends woul most certainly feel at home, she thought to herself, picturing the three of ther gathered around the table sharing treats and tea and conversation. Back in th kitchen, she poured the carrot-ginger soup into a tureen and lined all the foo neatly on the sideboard.

Now for the guests to arrive. She checked her pocket-watch—everything had timed out perfectly, and it was now eight minutes until noon, the official start time of their little lunch date. Angela went to the living room and perched on a velvet pouf, her eyes on the door.

At 11:56, her phone buzzed. It was a text from Jennifer: *"Hey, really sorry but I'm not going to be able to make it today, something came up. Another time maybe!"*

Angela sagged with disappointment. What had come up, she wondered. Odd of Jennifer to leave it so vague. She hoped everything was alright. But, she thought, trying to pluck her spirits back up, it wouldn't be so bad to enjoy some one-on-one time with Sofia, would it? They could swap stories about tours, chat about their coworkers, get to know each other. Angela was always meaning to get to know the other tour guides better. Maybe she could even impart some advice to the young woman, being, after all, many years her senior, both in age and experience.

12:00 came and went. There's no such thing as "on time" in New Orleans, Angela reminded herself with an inward chuckle, and she tried to relax. At 12:12, she went back to the kitchen to check on the food and found that the croquettes were losing their warmth, a shame because they were most delicious fresh out of the oven. Well, surely there would be more occasions like this, more occasions to cook and eat and socialize. Perhaps they could even make a weekly date of it.

At 12:28, she sent Sofia a text. *"Hello, lovely lady! Just checking on your E.T.A. Yummy treats await!"*

Five minutes later, she got a response. *"Omg was that today? Totally forgot, so sorry. I'm in Chalmette, don't think I can make it."*

"Don't worry about it. Another time, then."

"Def," Sofia wrote back.

Def.

It was a coincidence, surely, nothing more than an unfortunate coincidence. People live complicated lives with a myriad of commitments, people make mistakes in their schedules, sure there was nothing personal in it, Angela thought, trying to smooth the lump in her throat. Of course, she had given them both hand-printed invitations and reminded them several times, but, well, some people just weren't particularly reliable. She finished putting the croquettes into tupperware and glanced at the ginger-carrot soup, upon which a gummy film had formed. She poured it into the garbage. It was a delicate dish and would be no good reheated.

Angela now had many hours to pass before she had to be in the French Quarter for her tour. There were several options as to how to spend this time: she could experiment with some of the new eye palettes she'd ordered, she could do a bit of meal preparation for the upcoming week, she could work on her vampire blog, or she could read. With so many hobbies, there was always an engaging way to pass the time. She settled on trying the new eye palettes and sat down at her vanity. Today, she decided, she would do a nude lip, dark brows, and a smokey purple eye, a look a bit outside her comfort zone (especially the nude lip; generally, she chose saturated reds and purples) but worth a try. The palette she'd ordered was up to the task, a set of incredibly rich pigmented colors with just a hint of shimmer and micronized glitter flecks. One sweep of the wondrous stuff was enough to shade both her eyes. She was an expert at makeup, having completed an extensive Mary Kay course and always spending at least an hour per day crafting her look.

After finishing her face, Angela went to her wardrobe to select an appropriate outfit for the rest of the day. For the failed lunch, she had been wearing a silk kimono over a light shift, much more colorful than her usual style, and a shift back into her traditional darker hues felt *apropos*. In the back of her closet, she found a black velvet dress that she hadn't worn since a funeral last year, the deceased having been another young lady Angela had tried to befriend, but who had died in an accident, and she hadn't worn it since because it was so heavy—and, of course, the tragic association. But lately, the temperatures had been so cold that the dress seemed an apt choice, thick and warm as it was. She accessorized it with a burgundy cloche, a lace cravat, and false but convincing ruby chandelier earrings. Tour guests often commented on her style, which she believed added to the experience a level of drama and authenticity that frankly some of the other tour guides, in their more casual attire, did not provide. She'd mentioned this to some of them, suggested that their ratings on TripAdvisor might improve if they "upped their wardrobe game," so to speak, but no one ever implemented her advice. Ah, well; their loss.

When she was dressed, Angela sat down on the sofa and picked up her copy of Le Fanu's *Carmilla*, which she'd read several times and had recently plucked off the shelf again. It was the first vampire novel she'd ever been introduced to, and the last book she'd read aloud to her father before his death. It was a paperback, worn and faded, the pages yellowing. She was reading it again for the umpteenth time.

And why not? By this time, she was sure, Angela had read every vampire book ever written. She'd seen *Buffy* and *True Blood* and *The Vampire Diaries* and *The Originals*, knew every pop-culture reference, could quote Bram Stoker and Charlaine Harris and Anne Rice—even, she hated to say it, Stephanie Meyer—in her sleep. "I live for the undead," she liked to say, enjoying the clever play on words. Just thinking about vampires made her itch for her next tour.

She opened Carmilla to the fourth chapter where she'd left off, her fingers tracing the florid sentences on the soft, yellowing pages as she read.

> *"Sometimes after an hour of apathy, my strange and beautiful companion would take my hand and hold it with a fond pressure, renewed again and again; blushing softly, gazing in my face with languid and burning eyes, and breathing so fast that her dress rose and fell with the tumultuous respiration. It was like the ardour of a lover; it embarrassed me; it was hateful and yet overpowering; and with gloating eyes she drew me to her, and her hot lips travelled along my cheek in kisses; and she would whisper, almost in sobs, 'You are mine, you shall be mine, and you and I are one forever.'"*

The language flooded Angela with longing—but for what? The sensuality of it was engrossing, even mildly arousing, to be sure. When Angela had first read *Carmilla* in middle school, she'd been intrigued by the feelings the book had stirred in her, had even wondered whether she was a lesbian. But in high school she'd decided that at most she was bisexual, and as she'd aged into adulthood, she had realized that her bisexuality was really more a sort of bi-apathy. Neither men nor women were particularly sexually exciting to Angela, and she went on dates more for the conversation than anything else. No, the longing she'd felt when reading *Carmilla* for the first time when she was eleven years old was something other than sexual. And she still couldn't quite put her finger on what it was.

And so, she'd kept reading vampire novels. Her father, also an avid reader, had been happy to buy Angela every book she wanted, even the trashy stuff. He had been proud of her intelligence, happy to nurture her love of reading, always encouraging and supportive of her interests. Every evening, Angela would rush through her schoolwork so that she could join him in the living room, sit in his lap, and read aloud to him. Angela loved making a presentation of it: reading passionately, changing her voice to mirror the characters, letting the story carry both of them to another world. Angela had never felt as close to anyone as she had when reading aloud to her father. When he'd died, shortly after she'd dropped out of college, she'd lost her only friend.

Later that afternoon, Angela decided to leave the house. It was still two hours until tour time, but she could go down to the Quarter early, have a stroll, maybe run into someone she knew. She put on her kitten-heeled Victorian boots and brought along her black parasol to keep the sun off her skin—for obvious reasons, she preferred to remain very pale and went to great lengths to protect her skin from UV exposure.

Angela's apartment was not far from the French Quarter, and she usually walked there, head held high, stopping to smell flowers and snap pictures whenever the urge took her. She enjoyed listening to the tidy click-click-click of her own heels as she walked down the sidewalk, her arms clasped in front of her and her parasol dangling from one wrist. She thought, sometimes, of what it would have been like to exist one or two hundred years earlier, when people had taken more pride in things. Back then, people had put more effort into their day-to-day lives: into their speech, their attire, their social engagements. More care was placed in the simple things, for the simple things were the only things.

She crossed Jackson Square and climbed the steps of the levee to the riverwalk, which situated her directly between the country's longest river and its oldest church. *What a place to live,* she thought to herself, turning from the impressive vantage of St. Louis Cathedral to gaze at the murky, slow-moving water of the Mississippi. She loved this city. Despite its stench and its crime and its crumbling infrastructure, New Orleans was the most perfect city in the world: perfect in its imperfections. Only in a place like this could reality match—nay, *exceed*—imagination, only here could life jump off the page the way it did in novels. She inhaled deeply of the mud-scented air, opening her parasol to let the cold breeze tug at it.

"Lady, you lookin' like somethin' out of a *movie*," a homeless gentleman nearby called out. She turned to face him.

"Why, thank you, sir! I shall take that as a compliment."

"Say, you could spare fifty cents so I could get something to eat?"

She took two dollars out of her pocketbook and handed them to the man, and he gave her a gummy smile.

"God bless."

"Take care of yourself, sir," she said with a polite nod. All people, no matter what their lot in life, were deserving of cordiality and respect. She hoped that she had brightened his day.

The afternoon had passed more quickly than Angela had anticipated; the sky had grown cloudy and dusk was approaching. Peckish, she decided to stop into one of the touristy restaurants at the foot of the levee where she ordered a cup of gumbo and an iced tea. The gumbo was surprisingly tasty, though not as good as Angela's own, which she made with okra, celery, and peppers from her own garden. Angela really was a fantastic cook. She thought regretfully of the ginger-carrot soup she had tossed in the garbage earlier in the day; perhaps it could have been salvaged after all. She could have even packed some in a tupperware container and brought it to work for Sofia, wouldn't that have been a nice thing to do? Yes, she'd been hurt by the last-minute cancellations, but there was no point in holding grudges; Angela always did her best to take the high road, to give more than she took and to treat others with more kindness than necessary.

And hadn't the day turned out nicely after all, she thought, mopping up the last of her gumbo with a chunk of bread. The loss of the lunch date hadn't ruined the afternoon, far from it. Instead, she'd spent the time doing precisely what *she* wanted to do. Angela enjoyed her own company immensely and was grateful for the opportunity to spend a day in solitude, unbeholden to anyone else's expectations or agendas. Besides, her tour later that evening would allow ample opportunity for socializing.

She arrived at work an hour later, thoroughly pleased with herself and happy, for the sake of her delicate skin, that the sun had set. Ruby, Vik, Veda and Ralphie were there in the street, and she said hello to each of them. Making conversation with the other guides before tour time was always a pleasant precursor to the big show.

"Good evening, everyone!" she said. Ruby and Vik were talking, and Ralphie was looking at his phone; no one responded but Veda, who gestured at Angela's parasol and smiled.

"I like your umbrella," she said quietly. She was wearing a ship captain's hat covered in shells, and her top seemed to consist of a wedding veil pinned to a bra.

"Why, thank you!" Angela responded, always eager to discuss her favorite accessories. "Believe it or not, this was an eBay find. When I was younger, I always enjoyed thrifting and antiquing, and eBay has made it possible to enjoy the hunt from home. If you'd like a similar one, I can keep an eye out and send you a few listings as they come along."

"Oh!" Veda said, her eyes widening. "That's okay. I find most of my stuff on the street." So that explained it. Angela was never sure what to make of the girl and her bizarre, sloppy makeup and her strange, mismatched clothes, but she did her best to be friendly and supportive, especially since Veda seemed rather shy. Today, her eyebrows were painted white, her eyes circled raccoon-like in blue liner. Angela's heart went out to the girl—wasn't she trans? No wonder she didn't know anything about makeup. She'd have to invite Veda over when they rescheduled the ladies' lunch and give the girl a tutorial.

"And as soon as I started talking about the torture chamber, he went down.

Bam, face first into the street," she heard Ruby say to Vik. A familiar anecdote, to be sure. "A fainter?" Angela asked, turning to them.

"Yeah, somebody on my tour last night."

"I've had a total of eighteen fainters, over the years," Angela began. "There's a particularly gruesome moment in the LaLaurie story that always seems to get them. Luckily, I do have a bit of medical training and am generally able to get any unfortunate swooners swiftly revived."

"Yes, by all means, tell us more," Vik said.

Angela was eager to. "Well, most often the lapse is a result of dehydration. It's important that the person be offered water afterward, but even more crucially, he or she needs electrolytes. Gatorade, SmartWater, even a salty snack—"

"So anyway," Ruby interrupted. "I basically had to end the story there, didn't get to talk about the bodies under the floorboards—"

"Ah ah ah," Angela said, wagging her finger. "That's actually not at all verifiable. There is no evidence in the historical record that any bodies were ever found under the floorboards of the LaLaurie Mansion, in the 1890s, 1960s, or any other decade."

Vik frowned. "If you look at issues of the New Orleans *Bee*, there's mention of—"

"The *Bee*!" Angela laughed. "That's rich. The *Bee* was essentially the National Enquirer of its time, just a trash tabloid."

"Forget it," Vik said. He sounded annoyed, and Angela realized she may have embarrassed him. She spoke more gently.

"Forgive me. Certainly, I can understand why one would be led to believe those rumors, based on a surface-level skim of the historical documents in question. But those of us who have actually taken the time to delve deeper into the primary sources—"

Angela realized that Vik and Ruby were not, in fact, listening to her anymore. They had turned their backs and were laughing about something. Still talking, Angela glanced around. Ralphie was a few feet away still looking at his phone, and she directed her next few sentences to him. "—will realize that sometimes even the historical record must be taken with a grain of salt. It's important to establish the overall veracity of any particular historic source, as some are more reliable than others. I almost always try to cross-reference at least three sources before including any particular piece of information on my tour, because—"

Realizing she was talking to him, Ralphie looked up from his phone. "Oh, uh, I have to ask Graham something, actually," he said, and walked away.

"Well," Angela said to no one in particular. "It's a lovely night for a tour."

Ten minutes later, glowing with anticipation, she drank in the eager faces of her group.

"Good evening, ladies, gentlemen, and non-binary friends! My name is Angela, and I will be your storyteller for the evening. I simply cannot *wait* to get started, to spend the next two hours talking with you about my favorite subject in all the world and to introduce you to the darkness that lurks around every corner of these narrow streets. But before we begin, let me tell you a bit about myself. I'm an Aquarius sun, with a Scorpio moon and Gemini rising. This means I'm an eclectic chatterbox, so basically, I'm a perfect tour guide. For those of you who prefer a more academic approach, I'm an ENTP on the Meyers Briggs personality type indicator, and on the Gygax alignment grid, I'm Chaotic Good. For any LARPers out there, in *Vampire: the Masquerade*, I play as Toreador but I strongly identify as Brujah. Any questions?" The crowd laughed at the end of this little introduction, which she always delivered at top speed and with perfect diction. "In that case, let us begin!"

After her first story, a woman about Angela's age rushed up to chat as they walked. She was tall and pale, like Angela, and wore combat boots, black cargo pants, and a union-jack t-shirt.

"So, you talked about the French bringing vampire legends with them to New Orleans, but I'm wondering, like, where did those stories start, exactly? Would it have been Vlad the Impaler?"

"Excellent question," Angela said. "A *lot* of non-experts assume that it all started with Bram Stoker, who of course reportedly based the character of *Dracula* upon Vlad Tepes, the Romanian warlord. However, vampire lore actually goes much further back than that. In the Egyptian Book of the Dead, for example, if not all five parts of the soul receive offerings in death, those unattended pieces may wander out of the tomb to find nourishment by drinking the blood of the living."

"Wow, I didn't know that."

"In fact, you'll find elements of vampirism in many ancient cultures. The ancient Chinese had *jianshi*, blood-drinking deities, for example. And in Indian culture, you'll find the fanged goddess, *Kali*."

"And all that just sort of spread throughout Europe in the sixteen hundreds?"

"Essentially, yes. Of course, you had a lot of different myths and traditions, not all of which were consistent, but it was really in Europe around that time that the idea of the 'blood-sucking vampire' began to enter the common zeitgeist."

"Cool."

"What's your name, by the way?"

"I'm Dusty," the woman said, and they exchanged a firm handshake.

"Thank you so much for coming on the tour, Dusty."

"Oh yeah, I'm here with all my friends. We love this stuff."

"Nerds like me, then!"

"Definitely! And we were so excited to get you as our guide, after seeing all those amazing reviews you had on TripAdvisor."

"Why, thank you," Angela smiled. "I do take enormous pride in my work."

At the next stop, she pointed out the residence of the Carter Brothers, notorious serial-killers in the 1930s who'd tied up, exsanguinated, and drank the blood of their victims. She told the story with gruesome detail and tied it to much larger themes, painting a rich portrait of money, family, crime, and politics in the turn-of-the-century Big Easy. The crowd loved it, gasping at all the right moments, leaning in when Angela let her voice dwindle into a whisper, jumping when she spoke with a sudden loud punch. This was a good group, engaged and positive, and she felt their energy infusing her storytelling with vigor and animation. A guide and her group have a sort of symbiotic relationship, Angela liked to believe, in which the story feeds the group energy, and the group energy feeds the story and the better one is, the better the other becomes. In moments like this, when she could look out at the group and see every member of it engaged, listening, hanging on her every word, Angela felt nearly intoxicated with the sound of her own voice. But it wasn't a performance, no, a tour was something far more intimate than that: a dance, perhaps, a *pas de deux*, the balance constantly shifting as the tour guide competes with distractions for the tourist's attention, and the tourist allows him or herself to be drawn in, to surrender to the narrative, to become one with the story.

Between the next several stops, Angela got to know the woman Dusty and her three friends, all of whom were also vampire geeks. At the bar break, the five of them got a table together in the courtyard and talked, pining over their shared dreams of attending the Anne Rice ball, arguing about which *Supernatural* brother was the sexier, and discussing their opinions of the upcoming *Nosferatu* remake. But after a few minutes, they were interrupted by another fellow from the tour—a portly man in a fedora, who sidled up to the table with a smirk.

"So, you're a Toreador, huh? How's that working out for you?" he said.

"Excuse me," Angela said to Dusty and her friends, and turned to the man. "Do I detect an air of sarcasm in your voice, sir?"

"No, no," he said, smiling. "It's just not the clan for me. Too fake. All manners and civility, no substance."

"The Toreador have nothing *but* substance," she said. "We are artists."

"You're prisoners to beauty. You've become immobilized by it."

"That may be true," she said, with an air of wit. "If we have a weakness, I think you've certainly hit the nail on the head."

"I've played V:tM a few times," one of the women ventured. "I was in…uh, what was it…Clan Malkavian?"

"Oooh, so you're a little cuckoo, then!" Angela teased.

And so, for the next few minutes, the group of them discussed the finer points of *Vampire: the Masquerade*, laughing and arguing and bonding over their shared interest.

"My goodness!" Angela said finally, glancing at her pocket watch. "It's time to get back to our other friends!" The rest of the group had already gathered at the meeting-point outside the bar, and so she led them away once more, into the darkness.

They were in the lower Quarter now, dimly lit and quiet. There had been parades on the other side of town all day and into the evening, so the Quarter was emptier than normal, and there weren't many people on the streets but for the locals sitting on their stoops enjoying a glass of wine or a cigarette. Angela made sure to give each a warm hello, expressing tacit gratitude for their patience as she led her group past. The night was cold and breezy, the almost-full moon rising yellow in the clear sky. Low-hanging gas lanterns cast small pools of warm light onto the cracked and crumbling sidewalks below, illuminating the tops of their heads as they passed beneath. The ghastly white facade of the Old Ursuline Convent loomed up ahead of them on Chartres Street, and Angela parked her group on the corner to tell her favorite story.

"The year," she began grandly, "is 1728. *La Nouvelle Orleans* is in its tenth year as the capital of the colony of Louisiana, and here we stand in the *Rue Chartres*, surrounded by the stamping of horse hooves, the stench of the open sewage running through the streets, and the shouts of stevedores from the levee as they unload the contents of flatboats: tobacco, grain, cattle, indigo. But today, one of the ships in the port contains far more precious cargo. Off the gangplank and onto the dusty ground of the levee steps one dainty foot, then another. This pair of feet belongs to a young woman, no more than sixteen or seventeen years old, who has just arrived from France; she carries with her a coffin-shaped box, a *cassette*, containing all her worldly possessions, and she is followed by a procession of other young women, stepping off the boat and blinking as they take in the new world in which they have just arrived. They have been journeying nearly six months and are here to begin new lives in the colony.

"These young ladies are orphans, wards of the state, who lacked opportunities in France and thus have been selected by the Bishop of Quebec and sent to *La Nouvelle Orleans* for one reason: to make matches with the lonely colonists here, a whole generation of young men who have arrived over the last decade and have found themselves with no one to marry. But until those matches can be made, these girls will be kept under the supervision of the Ursuline nuns here at the Convent. My friends, this building is not simply one of the only three remaining French buildings in the Quarter today, it is *the* oldest structure in the entire Mississippi River Valley. Today, it is a museum, but back then...back then, this was the home of the Ursuline nuns, a Jesuit order of incredibly strong and resourceful women who almost single-handedly uplifted the illiterate, diseased, and ungodly population of French colonial New Orleans into civilization, education, and passable health. But forgive me—I've gotten off track. For what kind of ghost tour would this be if I spent an entire story espousing the merits of nuns?" Someone in the crowd laughed loudly.

"Nay, this story is not about the nuns, but their charges: these newly-arrived young ladies from France, who swiftly become nicknamed 'The Casket Girls' because of the little coffin-shaped boxes they brought with them off the boat. And no sooner have they settled here at the Convent that rumors begin to circulate about these girls. "*Très pâle*," the locals whisper, "how pale." So pale, in fact, that when these young ladies step out into the hot, subtropical New Orleans sun, their skin begins to blister and burn within minutes. They're sickly and gaunt; they are rarely seen to eat or drink, and if you look closely enough at the corners of their mouths, you may notice just the faintest lingering traces of dried blood. It seems that perhaps some of these girls contracted tuberculosis on the long voyage from France. *Yes, tuberculosis*, think the nuns. What other acceptable explanation can there be?

"Soon the matches are made, and many of the Casket Girls are married off to local men. But alas, a great number of these marriages do not end well. Some of the Casket Girls are discarded by their husbands within weeks, left to fend for themselves and forced into prostitution. Others are mistreated and abused. Around this time, the death rate in the city shoots suddenly upward; there are more murders, more grisly and gruesome deaths than ever before.

"Finally, the King of France receives word of how badly the experiment with the Casket Girls has turned out and orders their return home. The nuns are sent to retrieve the girls' caskets from the attic of the convent, where they have been stored; these caskets contain everything the young ladies brought with them from France, contents which will surely be required for the return journey. But when the nuns climb the creaky stairs to the attic and retrieve the caskets, they are startled to realize that most of the caskets contain nothing at all. No clothing, no books, no letters from loved ones; in fact, these casket-shaped boxes are entirely empty. Empty, that is, but for a few strands of hair.

"Rumors spread, and soon, whenever the Casket Girls are mentioned, another word is whispered as well...*vampire*. Of course, any historian will tell you this is just silly superstition. The Casket Girls were tragic figures, sent from France alone and underage and unprepared for the strange new world they found themselves in. They became malnourished, tubercular, and pale in the hold of the ship over their long journey; the sudden increase in the city's death rate after their arrival had nothing to do with these fragile young women, who certainly were too frail to even lift a finger against their unkind husbands."

The faces of her audience were rapt, hanging on every sentence. She leaned in close and spoke quietly.

"But answer me this. If it's just superstition, why did the Ursuline nuns—women of God, mind you—lock the empty caskets in the attic of the convent and order the windows permanently nailed shut? And another question. If it's just superstition, what happened to the paranormal investigators in 1978 who snuck into the attic one night to learn if the rumors were true, and who were found the next morning, ravaged and dismembered?

"And finally. If it's just superstition...please. Please, someone explain to me. Why is it that every so often, when I'm walking home after a tour in the middle of the night...those shutters up there on the attic windows, the ones that were nailed shut nearly three-hundred years ago...are hanging wide open?"

Angela felt a thrill course through her audience, heard the little barely audible gasps that she had grown so used to at this part of the story. She shifted her tone.

"Perhaps the Casket Girls were vampires after all. Or perhaps they were something else: odd young women, misfits, outcasts who could never seem to fit in. And if history has taught us anything, it's that women who stand out are punished for it. Society has such an incredibly narrow definition of what a woman should be, and when a woman steps outside of that narrow role, she suffers. This is a narrative that society tells us over and over. That women who don't meet society's expectations for propriety, for purity, for good behavior, deserve to be shunned, demeaned...and in some cases, murdered."

Many of the members of her group were nodding along.

"And so, folks, you know what? I hope that the Casket Girls *were* vampires. Because vampires don't care what society tells us is appropriate. In fact, vampires raise the ultimate middle finger to human convention, because they take the one thing we hate and fear above all else—death itself—and they make it beautiful. Sexy. Worshipped, fetishized, valued. And isn't that all any of us want, to be desired? To know that yes, you're different, yes, you're not what society wants or expects, and yes, people may find you grotesque, strange, even downright scary...but you're powerful. You're special. And you possess an undeniable magnetism that cannot be dimmed by any mere mortal, no matter how hard he or she may try.

"That's the beauty of being a vampire. But with that beauty, with that appeal, comes the most damning contradiction of all: a vampire's deep, undying loneliness. Because in order to survive, a vampire needs mortals—their companionship, their sexual partnership, their very blood—but most mortals, most ordinary human beings, are afraid to give those things. We've read about Carmilla, about Edward, we've watched Bill Compton and Angel and all sorts of other gorgeous, brooding vampires who earn the undying devotion of their mortal partners. But what of those who don't? What about the ugly vampires, the undesirable vampires, the just plain weird vampires? Eternally disliked, eternally alone. Certainly, they exist. Perhaps the Casket Girls were some of them. And perhaps, just perhaps...late at night, when all the tourists have gone, when the streets are quiet and the moon is dim and those sealed shutters are somehow open...perhaps they wander the streets of this very city. New Orleans is three-hundred years old, after all. And though that's not a particularly long time for a vampire...it's long enough to settle in."

Her group erupted in spontaneous applause. As she led them to the next stop, they all fought to be near her, to ask questions and make comments and give compliments, and she chatted with them and answered their questions and accepted their praise. Angela let her tour go late, past 10:00, throwing in an extra story because the group was enjoying it so much. Afterward, she stood around making the last vestiges of conversation as the guests trickled away.

"We loved it. We'll definitely leave you a five-star review!"

"That was so awesome, Angela. Thanks."

"Next time I'm in town, I'm going to bring my daughter! She would *love* you."

"Goodbye!" she called to each group as they departed. "Have a nice evening!" "It was a pleasure to meet you!"

And then they were all gone. She stood there for a minute or more, holding onto the post-tour glow as best she could. But soon it had faded, and she was simply alone.

Her purse stuffed with tips—at least a few twenties, she was sure, and plenty of tens and fives—Angela began her walk home. She crossed Bourbon, making her way through the crowds, brushing against people too drunk to even notice her. The Quarter Rathskeller was just half a block away. She stopped in the doorway, looking through the bar to the courtyard. She could see some of the other tour guides back there, Veda and Sofia and Ruby, Vik and James, all laughing and talking and drinking their beers. Socializing with the other guides wasn't something Angela did often, but she'd had a good time with them the night before; perhaps she could begin to join them regularly. She took a step into the bar, and Vik caught sight of her from the courtyard. Angela smiled and held up a hand in greeting. Vik didn't wave back; he just leaned over to say something to James, his eyes still on her, before looking away.

Angela put her hand down. She was tired anyway.

She returned to the street, heading toward Royal, parasol tapping on the pavement. Instead of dwelling on the look Vik had given her, she allowed her mind to return to the tour she'd just finished. *Such nice people they were*, she thought, smiling, replaying the best moments of the tour in her mind.

What a shame that I'll never see any of them again.

In just a few blocks, she was passing the Convent again, its white walls glowing faintly in the light of the moon. She glanced up at the shutters of the attic windows.

Angela had never actually seen them open, as she always told her tour groups that she had. But it was nice to pretend.

CHAPTER 4

The Pirate Boy

Ralphie sang along with the radio as he drove. He didn't know the lyrics to this particular song but was singing along anyway, just making it up because he loved music, especially loved driving while listening to music, even though he had a hard time keeping up with the words and making them come out in the right order when he sang. He drove with his left hand resting on the top of the steering wheel and his right hand on the gear shift, which over the years had been worn down smooth and soft by his palm because even though it was a Honda Civic, an automatic, he liked to pretend he was driving a Trans AM or a Mustang, like some drug-running greaser from the sixties or seventies. He was cruising up Wisner Boulevard, past the park and along the lakefront. This was one of his favorite drives, and he made it almost every morning after he had taken his medicine.

The big, gray expanse of the lake slid by as he drove, and the gears in his mind started to turn, slowly at first, then faster and faster, spinning images into ideas, ideas into stories. He was a long-distance trucker driving up along Lake Michigan out of Chicago, chewing on a plug of tobacco and shooting the shit on a CB radio, maybe glancing up at the picture of his pretty, tired wife clipped to the sun visor. No, not the sun visor—the rearview mirror, that was more poetic. Maybe they were separated, going through a rough time because of the accident–yeah, the accident, he'd lost his legs, he couldn't walk, but he could drive, and all these hours he spent on the road were how he ran away from his wife and his accident and all the other things that slowed him down. No, no. He wasn't running away. He was running *toward* something, something he didn't even know how to get to, something that maybe didn't even exist, but he had to try, didn't he, we all have to try to get where we're going even if all we're doing is going seventy on an empty highway that's bound to end somewhere, just like everything else.

It was a pretty good idea for a story, and just thinking about it made Ralphie speed through a couple yellow lights to get home. Things always started to click into place this time of morning. As soon as he got back to his house in Mid City, which he shared with a couple younger guys, he rushed to his room and sat on his bed with one of the dozens of crumpled notebooks that littered his desk and floor and began to write. Page after page he scribbled, the ideas leaping from his mind onto the paper. His phone buzzed, but he ignored it, one of his roommates called out from the kitchen but he didn't answer, the cat wanted to be let in, but he didn't have time for any of that, he needed to write, he needed to write, he needed to write.

> *I've always been what you would call a drifter, a ramblin man. But on that fateful night I drifted further than ever before, even though my body stayed in one place. When I felt my legs crumble like kindling underneath me I knew that nothing would ever be the same. That's when I turned to the sweet, sweet release that can only be found at the bottom of a bottle. Not a bottle of whiskey or gin—a bottle of pills. That's when the nightmare began.*

He wrote about the trucker for a while longer, and then he jotted down some ideas for a sci-fi story, and then he just journaled. He had to finish something, he reminded himself. He needed to stick to something and get it done, flesh it out, revise it, make it perfect, because how do you succeed as a writer if you don't have any finished stories to sell? But there were always so many ideas buzzing in his brain, like big, pretty iridescent insects, and as soon as he reached out to catch one, another landed on his hand, flexing its shimmery wings. Bugs, now he was thinking about bugs. A bug-catcher! Monster bugs! No; stop; slow down. He threw down his chewed-up pen and realized two hours had passed.

Now he was getting a headache, and the afternoon fatigue was beginning to settle in, the first slow-down of the day. He drew the blinds, crawled under the covers, and closed his eyes. This had always happened in school too, after recess, when bouncing-off-the-walls morning-Ralphie became sluggish-afternoon-Ralphie. His cheek would sag in his hand, and he would stare unblinking at the textbook on the desk, unable to read a word of it. It was all so *boring*. Letters seemed so stupid that he couldn't understand them, and he'd find himself reading the same sentence over and over again, losing focus every few words, not processing, not caring. He'd take out his pencil to underline the material because sometimes that helped, and five minutes later, he'd still be stuck in the task of sharpening it and accidentally breaking the point and sharpening it and breaking the point and sharpening it over and over and over until somebody yelled at him.

He just needed a nap now, a little quiet rest, just for an hour or two so he could find the energy to go to work and give a tour later in the evening. *No!* He thought, *no napping*, he couldn't waste his time like this. He was getting older, he was almost thirty now, and he wasn't any closer to being a real writer than he had been at twenty-two. In fact, he'd been *more* successful at that age, had written a couple funny articles for trashy magazines, college-humor type stuff that he wasn't particularly proud of, but hey, at least it was something, at least he could dig out the glossy copies from the box under his bed and see his name there in the table of contents. His friends had loved that stuff. Funny, wacky Ralphie, writing anecdotes about all the ridiculous shit that happened to him. And God, he'd been stupid back then, all the drinking and partying and doing lines of coke late into the night, his old group of buddies stealing cars, tripping on mushrooms in the woods, locking each other in port-a-potties at music festivals. And Ralphie could go harder and longer and weirder than anyone when he didn't take his medicine, flitting from each thing to the next to the next without ever stopping to rest, always the life of the party. It had been good material and he'd had a blog for a while, made people laugh, crazy Ralphie and his funny stories. "Poop Monster" had been a particularly good one.

But there was more in him, he knew there was. He had stories to tell, not just about himself and his stupid exploits, but stories about real things, moving things, dark things, stories that make you shiver, stories that make you think. Because somewhere deep inside him, beneath all the goofiness there was a voice, *his* voice, and he had to find it, he had to get it on the page, and he tried every day, he worked at it, he searched for it, where *was* it, how could he become the writer he wanted to be?

He forced himself to get out of bed. His room was a mess, as always, socks and cereal bowls and empty beer bottles and books scattered across every surface. He heard Kat's voice in his head, as always—*"Christ, Ralphie Roo, did a tornado touch down in here?"*—and told her to leave him alone. He made his way to the bathroom, swearing loudly as he stepped painfully on a stray phone charger, and took a piss. As he turned to go back to his room, he caught his reflection in the mirror, something he generally tried not to do. He'd always been a little different-looking, with droopy eyelids and a propensity for excessive sweating. "Frog boy," they'd called him in school. Shyly, as though approaching a blind date in a bar, he let himself look at his reflection full-on. He wasn't *that* hideous, was he? He had bright blue eyes and a nice smile. Just for fun, he growled like a bear at himself.

"Don't hurt me, Mister Bear!" his reflection cried out in a small, shrill voice.

"You know there's only one thing I want," Ralphie the bear responded.

"What is it?"

"A *bear* minimum," he growled.

"A *bear* minimum of what?"

"Respect!" the bear yelled, lunging at the mirror.

"Aiiiie!" shrieked the small voice.

There was a knock at the bathroom door. "Uh...can I get in there when you're done?"

"Gotta go," he whispered to his reflection, then grinned sheepishly at his roommate as he went back into the hall. It was always a little embarrassing when he let his imagination get the better of him and somebody noticed.

After heating up some frozen taquitos and playing with his roommate's cat for a little while—it was a good cat, it played fetch like a dog—Ralphie managed a second wind. He wrote for another two hours, this time forcing himself to stick to the story he was officially working on, one he'd started a few days ago and which he was pretty excited about. It was about a mob boss, Giorgio Calzone (pronounced *Cal-zone-ay*, of course, like in Italian), who runs a shitty pizza place as a front for his mob activities, but then, when his daughter gets killed, he has a come-to-Jesus moment and decides to quit the mob so he can actually just sell really good pizza. It was supposed to be kind of funny but moving too, and he had just gotten to the part where Giorgio Calzone sees a piece of pizza face-down on the ground and starts weeping in the street because it's a metaphor for his life. The story was going pretty good. *This could be it*, Ralphie thought. *This could be my big break.*

But his medicine tended to wear off around 6:00, and he began to feel the distractions rising up like vapors around him, seeping into his brain and fogging his focus. Whereas an hour ago his writing had been the only interesting thing in the world, now everything was interesting—but not quite interesting enough to keep him focused on anything for more than a couple of minutes. He opened his laptop and began to flip through tabs, consuming and dismissing bite-sized nuggets of information until he couldn't sit still anymore. Just as well, because it was almost time for work. He sang his "time for work" song while he showered, pulled on some pants he found on the floor (were those the clean ones or dirty ones? where was his belt? whatever) and took his vest from the back of his chair where he always so carefully hung it. It was a gray tuxedo vest he'd picked up at a thrift store, and he usually wore it over a t-shirt just to give his look a little extra something. It had a stain over the pocket, a little smudge of red, from two Halloweens ago when Kat had been the zombie Queen of Hearts and given him a hug, accidentally pressing her oozy bloody face against his chest. She'd tried to get the stain out for him, but it hadn't worked, and he'd kept wearing the vest anyway. "Kat's blood" is how he always thought of it, Kat's blood right over his own heart.

Things were looking pretty slow outside Madame Livaudais'. Graham was sitting in front of the shop on his stool, grinning, probably drunk, and old Max was standing on the street smoking. Ralphie went right over to him. He looked so stoic, standing there with his wide stance and patchy gray hair.

"Hey, buddy!" Ralphie beamed as he approached. Max cracked a smile.

"Hey there, young man. Give me a hug, would you? I could use it."

Ralphie embraced Max around his frail shoulders. "You doing okay?"

"Oh, you know. Hangin' in there," he said in his slow, grizzled way. Ralphie wanted to write a book about Max, or make him the hero of a movie. He knew Max had been in the Peace Corps and the Black Panthers, had lived overseas, had married a white woman back when interracial marriage was still seriously taboo. Just thinking about all the stories Max could tell got Ralphie's mind churning with excitement, and Ralphie wanted to sit him down in the bar sometime and talk to him, hear his life story, ask him all sorts of questions. Maybe in a few months, when he was doing better. Max had been having a hard time lately, Ralphie knew, ever since his wife had died. He wore her wedding ring on a chain around his neck.

James appeared from inside the bar. "Hey, Ralphie. Hi, Max," he said, sounding bored. "I like your acid-wash jeans," he added, gesturing at Max's pants.

"Is that what you call 'em? These old dungarees?"

"Yeah," James laughed.

"Been sitting in my closet for decades. Since the seventies, probably."

"True vintage! You've got such great style," James said. "Ralphie, you could learn a thing or two from Max about how to dress for work."

Ralphie looked down at the saggy t-shirt under his open vest. "I'll have you know, I have not spilled *anything* on this shirt since I started wearing it a few days ago."

"Charming," James said, then went into the street to talk to Ruby.

"So how was your day, kid?" Max asked.

"Not too bad! Been working on this new story, it's coming along pretty good, I think."

"You really put in the time, don't you?"

Ralphie smiled. "I try, yeah."

"So, when are you going to let me read it?"

"Aw, it's no good."

"I'm sure that's not true, if it's anything as unique as its author."

"You're serious? You would really want to read it?"

"Absolutely," Max said.

Ralphie's chest expanded with warmth; no one besides Kat had ever asked to read his stories. "Alright, I'll bring you a copy when it's done."

"You better."

"So how about you, buddy, what's new with you?" Ralphie asked Max.

"Well, I got to see my grandson last night. Came in with his dad from up North."

"That's great! How old is he now?"

"Just turned nine."

"Wow, getting big! You gonna teach him some moves?" Ralphie threw a few jabs in the air. He knew Max had once been a boxer.

"Honestly, I don't know what kind of moves I've got left in me. Feeling a bit frail these days. Losing weight."

Max did look even skinnier than normal. "You gotta eat, buddy!"

He shook his head. "I know, I just can't seem to...I get tired of the microwave meals, you know? Molly was such a good cook."

"She'd want you to stay strong, Max. You know that."

"Don't I know it," he said, and kissed her ring on its chain. "And I try."

"Well, on the bright side, there's tons of people here for your tour tonight!" Ralphie said brightly, gesturing at the empty sidewalk. "Actually," he continued, "I dunno…looks like tonight we may be giving a tour *to* ghosts, instead of about them, amirite?"

Max chuckled. "Round up some customers for us, would you, Ralphie? Anybody can do it, it's you."

"Yes, sir. *Ghost tours!*" He cried out in a corny, old-fashioned barker's voice. "*Git ya ghost tours heah! Hot tours, cold tours, half off yesterday's tours!*"

Ruby, who was standing in the street with James, rolled her eyes. "You're such a dork, Ralphie."

He went over to them. "Come on, we gotta get some customers! Don't you guys want tours tonight?"

"No," James said, his arms crossed. "My seniors wore me the fuck *out* today."

"Yeah, I'm gonna pass too," Ruby said. "Gotta get my shit ready for Troy."

"I didn't know you were in that." Troy was a new all-female krewe that threw hand-decorated crowns from their parade floats. "It rolls on Wednesday?"

"Yep. I have so many crowns to finish, ugh. My apartment is an *explosion* of glitter right now."

"Hey, James, catch me!" Ralphie exclaimed, running toward James like he was going to leap into his arms. This was a game they often played—well, that Ralphie played—and that James received with varying levels of patience. Apparently, that was not much tonight.

"Get *away* from me," he said, holding up his hand with disgust.

"Come on, you never want to catch me. I bet you could, you're strong, all that working out you do."

"Oh my God, do you ever simmer down?"

Ruby laughed. "Oh, Ralphie. Do one of your little dances if you're so hyper, get us some customers."

"Okay." And he did his Snoopy dance, palms pressed toward the ground, chin up, big smile, feet shuffling. James and Ruby laughed, and Ralphie felt good. He loved making people laugh.

A couple approached, looking around. "Here for a tour?" Ralphie asked.

"Excuse me?" the woman said. He was told that he spoke too fast and often had to repeat himself.

"Are you here for a ghost tour?"

"Oh, yes!" they said. Ralphie checked their confirmation print-out and handed them the Spirits of Yore stickers that acted as tickets. "Just put those anywhere on your person—"

"My purse?" the woman said, confused.

"No, your *person*, like your body. Just not on a leather jacket because it might get stuck. Anyway, yeah, put the sticker on then meet down the block under the green sign. Tour leaves right on the hour with or without you so don't be late, oh, and you get two for one hurricanes at The Quarter Rathskeller right there before or after the tour." They nodded, looking confused. He wondered if he should say it all again, but they wandered away.

James sighed. "Lord, Ralphie, do you talk that fast on your tours?"

"Yeah, dude, how can anyone understand you?" Ruby said.

"Beeeeecause I don't actually talk on my tours. I just communicate with my eyes," Ralphie said, wiggling his eyebrows and blinking rapidly. "See? Two blinks for LOOK, A GHOST. Three for JUST KIDDING, GHOSTS AREN'T REAL."

Ruby laughed in spite of herself. "You're ridiculous."

"Hey. Them's fighting words. Come on, put em up," he said, holding up his fists to Ruby. "Show me some of that *kai poop*." He knew she'd been taking self-defense classes.

"It's *krav maga*."

"Whatever. Show me what you got."

Grinning, she put her fists up, and for a few moments, they shadowboxed, laughing and calling each other names. She managed to sock him in the stomach.

"Owww!" he howled.

"Oh, don't be such a baby, Ralphie."

"Well. You may have beat me to the punch...but I punch you to the beat," he said, making a deep-house *untz, untz, untz* with his throat and hammering her lightly on the arm.

"Breaking two groups," Graham called out. "Max, you going?"

Max nodded; you could pass a tour down to a less-senior guide if you wanted to, but Max never did.

"Cool. James?"

James was next on the list for a tour, but he shook his head and so did Ruby.

"Sweeeet. Guess who's giving a tour tonight? This guy!" Ralphie said, doing another little dance.

"Have the time of your life," James drawled.

"I will, buddy!" Ralphie said, pinning James' arms to his side in a bear hug.

"Get *off* me."

"Have a good tour," Ruby said, extending her arms for a hug. Ralphie's heart leapt, and he gave her a little squeeze, a nice civilized one. It made him feel good to see her smile. These days, she rarely did.

Ralphie's group that night was small, just twelve people. "What's your name, buddy?" he asked the well-dressed guy who happened to be walking at the front of the group. They got to talking, and by the time they had rounded the corner and gone two blocks to where Ralphie gave his intro, he'd made a friend. The guy's name was Alan, and he was from Texas, a Southern-gentleman type, probably in the oil business, Ralphie thought, his mind wandering as the man described the business trip that had brought him to New Orleans, and soon he was picturing the man's cookie-cutter mansion and all his sports cars and the affair he was probably having with his kids' sexy young nanny, not that Ralphie was one to judge character. He knew deep down that if by chance he ever met someone and fell in love, *he* would never cheat, but people have all sorts of reasons for the things they do, and Ralphie always did his best to put himself in the other person's shoes, to understand things from perspectives other than his own.

He realized that Alan was looking at him expectantly.

"Sorry, what?" he said, wondering if he'd been asked a question and missed it. That happened a lot.

"I asked how long you'd been a tour guide."

"Oh! Yeah...about two years."

Two years giving tours—had it really been that long? The time before he'd moved to New Orleans had just dragged on and on, back in Indy where he'd tried so hard to lead the kind of life that was expected of upper-middle-class white people but that had always felt about as natural as banging your head against a wall. He had majored in Communications, and with help from his father, he'd gotten a job at a big media conglomerate as a copywriter, a 9-to-5 like you're supposed to have when your parents have spent a fortune on your degree and want you to have all the same things they do: a big house, fat IRAs, a quietly failing marriage held together by wealth and stubbornness. For a time, he'd thought that copywriting was what he wanted to do, that any writing was better than no writing at all, and he'd tried his best to climb that ladder to better things. But he'd always felt like he was treading water, barely managing to finish his tasks because he just couldn't make his mind stick to them. Eventually, he'd been fired from that job, and the one after that. It had been around this point that he'd realized the work on his desk could never be as interesting as what lay out the window beyond it. He had cousins in New Orleans, had spent summers down here as a kid, and one gray afternoon three years ago, he'd driven down and started a new life.

He was halfway through the first story on his tour now, the tale of Bienville's arrival in swampy, gator-infested Louisiana. Bienville was a particular favorite of Ralphie's, a character who really made his imagination run wild.

"They say that he was the only one of his men who could speak to the Indians without an interpreter, because he had learned their language. And get this—supposedly Bienville was actually covered in tattoos of snakes from the neck down to show the Indians he valued their traditions, and believe me, in those days, getting a tattoo was not fun. You'd have your skin punctured over and over by a needle made of bone, and then they would spread hot ash in the wounds to make the design. But Bienville ate it up. In fact, he was sometimes known to strip down to a loincloth, hop in a canoe, and visit the natives to hang out with them. Can you imagine! This French guy, you know, *Oui Oui Monsieur* and all that, showing up in this mosquito-infested swamp, making friends with the tribes everybody else is scared of, getting tattoos, running around naked…point being is, he's the badass who gave us New Orleans. Where you from, ma'am?" he asked the lady up front.

"Kansas City."

"Now, I don't know who founded Kansas City, but it wasn't Jean Baptiste Bienville is all I'm saying." They laughed.

What a perfect night, he thought, sucking in a breath of the cool evening air as he led his group around the side of the Cathedral toward their next stop. It was colder than all his friends liked, but Ralphie was pretty hot-blooded, and the chilly wind put a pep in his step that he had a hard time finding in the hot summer months. Goddamn, he felt so *good* right now! Sometimes he got so sluggish during the day. His medicine helped keep him on track, but it also slowed him down, made him tired, took him so deep into his own head that sometimes he got terribly lonely without even realizing it. Ralphie loved people, needed to be around people, and it felt damn good to give a tour and reconnect with humanity at the end of every day.

He felt a tug on his sleeve and realized there was a kid there, about seven or eight years old, a chubby little girl with messy hair. She had been near the back of the group with her parents at the first stop, and her dad was with her now.

"Hey, kiddo!" he exclaimed. "What's up?"

"Um, excuse me? Can I ask you a question?"

"Sure thing!"

"You were talking about the alligators in the swamp when that man came here. Did—um—did the alligators eat people?"

"Well," he said. "An alligator probably isn't going to bother you unless you bother it. It's gonna leave you alone unless you come along and poke it with a stick or something. Is that the kind of thing you would do?"

She grinned and shook her head.

"Are you sure? I dunno, you look like a bit of a troublemaker. You look like the type of person who might see a gator just minding its own business, lying out on a rock with its eyes closed, and decide to come along and just give it a good old poke."

"I wouldn't!" she exclaimed.

"Well, that's good. Because if you do, you know what's gonna happen?" Ralphie lunged suddenly at the little girl, sawing his arms up and down like alligator jaws as he shouted. "He's gonna BITE your arm off!"

The little girl shrieked and giggled.

"You hear that?" the dad said. "No harassing the alligators on our swamp tour tomorrow, or you might be going home with one less hand."

The little girl took quite a shine to Ralphie after that, walking with him between every stop, asking him questions and telling him stuff, at one point describing in detail a story her grandmother had once told her about a doll that kept reappearing in the house no matter how many times it was removed.

"Ooooh, that's too spooky for me!" Ralphie said, covering his ears with his hands.

"But you like scary stuff!"

"No, ma'am, I do not. You think I like all these ghost stories? I go home and have nightmares after every tour!"

"You do not," she teased.

"I do, it's torture! Pretty tragic, really...a ghost tour guide who's afraid of ghosts."

"That's okay," she said, patting his arm. "You're still doing a really good job."

That gave him a happy, warm feeling, which he decided to supplement with a whiskey on the rocks at the bar break. You weren't really supposed to drink on tour, but as long as you kept it on the down-low, didn't get hammered and made sure to tell your group it was ginger ale if anybody asked, it was a rule you could sort of slide by. Not to mention that drinks at the bar were free for tour guides, and who can turn down free booze? The bar, Lafitte's Blacksmith Shop, was pleasantly un-crowded tonight because everybody was uptown at the parades, and Ralphie actually managed to grab a seat at a table with a couple from his tour, shooting the shit for a few minutes while everybody else used the bathroom and got their drinks.

After the break, he gathered his group across the street. "How's everybody feeling? Good? Took a little break, got a drink...I see you opted for the Voodoo Daiquiri. I think it tastes like grape kool-aid, but that's just me, you do you..."

The little girl joined the group with her parents in tow, digging into a cup of ice cream from the sandwich shop down the street. "Ice cream! Excellent!" Ralphie exclaimed. "But uh...where's mine? Didn't you get me some?" The girl giggled and shook her head. "I'll never forgive you for this," he said sternly, and she flashed him a big chocolatey smile.

"Okay, everybody, welcome back! Like I said, I wanna tell you a little bit about this bar you were just in! First of all, this here is actually the oldest, continuously operating bar in America. Now, there was a brief period of time during Prohibition that it was technically a 'Hardware Store'...but I think we can all guess what kind of *screwdrivers* they were selling." He always hammed this joke up big time, and it usually got either a big laugh or a big groan.

"That's my dad-joke of the evening, thank you, thank you," he said, taking a little bow. "I'd also like to tell you a bit about the guy who owned this place. Very important figure in New Orleans history, his name was Jean Lafitte, and he was our city's most famous pirate." He always had to force himself to pronounce it correctly, like "John" instead of "Gene," because Vik had made a big show of making fun of him when he'd heard Ralphie say it wrong. Ralphie's brain often took shortcuts like that, and he had to force himself to slow down enough to get things right.

"He was a really legit pirate too, he had a pirate ship across the river at Barataria Bay, and he ran a giant smuggling operation, pretty much controlled all the illegal activity of this entire region, in fact. And this bar, which he owned, was his center of operations here in town. Was it ever actually a blacksmith shop? We're not really sure. Jean Lafitte's older brother, Pierre, was said to be a blacksmith, so, maybe, but others will tell you that's just a front for what it really was: a pirate bar, and the place where all black market activity went down in the early 1800s. Now listen. Anyone wanna hear a ghost story about this place?"

"Yeah," a few people in the group called out.

"Okay. So. Back around the time Jean Lafitte was running things, there was a young man here in town. Sort of an oddball, didn't really fit in, marched to the beat of his own tune, if you know what I mean. He was training to run his father's business, but as he got older, he realized more and more just how much it wasn't the life for him. This kid had bigger dreams than that. He wanted adventure, you see. He didn't want to waste his life crunching numbers in some boot shop, he wanted to see the world. And so, on a whim, he ran away from home and tried to make something of himself. And by make something, I mean he decided to become a pirate.

"But there was one problem: he didn't know how. Didn't know any pirates, wasn't really sure how to break into this career field. So, he decided to become a different kind of criminal first—a cat burglar. So, he starts breaking into people's houses to steal jewelry, money, trinkets, all that, and he was actually pretty good at it, never got caught, and after a couple weeks, he's got a pretty large collection of this stolen stuff. Phase two of his plan was to take all of these stolen goods into the notorious pirate bar—Lafitte's, right there—and try to use it to get some street cred. Now back then, this was a place you didn't go into if you didn't have legit black market business. But he thinks he's up for it. He's thinking he can go in there and make some sales, make some connections, and maybe one of the pirates will take a liking to him, take him under his wing, and they'll sail off on the high seas together. So, he goes in there with all his stolen jewelry, and he's trying to show it off. But no one's interested! All the pirates are just growling at him, sending him off, nobody cares. *Get lost, kid. We don't want what you're selling.* They're so mean! He thought this was the one place in the world he could maybe, maybe fit in...but no. Nobody wants him.

"Then he notices something. Sitting in the darkest corner of the bar, a particularly impressive looking pirate, with fine leather boots, one of those tricorn hats, the shirt, the sword, everything—is watching him. Staring at him, in fact. And then he holds up one finger and beckons the kid over."

Ralphie looked at the little girl and held up his finger, beckoning sinisterly to demonstrate.

"Well, that's hella creepy, right? So, he's nervous. But he's excited, too, because someone's finally paying attention to him! So, he takes over his tray of stolen jewelry, and silently, without a word, the pirate begins to examine each piece. He holds up every ring, every necklace, turning them over in his fingers, feeling their weight. Finally, he stops on one particular brooch, a cameo, circled in filigree gold, with the picture of a woman engraved in the center. You guys know what a cameo is?"

The group nodded.

"Yeah, like a picture of a lady. And the kid can tell the pirate *loves* this cameo. He won't stop looking at it. And the kid is thinking, this is it! This is his big break! He starts talking, babbling, he says, 'Oh sir, I see you've found that beautiful cameo brooch. It's a fine piece, one of the best I have. If you'd like to buy it, I can cut you a truly excellent deal. You have great taste because it really is worth a lot.'

"And then the pirate turns to him, makes eye contact for the very first time. Smiles a little. And then he says..." (Ralphie tried to do a French accent here; it never went well, but he didn't care), "'Yes, it is a beautiful piece. I do have great taste, don't I? And you're right, son, it is worth a lot. In fact, I know exactly how much it is worth because I am the one who bought it.' And he turns the brooch over in the light, and sure enough, there, engraved on the back, it says: For Abby, with love. *From your friend...JEAN LAFITTE.*"

Gasps from the crowd. The little girl had forgotten about her ice cream and was staring at Ralphie wide-eyed.

"The kid looks up into this man's face, says something along the lines of, 'Uh-Oh,' and before he knows it, Jean Lafitte has taken a knife from his belt and is plunging it into the kid's guts, over and over and over—" Ralphie acted this bit out "—before dropping him to bleed to death on the floor. Everyone else in the bar just glances over then goes about their business. It's a pirate bar, these things do happen, and for the rest of the night, they're all just stepping over the corpse of this poor kid in a pile of his own blood.

"But then, at the very end of the night...more like the wee hours of the morning...there's only one pirate left in there. An old pirate, who's seen a lot, and maybe the years have made him a little kinder to some degree. And this old pirate is finally decent enough to scoop up the young man's body..." Ralphie pantomimed this with great care. "And toss him out into the alley behind the bar!

"And they say...that if you're there late at night, over by the darkest corner of the bar, you may see a young man. He's in sort of an old-fashioned tunic, and he's doubled over, clutching his guts and groaning."

Ralphie demonstrated, staggering in the street, then straightened up and grinned.

"Now guys, keep in mind, this is the last bar on Bourbon Street, so seeing a young man in there doubled over clutching his guts groaning? Not that uncommon of a sight." The group laughed. "*But.* If you're a particularly nice person, maybe you'll reach out to him, see if he's okay, offer to call him an Uber or whatever. But of course, as soon as you do, either he'll disappear completely...or your hand will go right through him.

"So, moral of the story is: never give up on your dreams, kids! And if you make dumb decisions and your dreams get you killed, try to die somewhere like New Orleans, so you can at least hang out in a bar for eternity."

At the end of the tour, the little girl proudly presented him with a twenty dollar bill her parents had given her. "Hey, thanks! Give me a high five, kiddo!" Ralphie said, and she did. "Did you have fun on the tour?"

She grinned. "You're so funny!"

"You did a great job, man, thanks," said the dad. "And thanks for keeping her company. I know she can be a bit of a handful."

"No problem, buddy. I'm a bit of a handful myself at times."

Ralphie always ended at the Beauregard-Keyes House, which left him with a five-block walk back to the Quarter Rat. The night had a habit of taking him back in time as he walked, the shiny parked cars vanishing to reveal horses tied to the posts that still jutted out at odd angles from the curb, the pavement disappearing into wooden sidewalks edged by muddy open gutters. Sometimes he was a Creole blacksmith, sometimes a gunslinging carpetbagger, but tonight, Ralphie was a wealthy merchant, a man of great wealth and power who had voyaged across the sea from France.

"Go and bother someone else," he said under his breath in his best attempt at a French accent. A street urchin had come up and was begging for change, and Ralphie had to pull his cloak away from the boy with a flourish to keep him from grabbing it. "Dirty *Americains,*" he muttered. It was their first night in port and surely all of his men were drinking and gambling in the dirty pubs of the *Vieux Carre*, he thought as he rounded the corner and came suddenly into view of St. Louis Cathedral. Awestruck, he gazed upward at its spires and crossed himself. Such a beautiful church. For all its swampy miasma, dirty streets and loose women, *Nouvelle Orleans* did possess pockets of magnificence. He twirled his mustaches as he rapped his cane on the cobblestones. *"Hot tamale, hot tamale, hot tamale!"* cried the little Hispanic man who meandered between the bars at night, vending homemade tamales out of a cooler bag. To Ralphie, he was a Spanish immigrant, shabbily dressed, with a wicker basket of tamales wrapped in brown paper.

He shook off the fantasy as he went into the Rat, where the happy-go-lucky bartender Leela was working. "Hey love, how was your tour?" she asked as he pulled up a stool. Ralphie ordered a shot of Jack and an Abita Amber, and they chatted for a few minutes before he went back to the courtyard where Vik was drinking alone.

"Hey, buddy!" Ralphie called out, spilling a splash of beer on his shoe as he tripped over a jagged piece of flagstone.

"Oh, Ralphie, hey. I've been meaning to ask you something," Vik said quietly, patting the stool next to him.

Pleased, Ralphie sat. "What's up, buddy?"

"You take adderall, right?"

"Well, yeah."

"Can you give me some? I'll pay you."

"What do you want it for?" Ralphie didn't know that Vik took speed.

"Just, you know. It helps keep me on my toes."

"Well, I could spare a few I guess, but I do need it. You know, for my brain," he grinned, tapping the side of his head.

"That's fine. Just enough to get me through a few days, till my regular guy re-ups."

"Hang on. You take it every day? Do you have ADHD too?"

"I told you, it keeps me on my toes."

"'Cause I mean, you really shouldn't be taking it every day without a prescription, it'll do weird things to—"

Vik slammed his hands on the table and shouted suddenly. "What are you, the fucking thought police! Can you spare it or not?"

"Jeez—sure. Yeah. I'll bring some tomorrow, just give me like twenty bucks."

"Good." Vik stood abruptly and went to the bathroom as Ruby and Veda entered the courtyard from the bar.

"There they are!" he exclaimed. "Spirits of Yore's brightest shining stars."

Veda giggled. Ralphie was pretty sure he had absolutely nothing in common with Veda—she was really into mystical stuff, and he knew nothing about trans people or the "queer community," as she called it—but he could tell she was a good person. He could also tell she was pretty insecure, a little shy. Ralphie always tried to build her up and make her feel good.

"What are you guys doing here? Ruby, I thought you were going home to work on your purses for the parade," he said.

"Yeah, well, I'm doing that later," she snapped.

"Alright, no need to bite my head off. Just curious."

"We went and got phở at that new Vietnamese place," Veda said.

"And didn't invite me?"

"You were on tour."

"Oh, right."

The two girls sat and resumed whatever quiet conversation they'd been having before entering the bar. Ralphie looked around the courtyard impatiently, wondering if anyone else was going to show up. He still had plenty of energy and wanted people to socialize with.

"What are you guys talking about?"

"Nothing. Just friend stuff."

"I'm a friend," he grinned, hovering behind them on their stools. "I'm the friendliest friend of all, dontcha know!"

"Ralphie…"

"What are you talking about? I won't tell, I promise. Are you talking about boys? Politics? The latest dance craze?" He began to do the Charleston.

Ruby whirled around to face him, eyes flashing. "Oh my God, Ralphie, take a hint. You're being annoying as fuck!"

Ralphie went back into the bar, deflated.

"Everything okay, darlin?" Leela, the bartender, asked.

"Yeah, whatever. I think I'll just take a beer for the road."

She filled a go-cup under the Abita Amber tap. "Have a good night, love."

He went into the street, brooding. He and Ruby had been having so much fun earlier, out on the street before work, and now he'd gone and messed it up, just like he always did. People would laugh at his antics for a while, but eventually it always became, "Calm down, Ralphie," "Shut up, Ralphie," or worst of all, the A-word: "You're being *annoying*, Ralphie." And he'd been stupid enough to think he and Ruby had a real connection, that the silliness at work earlier had meant something. He knew Ruby had been hurting bad since her breakup, and Ralphie understood. He'd lost somebody important too, they'd all lost her, though Ralphie was probably the one who missed her most. He'd thought that maybe he and Ruby could have something. Just a friendship, that would be enough.

He chugged the beer and then stopped into a corner store to pick up a little bottle of Jack to suck on for the last couple blocks of his walk, watching the untied shoelaces of his beat-up sneakers drag along the concrete until he reached his car. It was a mess, as always, and smelled like stale beer. He took another pull from the bottle and tossed it into the passenger seat, cranked up the radio. *"Niggas can't see me!"* Tupac huffed, and Ralphie felt that toughness, that anger and independence, swelling inside him as he closed his eyes and tried to rap along. He couldn't rap, of course, not even sober, and settled for just swaying back and forth in his seat and pounding the steering wheel at the intersection. Whatever melancholy he had felt a few minutes ago was gone now, he was on top of the world, he was an East Coast rapper with a gun in his pants and poetry spewing like a blood spatter from his mouth, he had come from nothing, but he was everything now, unstoppable, invincible, king.

He tumbled out of his car into his driveway and banged open the back door of his house, went to his room, plugged in his million-year-old iPod. It was dark, and he didn't bother turning the lights on, just paced back and forth in the blackness, sucking down whiskey. He listened to more rap, drinking, drunk, until the words bypassed his mind completely and went straight into his bones. He was Marshall Mathers as a young boy, lost and hurt and neglected by his mother, he was Kanye, suicidal and megalomaniacal, he was Biggie mourning the loss of a friend turned mortal enemy. He knew them, he felt them, he *was* them, and it was in moments like this that he knew his imagination was worth something, that if he could feel it, he could write it, that if he could just put his mind into words, he could hold a mirror up to nature, the likes of which no one had ever seen, he could be Shakespeare, he could be Dostoevsky, he could be Dickens. It was *in* him. He knew it was.

Stabbing sloppily at the iPod, he put on Queen and turned the volume up high. Soon he wasn't pacing anymore but dancing, flailing, letting the rhythm take his body. He was no good at dancing, couldn't keep on top of a beat to save his life, but it didn't matter, he was soaring, holding his bottle up in the air as he stomped his legs and snapped his head back and forth, grinning, swaying, hammering on an invisible drum set. He danced through song after song until

"Don't Stop Me Now" came on, probably his favorite song of all time, and in celebration, he tipped the bottle *glug-glug-glug* into his throat and closed his eyes as he whirled through the room. It was pitch black, and he was alone with the music and the alcohol, and as he danced, all the characters that lived in his mind faded away. He wasn't Jean Lafitte, he wasn't a French merchant, he wasn't a trucker or a basketball star or a sharpshooter or a rapper, he was *himself,* he was Ralphie. Just Ralphie, alone and happy.

And across the room, you couldn't see it in the dark, but it was there, he knew it was, there was a bookshelf, and on the bookshelf, there was a row of books, all with his name on the spines. His life's work. And in front of the books there was a, what was it, a medal? No, it was a prize, *the* prize, the *Pulitzer* Prize, so pretty and heavy and clear, and next to that there was a picture, yes, a photo, a photo of Ralphie in a room full of the world's most successful writers, Stephen King, George R.R. Martin, all of them shaking his hand, slapping him on the back, smiling at him, *Ralphie,* this is the guy, see him, see how good he is? And next to that there was a picture of Ralphie with his girlfriend, beautiful and grinning and wild. Tonight, she was Ruby, but a *better* version of Ruby, someone who actually liked him, and he and this girl who actually liked him were together on a mountaintop, a mountaintop–yes, why not–looking out at the dawn. And she was here, too, in the room. Yes, of course. Ralphie's amazing girlfriend was on the bed, smiling, watching him dance in the dark, because she loved him fiercely, loved all his eccentricities, saw him and knew him and respected him, and his heart leapt to know that soon he would crawl into bed with her and hold her close, but now he needed to dance more, dance for hours, dance forever, Freddie Mercury was singing about being a rocket ship, a satellite, spinning out of control, and now the door was opening, and there were other people coming into the room. Who were they? Why, they were his friends, of course, his college buddies, all the other tour guides…even the little girl from the group tonight was there, along with all the other good people he'd met on his tours over the years. Yes, everyone he'd ever cared about was there in Ralphie's room—*hello,* Matt from middle school, kind of a jerk sometimes but still a good guy! *Hello,* Grandma Baker, sure, I would love a sandwich! Mom and Dad, holding hands like they still loved each other and beaming at Ralphie like they weren't disappointed in him. Max from work, with his wife at his side, still alive. His roommates from Indy all those years ago, all the friends he'd ever had, all of them, every one.

The very last person to enter was Kat. She was glowing, surrounded by fuzzy pink light, eyes smiling under her glasses. And he took her in his arms, and they held each other close for a long, long time, and he knew that she wasn't gone after all, it had all just been a bad dream, she was here, and she was real, and he would never let her go. And then she was flattening his cowlicky hair, she was tucking his pockets into his pants and smoothing his vest like she always did, and then she kissed him on the cheek and laughed and stepped away into the crowd. Ralphie held out his arms to welcome them all, all the good people, and together they laughed, and danced, and drank, and soon they were all shouting his name, "Ralphie, Ralphie, Ralphie!" And then there were hands around him, warm hands touching him, supporting him, lifting him, and soon he was aloft, in the air, being passed through the room like a superstar. He was completely vertical now, lying on his back, eyes closed.

The bottle lay beside him, empty.

CHAPTER 5
The Empty Courtyard

"I ran into him last night," Ruby says, working two fingers through a knot in her dreads. This is a fairly new look for her. I'm not sure if it was an intentional choice or not; after she broke up with her boyfriend, her hygiene went down the toilet, and the dreads may have sort of happened of their own accord.

"Did you talk to him?" Veda asks.

"No, of course not. It was pretty fucking triggering, though."

"I bet."

It's Monday night in the Quarter Rat courtyard. Tonight, Poppy's alone at one of the shorter tables, doing something with some herbs and sipping on brandy, and Ruby and Veda are at one of the hi-tops talking. Ruby's drinking vodka, and Veda is painting her nails. I'm over in the corner, as usual.

"I wish he'd just *move*. Like why the fuck is he still here, you know? Everybody knows his, you know his dirty laundry or whatever, why wouldn't he want to get out of town and start over somewhere else?"

"That's a good point."

"Poppy said she could put a curse on him."

Veda frowns. "Mmm...I wouldn't go that route if I were you."

"Why not?"

"It'll just bring you down to his level. Better to let the universe deal with him in its own way."

"But the universe isn't doing shit! He's still out there walking around!"

"He'll get his justice."

"There's no such fucking thing," Ruby muttered.

"Try not to take it personally. I don't think he's trying to hurt you. He's just...oblivious."

"Yeah, no shit. I think he's a sociopath."

"Really?"

"Why else would he have done it? Any of it?"

"Probably because he was hurting."

"You mean like, 'hurt people hurt people' or whatever?"

"Well, yeah."

"That's bullshit," Ruby says, her voice rising. "How can you think that?"

Veda shrugs. "Experience."

"I mean, I know you've been through some shit, more than me. But how can you look at the people who hurt you that way and say 'Oh, they just, they were mistreated, so—'"

"But they were."

"*You* were mistreated. *I* was mistreated. And look at us, we're not abusive assholes."

"That's true."

"And how was Brian mistreated, huh? What happened to him in his childhood? Nothing. He had a perfect life." Gesturing wildly, Ruby accidentally knocks over Veda's bottle of glittery nail polish. Veda picks it up.

"Maybe he just lacks empathy."

"Exactly. Sociopath."

I only met Ruby's boyfriend once, at a birthday party he threw for her, but he definitely gave off a weird vibe. He had this strange haughty attitude, barely talked to any of us, but had his arm clamped around Ruby's waist the whole time. He kept kissing her neck and playing with her hair, which was shiny and gorgeous then. "Doesn't my baby have the most beautiful hair?" I think he said to me, and I remember it was one of the only times he spoke to me the whole night. I wondered if he was high. But then I remembered that Ruby had told me how straight-edge he was—he hated alcohol and drugs, got mad when Ruby even smoked weed. She always used to rush home after work because he didn't like her hanging out in the bar with us. Needless to say, none of us really liked him. I'm sure she's much better off without him, but she can't seem to get over whatever it is that he did.

"I'm sorry you have to see him," Veda says.

"Whatever," Ruby mutters. "Let's go throw some shit in the river soon, yeah?"

Veda nods, then looks toward the bar, distracted, like she's expecting someone. A few seconds later, Jeremy comes into the courtyard. Veda draws back as he walks by and approaches Poppy at the table next to me. I don't normally see Jeremy this close up, and I notice how haggard he looks: dark circles around his eyes, his cheeks puffy and blotchy. His long hair is thinning at the top, making his forehead appear larger, and his loose white linen shirt is yellowing under the armpits. He sits across the table from her, sighing as he sets down his glass of wine.

"What's up, baby?" Poppy asks, not looking up from her herbs.

"Day off," he says under his breath. Jeremy always talks under his breath, even to his tour groups. Even now, from just a few feet away at my little table in the dark, I have to strain to hear him. "I've just been wandering."

"You look tired."

"Can't sleep."

"Yeah, join the club."

He raises an eyebrow. "You either?"

"The fibromyalgia's killing me," she says. "And you should see my feet. All swollen up, hurts to stand. Doc thinks I might have kidney disease."

"You're kidding."

She shakes her head. "Always something, ain't it?"

"How's Asmodeus?"

Anybody who's met Poppy knows the way to her heart is through her cats. Asmodeus is her favorite, and she keeps a picture of him in her wallet, right next to the one of Emmie, her daughter.

"Oh, he's an angel," Poppy smiles, and I see the gap where one of her teeth is missing. I asked her what happened once; she said it rotted, and she didn't have enough money to get it fixed.

"My sweet baby angel. But his health is starting to go too, you know. Kidneys, same as me. That's what always gets male cats, the kidneys."

"Sorry to hear it."

"Yeah, well. Nobody's immortal."

Jeremy takes a sip of wine and licks his fangs. "What's this," he says after a moment, gesturing to the herbs.

"Oh, just bundling some sage and things. Been selling it behind the Cathedral. Smudges, gris gris, dolls."

"Making some money?"

"A bit. Not enough, though. You know I can't hardly give tours no more, can't barely afford my rent."

"What about your paramour, doesn't he pitch in?"

"Bludwan? Took off."

"I'm sorry to hear that."

"Eh. Useless, just like the rest of 'em."

"They don't deserve you."

"They just feed on my energy, you know. No offense."

"None taken."

"Draining my light. I used to do much higher magick, you know, beautiful stuff."

"I remember."

"It's all gone now, almost all of it anyway. Stolen. These men come along, calling themselves warlocks, but they ain't got no power of their own."

"Well, maybe now you've learned your lesson."

"Eh, I never learn," she sighs. "Fall for it every time. But it's better than being alone, I guess." She finishes her brandy, and they sit quietly for a moment.

"You ever been to Colorado, J?" she asks.

He shakes his head.

"Beautiful. Clean, dry, the mountain air…not like this. Nothing like this dirty swamp."

"Mm."

"I been thinking…what if I got out of here, you know, made a fresh start."

"You mean leave New Orleans?"

She shrugs. "Yeah."

"That's an idea."

"Never happens, though, does it?"

"Good *eeeevening*," sings a voice from the other side of the courtyard, and I look over.

James and Vik have arrived, descending loudly upon the table where Ruby and Veda are sitting.

"Um, we're in the middle of a conversation?" Ruby says.

"Well, I'm sure it's quite boring," James says, plopping down on a stool.

"What have you two been doing?" Veda asks.

"Oh, galavanting through the Quarter like a couple of gay degenerates," James says with great flair. Overhearing this, Jeremy rolls his eyes so hard, his eyelids flicker.

"Oh, they're just kids," Poppy scolds.

"When *we* were that age—"

"Really? You're going to start with that shit?" she teases. "Let them have their fun."

"That one," he says quietly, jerking a thumb over his shoulder at James. "Doesn't he remind you of Mortimer?"

Poppy chuckles. "Maybe a little. Mortimer was much more fabulous, though."

Jeremy smiles. "I miss that freak."

"Yeah, well. Our little family's almost all gone now, isn't it?"

Jeremy nods and his smile fades to a scowl. I don't think about it much, but we're not the first group of weirdos to settle here, are we? There have been a dozen generations of Quarter Rats before us, misfits and dreamers and goths, little groups like ours gathered by necessity in the hole-in-the-wall bars to laugh and bitch and look for belonging. I wonder what has happened to the groups who came before. I wonder what will happen to us.

Jeremy sighs.

"What are you doing here on your day off, anyway?" Poppy asks him.

"Came to find you, actually."

"Oh yeah?"

"Like I said. Can't sleep. Wondering if you could help me out."

"Well, sure. I could make you a tea."

"What about something stronger? A spell? I'll pay."

Poppy sighs. "It's that bad, huh?" He nods.

"And not just sleep. Peace," he whispers.

Poppy laughs dully. "Oh, J. Even the strongest magick can't get you that."

"Do your best."

"Alright. I'll bring you something in the next couple days."

He picks up her leathery hand and kisses it meaningfully. "Knew I could count on you."

"Oh, stop," she smiles, and if they were both twenty years younger, she might be blushing.

Jeremy gets up to go, striding past the table of younger tour guides without so much as glancing at them. "Have a good night, Jeremy!" James calls after him. Jeremy doesn't acknowledge it, of course, and when he's gone, the whole table erupts into giggles. We're like children that way, always acting like he's Boo Radley or something. I wonder if it bothers him. I doubt it. I bet he actually likes it. I get the feeling that his creepy shtick is all he really has going for him these days. Funnily enough, the most scared I ever was of Jeremy was when I ran into him in the mall in Metairie, wearing jeans and shopping for cookware. When he saw me, he gave me the most vitriolically hateful look I've ever seen. I'm sure he was just embarrassed, but holy shit, it was terrifying. I straight up ran out of TJ Maxx.

"Wow, how drunk *are* you?" Ruby asks James.

"Oh, poo-poo," James says. "I'm not scared of that guy."

"You should be," Veda says.

"Why, because he's a '*vampire*'?"

Veda nods. I can't tell if she's being serious or not.

"Pffft," Vik says. "Jeremy's pathetic. I'm more afraid of Elijah next door." Elijah's the other vampire on the block, all of five feet tall, who works at the Curiosity Shop.

"Oh, Elijah's just the *cutest*," James gushes. "With his little fangs and his tiny combat boots? Where do you think he got those, OshKosh B'Goth?" Vik snorts in laughter.

"Elijah pissed me off the other day," Ruby begins.

"Literally everyone pisses you off every day," Vik says into his beer.

Ruby gets mad. "Ex*cuse* me?"

"Case in point."

"Speaking of adorable little weirdos, where's Ralphie?" James asks. "Didn't he have a tour tonight?"

"He was here, but he went home," Veda says.

"Yeah, he was being kind of annoying," Ruby adds.

"Shocking," Vik says.

"I love Ralphie," Veda smiles. "He has a very kind heart."

"That's true," Vik says. "Ralphie's far too good for the likes of us."

"Speak for yourself. I have a heart of fucking gold," James says, slurping down the last of his gin and tonic.

"You? Your heart is just a little ball of condom wrappers and dog hair."

"*Excuse me?* That's so rude. I don't even have a dog."

Poppy stands, beginning her long slow shuffle out of the courtyard toward the bar and the street.

"You out of here, Poppy?" Vik asks.

"Yep. G'night."

"Night," they chorus.

"Poppy's not doing too hot, is she?" Vik says when she's gone.

"No shit Sherlock, she weighs like two fifty and can barely walk," James says.

"Her energy too," Veda adds sadly. "You can tell her magick is waning."

James raises his eyebrows in amusement but says nothing. "It's a shame," Veda says. "She clearly used to be really powerful."

I haven't known Poppy long, just a few years, but it's hard to imagine her as anything other than what she is now. In my experience, people in the French Quarter don't change.

"By the way," James asks Veda, "How's the ghost in your house?"

"Oh, the old woman?" Veda says brightly. "I actually got her to move on."

"Opened a portal for her, huh?"

"No, there was already one there. But she's gone now, and I closed it."

"Coooool," James says, making little effort to disguise the sarcasm in his voice. When he's drunk, he's even more of a dick than usual. "I think there's a genie in my closet, maybe you could do something about that too."

"A genie?" Veda asks, looking confused.

"Shut up, asshole," Vik says. "There hasn't been anything in your closet since you were seven years old and sashayed out of it covered in glitter."

"You don't know my past!"

"I could take a look if you want," Veda says.

"No, don't pay attention to him," Ruby says. "He's just being a dick."

Vik gets a text and stands. "Gotta go," he says.

"Aw, why?" James whines.

"None of your business."

"Doth Her Majesty call?"

"I told her I'd pick her up from Chalmette."

"Doesn't she have a bike?"

"It's like forty degrees outside."

"Aw, *mamacita* can't handle the cold? Maybe she oughta go back to Mexico."

"She's from here, asshole," Vik frowns.

"Yeah, what the fuck, James?" Ruby says.

"Oh, hush. I'm just talking shit."

"Well, it gets old," Vik says.

"If you're heading that way, can you drop me at home?" Ruby asks Vik.

"Sure."

"You're *all* leaving?" James exclaims. "Come on, it's Monday night! Let's get lit!"

"I'll stay for a bit," Veda says.

Ruby gathers her things and Vik puts on his jacket. "Later, kids." They leave.

James and Veda are quiet for a moment, and he stirs the ice cubes in his former gin and tonic. "Want a drink?" he asks her.

"Oh, no thanks. Alcohol is a depressant."

"Honey, look around," he says, slurring a little as he gestures to the empty courtyard. "Everything here is a depressant. *Life* is a depressant."

"That's true. But I do my best to walk in the light."

"Good for you."

"It can be hard, though. It's not always easy to stay away from the shadow entities that want to drain our energy."

"You mean ghosts?" he says with a sour little smile.

"Oh, ghosts can definitely be draining. But mostly they just need guidance. The real shadow entities we need to worry about are here," she says, laying a palm across her chest.

"Our inner demons, or whatever?"

She nods.

"Yeah, well, I've got plenty of those," he mutters.

"I can tell."

James stiffens. "Oh, you can tell, huh? Why, am I that fucked up?"

"Pain recognizes pain."

"What do *you* know about pain?" he says. "Where'd you grow up? Let me guess, California? Suburbs? Parents wanted you to go to law school but instead you took your trust fund and came to New Orleans to 'find yourself?' Yeah, real traumatic."

She looks at him for a moment, then says quietly, "You know I'm trans, right?"

"Oh. Right."

She gets up. "It's getting late."

"No, don't—I'm sorry. I'm a dick."

"I'm just tired," she smiles, pulling on a furry pink coat over her pale-yellow coveralls and granny sweater. "I hope you can find your light tonight, James."

She goes. James slowly lowers his head, softly bangs it on the table once, twice, then leaves it there. A minute later, he sits up again.

He pulls out his phone, puts it to his ear, waits as it rings.

"Hey," he says. "Where are you?" He lays his cheek in his palm as the person on the other end talks, then asks, "Can you come to the Rat when you're done?"

He hangs up. We're alone now, me and James.

There's just one time in the past I can think of that James and I were alone together, and it must have been a couple years ago. We were over by the river together, smoking weed and talking. It's something I've done with most of the other tour guides at some point or another, and that they've probably all done together too, just one of those things that happens when two guides both don't get a tour and are looking to kill some time. We were talking about love, I guess, in all its elusiveness. And he told me that he had a soulmate. I was surprised, given what I've seen of James' romantic conduct over the past several years. I asked him who it was.

"It doesn't matter," he said, coughing a little as he exhaled smoke.

"What do you mean?" I asked. And James told me that this soulmate was so far away, and so out of his league, that he might as well be in another universe.

I got angry. "What the hell?" I think I said.

"Excuse me?"

"If he's the one, go get him. You go fucking get him."

"I can't," he said, looking out at the dark river.

"Why?" I asked.

"Because he's a perfect human being. And I'm trash."

He's sitting very quietly now, staring at the courtyard wall. Fifteen minutes pass. I've never seen James so still.

A little while later, that boy comes in, James' lover. Landon, I think his name is. He walks up behind James, smiling.

"Hey you," he says, laying a hand on James' shoulder. "Glad you called."

James turns around in his stool and buries his face in the boy's torso.

"Aw, what's wrong? You okay?"

James shakes his head. Landon pulls him close, cradling James against him. "Hey, shh, it's okay. Everything's gonna be okay."

"I missed you," James says, his voice muffled.

"I missed you too." Landon sits on the stool next to him and rubs his back. "What's the matter?" he asks. James lets out a long sigh and is silent for a moment.

"I'm just tired of being me," he says dully.

"I like that you're you," Landon smiles.

"I don't know why."

"You don't have to know why. You just have to like me back."

James sits up to look at him. "I do," he mutters. "Too much."

Landon nudges a piece of hair out of James' eyes. "I'm not going to hurt you, you know."

"Not if I hurt you first."

"Is that what you want?"

James shakes his head and mumbles something.

"What?" Landon asks.

"You're my light," James repeats. Landon squeezes his hand.

They sit there like that, quietly, for a long time. Eventually, Landon gets James up and they leave the courtyard, arms around each other.

I'm alone.

It always feels so strange, this late at night, to remember the tour you gave a few hours ago—back when you were sober, when you could speak so eloquently, when you were surrounded by a couple dozen people who liked you and trusted you and hung on your every word. I try to remember my last group. A family, I think, a petite guy with glasses and his smiling wife, two girls...a few college guys, here for somebody's birthday...that nice woman from California, a magazine editor, yes...I can barely remember her face now, any of their faces.

It's getting late.

The bars don't close in the French Quarter. Well, they do, but not till the last lonely sop has staggered home at 3 or 4 or 5 AM. Sometimes the tour guides are the last ones here, holding the tired bartenders hostage until enough of us have trickled home that whoever's left in the courtyard finds the drunken posturing no longer worth the effort. Avery and Leela don't mind us, though. We spend lots of money, and we're certainly more likeable than the groups of bachelorettes who wander in off Bourbon and tip nothing and the conventioneers who come in alone, middle-aged men who think pretty bartenders owe them smiles and conversation and who dawdle over choosing a draft beer just for attention. Tour guides are loud and insufferable, but we're service industry, so we get it. The bartenders like us. And sometimes we forget to close our tabs, but they always know we'll be back again tomorrow.

As always, I'm the last one back here. And I don't want to be. I should go home, get some rest. Maybe even quit. Instead, I stick around night after night, watching them, contributing nothing, over here in my self-imposed exile from the group. They don't even try to talk to me anymore; I think they gave up a long time ago. Not that I blame them. I'm not much fun.

Maybe I just don't want to be alone. Even though I'm always just over in the corner by myself, it's something, being around them. Human contact. Sort of like the human contact you get on a tour. It's not real, exactly, the people in your group aren't *actually* your friends, they don't really care about who you are or what you've been through or what your hopes and dreams are, no matter how much they might laugh at your jokes and chat with you between stops and hang on your every word when you're telling a story. But even so, there's a connection. A real connection, an exchange, based on shared truths and shared experiences. Stories can do that. Humanity by proximity, I guess.

My last tour feels very long ago. I don't know if I could give one now, if I could walk down the street with a big group following me, talk and gesture and joke and shout down the hecklers like usual. The idea of giving a tour seems very difficult, now that the night has grown so late. But I still know the stories. They're in me. Permanent.

They are as permanent as me in this empty bar.

CHAPTER 6
The Burnt Orphans

It always started with her feet. Little jolts of pain began to shoot from her toes up to her ankles, just lightly at first, blending into Poppy's dreams. Then the jolts got angrier, more painful, pulling her out of sleep. Next came the hurt in her lower back. Around 5 or 6 AM, she started to change positions every few minutes, trying to shift the ache, waking more and more every time she moved. By the time her neck and shoulders started to throb, Poppy had usually come to know that the short escape of sleep had ended and that it was time to hurt again.

Asmodeus was usually polite enough, thank Goddess, to not bug Poppy for breakfast while she was still asleep, but the meowing always started the second she opened her eyes.

"Gimme a sec, kids," she muttered, starting the slow process of hauling herself out of bed. Maven and Snowball fussed at her ankles as she made her way to the kitchen to shake food into their bowls. Good cats, they were. Snowball was getting old, though, wasn't she, Poppy thought, frowning as she watched them eat. Her white fur was the color of dishwater, now, and stuck up in dry patches around her bony rump. How fluffy she'd been as a kitten, those bright blue eyes—she was a present for Emmie's sixteenth birthday, who'd named her Snowball not for her pure white fur but because Poppy had taken her to Hansen's Sno-Bliz earlier that day. Snowballs had always been Emmie's favorite treat, more than birthday cake or ice cream, because they came in so many different colors. Emmie always got rainbow. Lime, Orange, Lemon, Blueberry, and Tiger's Blood, the syrup poured in stripes so thick that the ice caved in under its weight.

So, Snowball must be coming up on seventeen years old now. Long time for a cat to live. She'd always been healthy, not like Asmodeus with his kidney problems, which was a small blessing. Poppy had always thought of her as Emmie's cat, even now, and her health was a comfort. She hoped the cat would pass easily in her sleep when the time came. Poppy didn't think she could stand to watch Snowball suffer.

She pulled back a curtain and looked out the window, down onto Dumaine Street where a mule buggy, empty except for the driver, was plodding along. It looked cold out there. The two homeless guys who usually camped on the corner were buried under their blankets, unmoving gray lumps under an unmoving gray sky.

Poppy had lived in the Quarters almost all her life. She and her mom had moved into a little shithole on Lower Decatur in the early seventies because the boyfriend-of-the-moment had a barback job at the dive downstairs, and she'd never left. Back then, the French Quarter's rents had been cheaper than dirt and its people had been deep on the decline. When she wasn't mooching off her boyfriends, Poppy's mom worked at the clubs on Bourbon, which by the mid-seventies, had become seedy to the extreme; lots of them driven out of business by the porn industry. She brought Poppy to work on slow nights, stowing her up in the hazy dressing room while she danced. There Poppy would sit for hours, chewing on candy cigarettes and listening to the dancers shoot the shit as they smoked cigars and changed from their boyish clothes into threadbare g-strings. They were tough, masculine even, and swore constantly. Sometimes they let Poppy take sips of the cherry brandy they poured into paper cups from a bottle they kept stashed in one of the lockers.

Poppy had tried to do better with her own daughter. Sure, their apartment had been a shithole too, and Poppy's boyfriends weren't generally any better than her mom's had been, but she'd taken Emmie places, done things with her, the Zoo, the Aquarium, she'd even bought them two-day passes to the Six Flags when it opened, when Emmie was fourteen. Emmie had loved it. In fact, the picture Poppy carried in her wallet was from that weekend, Emmie wrapping her arms around a guy in a big Spongebob suit, smiling that smile that could melt your damn heart.

The dim light from the window lit up a swirl of dust particles in the air of Poppy's bedroom, and she watched as they settled on the sweaty covers of the unmade bed, the laundry and crystals and bundles of sage on the carpet, an old moldy cup of tea. She yanked the curtain closed, returning the apartment to its normal dimness. There was shit to do today, no point in wasting time. It took Poppy a while to get up and moving anyway, her joints painfully stiff after the paralysis of sleep, her brain still a little foggy. She made a cup of tea, ignoring the smell of cat piss in the carpeted corner by the kitchen door. Asmodeus had been pissing outside the litterbox lately; she suspected kidney problems but couldn't afford to take him to a real vet.

It was 9:00 before Poppy was out the door, inching her way down the apartment building's steep, dark stairway to the street. Bludwan wouldn't be awake yet; he always slept until noon like a damn nineteen-year-old, but that was a good thing. It meant she could get the jump on him. He'd been evading Poppy for a week now, somehow managing to duck out of his usual bars just before she arrived, spreading conflicting information about what he was up to. Someone had even told her he'd left town. But all her most reliable sources were sure he'd been shacking up with a hussy who read palms in Jackson Square, and Poppy happened to know where this hussy lived.

She pounded on the door. It took a few minutes, but eventually the girl answered, her hair in a lumpy bun, the acne on her cheeks red and angry.

"Is Bludwan here?"

"He's sleeping."

"Can you go get him? We got business."

"What business?"

"I'm not leaving till I talk to him," Poppy said. "You want an angry witch on your porch all day, be my guest."

The girl gave her a bratty frown and shut the door. After a minute, she came back and yanked it open again, Bludwan in tow. His eyes were gummy with sleep, and they widened when he saw Poppy.

"You woke me up for *this*?" he whined at the girl, who shrugged and went back into the dark recesses of the house.

Poppy crossed her arms. "You can't avoid me forever."

Bludwan pushed his long, thinning hair out of his face. He was in the loose linen tunic he always wore, chest hair spilling out the top and skinny legs in boxer shorts sticking out from under his fat paunch. His sideburns, which came all the way to his jaw, were swallowed in stubble. He wasn't wearing his earrings.

"I want my money, Bludwan."

"What money?"

"You took a hundred bucks out of my dresser."

"You said I could."

"When we were *together*. That's different."

"I'll pay you back, okay? Soon. Next week." He tried to close the door, but she held it open.

"And how about an explanation, huh? Will I get one of those next week too? Or ever?"

"Poppy…"

"Why'd you take off? Without a word, without even a note…"

Bludwan sighed.

"Come on, just…just talk to me. I'm not gonna hurt you or nothing."

"Fine. You wanna come in?" he said, and she followed him into the house.

It was dark like her place, all the windows covered with heavy curtains. Most of the front room was filled with the girl's palm reading stuff, a cart and a table and a big hand-painted sign that she dragged out to the square every day. Poppy had used to read cards in the square too, before Emmie, before she was a tour guide. Not very rewarding work, and it sucked having to sit in the sun all day. Her heart softened just a bit for the girl.

"So, you're seeing little miss palm reader now, huh?"

"Just crashing here for now."

"Yeah, well, I hope she clues up soon. God knows you're not gonna do nothin' but smoke her weed and steal her money." Bludwan glared, then shrugged, then lit the remnants of a joint.

"I didn't know what happened to you," Poppy said. "Didn't know if you'd gotten in trouble, or what."

"I just needed a change."

"You could have told me. I thought..." She'd promised herself that she wouldn't go soft like this, just demand the money and go, maybe chew him out a little. "I thought we had something good going."

He blew out a cloud of smoke. "Yeah, we had some fun." He coughed. "But it was never supposed to be permanent."

"I didn't say it was. But you didn't have to just take off like that."

"You know I've got a rambling soul."

She rolled her eyes. "Spare me."

"Besides, you were always talking about leaving too. Going out West or whatever."

"So? I've been saying that for years."

"Well, maybe you ought to quit saying it and just do it."

"How come?"

"You're not happy here."

Poppy scoffed. "I'm fine. I've got my practice, my tours—"

"You barely give tours anymore."

"I do. Couple times a week."

"That's not the point, Poppy, you know? It's just…" He took another hit from the joint and waved pensively at the smoke as he exhaled.

"It's just what?"

"Spiritually draining. Being around you."

"What do you mean?"

"You know what I mean. With your health troubles, and Emmie…"

"Don't bring her into this."

"How can I not? It hangs over everything."

"I will always put my daughter first. I'm not gonna apologize for that."

"You don't have to," he sighed, stroking the amulet that hung in his forest of chest hair. "I just hope you find some peace."

"Peace," she spat. "You're one to talk. Bouncing from woman to woman, lying constantly—"

"I'll give you your money."

"It's not about that."

"I will. Right now," he said, getting up and going to the girl's pile of stuff. He took a little box out of a tote bag and pulled out some cash, counting out a few twenties, some fives and tens.

"Is that even yours?"

"You need it, don't you?"

"You stole more than money from me, Bludwan! You took my energy. My magick."

He tossed the cash at her and shook his head. "Poppy, honey. Come on. You lost your magick years ago."

She swore at him then, just like she'd promised herself she would, and left. Later, she thought, she'd come back to this house and put a hex on it. Or maybe just leave some dog shit on the stoop.

The Quarters was still as cold and gray as it had been in the early morning, and the day's first tourists were hurrying off the street into the warmth of shops and restaurants. Poppy felt sour about their quickness, their laughter, the money they had to throw around on vacation. She didn't travel. In fact, the only other state Poppy had ever been to was Colorado, back when she was ten or eleven years old. Her mother's sister had been living out there and making decent money at the time and had flown them both out to visit one Christmas. It was the first time Poppy had ever seen snow, and she remembered sitting by the window the night they arrived just watching it come down, hypnotized by the tumbling white drifts lit up against the darkness by a single streetlight. In the morning, she'd gone to the same window and been startled to see mountains in the distance, rising above the town. Poppy had never even seen a real hill, being a native of flatter-than-flat Southeastern Louisiana. Looking at those mountains stirred something in her, a feeling hard to name. What would you call it? A sense of possibility, maybe. You could climb those mountains if you really wanted to. And even if you never did, they'd still always be there, daring you. Promising a future that was just out of reach but close enough to keep you dreaming.

It had always been there in the back of her mind, the idea of living somewhere with mountains someday. But she'd gotten pregnant just out of high school, and then she'd been a single mom, and of course it took everybody years to get their heads on straight again after Katrina. Lately, she'd been thinking about it more and more, though, that mountain view. A stupid idea, really. She had obligations.

Poppy went back home to get what she needed then made her way slowly down Royal to Canal. She didn't have to wait long for the streetcar, but her back was aching by the time she was finally able to sit down on one of its narrow benches. She settled her heavy bag on the floor next to her and looked down at her toes, which were angry red from the cold. Somebody at work had asked why she wore sandals in this weather, and she'd been too embarrassed to tell them that these were the only shoes her swollen feet fit in anymore. She'd been meaning to buy new shoes, maybe some sort of boots for winter, but money was tight. Bludwan was right—she didn't give nearly enough tours anymore.

The streetcar made its way up Canal Street, collecting and depositing people from the worn paths on the neutral ground that ran along its tracks. Half of them were locals like Poppy, just going about their business, sliding expressionless into the wood-slatted seats and rising expressionless again when their stops came. The other half were tourists who stood in clusters, laughing and taking selfies and losing their balance whenever the streetcar came to a stop. Fuck 'em.

Poppy got out at City Park, the end of the line. The art museum was there down the lane from the park's entrance, and next to it was the pond where folks rented paddleboats in springtime. The dull white water shooting from its fountain was the same color as the sky.

She left the path and made her way across the dry grass to the Singing Oak. Hung with dozens of heavy chimes, some as long as your arm, the tree made music as the wind blew. It was a live oak, green even in winter, and hundreds of years old. Poppy took a small blanket out of her tote bag and spread it on the ground then slowly and painfully lowered her heaviness down onto it.

Sage first, to cleanse the area. She lit a smudge and closed her eyes, letting its woodsy scent surround and purify her. Then she took out her candles, the tall glass kind with pictures of Catholic saints on them, which were good and sturdy but a pain in the ass to haul around. She set them in a circle around her and lit them, cupping her palm around the lighter's flame as it flickered in the wind. Next, she took out the mirror, a heavy old-fashioned thing about ten inches square, brass with its own stand. She was sitting with her back to the tree and set the mirror across from her on the blanket, adjusting it to reflect the branches behind. Directly in front of the mirror she placed a talisman, a Minnie Mouse doll that she always kept with her, the whites of its eyes and gloves gone brown with dirt and age and love. And then she took out her envelope of pictures, laying them down softly around her. Baby Emmie sleeping in the arms of her gaunt, old Gramma Beth. Emmie at a pool party with the five other kids in her class. Emmie and Poppy at Christmas with their arms around each other, Emmie on the teacup ride at Six Flags, Emmie in her dalmatian dress, fifteen years old. *101 Dalmatians* had always been her favorite movie, and when they'd seen the dress at Walmart, Poppy knew Emmie wouldn't be able to talk about anything else until she had it. Of course, Emmie was big then and the dress was for little girls; Poppy had driven to four Walmarts that week, one all the way out in Ascension Parish, to find it in an XXXL. Even then, the dress was too small, but Emmie wore it anyway. In fact, she'd worn that dress to the hospital, the very last time she'd been admitted. Congenital heart problems her whole life. Common in people with Down's.

"Hey, baby girl," Poppy whispered, touching each photograph. "Missing you." She closed her eyes and conjured the sensations that went with Emmie. Her thick laugh. The warmth of her chubby hand, always reaching out for Poppy's. Her bigness, the space she took up, the soft cotton of her brightly-colored clothes. Holding all this firmly in her consciousness, Poppy spoke.

"Hermanubis, Keeper of The Gate, Lord of The Hidden Road Between Life and Death, I call on you. Hermanubis, I summon you. A follower of the Old Ways calls out to you. Open the gate between the Realm of the Living and the Realm of the Dead, for I would traffick with the Departed."

After she spoke the words, Poppy felt herself growing heavier. It happened slowly at first, just a gentle sensation of sinking slightly toward the earth, but after several minutes of meditating on the invitation, she realized that she could barely lift her arms. She opened her eyes and allowed her focus to come to rest on the mirror, which no longer reflected the tree behind her but instead contained a pearlescent cloudiness.

"Sweetheart, you there?" she asked. Surely, this time, Emmie's face would appear in the mirror. Poppy stared into it, squeezing the memories close, waiting. Minutes passed. But the shapes in the mirror stayed cloudy, shifting and changing like cream settling into coffee, resolving into nothing.

A voice, then? Emmie's voice would come to her if she just listened close enough. Poppy shut her eyes again. "Talk to me," she whispered. "Mama's right here." But the only sound was the low tinkling of the chime tree, and as the wind settled, that too faded away.

Poppy clung to the trance for as long as she could, but gradually she felt herself coming back into her body, back to reality. The mirror had tilted slightly on its stand. When she looked into it now, all she saw was her own face.

One time she was sure she'd seen something. A disturbance in the air around the tree, a shimmer, like the shimmer Emmie's ashes had made in the wind when Poppy had scattered them here. But that had been years ago. And it probably hadn't been anything at all.

She blew out the candles and packed up her things, hauling herself to her feet with great difficulty. "I'll try again next week, baby," she said before turning to go back to the streetcar. "Whenever you're ready."

Poppy spent the rest of the afternoon shuffling around the apartment, taking care of business. There was laundry to be put away and a bit of spell work to do, various things that people had asked her for. She did it by rote, just going through the motions. She didn't take much joy in her magick anymore. In her youth, Poppy had been well-known in the community, maybe even revered, for her powerful spellcraft. Lately, though, she'd begun shifting toward more mundane types of magick: crystal work, tarot cards, runes. In fact, her favorite thing these days was making soap, which could hardly be called magick at all. She knew the other witches in the French Quarter laughed at her behind her back, joked about her weight, her fading looks, her waning power. But she was too tired to care.

Poppy lived just a few blocks from work. She arrived on the street outside the Curiosity Shop at 7:30, just as she had almost every night for the last twenty years, and waited there with the other guides for launch time to arrive.

"Evening, Poppy," said Max, buttoning up his coat.

"Max."

"Chilly this evening."

"Worse for a skinny guy like you," she joked. "At least I've got padding."

Max winked and squeezed her shoulder. "Any plans for the weekend?" he asked. "Going to see the parades?"

"Oh, I don't do parades anymore. Too old for that shit."

"You and me both. Rather just relax at home with my dog."

"How is the old boy? What's his name again, Sean?"

"Seamus. He's alright. Having some trouble with his hip, though."

"Sorry to hear that."

"Got a vet appointment tomorrow," he said. His brow furrowed. "I sure hope they can help him. He can't jump into the car anymore, and I can't lift him."

"Yeah, I've got a cat that's getting old. It's rough."

Max shook his head. "I can't lose him, not so soon after Moll. Don't know what I'd do."

Poppy wondered how Max's wife had gone. She knew it had been sudden, a case of pneumonia gone wrong. But had he been there when it happened? Had they been able to say goodbye? She thought of Emmie, then, of that last stay in the hospital. Emmie's IQ had been in the sixties, but somehow, she'd been able to come to terms with her sickness more easily than anybody else had. At the end, she'd been the one comforting Poppy. Saying, "It's alright, mama. I'll see you soon." Kissing her fingers.

Max wore the death in his body, just like Poppy did, though he was wasting away to nothing, whereas she'd swollen up, putting on a hundred pounds in the last decade and a half. She had half a mind to reach out to him, ask if he needed someone to talk to. But Poppy didn't see what she could possibly offer Max that would make any real difference. At least other people could tell him lies in their ignorance: that there was strength to be found, reason to keep going. But Poppy knew the truth. When a piece of your soul gets taken away like that, there's no recovering. No real reason to go on. But you do anyway.

Jeremy appeared from the shadows, which Poppy knew he did on purpose. Sometimes he'd go a block out of his way so he could approach from a low-lit area, which Poppy found both funny and obnoxious. In the old days, it had worked beautifully, his mysterious air coming across so effortless, though Poppy had always known how hard he worked at it. In fact, Jeremy had disliked Poppy in the early days because she'd seen right through him, never fallen for his shtick. Come to think of it, there'd been a time in the late eighties when Poppy was probably the only beautiful woman in the French Quarter who hadn't found herself in Jeremy's bed at some point, which she was sure had driven him crazy. Even more frustrating was the double bind he found himself in, the fact that he couldn't make any real effort to persuade her because that would have ruined the whole effect. But of course, he'd lost interest as Poppy had aged, and they were friends, now, good friends.

"Hello, J," she said, and he nodded. "Anything new in your neck of the woods?"

Jeremy scowled. "Elijah Horowitz is an absolute cretin, but other than that..."

"Oh right, you're living with the little guy from the shop now! How's that working out?"

"Terribly. He's like a gnat in my eye, tiny but infuriating."

"Sorry to hear that," she chuckled.

"Don't laugh. I'm at the end of my rope. I may be driven to desperate measures."

"Well, control yourself. I'm in no state to haul my ass over to OPP to bail you out."

"Duly noted."

"Poppy, you passing?" asked Graham from his stool.

"You know what, I think I'd better take it." The money situation was getting dire and she couldn't avoid giving tours forever.

"Up to you," he shrugged.

"I will. I'll give a tour tonight."

"Alright. Jeremy, Poppy, and Max, head up front. And Sofia, if we sell any more tickets, you're next. Though I doubt we will." The girl smiled and nodded. Such a pretty young thing she was. Poppy had once helped Emmie dye her hair that same turquoise; it had made such a mess of the tub.

A sudden burst of pain shot through Poppy's hip as she shuffled to the launch spot, and she stumbled a little. Jeremy laid a hand on her arm, gave her a concerned look.

"I'm fine. You know how it is with me, this old body..."

Jeremy nodded gravely. "I'm sorry."

"It'll pass," she said. She hoped it would.

"Is everything else alright?" he asked.

"What do you mean?"

"Your aura is a bit...cloudy...today," he murmured, his eyes searching her face.

She waved him off. "My aura's always cloudy."

"Not like this. Did something happen?"

"Oh, I dunno. Bludwan's a piece of shit, for one thing."

"You saw him?"

"He says being around me is spiritually draining."

"Want me to eat him?"

Poppy laughed. "He's not your type."

"Ladies and gentlemen here for the Tour of Lost Souls, it's time to get started!" Graham was shouting at the dozens of people gathered and waiting on the sidewalk. How many managers had they been through over the years, Poppy wondered. Graham was probably the eighth or ninth. He was a drunk and a sweetheart, a better combination than some. She liked him. He sent Jeremy off first, then Poppy.

There were twenty-two people in her group, all bright-eyed and bushy-tailed. She wished they didn't look so excited. "Good evening, everyone, and welcome to the tour. Tonight, we'll be visiting several places in the Quarter and talking about ghosts and hauntings. There will be a break at a bar, and the tour will last about two hours. If you have any questions along the way, just let me know."

Poppy had been giving the same tour for nearly twenty years, and no longer made an effort to hide the apathy in her voice. She showed up, did her spiel, went home. It was routine, boring even. The hecklers in the street didn't faze her, it didn't matter to her whether the group listened or not, and she'd given up on caring about tips long ago. She also hadn't changed her route in all that time. She always started with the Bourbon Orleans hotel, which back in the day had been the Orleans Ballroom. First, she talked about quadroon balls where young white men competed for the hands of free women of color, then about the duels in the Cathedral's back garden across the street. She told them that if they came back late at night, they may hear the clinks of rapiers and shouts of *"en garde!"* from within.

"Have you ever heard it?" a young woman asked eagerly as she led them away.

"Nope," Poppy replied, and left it at that.

By the end of the Swamp Witch story, Poppy's lower back was killing her. She tried to keep her voice pleasant, but she knew they could hear the strain in it.

"And so, Kate moved out to the swamp with her nanny Labasse where she learned the art of witchcraft." Normally Poppy would pause here and tell them about her own work as a witch, about the world's misconceptions about magick, about New Orleans' pagan traditions. But tonight, she was just in too much pain. She hurried to get to the end of the story, though there wasn't any point in that because walking felt just as bad as standing. The next hour and a half would be agony whether she rushed through the stories or not.

Poppy decided to take her bar break early, after the next story. Normally, she went to Lafitte's Blacksmith Shop like everyone else, but she didn't want to walk the three blocks. Instead, she took them to the closest little dive bar on Chartres Street, which smelled like mildew and only had a few regulars. "Is it haunted?" someone asked, as she prepared to dismiss them for the break.

"Doubt it," she said. "They've got cheap beer, though."

Inside the bar, she lowered herself onto a stool by the video poker machine and sank back against the wall. She wondered if she ought to get a shot of whiskey, just to help with the pain. She decided against it; the bartender here was new, probably wouldn't give her one for free, and she certainly didn't have five bucks to spare.

"It's a little boring," she heard someone saying from the line to the women's bathroom. "Is it just me, or does she not seem to care very much?"

"She seems bitter."

"Can you blame her? I'd be bitter too if I weighed that much and had to walk around giving tours."

"Do you believe what she said at the beginning of the tour? About being a witch or a psychic medium or whatever?"

"Psychic medium, hah. More like psychic extra-extra-large."

Poppy got up and bought that shot of whiskey after all.

About half the group didn't come back from the bar break, including the women from the bathroom line. Poppy didn't care but hoped they wouldn't ask the company for refunds. The last thing she needed was to get in trouble with management.

She led the rest of them down Chartres to Governor Nicholls Street, passing Jeremy along the way. He still had his full group and was whispering dramatically about the Convent, holding their attention easily. Admirable, really, that he still cared so much about his tours. Poppy figured she might too if things had turned out differently.

Her next stop was the LaLaurie Mansion, the longest story on the tour. Standing for so long was agony, but at least the group didn't notice. The story was so fascinating, so horrifying, that even the worst tour guide could hold a group's attention here. Her mind wandered as she spoke. As she described Madame LaLaurie's torture methods, the peeled-off skin, the drilled-through skull, all she could think about was the pain in her swollen feet and lower back, barely registering the disgusted expressions of the people in her group. If they'd all been replaced with different people every time she looked away, she wouldn't have noticed. Twenty years of tours, hundreds of thousands of faces, none of them worth remembering. She looked right through them.

Poppy always finished at the Andrew Jackson Hotel on Royal Street. It was across from a vet's office, and sometimes its resident cat, Gris-Gris, was lounging in the window when she approached with her group. People were often distracted by him, but she didn't make any effort to prevent it. The cat was surely more interesting than her story.

"Take a look across the street here at this little yellow building, the Andrew Jackson Hotel. This place is notoriously haunted by the ghosts of young children."

The people in the group who were still managing to care "ooo'ed" in anticipation.

"In 1788, there was a fire here in New Orleans that destroyed about eighty percent of our original French buildings, and also killed quite a few people, leaving the city with a bunch of orphans to care for. The girls were sent to the Convent, but the boys were sent here. Before this place was a hotel, it was an orphanage. So, for several years there were little boys running around here.

"But just six years after that fire, there was another fire. Didn't kill as many people, but it did burn down the orphanage. So many of these young boys who'd lost their whole families in the first fire went on to lose their own lives just six years later in the second one."

"That's sad," a girl in the group murmured.

That's life, Poppy thought. "Now, I knew someone who used to work here, worked the night shift." And this story was actually true: she *had* known this guy, a guy named Bard, back in the nineties. Every other tour guide told this exact same story, but Poppy was the one who'd originated it. She took at least some care in telling it, more than she had for the rest of the tour.

"Now keep in mind, this guy was completely strait-laced, new in town, didn't even believe in ghosts when he started. But he said when he was here alone at the desk at night, strange things would sometimes happen. Usually started with the lamps flickering. And he said whenever the lamps flickered, he'd have some encounter with these little ghosts. Most often, it was just little footsteps running through the halls above his head. But sometimes they'd be giggling…sometimes he'd hear nursery rhymes…in fact, sometimes these little shits would get so worked up that they'd start to bang on the doors, and he'd get calls from guests in the hotel, 'Hey, why are there kids running around, it's midnight, get them back to their rooms!' And of course, he had to explain that there were no kids *staying* at the hotel that night. No living ones anyway.

"But you know what he told me? Said eventually he got used to it. To the point where the hauntings didn't really freak him out anymore, didn't really bother him. Until something happened. He says one night he's here, alone at the desk, late at night, as usual. But he's just worked the day shift too, so he's exhausted. Trying to pass the time, just watching the news quietly on the TV there in the lobby. Well…the lights start to flicker. And he knows something weird's gonna happen."

Poppy enjoyed this story. "And sure enough, a few seconds later, the channel on the television suddenly *changes*. All by itself. From CNN…to Cartoon Network."

The group laughed. "So, he changes it back to CNN. A few seconds later, Cartoon Network comes back on. He changes it back. CNN. Cartoon Network! CNN. Cartoon Network! This guy gets in a channel fight with these orphans from the 1700s.

"Now look...he's not scared. He's not freaked out. *He's pissed off.*" The group laughed again. "He doesn't wanna deal with it! And he always said he wasn't totally sure why he did what he did next, but the urge just came over him, and he stood up and yelled out, '*Boys! Enough! Go to bed!*'

"And he said it worked. No more flickering lights, no more channel changing, everything was peaceful and quiet for the rest of the night."

The people in the group were smiling, and Poppy found herself smiling too. "And I love that story, right? Because what that story tells me is that these little ghosts…they're not evil. They don't want to hurt you. They're just kids! They want to have a little fun. Because they've been in here for hundreds of years, and they are…forgive the pun…bored to death." The group laughed again. They were more engaged than they'd been all night.

"Here's the thing. When children die, particularly in painful or violent ways, they're more likely to stick around than adults. Because they don't really understand the line between life and death, don't understand where they're supposed to go.

"And a lot of people think the ghosts of children are creepy, more creepy than the ghosts of adults. Right?" The group nodded. "So why is that, what is it we don't like about them? Well…kids are supposed to be the opposite of death. Kids are new life. So the ghost of a child, it's doing the wrong thing. It's staying small forever, when it's supposed to grow. It freaks us out. It doesn't feel right." Poppy didn't usually talk like this. She usually just ended on the "bored to death" joke and said goodnight. But some people in the group were nodding, and so she kept going.

"And we don't like to be reminded, do we? That our children are going to die. Maybe not *when* they're children, but it's gonna happen eventually. We hate to face that fact. They talk about making new life when you bring a child into the world, but when you have a baby, you're not just creating a life, are you? You're creating a death. You're creating a person who is going to die, and all you can do is hope you're not around when it happens.

"So maybe that's why we don't like kid ghosts. It's our greatest fear, the death of our children. Our greatest fear and our greatest failing.

"But these little orphans? They don't know that. Hell, all they wanna do is watch TV." She smiled a little.

"And that's all I got for you, folks. Thanks for coming." She didn't even bother asking for tips anymore, but a few people pressed money into her hands. They really had been a nice group, in the end. Poppy regretted that she hadn't been able to give them a better tour.

She went back to the Quarter Rat and sank down into one of the chairs in the courtyard. There had been a time, long ago, that giving tours had felt like the greatest job in the world. Poppy had come from a long line of service industry women and blue collar men and had spent the first two decades of her working life slinging cheap beer, cleaning bathrooms, waiting tables, whatever needed doing in the Quarter to keep the tourists fed and drunk. She'd learned plenty about humanity in those days, including how eager most people are for the opportunity to treat another person like dirt. Poppy had never let herself get pulled to that level. "Kindness is free," that was her motto, and she'd always kept a smile on her face through the shit people threw. Easier to be kind when you're young and beautiful, though.

Jeremy appeared in the doorway of the courtyard and plinked a little glass of brandy down on the table in front of Poppy.

"That's for you," he said. "And so are these." From behind his back, he pulled out a bouquet of white roses.

"What?"

"I know black dahlias are your favorite, but I couldn't find any. And white is nice. I figured you could use some light in your life."

"Jeremy! Flowers? What's this about?"

He lay the bouquet on the table and sat.

"I told you, your aura's cloudy today. Wanted to lift your spirits."

"Psht. Save your romance for someone who deserves it."

"It's not romance. And you do deserve it."

"You're ridiculous," she said, reaching out to touch the roses' soft folds. They were perfect.

"I'm sorry about Bludwan. He's vermin."

"I'm sure you were just waiting for us to break up so you could say that."

"Well, they all are."

"I know."

"If you're so intent on having a man, there are better ones out there."

"Like you?"

"No, definitely not like me," he laughed darkly. "But someone, surely."

"You attract what you put out. And it's not like my energy's in great shape these days."

Jeremy looked at her pensively, palms pressed together in front of his lips. "What are you going to do about that?"

"Do about it? I don't know. There's nothing *to* do."

"You could make a change. If you really wanted to."

"I don't really want to. I don't really want anything."

"What about Colorado? The mountains."

"How would I get there? What would I *do* there?"

He shrugged. "You'd figure something out."

She sighed and took a sip of her brandy. "Even so. I can't."

They sat quietly for a moment.

"Oh! Your tincture," she said, pulling a small jar out of her bag. She'd made it for him earlier in the day.

"A tincture?"

"To help you sleep, like you asked. Yarrow flowers, catnip, oatstraw, some other things. Should help."

"I'll give it a try," he said. "Thanks."

"And I've been lighting a candle for you in my ritual work. Mentioning you when I contact the entities."

"I appreciate that." He stood.

"You leaving?"

"I only came to drop those off," he said, gesturing at the roses.

"You're crazy," she smiled, and shook her head. "Three droppers of that tincture before bed, yeah?"

He nodded and stood. "Thanks, Poppy. Goodnight."

Jeremy left the courtyard. He'd always been so strange, so lonely, despite all the seduction and sex. Lately, he was clearly struggling to maintain his grip. Poppy couldn't muster the energy to worry about him, though. She couldn't even manage to worry about herself.

"Hey, Poppy, come sit with us," Vik called from the tall table where a few of them were gathered on the other side of the courtyard.

"Nah. I think I'd better be getting home."

"Come on, just one drink."

Home was only a few blocks away, but the thought of getting up and walking any kind of distance at all made Poppy wince. Just one more little snifter of brandy, then, something to dull the pain first.

"Alright, fine." She got up and went to them. It was Vik, Sofia and Veda sitting there, all of them hunched forward in the cold with their elbows on the table by their drinks.

"What are you drinking?" Vik asked.

"Brandy."

"I'll get it," he said, and went into the bar.

"Brandy? I've never had brandy," Veda said. She was a weird kid, always halfway to some other planet, and the only tour guide who didn't dress in some variation of all-black. Tonight, she was wearing a white feather boa and a big furry pink coat.

"It's pretty gross," Sofia said. "No offense."

Poppy shrugged. "I got a taste for it when I was a kid, some strippers turned me on to it."

"Strippers?"

"My ma worked at one of the clubs on Bourbon, back in the seventies."

"Which one?"

"It's not there anymore. All them old places are gone now."

"Bourbon Street in the seventies, wow," Veda smiled. "What was it like?"

Poppy grunted. "Same as it ever was."

Vik came back from the bar. "Here you go." He set a glass of brandy in front of her, and she took a sip.

"Thanks. I owe you one."

"Don't worry about it, mama."

"Not your mama."

"Did you know Poppy's mom was a stripper on Bourbon back in the seventies?" Sofia asked Vik.

"Oh yeah? That must have been an interesting time."

They were all looking at her, eyes full of expectation, waiting for her to tell some story about the way things used to be. She wasn't in the mood to play the wise elder, though, never liked when they wanted that from her. She liked these people best when they treated her like one of their own. They were tour guides, and she was a tour guide, and that's all there was to it. When age came into it, or experience…it was too easy to look at them and see something she didn't want to think about.

When she didn't say anything else, they struck up a conversation about the night's tours. How they never got sick of talking about work, Poppy couldn't understand.

Veda turned to Poppy. "Have you always practiced magick?" she asked.

"Sure."

"I've been working on my powers of manifestation," Veda said.

"Good for you."

"Yeah. Manifesting what I need, working through some things. I wouldn't call myself a witch yet, but I'm trying to learn more."

"Uh huh."

"You read tarot, right?"

"Yep."

"I was wondering…well, I was wondering, actually, if you could teach me."

"Teach you to read tarot?"

"Yeah."

"Just get online, look at some videos or something."

Veda shrank back and went quiet, and Poppy looked down into her brandy to take a sip of it. She hadn't meant anything by it. The girl was just so damn young, barely more than a teenager, and the sweetness of her was frustrating. She glanced back up from her brandy at Veda. Emmie would have liked that furry pink coat.

It was hard, sometimes, for Poppy to be around young women. They were all Emmie, and all not Emmie. And then she'd remember that if Emmie were alive, she'd be much much older than that by now. Probably closer to Vik's age, a full-grown adult. Not like Veda, who was just a baby.

"Maybe," she sighed. "I guess I could teach you a couple things, sometime when we're both back here after tours."

"Really?" Veda's face lit up.

"Sure. I'm not the best there is, but throw me ten bucks or something and we can sit down with a deck for a bit."

"Okay!"

"Alright, I'd better get home," Poppy sighed, tossing back the last of her brandy and inching off the barstool to get to her feet. "Goodnight."

"Goodnight, Poppy." Like a chorus of schoolchildren.

It took the better part of ten minutes to make her way back to the apartment, each step painful even despite the brandy. She could hear the cats meowing behind the apartment door as she climbed the stairs, whining about how hungry they were. "Yeah, yeah, here you go," she murmured as she fed them. "Kibbles for my babies."

She sank down in her armchair and pulled off her sandals. Her toes had gone a bluish color—the circulation in her feet was all messed up. She massaged them, trying to get the blood flowing again.

After ten minutes of just sitting and being in pain, she pulled herself up and went back to the kitchen to make her nighttime tea. The roses were on the kitchen table where she'd tossed them when she'd fed the cats. Better put them in some water. She didn't have any vases, so she cut off the bottom of an orange juice carton from the recycling bin and stuck them in that. Every surface in the house was scattered with crap, mail and soap-making supplies on the kitchen table, candles and old cups of tea on the nightstands, bundles of herbs all over the counter. Looking for somewhere to put the roses, she noticed a small empty space on Emmie's altar.

"Mind if I put these here, baby?" she asked, smiling at Emmie's picture and setting the roses next to one of the candles, their petals lit up pretty by the glow. "There. Flowers for my girl."

Her smile faded. She wished Jeremy hadn't bought them. They were beautiful now, but in a day or two they'd start to wilt, and not long after that they'd be brown and brittle, just trash to throw out with the tea dregs and toilet paper rolls. Better never to have them at all than to have to watch them die.

Poppy gazed at the photo of her daughter in its frame. She'd known. Eleven weeks in, belly just starting to show, the doctor had sat Poppy down and talked about plasma proteins, hormones, some sort of fluid in the baby's neck. "We'll have to do more tests, but at this point, I'd say there's about a fifty percent likelihood that your baby will be born with an extra copy of chromosome 21." In the next few weeks, there were more blood tests, more samples, and fifty percent went up to seventy-five, then ninety, then nearly one-hundred. Four months in, the ultrasound found the possibility of a heart defect.

That was the same day they'd told Poppy that her baby was a girl. And Poppy wanted her. More than anything she'd ever wanted in her life, Poppy wanted this baby. She might as well have stuck her fingers in her ears for all the attention she paid the doctors, their warnings, those sad pitying looks on their faces. She hated them. Didn't they understand that this was her child, her daughter, her own flesh-and-blood?

Maybe it had been selfish, bringing a sick child into the world. There had been almost no chance that Emmie would make it to adulthood, and Poppy had known that, but she'd done it anyway. The sixteen years that followed hadn't been easy. But they were joyful, so joyful, and full of beauty and meaning that Poppy hadn't known before or since. It was all borrowed time, of course, happiness borrowed from her own future. Because now there was no joy, no beauty, no meaning, just a long, pale march toward nothing. If bringing Emmie into the world had been a selfish decision, Poppy paid for it karmically every day.

She finished making her tea and went back to her chair but found it occupied by Snowball. The old cat was curled up asleep, slender tail wrapped around bony hips, a little puff of shed white hair on the cushion next to her. Seventeen years, almost. Seventeen years since Snowball came into the world and Emmie left it. And soon, the old cat would be gone too.

Poppy didn't move Snowball so she could sit. Instead, she drank her tea in bed, Asmodeus by her side, Maven at her feet. When her eyes started to close, she found herself dreaming that she was in Colorado, curled up by the fire in a little mountain chalet, snow falling in drifts through the dark outside the window.

But then a voice shouted drunkenly from the street, and a charley horse shot through her foot, and Poppy was right back where she'd always been.

CHAPTER 7

The Frozen Lover

It was dark in the room. It was always dark in Vik's room; he had those big black-out curtains that make noon feel like nighttime, make you sleep for ten or twelve hours straight if you don't set an alarm. He was on his side, breathing softly, and Sofia was pressed up against his cool, dry back. "Babe," she whispered. He didn't wake. "Babe," again, louder. Still nothing. She started to play her little connect-the-dots game on his back, making constellations of his freckles, tracing lines from one to the next. That usually woke him up, and sure enough, soon he turned over to face her, his eyes still closed.

"Time is it," he muttered.

"10:45."

He stretched out and made a big show of yawning loudly, rubbing the dark circles around his eyes where yesterday's eyeliner had gone smudgy. She began to trace the hair on his belly down to his waist, and his dick stiffened predictably as she slipped her fingers under his boxers. They had sex almost every morning that she stayed over, as regular and necessary as a cup of coffee. He pulled her up onto him, and she peppered his neck with kisses as he fumbled to get their underwear off.

"Whatcha doin' today?" she asked after they'd finished, laying her head on his sweaty chest.

"Oh, I dunno. Hanging out."

"Want to go for a walk at the cemetery?"

"Uh, kind of had some stuff around here I wanted to get done," he said, moving her head off him and getting out of bed.

"What stuff?"

"Chores. Reading. I dunno." He pulled on jeans.

"You look so sexy in jeans and no shirt."

"Yeah?" He flexed in the mirror. "That is pretty hot, huh?"

His phone buzzed next to her on the nightstand, and she glanced at it, trying to make out the name on the notification before he grabbed it.

"Who is it?" she asked as he stood there texting.

"James."

"What does he want?"

But Vik was doing that deaf-to-the-world thing that comes over people sometimes when they're on their phones and didn't answer her. When he was finished, he threw a pillow at her.

"What are you doing? Come on, get up. It's after eleven."

"Why are you in such a hurry to get rid of me?" she teased.

"I told you, I have stuff to do." He was over by the dresser, crushing up a pill. Adderall. These days it seemed like he needed forty milligrams to even get going in the morning.

"You're not going to *snort* that, are you?" she frowned.

"None of your business."

It scared her a little, this developing dependency. He'd been out of adderall for the last few days and had finally resorted to driving all the way to Kenner to pick some up from a sketchy friend-of-a-friend-of-a-friend. Turned out the guy had only given Vik a handful of pills and just written him a fake prescription for the rest.

"Are you kidding?" Sofia had yelled at him when she found the piece of paper on his nightstand.

"What's the problem? It looks totally legit."

"You can get away with that one time, Vik, *one time!* And then they figure it out, mark you as drug-seeking, and your whole life gets fucked up!"

"Calm down! I'm not even going to use it. My regular guy is going to re-up soon anyway."

Stupid white boy, she'd fumed inside. *Thinking he can just get away with anything.*

"That's really not good for you," she said as calmly as she could manage, watching as he crushed up the pill on his dresser.

"Oh, fuck off," he muttered. "It's not even that much."

Ten minutes later, she was at the front door with her tour clothes from the night before rolled into a bundle under her arm. She was wearing one of Vik's t-shirts, which he didn't like for her to do (he was very protective of his wardrobe), but that's what he got for not wanting her to leave a change of clothes at his place.

"See ya later," he said, still shirtless, giving her a peck on the lips. He closed the door.

Sofia didn't have a car and usually had to walk or take the streetcar home unless Vik drove her, which he only did in bad weather. It was cold today, had been for weeks, and she didn't have a good jacket. She wrapped her arms around herself and walked fast through Vik's neighborhood toward the streetcar line. Vik lived at the very top of Canal Street, a straight shot up a couple miles from the Quarter, near a cluster of cemeteries. There was one directly across the street from his house, in fact, and sometimes they'd sit on the porch and watch the sun come up or go down behind it. It was a pretty spot, and quiet. Vik lived alone. Sofia was waiting for him to ask her to move in with him, but it hadn't happened yet.

By the time the streetcar came, rattled a mile down Canal, and deposited Sofia at the corner of Rampart for her twenty-minute walk home to the Tremé, it was almost noon. Her cat, Monster, was mad at her when she walked in. He had every right to be, seeing as how she hadn't fed him since 5:00 the night before. This always happened. She meant to come home after work but ended up staying at Vik's and didn't get back until late morning the next day. "I'm sorry, baby," she said, picking Monster up as he huffed and puffed. "I should have told those girls to feed you."

Her roommates were students at UNO, the same age as Sofia, and they were usually gone when she got home in the morning, off to their classes. In the beginning, she'd tried to be friends with them, but college life seemed to be a whole world that Sofia didn't fit into or understand. "Sorry, too much work tonight," always seemed to be the answer when she invited them out to the bar or asked if they wanted to watch a movie. *Work. You mean homework,* she thought to herself. *Work is what real adults do, those of us who actually have to pay our own bills.*

She shook some food into Monster's bowl, and he gobbled it up. Then, before she got a chance to take a shower or even change clothes, her phone rang. "Hey, mama," she answered. Her mom called her every day around lunchtime, sometimes just to complain, sometimes to ask for something.

"Baby, I need some help, *si?*"

"What you need help with, mama?" she asked, not in the mood to bike all the way to Chalmette.

"The TV's broken. Something's wrong with the channels, I can't get it to show what I want."

"Could you ask one of the neighbors to help?"

"I can't do it, I just can't." She sounded exhausted. "Come on, baby, please? Come and help your mother, *por favor.*"

"Okay. I'll be there soon."

Sofia's family had left after the storm, spent a couple years in Houston, and when they'd come back, they'd rented a house in Chalmette, on the outskirts of the city just beyond the Lower Ninth Ward. It was around that time the doctors had diagnosed Sofia's mom with PTSD, made worse by the bipolar. Sofia had gotten out before Katrina with her dad and big brother, but her mom had stayed with some other church volunteers to take care of the old people who couldn't evacuate. She'd seen people die.

The bike ride to Chalmette was cold and windy, twenty-five minutes down St. Claude through the Lower Ninth and Arabi, past abandoned parking lots and shitty dollar stores. She knocked, but her mom didn't answer—no surprise there, so she let herself in. Her mother was on the couch in her bathrobe, staring blankly at the dark TV. Sofia went to her and pulled a cigarette out of her mouth.

"Don't smoke in the house, ma."

"You smoke."

"Yeah, but not in the house. It's gross."

Sofia's mom stared at the cigarette in the ashtray like she was searching for the will to pick it up again. She was only forty-five years old but looked much older, her hair already graying, her eyes and cheeks saggy. She lived on her disability checks and didn't work.

"So, how's today?" Sofia asked, picking up the remnants of her mom's breakfast and what looked like the previous night's dinner and taking the dishes to the kitchen, disturbing a half dozen flies in the sink.

"A lot better if I could get the television to work."

"Alright. Let me take a look at it." Sofia fixed it just by pressing a few buttons on the remote, changing the input selection. Then she made tuna salad sandwiches for both of them.

"Mardi Gras coming up," she said as she sat down next to her mother on the sagging couch.

"Already?"

"Next week. Want to go to some of the parades? I can drive us in your car, maybe some of the Saturday ones?"

"I don't like parades."

"Sure you do."

"No, I don't." Her mom lit another cigarette.

When Sofia was a kid, they'd always gone to every parade. Not just the Superkrewes, either, but the ones like Femme Fatale, King Arthur, Okeanos, the ones that the transplants like Vik didn't care about. Sometimes her brother and dad came and sometimes they didn't, but Sofia and her mom never missed one. They'd pack chairs and a cooler full of store-brand Sprite and string cheese and get out on the route early, hours before the parades, and Sofia's mom would braid her hair while they waited, and when the floats came, they'd shout themselves hoarse, waving at the people in the krewes, calling out for throws. They'd never had the fancy ladders like some families did, the ones with seats up top for the kids, and when Sofia was little, her mom had put her right on her shoulders so the float riders would see her and throw to her. Sometimes they got into squabbles with other families or other kids over throws, and Sofia's mom was pretty fierce about it. She'd always yank back a throw Sofia had caught if some other kid grabbed it from her, and sometimes she even got up in people's faces, saying, "Excuse me, that was for my daughter! He threw it right to her," holding out her hand to demand a string of beads or a plushie that somebody else had snatched out of the air. When they got home, they'd always count the strands of beads around their necks, whoever had the most won, and dump out all their throws from the duffel bag Sofia's mom always brought to the parades. The stuffed animals, the little nerf footballs, the frisbees—those would be Sofia's toys for the year until she got a gift or two at Christmas time. And the special throws, the things like porcelain beads from Rex, shoes from Muses, Zulu coconuts, hand-bedazzled toilet plungers from Tucks, those went on a shelf in Sofia's room. They were her prized possessions, collected over years and years.

It had all been lost in the storm. Six feet of water, mildew covering the furniture and crawling up the walls, part of the living room crushed by a tree. Of course, that was nothing compared to what they lost down in Cajun country, Plaquemines Parish where Sofia's dad's people were. The houses, the fishing boats, the little tackle store Sofia's Papaw had run for thirty years, all of it wrecked in the twenty-foot storm surge. Sofia's cousin, Tiny, had owned a little gator ranch down there, and whenever they'd gone down to visit, he'd let her play with the babies. They were cold and compact, and she liked to carry them around. Tiny gave them names like *Petit Babette* and *Ma Chére Vert*, and Sofia knew enough Cajun French to understand. Sometimes when there were new hatchlings, Tiny let Sofia name them. Her favorite was a runt whom she called Channing Tatum because he was so cute.

Of course, Katrina took the gator ranch. Tiny told her that they'd gone back to find the big ones dead and the little ones just gone. Probably blown away, he said. Sofia pictured Channing Tatum ripped away from his mother by the wind, those little yellow eyes watching the world tumble by upside down and then go dark.

"It's so rank in here, mom," Sofia said, fanning the smoke from her cigarette away. "I'm serious. When was the last time you showered?"

Her mother shrugged. "What does it matter?"

She'd been depressed like this for weeks now, and you just had to ride it out until the flipside came. At some point, her mood would change, and she'd become hyperactive and unpredictable, which wasn't much better, honestly.

Sofia didn't blame her dad for giving up. After the storm, he moved down to Delacroix full time, and a couple years later, her brother, Andrew Jr., quit school and took a job on an oil rig. It had just been the two of them, Sofia and her mom, since seventh grade. She was basically a zombie after Sofia's dad left, stuck in a depressive episode for a year or more. Sofia didn't handle it well. She took water bottles full of Smirnoff to school, threw ragers, fucked boys on the couch while her mom was right upstairs. How she managed to graduate was anyone's guess. Of course, college had been out of the question.

"What's on that shirt, baby? What is that?" her mom asked as she ate her sandwich, squinting at the t-shirt Sofia had borrowed from Vik. She wished she'd remembered to change.

"Oh. It's Vik's. *A Clockwork Orange*, it's a movie."

"More of that Satanic stuff, ah?"

Her mom had seen a picture of Vik wearing his pentagram hoodie and spiky earrings, and since then, it had been all Sofia could do to convince her that he wasn't a devil worshipper.

"It's just a style thing, mom. It's a look."

Her mom mumbled under her breath in Spanish.

"What was that?"

"I just don't like it."

"It's not a big deal." Sofia wiped away a fleck of tuna salad that was stuck to the corner of her mom's mouth.

"You've always been terrible at picking boys."

"Mom..."

"Why can't you just find a nice one? For once."

"Vik *is* nice."

"Why don't you bring him over here, then?"

"He's busy." Frankly, Sofia had no interest in showing Vik this dump or introducing him to her mess of a mother. And even if she wanted to, he probably wouldn't agree to it anyway.

"He's bad news. Just like the last one," her mom said ominously.

"He is *not* like Donny."

"Whatever you say."

She'd met Donny the summer after graduation and moved in with him and his roommates just a few months later. He was twenty-five, worked in the strip mall Sam Goody's, and was cute—very skinny, with bad teeth like hers, but cute.

He had Justin Bieber hair, and at first, he was really nice. He stole stuff for Sofia from his job, paid for her first tattoo, always brought her pizza and beer after her waitressing shifts. He shared his cocaine and sometimes his heroin.

Sofia had seen what smack could do to people. Her mom's friend had OD'd a while back, so had a guy at school. But of course, living with three users, she had to know what the fuss was about. And she'd been amazed to find that it didn't feel like anything at all, really. Heroin was just...chill. No comedown, no hangover, no wild shenanigans. It just made everything feel a little better. On heroin, Sofia could still go over and take care of her mom, help her out around the house without getting sucked into her crazy ups and downs, she could wait tables without wanting to murder the old creeps who slapped her ass, she could exist in Donny's shithole of an apartment without really noticing the roaches and the cigarette-burned drapes and Donny's temper, a temper that was getting worse, so that soon he wasn't just yelling about what Sofia spent her paychecks on, he was punching the walls, he was throwing her phone across the room, he was shoving her head as she drove so that the car swung wildly into the other lane. Twenty bucks for enough smack that she could just chill out for a night, not really have to deal with it, not really have to feel scared or upset around him? Worth it.

Monster was just a kitten then, a little dumpster baby Sofia found behind the daiquiri place in the strip mall. And if it hadn't been for Monster, who knew. Maybe she'd still be stuck there in Donny's apartment in Arabi, getting yelled at and beat up. It was one thing to let him smack her around, though; it got real different real fast when he started smacking around her little kitten. She found out they were hiring at the Clover Grill on Bourbon Street, packed her shit, and left. Sofia got the job and slept in her car, little black Monster curled up with her on the backseat, until she found a room in somebody's shotgun house on North Derbigny. She didn't have anything, really, just a pile of clothes on the floor to sleep on. With her first paycheck, she went to Walgreens and got a folding camp chair and a toothbrush. She hadn't brushed her teeth at all when she lived with Donny, and when she finally got on Medicaid, she had to have three pulled.

It was slow-going those first few months, but she'd done it, managed to get sober: all the way off the dope, and she'd seriously cut down on booze and casual drugs. She worked her shifts, paid her rent, saved up for the little fairy tattoo she'd gotten on her lower back to signify getting clean. She had her black cat and her little room and a couple work friends. It wasn't much, but it was better than Donny.

And then she'd met Vik. He'd come into the restaurant one day and flirted with her, told her he liked her hair—it had been pink at the time; she was always changing it—and given her his number. Sofia was used to the boys in Chalmette, dumb high-school kids who didn't do anything but smoke weed and drive ATVs or older guys like Donny with no future, and she'd never met anybody like Vik before. He was confident, funny, and so much smarter than Donny, smarter than anybody she'd ever met, actually, because he'd gone to college. And he was hot, too, and edgy as hell. He wore eyeliner. She didn't know he was nine years older until they'd already been hanging out for a week or two, but it didn't matter. "Age is just a social construct," he'd told her. "As long as you're old enough to drink and fuck, you're cool with me."

Sofia had probably been drinking and fucking for longer than Vik had, even with the age difference, but she didn't feel the need to tell him that. She'd also never told him about Donny, or being an addict, or any of it, really. He hadn't asked.

Her mom had discarded most of the sandwich Sofia had made her and picked up her cigarette again.

"You don't want any more of your food, mom?"

"Don't feel like eating."

"Come on. You have to take care of yourself."

"Why? Who for? Your father's gone, Andrew never comes to visit."

"Me, then."

She took a deep drag of the cigarette and licked her teeth. "You don't care about me."

"Well, mama," Sofia said, standing. "If you don't think I care about you, I guess there's no reason to stay."

"That's fine. I got my TV now."

"You're welcome, by the way. For fixing it."

"Oh, now I've gotta thank you? For taking fifteen minutes out of your day to help your mother, your mother who's got nobody else?"

"That's right. You've got nobody else. I'm the one who's stuck by you, mama, *me*, I always come when you—"

"*Ingrata*! I kept you fed and clothed, didn't I? Taught you stuff, took you places, all the parades—"

"Yeah, when you weren't lying in bed so long, I had to give you fucking sponge baths!"

"What do you want me to say, ah? I'm sorry? I'm sorry for being such a bad mother, for being so selfish, you think I like this, ah?" Her voice was faltering. "You think I like missing church, missing Mardi Gras…you think I like being *stuck* like this..."

"No, ma. I don't think you like being stuck like this," Sofia said quietly. There was silence for a moment. She opened the door. "I'd better go."

"Wait," her mom said.

"What?"

"What day is it?"

"Um. Tuesday."

"Muses is Thursday?"

"Yeah."

Her mom was staring at nothing now, speaking softly. "That was always our favorite parade, remember? All the ladies, all those pretty ladies. I said, 'Someday that'll be you and me up there, *mariposa*, riding in that float.' Remember?"

"Yeah."

"Bring me a shoe, *si*? Like you always do."

Sofia glanced over at the shelf where the hand-decorated Muses shoes she'd brought her mom for the last five years were sitting in a pile of junk. Two of them had fallen over, and there were gobs of dust stuck in the glitter, impossible to clean off.

"I didn't know it mattered that much to you."

But her mom was gone now, lost in her own darkness, staring blankly at the ceiling. Sofia went to her, kissed her on the forehead, and left.

She got to the bar before work that night and found Vik in the courtyard, eating chicken wings with James.

"Hey," Vik said, nonchalant.

"How was your day?" she asked, pulling up a stool next to him.

"Pretty good. We watched *Mother.*"

"You and me were supposed to watch that together!"

"Oops," James said. "Did I ruin y'all's plans?"

"It's no big deal," Vik said. "There's plenty of other stuff we can watch."

"I wanted to see that one, though," Sofia pouted.

"Big Aronofsky fan?" James asked.

"Who's that?"

"Uh...the guy who made the film?"

James and Vik both snickered. "Nah," Vik said, "I think she just loves Jennifer Lawrence."

James rolled his eyes. "All basic bitches love Jennifer Lawrence."

"I just wanted to see the frickin movie," Sofia said, standing.

"Aw, did I hurt baby girl's feelings?" she heard James tease as she went back into the bar. Vik muttered something she didn't catch, and they both laughed. James was always being such an asshole to her for no reason, and Vik never defended her. It hurt.

It wasn't time to be on the street for work yet, but she went out anyway. The only other people out there were the manager Graham, the weird girl Veda, and Jeremy. Not exactly Sofia's closest friends—she had been hoping Ruby would be there, so she could vent about Vik and James—but Veda would do.

"Hi, Sofia. How are you?" Veda asked. She was wearing threadbare red suspenders, big, pleated mom shorts, and a too-small striped shirt that showed her plump little tummy and its line of dark hair trailing down from her belly button. Sofia sometimes forgot that Veda was born a boy.

"Oh, I'm just annoyed. Vik was supposed to watch that movie *Mother* with me, and he watched it with James instead."

"Yeah, those two do seem to have quite the psychic connection."

"I get that they're friends, but like, I'm his girlfriend. You know?"

"I don't know much about that," Veda said pensively. "I've never been in a relationship."

"Never?"

"You have to love yourself before you can love someone else," she shrugged. "And I'm not sure I do yet."

James came out from the bar, and Sofia glared at him. "What? Are you actually mad at me?" he laughed.

"It's fine."

"Look," he said, taking her aside. "It was my idea to watch the movie. Don't take it personally, I know Vik's really serious about you."

"You think?"

"Yeah. I think he might even pop the question soon."

Sofia's heart painfully skipped a beat. "What?"

"Yeah, you know…'Can we start sleeping with other people?'" He cackled, and Sofia pushed him.

"You're such a dick."

"Maybe," he shrugged. "But in my defense, it's only because I think it's funny."

She walked away from James, down the darkening street. "What?" he called after her. "Girl…come on, it was just a joke."

She stared at the ground as she walked, her vision blurry and wet, and almost bumped into Jeremy, who seemed to appear from out of nowhere. He was tall, with a mane of long black hair, and always wore billowy red pirate shirts and skin-tight black pants tucked into boots. Everyone was kind of afraid of him, Sofia included.

"Oh! Sorry," she said, blinking back her tears. He paused for a moment then smiled.

"An Aronofsky fan, are you?" he asked. He must have overheard the earlier conversation, though she hadn't remembered seeing him nearby.

"Oh…I dunno. I just thought the trailer looked interesting."

"It's a very dark film. I wouldn't guess that a girl like you would be interested." His voice was quiet and low, almost inaudible.

"I like dark stuff," she shrugged. "I mean, I do tell ghost stories for a living."

He smiled mysteriously. "So, you're enjoying the work?"

"Yeah, definitely."

He paused for a moment, holding eye contact with her, then looked her up and down. "That's a nice dress you're wearing."

It was a black long-sleeved dress with a white collar, like the one Wednesday Addams wears. "Thanks," she smiled. "It's new." She had been waiting for Vik to say something about it, but he hadn't. Jeremy turned with a mysterious smile and swept away down the street.

Sofia went back over to Veda. "Did you see that?" she whispered. "Jeremy just talked to me. He never talks to me."

Veda frowned. "Be careful."

"What do you mean?"

"That man is on a much lower psychic channel."

"What?"

"Just be careful. He wants to feed on your energy."

Okay, O Weird One. "I'll keep that in mind."

Twenty minutes later, Sofia was sent out with her group. They were a quiet bunch, and she could tell they were smart; her group the night before had been a bunch of drunk idiots, who kept asking her questions she'd already answered and peering into people's windows when she told them not to.

"So how long have you been doing this?" a young black guy asked her as they walked away from the first stop. He was cute, a bit hipster for her taste with those round glasses, but cute, nonetheless.

"Just about six months, actually."

"You're a great storyteller."

"Thanks, that means a lot."

"Were you a history major?"

"Oh, no."

"Theatre?"

"No, just…naturally talented, I guess," she said with a weak smile. She hated having to deal with people thinking that she'd gone to college.

"New Orleans is such an amazing place," he said, looking around as they made their way through Jackson Square. "Have you lived here your whole life?"

"Pretty much." And now, she was sure, she'd be asked her other least-favorite personal question, about her experience during Katrina. The questions that drunk people, even sober people, sometimes asked about it were disturbingly tasteless. *Did anybody in your family die? Do you know any Katrina ghost stories?* But to her surprise, he didn't ask about it, just kept chatting with her about the city and its charms.

At the next stop, the Hotel Provincial, Sofia described the amputation practices of Civil War surgeons. The hotel had supposedly been a hospital back then and was haunted by the ghosts of soldiers and doctors. But just as she began to saw off her own arm with an imaginary bone saw, a drunk man who'd been staggering down the street stopped directly behind her and stood there, leering.

"Can I help you?" she said, turning to him.

His eyes moved slowly from her groin to her face. "Yeah, you can gimme some of that pussy," he mumbled with a sour grin. Sofia's heart began to pound.

"You need to leave," she said, less authoritatively than she would have liked.

"Hey," said a voice from behind her. "Fuck off."

She glanced over her shoulder and saw the young guy from her tour, who'd stepped forward.

"Who are you?" the drunk sneered.

"I'm the guy who's gonna beat your ass into the ground if you don't move along."

"This cunt is just lying to you, you know," the man said to the group, swaying on his feet. "Buncha fuckin' lies."

"Fuck. Off." the young guy said more forcefully. The drunk spat on the street and finally wandered away. The group began to clap.

Sofia did her best to finish her story as her pounding heart slowly settled. Shit like this happened sometimes, every tour guide had to deal with hecklers occasionally, but it wasn't usually this bad. This was also the first time someone in her group had come to her defense. At the bar break, she noticed some of the other people in her group patting the guy on the back, thanking him.

"You said what we were all thinking!" an old lady laughed before going into the bar. Sofia went over to him as he was cleaning his glasses.

"Hey, thanks so much for doing that. I was just at a loss; I didn't know what to say."

"I'm just surprised nobody else in the group spoke up. Does that kind of thing happen a lot?"

"Sometimes. It's not usually that bad, though. Thanks again."

They talked for the rest of the bar break, and she learned that the young man was a public defender in Los Angeles.

"This might sound weird, but have you ever considered going into law?" he asked.

She laughed. "Law? No."

"You'd be great at it. You have a really strong presence, you're very charismatic...you could do good things in the world if you wanted to. Make a difference."

"Doubt it," she muttered.

"What do you mean?"

"I, uh...I don't even have a degree."

"That's okay," he shrugged. "I was a high school dropout."

"You were?"

"Yeah. I hated school. But I saw my cousin get twenty years for selling pot, have his future completely stolen, so I decided to do something with mine. Try to change the system."

"That's really cool."

"I'm not trying to brag. I'm just saying, it's never too late to start something new."

"Alright. Cool. I mean—thanks."

"I'm Abraham, by the way." They shook hands.

"Like Lincoln?"

"Yeah, if you like," he laughed.

Sofia gathered everyone back from the bar break. The tour was going great so far; the experience with the drunk heckler seemed to have bonded everyone together, and she could tell they all liked her. "We only have one more stop, guys," she said after she did the Andrew Jackson Hotel. "Y'all gonna stick with me to the end?" They shouted "yes" with enthusiasm, and she led them to Père Antoine alley by the Cathedral, drawing the group in close around her.

"Alright," she said quietly. "This is our last stop on the tour. And I like to save it for last because it's actually my favorite." They were all smiling. She loved this feeling, the feeling that they all respected her and cared about what she had to say.

"But first some history. See, in the 17- and 1800s, New Orleans had a big population of free people of color. They were usually well-educated, owned property, some even owned businesses...but there was a law against interracial marriage. Of course, the law didn't stop some wealthy white men from wanting to have relationships with free women of color. And if the rest of American history has taught us anything, it's that rich white guys usually get what they want..." This usually got a laugh, and she could see Abraham chuckling. "Which leads us to a social custom called *plaçage*. It's French, basically it means 'placement,' and it was a legal contract between a white man and a free woman of color negotiating the terms of a romantic relationship. He gave her a monthly allowance and put her up in a little apartment somewhere, and she served as his companion for as long as he wanted one."

"Now, I want to tell you about the guy who was living here in this house in the 1830s." Their eyes searched the plain brick building behind her. "He was a young white Frenchman named Michie. He's young, he's smart, he owns a pretty successful business...but he's shy. Really shy. He hasn't met the right girl yet, and he's getting lonely. So, he goes to what's known as a Quadroon Ball, where white men can meet free women of color. And there, he makes the acquaintance of a beautiful young lady named Julie, who's also smart, funny, and talented. They dance together all night, and at the end of the ball, they sign a contract and begin a relationship.

"But pretty early on in this contractual romance, something a little untraditional happens. Michie, a white man, and Julie, a free woman of color, actually fall in love."

Some "awws" from the crowd. They always ate up the happy stuff, but you could tell they were nervous, always waiting for the other shoe to drop. This was a ghost tour, after all, and they knew deep down that someone was going to end up dead. But it never seemed to stop them entirely from hoping for the possibility of a happy ending.

"They are so in love, in fact, that Julie decides to get rid of the house that he bought her so she can move in with him here. But just a month or two after she moves in, Julie comes to Michie with a question. And it goes like this." Sofia batted her eyelashes, struck a seductive pose. The group giggled. *"Michie...won't you take me to the church and marry me?"* She said it in her best French accent, one she'd been working on for months.

"And he says, *Julie, my love! You know there is nothing I would like more than to be your husband. But alas, my love, this is not the world we live in. To marry would be against the law.*"

She described the back and forth, Julie's persistence in asking, his continued refusal. *"I could lose my business; I could lose my reputation! I will not take the risk, my love. I will not marry you."*

And Julie's final plea: "*We can get a priest from outside the parish to marry us in secret! And no one will have to know that we are wed. No one but us…and God.*" But Michie still wouldn't do it.

"A couple more months pass, until a very important night: New Year's Eve. Every New Year's Eve, Michie throws a business party where people from other companies come to eat, drink, make deals, and sign contracts for the upcoming year. It's very important that this party go well. But he's unlucky because this particular New Year's Eve happens to be the coldest night of the year. Sleet falling, ice on the roads…" This part of the story was always much easier to sell this time of year when it was actually cold outside. "The wind is howling, and the temperature is way below freezing. Michie's big party was supposed to start at 8:00, but by 9:00, no one had arrived because of the terrible weather. By 10:00, he's super upset. He comes out onto the balcony—" she gestured behind her, watched their eyes rise up to it, "—and starts pacing back and forth, looking down the street. But it's covered in ice, and he's sure no one is going to come."

"And as he's up there, pacing, in an awful mood, Julie comes out onto the balcony with him. Sobbing. She's been crying a lot lately."

"*Julie, what is it? What now?*" Sofia said in Michie's gruff, annoyed voice, then let her shoulders sag and her eyes plead. "*Michie, please. Please. I do not know what else to do but beg. I swear I will not ask you for anything else, as long as I live, but I need you to marry me. And I need you to marry me soon.*"

Sometimes people snickered quietly here, at her French accent and her acting. And that hurt, when she could tell they thought it was cheesy. But most of the time, their eyes widened, and they leaned in closer.

She described Michie's angry refusal, Julie's tears, the sound of one of his guest's carriages finally clip-clopping down the street, Michie turning to rush inside so he can meet it downstairs. Julie, throwing herself against the balcony door to block his path.

"*I will not move from this spot, Michie, she says. I will not move until you tell me that you will marry me, and until you tell me when.*"

Michie's calculated response. "*Fine,*" he spits bitterly. *Fine. You want me to marry you, fine, I will do this thing for you, you selfish woman. But if you want me to marry you—to make this sacrifice, to put my reputation at risk—then you too must make a sacrifice for me. Prove your love for me, Julie. If you want me to marry you, then you must go…. He thinks for a moment. …go up to the roof. Yes! Go up to the roof, stay out of my way for the rest of the night, and wait for me. If you can do this, well, then I will know that you love me truly, and I will marry you. Tomorrow.*

"Julie runs back into the house crying. Michie feels awful, and he almost goes to tell her he didn't mean it, that he was just being foolish, but he doesn't. No, he gets distracted because the doorbell rings, and he has to go greet his first guest. And over the next couple of hours, the rest of them show up too; they were late because of the weather, but no one wants to miss the best New Year's party in town."

Sofia lowered her voice. "And because it's so cold outside, everyone gathers very close around the fire. They eat a lot, they drink a lot of wine, they make all those deals, and they sign all those contracts. The party goes perfectly! And the party goes late. Things don't wind down until three or four in the morning because no one can bear the idea of going back out into the terrible cold. But finally, Michie bids *Adieu* to his guests. And he's feeling great. He's happy, he's drunk, he can't *wait* to get upstairs and tell Julie about the party. But the bedroom is dark...it's empty..."

She described how Michie, confused in his drunkenness, wandered the house, searching every room for his lover. "Finally, he realizes she's just not there. And he remembers that stupid thing he said earlier...*something about the roof?*

"So Michie goes to the roof. Climbs out a little attic window. And it's slippery up there, and dark, and cold, even colder than it is down here on the street. It's wet, it's icy, the wind is howling...and he's up there, looking around. Finally, he notices, lying on the roof near the chimney, a woman. All curled up."

Sofia mimicked Michie staggering drunk to the body. "*Julie, have you been up here all night? Oh, my love, I am so sorry, I did not mean what I said...come in, please, we'll get you warm...come in...I will make it up to you, my love, I promise.*

"But she doesn't respond. So Michie reaches out to touch her. And when he does, he realizes three things. First...her skin is cold." Sofia traced her index finger ever so softly down her own cheek. "Tears have frozen on her face."

"Secondly, she's naked. Her clothes are neatly folded in a pile next to her." Confusion on the faces of her group.

"And finally, he realizes what y'all have probably already guessed...Julie is dead.

"Here's a little fact about hypothermia," she said gravely, after a brief pause. "As you're freezing to death, you might start to feel warm. Hot, even. In fact, sometimes people who are freezing begin to take off their clothes. It seems that's what happened to Julie. She went up to the roof, determined to wait all night for him, and she froze to death.

"And Michie, of course, is just destroyed. Finally, he does the one thing she always asked him to do, but he never would…he calls a priest." She could see visions of *The Corpse Bride* forming in their minds, the disturbed expressions. "But not to take her to the wedding chapel," she added. "You can't marry a dead person. Even in New Orleans." A laugh—her last joke of the tour. "No, he has the priest take her to the morgue. There they do an autopsy on Julie's body, and they learn something really sad. Any ideas?"

They all knew. They always knew. She's *pregnant*, they murmured. Sofia nodded.

"She's pregnant. Three or four months pregnant. And of course…now it all makes sense. Julie was Catholic, like most free women of color at the time. It was very important to her to be married to the father of her child, *at least* in God's eyes. Not for his money, or his name…no. For the sake of her child's eternal soul.

"And now, Michie, learning what he has truly done—not only has he killed the love of his life, he's killed his *child*—he's destroyed. He retreats into himself, he retreats into his house, he becomes an alcoholic, and he drinks himself to death within three months."

She leaned in a little closer, dropped her voice down quiet. "And if you're here in the alley on a chilly night, you might see something, just out of the corner of your eye. Up on that balcony…a figure. Pacing back and forth. And that's Michie, waiting for his party guests. But also reliving over and over the last precious moments he saw Julie alive."

She stepped in even closer, speaking in a whisper now. "And if you're here on a *very* cold night. They say it has to be below freezing, and it has to be after midnight. But if you're here, and you look up at that roof, you might see, for just a second…a beautiful woman, standing up there, looking out into the wind." They all looked up. They didn't see anything, but it didn't matter. Her words painted a picture on the night, clear as anything.

Sofia put her hand on her heart. "And that's Julie. My favorite French Quarter ghost. Up there, waiting. Just waiting, and waiting, to this day, for the love of her life to come and fulfill a promise...that he never will."

When it was a good group, when they were engaged, this was the best moment of the tour. Time stopped for just a moment, hung suspended in the air, as together they mourned a ghost. Sometimes she got chills. And she knew they did too.

"And that's the end of the tour!" Sofia exclaimed with a big grin, and they collectively exhaled, shaking the story off. She gave her tip line, said goodbye to the group, stood around smiling until there was no one left but Abraham.

"That was fantastic," he said.

"Thank you," she grinned.

"I mean it. You're really gifted at what you do."

She got this compliment often but found herself blushing. "Thanks."

"So, uh…the interracial dating thing, that's not still a rule here, is it?"

Sofia laughed. "No, no, it's not."

"So can I buy you a drink?"

"Um…" *That's so nice of you. I would love to, but I'm involved with someone. In love with someone. Wrapped up in a whole, big dramatic mess of a relationship with someone.* "Sure."

She took him to the Rat because she didn't know where else to go. They sat at the front of the bar by the door, far from the courtyard where the other guides were beginning to gather. For twenty minutes, they sat sipping beer and chatting. He asked her about herself, described his favorite parts of the tour, complimented her. She was aware of their knees inching closer and closer under the bar.

"So how long are you in town?" she asked.

"Just until Thursday."

"Are you going to catch the parade tomorrow?"

"There's a parade?"

"Yeah, Troy. An all-female krewe. It's pretty fun."

"Would you, uh…would you want to go together?"

"Oh..."

"Of course," he said, slapping his forehead. "You probably have to give a tour."

"Yeah."

"Well, how about dinner beforehand, then? Or another drink?"

"I, uh—"

He looked down, embarrassed. "I'm sorry, I know you probably get asked out all the time by guys on your tour."

She didn't. "No pressure. But here's my number," he said.

He jotted it down on a napkin. How quaint, she thought, smiling to herself. As if smartphones didn't exist.

"Thanks."

"I mean, we live two-thousand miles away from each other, it's not like… you know."

"Yeah."

"But it could be fun to hang out. I'd love to get to know you more."

She pocketed the napkin.

Vik had come in from the courtyard and was at the other end of the bar, talking to the bartender, Leela. He did a double take as he noticed her sitting there with Abraham and came over.

"Hi," he said loudly, shoving out his hand to Abraham. "I'm Vik." They shook.

"Abraham. Are you a friend of Sofia's?"

"Yeah, I am."

"I just took her tour. It was fantastic."

"So, uh, you ready to head out?" Vik put a hand on Sofia's leg. She watched Abraham look down, register it, look back up again.

"Right now?" she asked.

"Yep," he said firmly.

"Um, okay." She slid off the stool. "Well, it was nice to meet you," she said to Abraham.

"You too." He held up a hand in a resigned wave. "I'll see you in the courtroom, yeah?"

"Maybe," she laughed.

She hurried to keep up with Vik as they walked briskly to his car. "The courtroom? What was that about?"

"Oh. He told me I should become a lawyer."

"Hah," Vik said. "Gross."

That night, in bed, she could feel a question in him as he pressed his body against hers, but he didn't ask it. She turned out the light.

Vik pulled her close under the covers, wrapping his arms all the way around her, kissing her neck. Her back was to him, they were spooning, and she could feel his gentle breath on her ear. They lay there like that for fifteen or twenty minutes in the cool, dark room.

"I love you," he whispered, long after she thought he was already asleep, and so quietly she wasn't sure if she'd really heard it or not. Her heart stabbed at her ribcage.

"I love you," Sofia whispered back. She'd said it a million times before, but always silently. She'd always just mouthed it into his back while he slept, or as he walked away, or after he hung up the phone. This was the first time he'd said the words. And the first time she'd let him hear them.

In the morning, she threw the napkin away.

CHAPTER 8

The Watcher from the Wings

A lot of us take Wednesdays off. Giving tours isn't like a regular job, you don't get weekends and holidays off work; in fact, weekends and holidays are when tour guides work the most. We're independent contractors, so we can pretty much be available or not available whenever, but woe betide anybody who tries to take off Friday or Saturday nights on a regular basis. Most of us prefer to take off Tuesdays or Wednesdays, the slowest days for tours, a nice break in the middle of the week before the rush of the weekend.

Usually, people don't congregate in the courtyard until tours end at 10:00, but since they're all off tonight, they're back here early. Out on the street, the tour was just launched. It must have just been one group, and I think Jeremy took it. I know James, Vik, Ralphie and Sofia got back a little while ago from watching Ruby ride in the parade, and Max is with them, having come in a few minutes ago when he didn't get a tour. Poppy is sitting alone with Veda at one of the other hi-tops, doing a tarot reading. And Angela's here too, at the only other two-top table besides mine. She's been here since before the others came back, talking to a man I've never seen, a sort of bland looking guy in a button-up and tie with a couple empty beer bottles in front of him. I've been eavesdropping on their conversation, which isn't hard to do because Angela is talking very loudly and grandly, as always.

"Many might hear the phrase 'ghost tour' and assume that my work is rather kitschy, perhaps even a bit ridiculous. But believe me when I say that it is as legitimate, fulfilling, and even demanding a career as any other. Many of my coworkers hold graduate degrees and PhDs in folklore or history, and though I myself never had the opportunity to complete any post-graduate studies, I am highly dedicated to my craft and am continuously researching and expanding my knowledge to make my tour a once-in-a-lifetime experience for my guests."

"That's cool. So, you ever see any ghosts?"

"That's always the million-dollar question," she smiles. "I'm not sure I could say that I, or anyone else at my company for that matter, have ever witnessed a 'spirit' go floating by in a haze of ectoplasm, *a la* Casper. I do, however—"

"So that's a no," he says, looking bored.

My attention wanders over to Poppy and Veda, who are sitting across the table from each other with the deck of tarot cards in between them. "Cut it," Poppy says, and Veda does so with formality. The deck is old and worn, soft around the edges. "I'm going to teach you a layout called the Celtic Cross. Pick up the top card and lay it down."

She does.

"This first card is the central issue, the heart of the matter. Understand?"

"Yes."

"So, you've been studying. What is it?"

"Nine of Swords," Veda says.

"What does it mean?"

"Um...anxiety. Bad things happening, hopelessness, trauma."

"That's right. So that's sort of the frame for the whole reading, you get me?"

"Yeah."

"Now draw what crosses you."

Veda draws another card and lays it horizontally across the first one.

"Ah. The Hanged Man," Poppy says. "Tell me about him."

"The Hanged Man represents sacrifice. No, not sacrifice...surrender?"

Poppy nods. "Look at him, he's hanging upside down. So, think about that: upside down, viewing the world from a totally new perspective. But see the expression on his face? Calm. He's surrendered himself completely. Now here's the thing. Maybe it's needless, this sacrifice, or maybe it achieves something. If this is the thing that crosses you, that's what you need to ask yourself. The sacrifices you're making, do they lead to enlightenment, or martyrdom?"

Veda nods.

"Draw another card. Place it below the first," Poppy says, and she does.

"What lies below. This is your foundation, what makes you who you are. The thing you fall back on, the thing that roots you. Or maybe it doesn't root you—maybe it holds you down. What did you draw?"

"My greatest friend," Veda smiles. "The Moon."

"Tell me about the Moon."

"She is the Unconscious. Our deepest intuition. The Moon represents the veil between illusion and reality."

"The Moon can mean many things," Poppy says. "It can symbolize your imagination getting the better of you. In the dark of the night, when you're taking a path you're unsure of, the moon can play tricks on your eyes. But the moon can also be your light. She can guide you through the dark."

"Yes, she can."

"Next, your past," Poppy says, and the smile fades from Veda's face.

"Well, go on. Draw another card, put it down there to the left of the first one."

Haltingly, Veda picks a card from the deck and lays it down. She stares at it, swallows.

"Well?" Poppy waits several moments for her to speak, then identifies the card herself. "The Ten of Swords. Not a difficult one...you don't recognize it?"

"I just knew," Veda whispers. "I knew that's what I would draw."

"Well, good. It's good to know your own past. You want to tell me about the card?"

Veda shakes her head.

"Okay," Poppy says. "Ten of Swords. You've got a man lying here facedown in the dirt, ten swords through his back. Can't get much worse than that, huh?" She laughs a little, but Veda's face is ashen.

"Major disaster, obviously. Betrayal. Death. Unavoidable tragedy. And the swords, the weapons...they're a part of him now. He has become his wounds. He has become death."

Veda looks so upset that lines of concern start to gather on Poppy's forehead.

"Hey, come on. It's not so bad." Poppy says. "Look at it. Come on, just *look* at it."

Veda finally looks down at the card.

"See here?" Poppy says, tapping at it with a stubby finger. "The sun's rising. And the weather, see how calm it is? Even despite the darkness. When you hit rock bottom, there's nowhere you can go but up. Yeah?"

Veda nods.

"You've had some bad things happen to you, huh?" Poppy says.

The opening chords of "A Hard Day's Night" play over the courtyard speaker. James is in charge of the music, as always, and it's been the Beatles for the last half hour straight. I glance over at the other hi-top, where he and Vik are arguing.

"The Stones are the definition of rock n' roll," Vik says loudly. "There is no better rock band in history, ever, period, end of discussion. Right? Back me up on this, Max."

"I'm a Zeppelin man myself," Max says.

James shakes his head. "But I'm not talking about who's a better rock band. I'm talking about who made a more important contribution to modern music."

"Pah," Vik scoffs. "The Stones beat the Beatles any day, you're not gonna convince me otherwise." He runs a hand through his shiny dark hair and takes a gulp of beer, his rings clinking against the glass.

I think Vik and I went on a date once. Well, I'm not sure what it was, exactly, but it was just the two of us and he footed the bill. This was before Sofia, of course, back when I was pretty new at the company. I'd had a bad day and a bad tour, and he invited me to come see a punk-rock show with him at a new place on Lower Decatur. I told him I couldn't afford it, tips had been shit that night, so he paid my $20 cover and bought my drinks. We stood around the club's courtyard, and he showed me how to vape and listened to me whine about whatever shit was bothering me, and then the show started and we headbanged in a big mosh pit for an hour and got all covered in splashed beer and sweat, and then he drove me home. It was strange, being around each other just as two ordinary human beings and not part of this dramatic, loud gathering always so firmly entrenched at the bar. It felt oddly vulnerable. Sometimes you want your understanding of someone to just stay what it is, you know?

"But the Stones' music never *changed,*" James says. "In the sixties, you have 'Let's Spend the Night Together,' in the eighties, what, 'Start Me Up?' Basically the same thing. Whereas from '62 to '70, the Beatles go from 'Love Me Do' to 'Across the Universe.' Holy shit, no comparison."

"The Beatles got way too experimental, and everyone knows it," Vik says.

"You just hate growth."

Vik rolls his eyes. "We get it, James Baker. You're deep."

"I like the Beatles. 'Fixing a Hole' is my favorite," Ralphie says with a dumb grin. He's been pretty drunk since they got here.

"Ralphie, my man. How's it going with your story?" Max asks.

"My story? My story. Mm. Kinda stuck, you know? Can't make the…the characters…do the things."

"Well, you keep working on it, hear?"

"I'll try."

"I mean it. I want my copy. One I can hang onto, that you can sign for me when you're a famous author," he winks. Ralphie gives him a vague thumbs up and takes a big gulp of beer, spilling some down his shirt.

Sofia changes the subject. "Hey, what do you think's going on over here?" she asks confidentially, jerking a thumb toward Angela and the random guy.

"She's on a date," Max says. "They came in before y'all got back."

"A date? Angela dates?"

"I wonder if she's let him get a word in yet," Vik mutters.

I can confirm that the answer is no. Angela doesn't seem to have taken a pause for the last two or three minutes, at least.

"Next, your future," I hear Poppy say, and my attention wanders back to the tarot reading. I watch Veda draw a card. They both stare at it silently for a moment.

"Death," Veda says quietly.

"One of the most feared cards in the deck," Poppy says. "And one of the most misunderstood."

Veda gazes at Poppy, waiting for answers.

"It doesn't mean you're going to die. Well—course you are, everybody dies. But the Death of the Major Arcana isn't supposed to be taken literally."

"It's about...transition."

"That's right. Rebirth. New beginnings, transformation. Out with the old, in with the new. That make sense?"

Veda nods.

"The other thing about death: it's inevitable. See his armor?"

Veda peers at the card.

"Nobody beats death. But see, also, he's riding a white horse."

"Purity."

"Death cleanses, see? Purifies. Puts us all on the same level. But if it's reversed..." Poppy turns the card around. "Fear of change. Stagnation. Feeling stuck. See?" Veda nods.

I look back over at Angela and her date.

"Oh, hardly," she's saying. "The reputation that Voodoo has as some sort of evil, arcane black magic is actually a complete misconception, sensationalized by Hollywood in the 1920s. Voodoo is a religion just like any other. Many people find this difficult to believe, but it is actually quite closely linked with Catholicism. They're very structurally similar religions; both are monotheistic, and both employ a system of divine intermediaries, known as the *Loa* in Voodoo, and of course, the Saints in Catholicism. And so, when enslaved people were brought to New Orleans from West Africa and forced to practice Catholicism, they actually began to integrate their religious traditions into it. This led to the creation of modern-day Louisiana Voodoo: a hybrid religion with a core of traditional West African beliefs, wrapped in the imagery and liturgy of Catholicism."

"That's cool. So, uh, do you want another drink, or?"

"And believe it or not, many practitioners of Voodoo—who were primarily women of color, mind you—also considered themselves devout Catholics. In fact, on any given Sunday mass at St. Louis Cathedral in the 1800s, a majority of the congregants there would have been women of color as well."

"My cousin just got married there."

"Oh?" Angela looked deflated at the change in subject.

"Yeah, and it was a total disaster. Turned out the maid of honor was screwing the best man's wife."

"You know, I think I will have another drink, thanks. A white wine, please, Pinot Grigio. I love a nice Pinot, even an inexpensive one. But the best I ever had was Greek, actually. Have you ever been to Greece?"

"Yeah, I spent a month there."

"Lovely vineyards. I had several bottles shipped back, which of course was costly, but given the comparative inexpensiveness of fine wines in Europe, the cost/benefit actually skewed toward—"

"I'll go get those drinks." The guy gets up and goes into the bar.

Sofia leans over toward Angela from the hi-top. "How's your date going?"

"Oh, uneventful," Angela sighs, smoothing the black kimono she's wearing.

"Do you like him?" Sofia asks.

"He's not very interesting, actually."

"How do you know?" Vik says.

"Pardon?"

"I mean, how do you know if he's interesting, the guy hasn't said two words."

"Yes…he's a bit quiet, isn't he…"

James snorts into his gin and tonic, and Sofia whacks him on the arm, just as the guy comes back carrying two shot glasses. "They're out of Pinot Grigio."

"Oh, really?" Angela frowns.

"Hope you like shots!"

"No…I stay away from hard liquor, actually. I like to keep my wits about me."

"Ah, bummer. Guess I'll have to drink them both myself," he says, holding one up and shooting it. He grimaces then immediately shoots the other.

Angela is talking again. "As I was saying, when I visited Greece…"

Poppy and Veda seem to be finishing up their tarot reading.

"Final card in the Celtic Cross is the Outcome. This isn't just your future, the events that happen to you—we drew that one already."

"So, what is it?"

"Well, the Outcome is your highest manifestation of being. The best possibility, the best you."

Veda draws a card. "The Knight of Cups," she says.

Poppy smiles. "That's a good one. Tell me about him."

"I'm trying to remember..."

"Well, if you can't remember, just describe the card."

"It's a knight on a white horse."

"How's he moving? Is he galloping?"

"No. He's moving slowly."

"That's right. He's calm. He's at peace. And he's totally in control of himself. What color is the horse?"

"White."

"Light. Goodness. Purity. Even though it's got a picture of a male knight, this is actually one of the most feminine cards in the deck."

"Really?"

"He's in touch with his emotions, he's got deep intuition. See that cup he's holding?"

"Yeah?"

"That's his gift. He's offering it to the world."

"What's in the cup?"

"Well, that's up to you. What's your gift?"

"I don't know."

"Something to think about, then."

Back at the other table, everyone's getting a little tipsy. Especially Ralphie, whose eyes have gone sort of soft and hazy.

"Guys," Sofa says, beaming her sweet, crooked smile.

"What?"

"Less than a week till Mardi Gras!"

"Thank *Gawd*," James says dramatically. "I need to unwind."

Vik sneers. "All you ever *do* is unwind."

"So, what days did you guys take off?" Sofia asks.

"Sunday and Lundi Gras," Vik grunts.

"I'm working through the weekend. All the way till Tuesday," Max says.

James nods. "Same. Trying to save up some money."

"For what? More butt plugs?" Vik says.

"My butt plug collection is quite robust already, thanks."

"For what, then?"

"None of your beeswax."

"Guys!" Sofia says with an alarmed look, jerking her head toward Max.

He chuckles. "Oh, don't y'all feel the need to censor yourselves 'round me, I've been around the block a few times. Heard it all."

"Yeah, buddy! That's my buddy, Max," Ralphie says, drunkenly slapping him on the back. I wince. Max is so frail it looks like it hurts.

"Oh, speaking of Mardi Gras. Are we doing Krewe du Tour this year?" Vik asks.

Everyone looks at Ralphie. "You're asking me?" he says. "Uh…don't see why not."

"You'll have to fill me in," Max says. "Krewe du Tour?"

"Just a thing we do on Mardi Gras," James says. "Get dressed up, go to the river."

"But wasn't it you-know-who that started it?" Sofia asks.

"She's not Lord Voldemort," Vik scoffs. "You can say her name."

"We can do it without her, can't we?" James says. "I mean, we could even make a thing of it. Like…do something cute."

"Yeah," Vik says. "That's a good idea. Say goodbye, or whatever."

Ralphie hiccups. He's beginning to get lost in his own mind, I can tell. "You think Ruby will come?" he says vaguely, not making eye contact with anyone.

"To what, Krewe du Tour? Why wouldn't she?"

"Because she's too good for us."

"Ruby? Hardly. Ruby's a hot mess," Vik says.

"Oh, be nice. She's going through a rough time," Sofia scolds.

"We're *all* going through a rough time!" Ralphie slurs. "Doesn't mean you gotta…ignore people."

"Are you mad because she didn't throw you a crown during the parade?"

"Maybe."

"Ralphie, what do *you* need a crown for?"

"Issa gesture. And I've been texting her, and she—"

"You've been texting her? While she's on a parade float?" James says. "Leave that girl alone, Ralphie, you know she's on like a million drugs right now."

"Can we listen to something else?" Sofia asks, wrinkling her nose as "Helter Skelter" comes on.

"NO," James says, pounding a fist on the table. "We're listening to the Beatles forever."

"This is the Beatles?"

"That's what I'm *saying*!" James screeches, jabbing a finger at Vik. "They have *range*!"

Poppy is putting the cards away now, and Veda is pulling on her furry pink coat.

"Thank you," she says. "That was so helpful. And really accurate. Like, crazy accurate."

"Eh, that's what they all say," Poppy says, rising from the table. "I'll let you in on a little secret: nothing particularly magical about tarot. People see what they want to see in the cards."

"You don't think it takes skill?"

"Skill, sure. Knowledge, yeah, you've got to be fluent in the language to some degree. But it's all just archetypes. We all been seeing the sun and the moon and knights and sorcerers since we were babies, we know what they mean. But do you gotta have magick to read tarot? No. That's why I still do it," she shrugs.

"I think you have magick," Veda says.

Poppy laughs dully. "Ain't you sweet."

"Oh! Some money—" Veda reaches into her bag and starts to pull out crumpled bills.

"Eh, don't worry about it."

"But I—you said—I'll pay you, really, it's okay!"

Poppy waves her off. "It's no biggie."

"But—"

"Didn't your mama teach you not to argue with your elders?"

"My mama didn't teach me anything," Veda says earnestly.

"Oh, come on. Your mama must have taught you *something*."

"How to hate myself, I guess," she shrugs.

"Ya serious?"

Veda nods.

"Well, that's terrible," Poppy says. "Come—come here." She holds her arms out awkwardly for a hug, and Veda folds her little body into it. I've never seen Poppy hug anyone. She gingerly pats Veda's hair.

"You're gonna be alright, sweetheart," she says quietly. "Just like the cards said, you're gonna be alright."

"Really?"

"Yeah. And if you ever need anything, you just…you just let me know."

The guy Angela's with finally interrupts her ongoing monologue. "Hey, so… you want to get out of here? We could go back to my place, have a nightcap?"

"Oh," she frowns. "You're not enjoying yourself here?"

"Well, I do work in the morning, and it's getting kind of late."

"In that case, let's call it a night, then."

"Alright. Well, do you want me to…call you? Sometime?"

"Mm, I think I'll decline," she says politely.

"Oh. Okay," he says, taken aback.

"Please don't take it personally," she says. "I just don't get the sense that we're very compatible."

"But...you don't know anything about me."

"I have a good sense for these things."

The others are doing their best to pretend not to listen, but their conversation has ceased, and they're all exchanging glances with each other.

The guy stands. "I just listened to you babble for two hours straight, and you don't think we're compatible? Well, newsflash, lady, *nobody's* compatible with someone who never shuts up."

"He's got a point," Vik mutters, and I see Sofia kick his shin under the table. For once, Angela is at a loss for words.

"I mean, I would've taken off an hour ago, but I at least thought you'd want to fool around! Jesus."

"Hey!" Ralphie says, getting haphazardly to his feet. He bumps against the courtyard wall as he goes to them.

"What do you want?" the guy says, looking Ralphie up and down: his stained t-shirt, sagging pants, untied shoes.

"Don't you talk to her like that," Ralphie says. "Angela is one of the most… most smartest people. Didn't you hear all that stuff she knows? What do *you* know? You look like you sell…sell insurance for a living, and people who sell insurance don't belong in the Quarter Rat!"

"The fuck?"

"So, you just take your stupid entitled face and your stupid…tie…and get out, okay? And don't ever try to talk to Angela—or any of us!—ever. Ever again."

"Gladly," the guy says, turning to leave the courtyard. "Buncha freaks," he mutters under his breath as he goes.

"Jesus, Ralphie," James says, looking slightly impressed.

Ralphie sinks down in the chair across the table from Angela and smiles vacantly.

"That was very sweet of you," Angela says.

"I've got your back," he slurs, gesturing vaguely at them. "All of you. Got your back."

This is not the first time I've seen drunk Ralphie perform an ill-advised act of valor. I once had to pick him up at the hospital because he'd picked a fight with a guy who was screaming at his girlfriend on Bourbon. From what I understand, there weren't even blows involved; the guy just pushed Ralphie over, and he hit his head on the curb and blacked out. He was concussed badly, and they'd had to shave his head to staple his wound, and the first thing James said to him when he saw him at work the next day was, "Jesus, Ralphie, you look like a thumb with a face." That pissed me off. I spat back, "So does your dick."

Poppy seems unfazed by the whole exchange. I guess at that age you've seen it all. "Night, folks. I'm going home," she says, shuffling toward the bar.

"Me too," Veda smiles. "Goodnight, everyone."

"I'm gonna get out of here too," Vik says, standing.

"What? Why? You keep going home so early," James frowns.

"I'm tired."

"Do you want me to come with you?" Sofia asks.

"Nah. Not tonight."

"Are you sure? I—"

"I *said* not tonight," he says, an edge in his voice.

"Okay, jeez."

He rubs his temples. "You don't have to fucking take it personally, Sofia. I'm just tired, okay?"

"Okay."

"See y'all tomorrow." He gets his bag, runs a hand through his hair, and leaves as Poppy and Veda do. James makes a sour face as he watches Vik go then turns to Sofia. "Is it just me, or is he a little saltier than usual these days?"

She sighs deeply and nods.

"What's that about?"

"He gets like this when he's out of adderall."

"Woof. Has he been taking a lot?"

"Like forty mil every morning."

"Is that a lot?"

"How much do you take, Ralphie?" Sofia calls over to him.

"Hmm?"

"Adderall."

"Fifteen mill—milligrams," he slurs.

"See?"

"Yikes."

"And his guy's out, so he's basically on withdrawal right now. He's been sleeping like twelve or thirteen hours a day. I bet once he gets more, he'll go up to fifty."

Max leans in, looking concerned. "Addiction's no joke. Especially pills…I've seen good people get in a bad, bad way."

"So…should we like, *do* something?" James asks.

"You know he doesn't listen to me," Sofia says.

"Hmm," James says, and she gives him a meaningful look.

"What, me?" he says, his eyes widening. "You think *I* should talk to him?"

"You're like his only real friend..."

"Oh, stop; no, I'm not," he says, his hand fluttering to his chest. "Am I?"

"Um, who else does he even talk to?"

"Ugh," James says, standing. "Fine, I'll go after him."

"Attaboy," Max smiles.

"See y'all later. Bye Ralphie."

Ralphie lifts a hand in a sort of half-wave.

"Have a good night, James," Angela says.

It's just her and Ralphie at the two-top now, and Max and Sofia are up on their stools at the big table. Angela looks at Ralphie, sitting there with his eyelids drooping and a big wet stain on his t-shirt from where he spilled some beer a few minutes ago.

"Ralphie," she says.

"Hmm?"

"Your shoes are untied."

He looks down at them, the laces grubby and shredded from dragging the ground. "Oh. Yeah. They're always like that," he mumbles.

"Here, let me help." She gets up, kneels, and ties his shoes.

He smiles sleepily. "Thanks."

"And your vest is inside out. Sit up a little?" He's docile as a puppy as she leans him forward, takes off his vest, and rights it. "And you know, we could probably find one that fits you a little better too. This one's a bit tight."

"I'm not very good at…stuff," he mutters.

She squeezes his shoulder. "You're good at lots of things."

"Thanks."

"Well," she says, addressing Max and Sofia. "It's been quite an evening. I think I'll turn in."

"Get home safe," Max says, and Sofia waves and smiles.

I watch her go, head held high, impeccable posture. Her tiny heels click on the stones as she leaves the courtyard.

"Ralphie, want to come sit with us?" Sofia asks.

"I'm good," he says. After a moment, he gets up and starts to pace the courtyard like he does, lurching and stumbling, acting out some little scene under his breath. Sofia turns to Max.

"You don't usually hang out after work."

"No, I usually don't," he says. "But there's not much to do at my place, with Molly gone."

Sofia's big eyes grow sorrowful.

"Oh, Max," she says, putting a hand on his. "I'm sorry. Well, you can chill with us in the courtyard anytime!"

"Doubt I'm very good company."

"Are you kidding? We love you. Vik's always talking about how cool you are."

Max smiles, then asks, "You two are an item, huh?"

"Oh. Yeah. I mean, kind of. He's weird about it."

"What do you mean?"

She shrugs. "He just doesn't like labels, I guess."

"Labels?"

"Yeah. You know, 'boyfriend,' 'girlfriend.'"

Max raises an eyebrow. "You're going steady, but he doesn't want to call you his girlfriend?"

"Guess not."

"Call me old fashioned, but that seems a little strange to me."

Sofia sighs. "It's whatever."

Max looks upward as "Norwegian Wood" comes on. A smile flashes across his face then fades. "Do you know this song?" he asks Sofia.

"I know it's the Beatles?"

"'Norwegian Wood.' Molly loved this song."

Sofia listens for a moment. "It's pretty."

Max closes his eyes and hums along. There's wetness in the corners of his eyes.

Sofia stands and goes around the table to him. When he opens his eyes, she's holding out her hand.

"Want to dance?"

He smiles, nods, and stands. He puts a hand high up on her back, she gives him her right hand, and they slow-dance in the courtyard between the tables.

"Molly loved to dance," he says.

"I do too. Vik never wants to, though."

"I didn't want to either. But I learned. For my bride."

"That's sweet that you call her your bride."

"That's what she was."

"I wish I could have met her. What was she like?"

"My girl, Moll? Well..." Max says, taking his time to think about it. "She was kind. Very kind. But stubborn. And she always knew how to make me laugh."

"How old were you when you got married?"

"Twenty-five, I think?"

"So young."

"I reckon."

"And you were sure you wanted to spend the rest of your life with her?"

"Oh yeah."

"How?"

"When you find the one, you just know."

A moment passes, and Sofia leans into his frail chest.

"What if I know, but he doesn't?" she says quietly. Max sighs.

"Then he's not the one."

The song ends. He kisses her head.

"Thank you for the dance," Max says. "You're an angel."

"Aw, stop. I'm just whatever."

"You're a lot more than whatever. And Vik's got his head up his ass."

"Max!"

He chuckles. "Just my two cents. Well, I think it's past my bedtime. Better head home."

"Me too," she says, then shivers suddenly. "God, it's so cold!"

"Cuts right through you, doesn't it?"

I can see their breath, little steamy puffs of life hanging momentarily in the still air. Everyone has been talking, lately, about how it's a much worse winter than usual. But I don't feel cold. At all. Which is strange, I guess. When I was living on the streets in Shreveport at age nineteen, I was cold all the time, even in spring. Maybe I've changed since then. Developed a tolerance. Or maybe I'm just losing my mind.

"How are you getting home, kiddo?" Max asks Sofia.

"Well, normally I would bike…but it's so chilly, I think I'll probably take the bus."

"Me too," he says. "Want to walk up to Rampart together?"

"Yeah," she smiles.

Before they go, Sofia looks over at Ralphie, who's still pacing near my dark corner. He's singing off-key under his breath: *"Fixing a hole where the rain gets in, to keep my mind from wandering…"*

"Ralphie," she calls. He doesn't look up.

"Ralphie, you gonna be okay?"

He waves her off. She furrows her brow, then shrugs, then turns to follow Max into the bar. Ralphie and I are alone.

I remember the very first time I hung out with Ralphie. It was a bad day; I'd just found out my father had been arrested again, and I'd spent the whole afternoon wandering around by the railroad tracks in Lakeview, staring through that ashy dark veil into the void. It was hot that day, one of the first really hot days of the summer, and Ralphie was soaked with perspiration when he arrived on the street for work. "I'm a sweater," he told me, and I said, "What kind, wool or cashmere?"

I think that was probably one of the only times in Ralphie's life that someone had made a joke as dumb as the shit he usually comes up with, and it forged some sort of magic bond between us. We went and got tacos after work, and in that hour we spent together, the darkness faded and I sort of just forgot to be numb.

On Halloween night that first year I met him, I got too drunk on hurricanes and asked him if he'd be my best friend. He agreed. There were moments, with Ralphie—moments when we were laughing, or philosophizing about life, or just roughhousing like schoolkids—in which the void seemed very far away, and not all that important. We went for long drives out to the spooky oil refineries in Harahan, danced in his room with the lights off, hung out by the river and talked. We used to have a reading club together, just the two of us. We'd alternate between ridiculously difficult literature and fluff. We started with *Infinite Jest*, then *The DaVinci Code*, then *Gravity's Rainbow*, then *Jurassic Park*. Ralphie is probably the most well-read person I've ever met, though Vik and James never seem to include him in their impromptu debates about literature. They think he's a dope.

And he plays along with it because he likes to be liked. But I know it tears him up inside, and he starts to internalize it, and he gets destructive. It's usually directed toward himself; he can't bear to hurt anyone else. But sometimes, because I'm the only person who really cared enough to get to know him, he lashes out at me, makes me a scapegoat for his loneliness, his struggles with ADHD, his low self-esteem. Last year, he drunk-dialed me to tell me that I was cruel and selfish and a terrible friend. I could see it for what it was—just drunk Ralphie acting a fool—but it hurt a lot. I'd just gotten out of the hospital a month or so prior.

We haven't really spoken since then. But maybe it's time to break the silence.

"Just you and me now," I say. He doesn't acknowledge me. He's completely shitfaced, maybe doesn't even register that I'm still here. Or maybe he's still angry.

He paces for another minute then goes into the bar. I watch him stand there, order a shot, down it. When he comes back, he can barely stand upright. He starts to fumble in his pockets for his car keys, finds them, drops them, picks them up.

"You can't keep driving drunk, Ralphie," I say.

"Stop with that," he mutters. "Don't need it. Always in my head, don't need it. S'busy enough in here without you."

"It's really dangerous. You could hurt someone."

He closes his eyes, swaying on his feet. He burps. "Can I just…can I just… live? It's hard, you know? You think I don't—I'll just—"

"I'm serious, you can't drive like this."

He holds up a hand, but he's so drunk that he's not even facing me. "Gonna sit in the car for a while, sober up."

"No, Ralphie, you're not gonna be sober for hours—"

"Sober up," he mutters. "Just for you. Sober up." He wanders toward the door of the bar, a beer dangling from his fingertips. More than anything, I want to go after him, take the bottle away, take the keys. Take him home and put on a movie and let him fall asleep in my lap, like old times. But some part of me knows it would be pointless to try.

Ralphie bumps into someone hard as he reaches the doorway to the bar. "Oh! Ralphie," Angela says, coming into view.

He teeters on the balls of his feet. "Angela? But you went home."

"I think I left my book here," she says. "Ah, there it is." She goes to retrieve a worn paperback from the table where she was sitting. "You're here by yourself?"

"I've got people," he says, tapping his head.

"You're quite drunk."

He grins. "I like drinks."

"My my. How are you getting home?"

"My car."

"Oh no, certainly not. We'll have to call you an Uber."

"Oh."

"I can do that for you," she says, pulling out her phone. "You'll just have to tell me your address."

He mumbles it to her then stands there swaying as she types into the app.

"There," she says when she's done. "Monique is en route in a white Ford Taurus."

Ralphie starts to giggle.

"What's funny?" Angela smiles.

"You're so fancy."

"Oh! Well. I do pride myself on my…attention to detail, I suppose you could call it."

"Everybody thinks…everybody thinks," he slurs. "But y'know what? Screw them. You just be yourself. I'll be myself, you be yourself, screw what they think."

Her smile falters. "They don't like me, do they?" she says.

"They don't like anybody."

"Ah."

"I like you, though. You helped me with my vest."

"Which, by the way, you've buttoned incorrectly."

He looks down and burps as she reaches out to fix it. "Oops. Silly me. Silly silly dumb dumb Ralphie. You prolly think I'm pretty stupid, huh?"

"I don't think that, no. I don't *know* you very well, but I'm sure you're not stupid."

"I'm not. I'm very intell—" he hiccups, "—elligent."

Angela is examining his vest. "One of the buttons is missing entirely," she frowns. "I'll take you shopping soon, what do you say? We can get you some new things."

"Okay." Ralphie mumbles. "You're nice."

"I try to be."

"People shouldn't be dicks to each other."

"No, they shouldn't."

"And that's all that—" he hiccups again. "—All that really matters. Smart, stupid, whatever. Just be nice."

Angela's phone dings. "Ah! Your car is here. Let's get you out to meet it, shall we?"

"Mmkay." He takes a few lurching steps forward, nearly falling.

"Why don't I help you?" Angela reaches out to him and puts an arm around his waist. She's taller than Ralphie, and he leans on her as she guides him out.

Like everybody else, I've always found Angela pretty tiresome. She talks constantly, usually about herself, and I get the feeling she just can't manage to see other people as real human beings. I don't have a ton of patience for those narcissistic types because I was raised by one, and it fucked me up pretty bad. It's fine when you're little, when they love you almost obsessively because you're an extension of them, but as soon as you get older, start to develop your own identity…things go downhill quickly. They tend to blame you for all their problems, get emotionally abusive, and throw you out of the house.

But Angela invited me over for lunch, once, and I went, just because I was broke and out of food. She's a good cook. I think she assumed that because I'm a tour guide too, I'm obsessed with vampires the way she is, and after lunch, she read several pages of some vampire novel from the 1800s. Aloud. It was weird.

But as I sat there, listening to her read, watching her glance up at me every so often to see what I thought, I realized something about Angela. She's not totally the same as my dad. It's true, I think, that she doesn't see other people as real, can't understand that anyone else actually has an inner life as rich as her own. But that afternoon, I realized that she really, really wants to.

Her paperback is still sitting on the table where she left it earlier. I can just make out the title: *Carmilla*. That's the one, I realize, that's the one she read aloud to me. She must really like that book if she's still carrying it around. But she got so busy taking care of Ralphie that she forgot it again. I'll have to keep an eye on it for her.

From here in my dark corner, I've begun to figure something out. About these people, this strange collection of adjacent individuals whom I've watched commit countless small cruelties against each other, blind to any suffering but their own, resistant to change, insisting on performing their maudlin little tragedy every night between approximately 8:00 and midnight in the Quarter Rat courtyard. And I think the realization I've made has something to do with the fact that I don't have a role in the play anymore. Instead, I'm watching it from the wings, from the cool darkness behind the unpainted sides of the scenery, able for the first time to see them step offstage when they're not in character. Sometimes they help each other practice their lines. And other times, they help each other take off their costumes.

I've realized that they're not quite as blind as I thought they were.

So why do they look right through me?

CHAPTER 9

The Witch of the Irish Bayou

Coffee. Ruby needed coffee. It was already 1 PM when she woke up, and she'd only slept five hours, pretty typical, but caffeine was an immediate necessity. She staggered to the kitchen, found a stained mug, and remembered that her stupid Mr. Coffee wasn't working. "Goddammit," she muttered, tossing the mug into the sink. The clattering sound of it hurt. Her brain felt dry; she never drank enough water.

Ruby pulled on a top and a long cardigan over the leggings she'd worn to bed and went outside, her breath condensing in the cold as she fished a half-finished joint out of an ashtray. Ruby's porch was a good twelve or thirteen feet above sidewalk level and the vantage was pretty nice, an unobstructed view of the wide street and its tree-lined neutral ground. Of course, it was winter and everything was dead now, the grassy neutral ground brown and ugly, and there were big soggy patches in the grass from a late-night thunderstorm.

She leaned on the wet railing and dragged deep on the joint, trying to ignore the tiredness behind her eyes and the slight tickle in her throat. She probably should have been wearing more than long gloves and a crop top for the parade last night—God, she *couldn't* get sick now, not less than a week before Mardi Gras—but whatever, what the hell, so what if she did? She'd power through it. Sonic the Hedgehog, that's what she liked to call herself, zooming nonstop through life, rolling, rolling, rolling, smashing through raves and parties and drug trips like so many golden rings.

She pulled out her phone for the first time since before the parade and checked her notifications. "What the fuck?" she muttered, the joint stuck to her bottom lip. There were five texts from Ralphie, of all people, from the night before.

"Hey we're at your parade. Throw me something mister!"

"Aw man I wanted a crown lol"

And then, thirty minutes later:

"I'm sorry i annoyed u with my friendshio"

2:00 AM:

"I care about u but ur so hateful"

"3"

Ruby rapid-fired a response. *"Get your shit together Ralphie. I'm not Kat."* She had zero interest in getting sucked into Ralphie's drunken drama.

She went back in, hoping to get a few things done before work. The hours passed quickly as she finished most of another joint and worked on her costume. She couldn't wait to wear it. All she had to do now was get through the next couple nights of work, and then it would be Mardi Gras weekend, "deep Gras," as she and her raver friends called it, and she wouldn't have to think about anything unpleasant, wouldn't have to even be sober at all, for four days straight.

6:30, shit. Ruby still hadn't eaten anything, and now there wasn't time. It was more important to have a minute to put together her look for the night because there would be tons of parties to go to after the Muses parade. She decided on a glam pirate look, an outfit involving a leatherette crop top, sequin booty shorts, knee-high boots, and a big purple pirate hat with a white feather. The hat was one of her favorite accessories, a gift from Kat. She spread black glitter in thick streaks like war paint under her eyes, put on some silver mascara, and finished the look with metallic purple lipstick. *Fierce as fuck*, she thought, jutting her bony hips out at the mirror.

And would you look at that, shit, she was going to be late for work. Ruby dashed around the house, grabbing everything she'd need that night: credit cards, keys, tour guide license, lighter. She made sure she had enough weed in her dugout, quickly lit some sage and smudged herself to cleanse her aura like Veda had taught her and grabbed the little bag of molly from her freezer. Hopped on her bike—fuck, it was pretty cold, oh well—and rode like mad down the Lafitte Greenway to the Quarter.

"Well look who finally decides to grace us with her presence," Vik smirked as she hurried down the street to the Curiosity Shop, twelve minutes late.

"Shut up. You know I have like three other jobs."

"Oh, really? And what are they?" Vik always gave her shit.

"Kicking ass, taking names, and fuck you," she said, counting them off on her fingers.

"Kicking ass, taking names, and fucking me? I can get on board with that."

"Gross."

Veda approached from Bourbon Street, wearing a threadbare rhinestone-studded green leotard, dirty mismatched thigh-high socks, and chunky nineties platform boots that she'd hand-painted pink. Her take on fashion was simultaneously aggravating and delightful; on the one hand, Ruby had no idea why Veda was allowed to dress like that at work, for a *ghost tour* no less, but on the other hand—fuck everybody, and Slay, Queen.

"That *leotard*!" Ruby exclaimed as Veda walked up.

"Oh, do you like it? I found it on my porch; I dunno who left it there."

"You always have the most amazing stuff."

Ruby hadn't known what to make of Veda at first, but lately they'd been hanging out. A couple months ago, Ruby had been over at the river smoking a bowl when she'd noticed Veda down by the water's edge, and she'd approached, watching Veda pensively throw a handful of small objects into the river one by one.

"What are you doing?" she'd asked.

"It's a releasing ritual," Veda said. "The moon is my guide; I do it whenever she's full."

"Releasing what?"

"My trauma."

They'd ended up sitting on the rocks by the river for the next two hours, talking about the shit they'd been through. Veda was one of the first people Ruby told the full story to; she was still one of the only people who knew, and Ruby knew things about Veda's past she was pretty sure none of the other tour guides did. They held each other's secrets close. Ever since then, they'd gone together to the river every full moon to throw things into it and try to let go. Ruby told herself it was working.

"Can I have a dollar?" Veda asked Graham, who handed one over from the stack of cash he was holding. There was no cash register at Spirits of Yore, the manager on duty just sat on a stool with a roll of tickets in one hand and a sweaty stack of bills in the other.

"Here, take another," he smiled, handing her an extra dollar. Veda went into the Curiosity Shop and came back with a bag of gummy worms. "Want some?" she asked Ruby, and when Ruby declined, she ate the whole bag herself. Ruby noticed that Veda was putting on weight, her tummy round and plump under her leotard. Every night before tours, she asked Graham for a dollar so she could buy candy from the Curiosity Shop, and she was always spending her tips on rotisserie chickens and cakes and lasagnas from the grocery on the corner. The thought of eating so much made Ruby nauseous, but Veda deserved to have whatever she wanted. Ruby knew she'd grown up so poor her family had to eat cat food.

Ruby yawned and wondered if she'd be giving a tour tonight. "How many groups so far?" she asked Graham.

"Uh…two? And I think that's you. Vik passed."

She turned to Vik, angry. "Why'd you pass, asshole?"

"I gave two Cemetery tours today already, probably before you even woke up."

Graham shrugged. "Fight amongst yourselves; I don't care who takes it."

"It's fine, I'll do it." Ruby said. She hadn't been expecting a tour—they'd been so dead lately, with all the tourists uptown at the parades—but it wasn't the end of the world to have to give one. All it meant was that she'd start partying at ten that night instead of eight, and when you're up till sunrise anyway, that's not much of a difference.

Ruby hurried into the bar. "How's it going, love?" Leela asked. "Need something before your tour?"

"Yes, please. Coffee."

"Irish?"

"Mmmyeah."

They kept a coffee maker plugged in just for Ruby. She propped her elbows up on the bar and watched Leela pour a cup then upturn a bottle of Jameson over it.

"Thanks girl. And—you know."

"Our little secret," Leela winked.

You weren't supposed to drink before or during tours. Everyone did, but it was better not to let on. Ruby went back out to the street, hands wrapped around her steaming styrofoam cup, inhaling its warmth.

"You ready?" Graham asked.

"It's not even 7:50."

"It's getting crowded; I want to get a group out."

"Alright, let's do this." She checked her reflection in the window of a parked car and gulped down the rest of her coffee, feeling the warmth of the whiskey wind its way through her ribcage and into her core.

"Ladies and gentlemen here for the Tour of Lost Souls!" Graham shouted at the top of his lungs to the people congregated on the sidewalk. "We're going to go ahead and get started. Your tour guide tonight is Ruby, say 'Hi, Ruby!'" She waved at them. A lackluster chorus of "Hi, Ruby" from the group.

"That was pathetic! Hopefully you can whip em into shape."

"Oh, I will. Come on, people, follow me." Ruby turned and led the group down the sidewalk.

"Okay everybody, welcome to the tour!" she said when they got to the corner of Orleans and Royal, gathering her group to the edge of the curb. Ruby always began by going over the rules. "There are a few city regulations we need to follow tonight. First of all, stay on the sidewalk during the tour. Don't walk in the street, don't stand in the street. If you get hit by a car, it's a huge liability for the company. A lot of times you'll see me standing in the street, but that's because I have a city license allowing me to do so, and let's be honest, if *I* get hit by a car, all it means is I don't have to pay my student loans." Ruby felt a little weird about this joke, after what had happened last year, and she'd tried to cut it out of her intro—but sometimes it managed to slip back in. It did always get a laugh.

"Second thing, don't lean on the buildings. They're homes, they're businesses, they're very historic, we can't be putting our hands and feet and backs all over them. In fact, what I need you to do is come all the way to the front of the curb, leaving several feet behind you so we're not obstructing the sidewalk."

Some jackass in an Iowa hat was leaning on the wall of the Bourbon Orleans Hotel, apparently too stupid or just too much of an asshole to follow directions. "So, yeah. Sir? I'm going to need you to come away from that wall." He looked around then slowly stood up straight. "And *away* from it, please. Like I *just* said." She could hear the people he was with muttering, but she didn't give a shit. Ruby did not suffer fools on her tours.

After the intro, she launched into her story about the Bourbon Orleans: the quadroon balls that had been held there, the duels that were fought in the garden across the street when competing Creole men at the balls got feisty, the ghosts of the nuns from the time it had been a convent who smacked you in the stairwells if you swore. And goddammit, that motherfucker was leaning again.

"SIR. Away from the wall. It's not a difficult concept." He rolled his eyes, and one of the women he was with gave an offended little scoff in Ruby's direction as he slowly peeled himself off the wall again. "Like I said, it is a CI-TY-RE-GU-LA-TION," Ruby said, hammering out each syllable for him like he was a child. "I'm not trying to be a bitch, here."

"Well, you are," she thought she heard somebody mutter. She gave the whole group a glare and turned on her heel to take them across Bourbon Street.

At the next stop, a little Creole Cottage at Dauphine and St. Ann where she talked about Voodoo; she was hardly half a sentence into the story when a heckler showed up.

"She's lying to you!" he yelled. The group turned to look at a little man in a mussed shirt and undone tie, shuffling down the street with a bottle of booze in his hand. This happened from time to time, and Ruby had half a dozen comebacks in her pocket.

"You're right," she spat back. "I *am* lying to them. I lied and told them your life has value, you worthless piece of shit." This stopped him in his tracks. Someone in the group let out a long, low whistle.

"Shall we continue?" Ruby asked the group. A few of them muttered assent.

"Fuck you, whore!" the drunk called out as he wandered away.

"Eat glass and die, fuckface," she called after him. Tour guides were definitely not supposed to swear in front of their groups. *Let someone complain,* she dared them darkly in her mind. *Just let somebody fucking complain.*

She finished her story, did the Sultan's Palace, then took the group back across Bourbon to the dim little spot where she liked to tell the story of the Witch of the Irish Bayou. Nobody was trying to make small talk with her as they walked, she'd probably scared them too much. Just as well. *Don't like intense personalities, don't come to the fucking French Quarter.* She hoped vaguely that she wouldn't get any bad reviews after this tour, not that it mattered. Reviews were a poor measure of a tour guide's abilities. There were so many times on tour that people just hadn't liked her for stupid reasons, nothing to do with the quality of her storytelling, like this Iowa asshole who wouldn't stop leaning on the walls and probably hated her now. Whatever. They could all go to hell. Or just back to the Midwest, that was probably just as bad. Ha.

"Our next story takes place in the year 1880," she said abruptly as they stopped, and the group instantly quieted. "A lawyer named Dan Weynman, who had been disbarred in his native Atlanta, arrived in New Orleans. He was smart, handsome, early thirties…and he had left an unhappy wife behind. He came here looking for a job, but when he couldn't break into our city's most popular profession as an attorney, he settled for our second most popular profession: fall down drunk. And one evening, he happened to pass out shitfaced in front of this building behind me, where a well-to-do Irish family by the name of Mulvaney lived. The Mulvaneys had a beautiful redheaded daughter named Kate, about twenty-five years old, with a voice like sparrow's song." Ruby sometimes thought of herself when she described Kate. Her hair was red too—well, reddish—and she had once loved to sing. She didn't do it much these days, though.

"It was Kate who found Dan passed out on the stoop, and instead of sending for the police, she brought him in, fed him breakfast, and got him cleaned up. When her father returned home, he ordered Dan to leave, which he did—but he took Kate's heart with him. He and Kate began to see each other around town. Secret glances became stolen kisses, and romance blossomed. Dan cleaned up his act and rented a small apartment, asking Kate to move in with him. She agreed, but there was a cost: Kate's father disowned her and wrote her out of the will.

"Dan was honest with Kate and told her about his wife back in Atlanta. But he promised that he'd get divorced soon, and also told her of a rich uncle who would leave him his inheritance eventually. Things started out well, but after a few months of clean living, Dan falls back to his old ways. He starts drinking, starts gambling, burns through the little money they have. Kate starts to think maybe she'd made a mistake by shacking up with this guy, but there's no family to go back to, now…she's thrown that life away. She has no one but Dan. And so, the years pass, and they get poorer and poorer, and there's never quite enough to eat."

A teenage boy in the group had stepped off the sidewalk into the street to get a better view. "I need you on the sidewalk," Ruby said, and he jumped back up like a scared rabbit.

"So, Kate is forced to provide for both of them by selling homemade ointments and salves, which her devoted nanny Lebasse taught her to make at a young age. Her resentment toward Dan, who still has not divorced his wife in Atlanta, grows and grows. He spends all her money and seems not to care how hard she is working to keep things afloat. 'Things will change,' he says. 'I always land on my feet.' Silently, Kate thinks *Yes—but your feet are on me*.

"Things continue like this for fifteen years, until finally Dan's uncle does indeed die, leaving Dan his entire inheritance. Kate rejoices, thinking their money problems have finally been solved, but this is not to be. Dan comes to her solemnly, apologizing for his failures as a partner, and he tells her that the best reward he can give her for her years of struggle is to 'relieve her of the burden of caring for him.' He takes the money and abandons Kate, leaving her destitute—and not only that, but she is now forty years old and has no chance whatsoever of starting over with someone respectable.

"Within a few months, Dan marries the nineteen-year-old daughter of one of his business associates, who gives birth to twin girls a few years later. Kate, bitter and alone, is left with nothing and no one but her elderly nanny Lebasse, who comes to live with her after Kate's estranged father dies. Unable to afford the rent in New Orleans proper, they decide to purchase a tiny cabin out in a swamp called the Irish Bayou. There they live together, continuing to make and sell their ointments and salves, experimenting with Voodoo and curses as well. People around town begin to venture out to the swamp to purchase potions and learn Kate's secrets, and they begin to call her the Witch of the Irish Bayou, or just the Swamp Witch. Kate and Labasse live in the swamp for many years, and people start to mutter that she's gone mad out there, her once beautiful red locks now thin and tangled gray.

"Well, in 1905, Kate came down with smallpox. Y'all probably know that smallpox is highly contagious and covers its victims' skin in horrible red lesions. These lesions grow bigger and bigger, oozing pus, until finally they scab over, leaving terrible scars. In her insanity, Kate peeled off each of these scabs as they healed and tucked them under her pillow. But thanks to the care of her devoted friend Labasse, Kate survived the disease."

Survived. Survived. The word echoed in Ruby's mind as she talked, her thoughts wandering to Brian.

"Ten years later, Kate fell ill again, and this time it looked like she wouldn't make it. On her deathbed, she called Labasse to her side, and she handed Labasse a package wrapped in brown paper. 'Go into New Orleans today,' she said, 'and give this to my Dan.' So Labasse went into town, to the law firm where Dan worked, and gave the package to a clerk.

"When Dan was given the package, he unwrapped it to find an ornate wooden keepsake box. Always a greedy man, Dan opened it hastily, expecting to find a gift from one of his clients, jewelry perhaps, or money. But what falls out into his hands instead? Dozens of small, hard smallpox scabs. You see, smallpox scabs stay contagious indefinitely."

The crowd looked horrified and grossed out: good.

"Normally, smallpox takes weeks to kill its victims. Not in this case, though. Because these scabs were sent by the Swamp Witch, who had lived for decades thinking of nothing but revenge, Dan and his entire family—including his two young girls—are dead in two days."

"Serves him right," a woman at the front of the group muttered.

Ruby smiled. "Yeah. I think Shakespeare summed it up nicely when he said *Hell hath no fury like a woman scorned.* That man stole the best years of her life. And it may have taken decades, but Kate got her revenge in the end."

The story always left Ruby with an uncomfortable feeling: a tightness in her chest, a little hotness in her cheeks. She ignored it and took them around the corner, did the story of the Singing Rain by the Cathedral, took them to a quiet little bar on Chartres for the bar break, finished with the Provincial Hotel and the LaLaurie Mansion. After the tour, a bunch of them walked off without tipping, which pissed her off to no end. "Thanks, guys, really appreciate it!" she called out after them passive-aggressively.

She went to the bar, a fistful of ones and fives in hand. "Help the homeless?" a drunk on the sidewalk whined, looking hungrily at the money.

"Like I tell you every night, no."

"Bitch."

"Fuck you."

A group of other guides were in the bar already. Ruby ordered a vodka red bull and sat down to count her tips.

"This is shit. Thirty bucks? Fuck." She felt a lump in her throat, a lump that had been there since the swamp witch story. Maybe she ought to stop telling it.

"Thirty bucks, that isn't so bad! Better than me," Ralphie said. She could see in his expression that he was embarrassed about the texts, that he wanted to make up, but she wasn't having it. She downed half her drink in one long slurp then ducked into the bathroom, fumbling in her purse for the molly. She dipped a wet pinky into the little bag, spread a fat nugget of powder across her gums, grimaced at the sour taste as she flicked her tongue across her teeth. It would be a little while before it kicked in, but she was starting to feel the booze now, and that would do for now. She remembered that she hadn't eaten anything yet that day.

When she came out of the bathroom, Ralphie had gone into the bar, and Sofia had entered the courtyard.

"Hey, girl."

"Hey." Sofia looked sad.

"You didn't work tonight, right?"

"No, I went to Muses."

"Oh, cool. How was it?"

Sofia shrugged. "Fine."

"What's wrong?"

"I didn't get a shoe."

"Aw, bummer."

Were those tears in Sofia's eyes? Yes, they were tears, and one had spilled down onto her cheek. "I really wanted one because—"

Sofia always took parades way too seriously, and Ruby didn't have the mental bandwidth to hear her whine about it right now. "Well, there's always next year," she interrupted.

"Yeah, I guess." Sofia was quiet for a moment.

"Anyway." Ruby made a smoking gesture. "Safety meeting?"

Sofia shrugged. "Okay."

Ruby sucked her drink down to the ice cubes and tossed the cup in the trash. "Let's go." Ralphie made a move to stop her as she passed him in the bar, "Listen, Ruby, I—" he started, but she dodged him, avoiding eye contact. She and Sofia went out to the street.

There were a bunch of tourist bros in Pirates Alley at their usual smoking spot. Ruby could tell they were making moves to flirt, but her glare made them think better of it, and they soon dispersed.

"So, how was your tour?" Sofia asked as they passed Ruby's little pipe back and forth.

"Ugh. Stupid. People suck."

"Yeah, totally."

"And every time I tell certain stories, I think about him."

"Brian?"

Ruby flooded with anger. "I just fucking hate him. I wish I could take a baseball bat and just—"

"Please don't. I don't want you to go to jail."

"*He's* the one who should be in jail! I can't believe he's still just walking around. And as soon as he found out, you know, that they weren't pressing charges, oh my God. The smugness in his stupid voice when he told me."

"Jesus."

"'*I'm just so grateful to get a fresh start.*' Yeah, well, where's *my* fresh start, asshole? Where are the last six years of my life?"

"I'm so sorry."

Ruby's nerves were settling ever so slightly as she smoked, and she fell quiet. She didn't want to talk about Brian anymore.

"It's fine," she said. "Screw him, right? That loser's not worth my mental energy."

"There you go! That's exactly right."

"Seriously, I'm so much better off without him. I'm so much happier now, you know, just doing my *own* thing, living life to the fullest, having fun..."

"That's awesome. You should."

Ruby took a deep breath of the chilly night air and felt a tinge of anticipation. "You coming out tonight? I think I'm gonna go dancing, maybe hit up a party or two."

"Maybe," Sofia said. "I'll see what Vik wants to do."

"You don't have to do everything together, you know."

"Well he *is* my boyfriend…"

"Yeah. Sure."

"What's that supposed to mean? *Yeah*, sure?"

Ruby rolled her eyes. "I meant, 'Yeah, he's your boyfriend. Sure, do what you want.'"

Sofia handed Ruby the pipe. "I think I'm gonna go back to the Rat."

"Okay, whatever," Ruby called after Sofia as she started to walk away. "Have a fucking *blast*."

Sofia stopped and turned. "Why do you do that, Ruby?"

"Do what?"

Sofia shook her head and left.

Ruby rolled her eyes again and went into the little bar in the alley. More drama, great. But everybody knew Sofia's thing with Vik wouldn't last. Why couldn't she just face reality? Oh well. It didn't matter; she wouldn't let other people's stupid immature nonsense get in the way of a good time tonight. She ordered another drink and got on her bike to go to the club.

The streets of the Quarter were ragged with potholes, but she managed to get most of the way to Canal Street with just her left fingertips on the handlebar, the drink in her right hand. Things were starting to look kind of blurry now, soft around the edges, and she knew that everything was okay, would be okay, now that the molly was kicking in. She took her hands off the handlebars completely and spread her arms out wide, laughing, the drink spilling into the street. Her bike wheel was spinning, spinning, spinning, and she watched its revolutions on the dark flecked asphalt for what felt like just a second but was apparently long enough to send the bike careening toward a parked car, *oops*, she giggled as she jerked it back into the right direction, overcorrected, slammed on the brakes as a big SUV thundered down the street she was about to cross. It honked.

"Honk honk," she repeated, grinning. Normally, it would piss Ruby off to get honked at, but now it seemed funny, like the car itself was a sentient creature, and it could only communicate with this one word, honk, this one angry syllable, and how tragic it was, really, tragic because surely it had lots more to say. *What if,* Ruby thought, giggling to herself, *what if from now on I only said the word Honk?* She'd lose her tour guide job pretty fast, she thought, letting the empty cup fly out of her hand into the street. But other than that, well, would anybody really notice a difference? She was just a nuisance to her friends anyway, an annoyance, *none of them really like you that much,* Brian had told her once with that sweet, sad little smile. *But I do. I love you.* He'd put up with all her crazy shit, tolerated everything that was wrong with her, loved her when probably no one else ever would—

Oh. She'd passed the club. Ruby jerked her bike into a u-turn and another car honked, a long, drawn-out sound that continued into the night as she sped away from it, laughing, imagining its long, low fading moan as an outcry of her soul.

The bouncer on his throne smiled when she approached. "Hey, baby girl, what's up?" She reached out to give him the fist bump he wanted, missing at first, trying again, her chapped white knuckles moving slow-motion toward his chubby brown ones. "You early tonight."

"Oh, y'know. Nobody wanted to hang out with me at my regular spot."

"You know I'd hang out witchu, baby." A suggestive raised eyebrow, a flash of gold tooth.

"Thanks," she said, and she knew it was half-hearted but why shouldn't it be, she was just trying to get into the club, go about her business and now he was acting fake hurt, "What, you don't like me? Come on, where's that smile?"

People—men—bouncers, bartenders, waiters, cashiers, Uber drivers, *fuck*! Did they ever not say these things? Tired, it made her tired—beat down, worn out, angry tired.

But she did it. Smiled. A reflex. *Fuck you, don't tell me to smile, don't you ever tell a woman what to do, here's your smile* with her middle fingers shoving up the corners of her mouth. Yes, she'd said those things plenty of times before, every fucking day walking to work; she was a fortress then, but she was drunk now, and there was a drawbridge coming down, rattling down, creaking down over the moat, and the drawbridge was the part of her that knew maybe they were right, maybe it's all she was. Beautiful face. Piece of ass. And was she even that? *Children under ten*

Ruby was inside the club now, trance music thumping, dark and anonymous, bodies radiating heat and it felt good, the beat, *untz, untz, untz,* the pulse of life, loud, raw. Here she fit. First, just a little stomp, foot to foot, stomach contracting, sway the hips a little. Arms now, right angles in front of her face, criss crossing building a wall a shield *I am untouchable* then throw the arms back, chest forward, heart open brave to the world but just for a second, now contracting, folding, head turned profile, arms up again hands like blades right angles. *Untz, untz, untz* then lower, lower, the music driving her down lower into the ground, hips drawn magnetic to the earth, legs wide, thighs burning going lower, lower, throw it down, throw it all away. Up again, stepping forward stepping back heart open eyes closed, beat dwindling away into nothing, just a sweet suggestion, absence absence bodies drifting anticipation anticipation anticipation until UNNG the bass dropped hard and the bodies all slammed down with it, mouth open in ecstasy, head banging, sound in her veins vibration in her soul. *Untz, untz, untz* yes, yesssss, she was rolling now, rolling hard the air sweet on her face, everything perfect, she was the final piece of life's puzzle and this was the empty space that needed filling, a perfect fit, curved edges fitting around her like her body among these others, this guy's butt in front of her, arms brushing hers, somebody with mesmerizing pink hair, shapes, bodies bodies around the periphery surrounding her framing her Ruby at the center of all of them, center of the universe, flying.

Sweat. Pouring down her temples to her chin to her chest to her stomach, a river of life. Fingers tracing the rivulets down, down, down her back to the top of her butt, shuddering at the touch, not her fingers? Not her fingers. Turning, lights streaking purple swaths along her eyeballs, turning to face a face, dim, jaw, hair, smile. Palm held up toward her, fingers wet.

"Sorry," the face said. It had a voice too.

"That was you?" Words came out of her mouth like she knew how to speak English.

Wet hand around Ruby's waist, fingers on hip bone. Ten million years later, "Yeah. That was me." Two bodies becoming one. Hips to hips, arms playing in and out, Ruby's hand on his chest, sweat-soaked t-shirt, grinding.

"You on something?"

Smiling at the sounds.

"You on something?"

Oh. Words. "Molly."

"Got any more?"

Holding hands like school kids, field trip to the bathroom. Familiar shape round head stubby arms triangle skirt she pulled him into the women's room, stashed him in a stall. Harsh dim light, she didn't look at his face. Where was it, where was it, tiny baggie so difficult to find like every time she closed her purse it crawled off to another dimension, took its time to come scooting back when she opened the clasp again, there, found it. Shoving white crummy powder finger at his face, missing, laughing as he licked it off the hair at the corners of his mouth.

"I've got coke," he said. Another baggie, another white powder, pen cap, up the nose, back of the throat, that sour drip drip drip in the sinuses. Stars.

Back in the dark heat with the other bodies. "Want another drink?"

"Vodka!"

He brought vodka back, and she drank it in one gulp, crushing the plastic cup in her hands, dropping it on the dancefloor. Playground. More dancing. Grinding, hips, hands, hands, holding, touching, sweating, grabbing, hands. Lips. His lips were on hers, fat and wet like slugs, such big lips. Brian's had been thin. Brian. Fuck Brian. She shoved her tongue down the throat, this random human throat, and he was grabbing her, not dancing anymore just grabbing, hands, too many hands. Her body wanted away now, away from the face and the hands that kept touching her, shoulders pulling her like wings toward the exit, moving through bodies but he was always there, inches away, hands. She turned and pushed, clawed, so many more bodies now, too many, glimpses of his white t-shirt always behind her till she got to the door, out into the cold. The bouncer.

"Look like you having fun in there, baby."

Beeline for the curb, body inside the ground, head up high, way up there, head high inside the night sky. Her body and her head were stretching away from each other and it hurt, she was going to split apart, she sat. The white-hot screen of her phone was screaming 1:29! 1:29! 1:29! Numbers pummeling her brain, making her squint, frown, 1:29. One hundred and twenty-nine days. Was that right? Not just a coincidence, no, it really had been 129 days, she knew it in her bones, 129 days since that perfect October morning when the world had ripped apart at the seams. It had been so early, 6 AM, back when she went to sleep at a normal hour, back when 6 AM was early not late, back when back when back when

That bouncer's thick voice. "Your boyfriend's looking for you."

Brian? Where?

White t-shirt coming out of the club. Not Brian.

"Hey." Strange body looming up over her. Ruby small on the curb.

"You ran out of there so fast, you okay?"

"One twenty-nine."

"What?"

"I found out. One hundred twenty-nine days ago. And that's what time it is."

"Okay...so, like, you wanna dance more, or what?"

Stars and streaks and the vast empty void of the universe swung behind Ruby's eyelids as she shook her head.

"You wanna go home?"

Nod. Home.

"Come on, then. Let's go."

She watched the phone. 1:29. 1:30. 1:31. 1:32. It went all the way up to 1:38, and there was a bug on her neck, she'd known for ages there was a bug on her neck but she hadn't done anything about it, finally she moved her hand through molasses to swat it away and it had fingers, it was his hand, fingers on her neck more fingers on her leg.

"Uber's here."

She was crawling into a seat, a backseat, a car. Her bike? Her bike. "My bike."

"You can get it later." The car was moving now, fast air on her cheeks hanging out the window, and she pretended to be a dog, or an alien, or herself a long long long time in the future when she wouldn't feel any of this anymore. Cars were so great. Cars took you away. Away, away, away.

Then she wasn't in a car anymore. A staircase, stairs up to a balcony, hands behind her, steadying her. "You okay? Don't fall." Night air so cold she wanted to run through it. She looked down at her feet, plodding, *clang clang clang* up the metal stairs, what was this, a fire escape? Why wasn't she running? She needed air on her face, cold in her lungs, and what was this, this was a door opening, a wave of stale air, carpet, a dog barking.

"Donner, shut up."

Donner. Wasn't that…a reindeer? Ruby's thoughts wandered to Santa, to Christmas morning, to children under ten, and it took a minute for her to get back to the right thought, to say it out loud. "This isn't—I don't live here."

"Yeah, no shit." Those slugs again, lips on her lips, so fat and wet she could see the trails of slime they left on picnic tables in the dawn. On the wall, there was a shelf with boxes of cereal and a little robot, what was it, a rice cooker maybe, all of it sliding down out of view replaced by ceiling as she fell backward, water stains like witches' fingers on the ceiling, lumpy blankets under her back. White t-shirt where ceiling had been. Hairy purple nipples where white t-shirt had been.

Belt coming off pants coming off sequin shorts coming off, ripped, the sound of ripping, all the sequins popping off in a million directions, lost, shorts naked and threadbare, hands clutching the sheets searching searching for the lost sequins and finding nothing, empty, and then something where emptiness had been, something unwanted, burning inside her, painful, and Ruby was lost but there was enough to know No, to say No, crying, struggling, losing. Wet lips, dry friction, pushing, groaning—

It went on and on and on and on and then it was over.

Sleep? Not sleep. Darkness, dizziness, flashing lines, buzzing sounds. Dog; TV; smell of food, coming back into focus. He was there on the couch, and she was in the bed. A lifetime had passed. Getting up took another lifetime. Finding her clothes. Shirt still on. Boots still on. Purse strap across her chest. Sequin shorts and thong around one ankle. Pulling them up around hurting thighs.

"You leaving?" He had nachos. Yellow cheese on his chin.

Dog staring. Door closing. Back down the stairs to the sidewalk below.

Phone. 3:38. Feet walking. Her mouth tasted hot and wet, coppery, like blood. She ran a finger along her gums to see if she was bleeding. Nothing. Dry.

It was cold now, really cold. All the forty-degree nights she'd come to work in a crop top, every shiver she'd banished with drugs and alcohol, well, the cold had noticed, noticed and kept track, and now it was getting its revenge. Real cold, evil cold, shooting blue ice into her bones. She wanted to fall down on the hard sidewalk and break into a million pieces, shards of human icicle skittering across the pavement until they came to rest in the gutter.

But she kept walking. The tall buildings of the business district were there in the distance, not so far, really, she could make it a few more steps before she froze. A few more steps, and then a few more after that. And a few more after that. She was warming up a little now. Head clearing. Her bike was there, somewhere among those tall buildings, and she had to get to it.

The phone—the phone knew. She spoke into it, asked it how to get back, holding its thin rectangle up to her mouth like she was about to bite into it. It told her where to go. Robot voice on the hushed Thursday streets. She hoped it didn't wake up any families, any kids asleep in their beds, sweet baby angels *children under ten*

And somehow. Somehow, Ruby's feet closed the distance between 1:29 and 3:38, all the way back to where she'd started, every step made with the intentionality that had been stolen by white t-shirt and his Uber, his stairs, his bed. The club was closed now, closed or at least the bouncer had gone home. And there was her bike, still and dewy, locked to the One Way sign at the end of the block. She wanted to kiss it and so she did, its thin hollow frame cold on her lips. Her mouth still tasted bloody, hot, and the bike felt numb and cool. She got on.

Amazing how the human body knows how to make a bicycle go. Lose your sobriety, your wits, yourself, but still, you can climb on and make those wheels turn. You don't forget.

Cold air skimmed Ruby's knuckles as the bike cut through space, the whirr of her tires on the pavement the only sound. It wasn't far to Canal Street, wide and empty and scattered with parade debris. To think that Muses had rolled by earlier in the night made Ruby feel very lonely. She couldn't picture it now, the crowds, the lights, the joy, when now there was nothing but broken beads and trash, broken beads and silence. The Mardi Gras Spirit, that elusive genie that all New Orleanians find themselves searching for somewhere between Krewe du Vieux and Muses every year, felt small and far away. Ruby didn't know when or if she would find it now.

She did laps on her bike up and down the streets of the French Quarter, Royal all the way to Barracks, back up Dauphine, back down Burgundy. Streets empty, houses shuttered, narrow carriageways leading to courtyards darker than dark had any business being. Occasional shapes of homeless human bodies elongated in doorways, headless under blankets, feet and legs tossed out at twisted angles. *Do we all sleep like that,* she wondered. *Or is something wrong with them.* And then: *Maybe they are dead.*

The French Quarter was so small on a bike. And to think this had been all there was once, thousands and thousands of sweaty people packed together with their horses and livestock and slaves in stifling rooms in stuffy clothes on the open-sewer streets of this vaporous swamp-turned-city, disease blooming every summer, spitting out wet bloated corpses with nowhere to go, walls on three sides, no escape but the river.

The river. She'd go to the river.

She turned off Burgundy onto Gov Nicholls. The LaLaurie Mansion loomed up on her right, and something felt very strange about it, very sinister, and she realized it was because there were no tour groups surrounding it, no battling cacophony of "*On April 10th, 1834,*" no hundreds of people crowding every inch of sidewalk to hear stories of torture. Empty streets, a tour guide's dream. God, had she given a tour that night? More than anything, she wished she could be that Ruby again, that girl from 10 PM, angry and capable and whole.

The little deli across the street from LaLaurie was open 24/7. Something to eat, some water, maybe, something to wash this taste of blood out of her mouth. She got off her bike and wheeled it over to a signpost. Another One Way sign, this one pointing a different direction.

She got a Powerade and a cup of lukewarm jambalaya and fished tips out of her purse to pay the cashier, a little old lady with yellowing plastic bifocals who looked as tired as Ruby felt. They didn't speak. The lady was eating Zapp's chips and sucked the crumbs off her fingertips before she handed Ruby her change, leaving little wet spots on the bills.

She sat on the curb and drank some of the Powerade then took the top off the jambalaya. It was wriggling, like maggots, and she felt vomit rise to her throat. She threw it away.

The river. She was going to the river. Ruby got back on her bike, wheeling silent again down dark streets. She had to keep reminding herself that her mouth wasn't full of blood.

Out of the corner of her eye, she saw a young woman sitting in the shadows at the base of a tree, legs spread wide, shoulders hunched, crying. But when she turned to look, the woman was gone. Just the drugs. Not real. She kept pedaling, but soon something dark and sinewy was slithering out from under a car next to her. Also not real. Her heart was pounding. There were faces looming up dark from inside the windows, sinister figures at every corner. Up ahead there was a man, this one had to be real, *surely*, he was crouched in one of the courtyard alleyways, ready to leap into the street—but as she got closer, she realized it was a post with a broom next to it. Just objects, she told herself over and over, just ordinary things. But there was no such thing as ordinary, anymore, not since last October. Why shouldn't there be ghosts and vampires and murderers lurking around every turn?

Ruby's legs nearly buckled underneath her as she climbed the steps of the levee. Her vagina ached. The Mississippi came into view.

America's beating heart, Ralphie had once called it. How poetic he could sometimes be. Wide and murky, usually some sort of non-color between brown and green, tonight the river was flinty gray under the starless late-night sky. Ruby crossed the riverwalk, where a few ghostly shapes lay dark and huddled under benches, and she climbed down the boulders on the other side of the levee to the river's edge. She sat on one of them, letting her fingertips brush the gentle edge of the water as it lapped at the garbage that had washed up there. Frost had formed on the rocks.

She and Brian had come here together once. At the beginning of freshman year, right before they'd started dating, when the French Quarter had still been such a novelty. Some people in their English Comp class had gotten together for a little outing; there had been a project of some kind, "narratives of place" or something like that, and a bunch of them had taken the streetcar from Tulane to the Quarter to "do research," but really just to drink and talk and come to terms with the fact that this legendary city was really where they lived now. But could you ever come to terms with it, really, truly? The fact still sometimes caught Ruby by surprise, six years later.

That year there had been a beach. The tide had been so low that the river had pulled away from the rocks and left a little sandbar where you could go and climb on stray driftwood and watch your footprints get sucked into the wet sand. It was the first time Ruby and Brian had ever hung out. There had been a bagpiper playing atop the rocks, and the sun had been setting, and everything about the situation felt ridiculously romantic, so much that they'd looked at each other and started laughing.

"This feels like a date," he'd said.

"Yeah, it does."

"Do you want it to be?"

She'd laughed again. Just laughed because she'd thought he was joking. Date *him*? He was a total nerd, not her type at all, and at that moment, she never could have imagined that she would fall in love with him, that they'd date all through college, move in together afterward.

It had been unthinkable.

Just as unthinkable.

Children under ten.

The sky was beginning to lighten. Streaks of lavender were creeping in from the east, and she could see more detail in the rocks around her, cigarette butts in the crevices, the startling brown quickness of a rat disappearing down a hole. The twinkling lights of the bridge were fading, and she could hear the homeless people on the riverwalk above beginning to stir. Mornings always came so suddenly. When the FBI had come last October, pounding on the door, guns drawn, hauling them both out barefooted to the curb, Ruby had thought it was the middle of the night. But just a little while later, the deep brown sky had started to shift and change, lightening into the beginnings of the gray overcast day it would become. It had looked like this.

Ruby's mind was calm now. "Do you know what child pornography is?" the agent had asked her after wrapping her in a blanket he'd gotten from inside the house.

"Um...sexual images of, like...people under eighteen?"

"In your boyfriend's case, we're talking children under ten."

She was past the denial phase now. Obviously.

The light was coming rapidly, faster than she was ready for, the dim shapes of her limbs growing pale and ugly with detail in the weak dawn. "There's no such thing as morning in New Orleans," Ruby remembered Poppy once saying. "Just the end of the night."

Ruby looked up and down at her body. She looked like a skeleton, her stomach gaunt, her bony hips like jagged cliffs at the top of her shorts. She realized suddenly that her pirate hat was gone. Lost. Gone like Kat who had given it to her, lost like the last six years. Ruby lost most things; she was used to it now. What else had she lost in that carpeted apartment, she wondered. Apart from the obvious.

She couldn't remember much. Maybe it wasn't so bad? The boy had been nice enough in the club, shared his drugs, bought her a drink. And he hadn't been bad looking; if she'd been sober, maybe she would have agreed, maybe he'd *thought* she agreed. And she'd been drinking, rolling, so even if she raised shit about it, tried to press charges or whatever, surely they'd all say it was her fault, just like Brian had said it was her fault, *If you didn't turn me down for sex so much, I wouldn't have been driven to it,* even though she was sure she had been crying, and who fucks a crying person, who fucks a helpless crying girl, a helpless crying little girl *children under ten children under ten FUCK*

She felt wet streaks on her cheeks. Blood? Like the blood in her mouth? No, her mouth wasn't bleeding—she kept forgetting—and the wetness in her eyes, that was normal, that was tears. Normal human tears. She was crying.

Ruby realized then that she hadn't cried in one hundred and twenty-nine days.

CHAPTER 10

The Axeman's Jazz

Vik spent his mornings in the cemeteries. There were many near his house, most of them traditional above-ground cemeteries, with rows of stately stone vaults like little houses jutting up from a plane of broken asphalt. Les cites des mortes. Vik liked living here, at the top of Canal Street, so close to the dead. Most mornings, like today, he walked across the street to St. Patrick Cemetery #1 as soon as he'd had his coffee and adderall, though there had been no adderall this morning. He was out of it again and needed a distraction.

Everything was much neater here in St. Patrick than in maze-like St. Louis #1, the oldest and most famous New Orleans cemetery, where Vik gave tours on Sunday and Monday afternoons. There, half the tombs were just piles of rubble crumbling into uneven concrete and there were no trees, no shade, no neat rows. There was some charm in the disorderliness of it, to be sure—St. Louis #1 was a product of its time, those filthy and chaotic colonial days when duels and yellow fever and heat stroke were expunging people from the fitful, humid city just as quickly as Saint Dominguan refugees and American carpetbaggers and European merchants could swarm into it—but it was nice to come here to St. Patrick #1, where "rest in peace" seemed to be something the dead could actually manage to do.

Once he had made his rounds of St. Patrick, Vik crossed City Park Ave and went into Greenwood Cemetery. He walked past the tombs, glancing at the names and dates, stopping to linger on anything interesting. "Our Little Henry, 1892-1894." Just a baby, but that was normal. William Mathers here, though, he'd lived to be ninety-four. An impossibly long time for someone born in the nineteenth century. Vik passed some of his darlings: Philomene Bajoliere, sharing a tomb with a man who didn't bear the same name—clearly a plaçage relationship—and Lucretia Paris, departed at age seventeen, whose inscription read, "She is not dead, but only sleeping." Vik had a funny little imagining of coming back some night to pry open the marble faceplate on her family's tomb, finding her lying so perfect and still inside, waking her with a kiss. But then what? Get to know her, make her fall in love with him, and then disappoint her like he disappointed every girl? Besides, her body was nothing but ash by now.

Holt Cemetery was always the last he visited. Tucked behind some nondescript outbuildings of the community college, it didn't get a lot of foot traffic. No tourists came to Holt, and the only locals who visited were morbid weirdos like him and the families of the dead. This was where the poor were buried. It was an in-ground cemetery—dig a hole six feet deep and toss 'em in, just like anywhere else in the country—but a sad excuse for one. Most of the headstones were just slabs of plaster or cement, the names and dates scratched in by hand or written with Sharpie, and some of the graves just had wooden crosses instead, a couple cheap pieces of wood nailed together. Each gravesite was rectangular, outlined by whatever low barriers the family of the dead had laid down around it: two-by-fours, cement blocks, in some cases just PVC pipe, dull white plastic tubes half-sunk in the wet dirt. Some still had barcode stickers, faded by the sun and peeling. Vik imagined the trip somebody had made to Lowe's: batteries, trash bags, oh and don't forget the PVC to mark Cousin Willy's grave.

Vik wandered the grounds in the weak February sun, reading the names of the dead. Some were barely legible. One headstone—if you could call it that, it was just a thin piece of plaster—had been marked with those sticky letters you use to spell something out on your yard sale sign. Some of them had peeled off, leaving an indecipherable remembrance:

E LOVE Y
THEL A MOM
DO MICK
1925
TO
19 7

A few rows away, a young black man was digging a grave. He was wearing a dirty t-shirt and a Pelicans baseball cap, and he was alone, chewing on sunflower seeds and spitting them into the hole as he dug. The shovel made a sharp crunching sound every time he drove it into the earth, and his breath was visible in the cold air. He was young, maybe in his early twenties.

"How you doin?" he said with a nod as Vik passed. The phrase was the New Orleans equivalent of "hello," nothing more and nothing less, but Vik took it as an invitation to stop and chat for a minute.

"Fine, yourself?"

"Aright, aright."

"Lot of work for one person," Vik said, gesturing at the hole.

"Ain't nobody else gonna do it."

"Who's it for? If you don't mind my asking."

"My grandma. She just passed."

"I'm sorry to hear that."

The man shrugged. "Least she get to be with her people. That all she ever wanted, just be around her family, you know?"

"You've got other people buried here?"

"Yeah. My grandpa, my daddy, my auntie...and over there, my little cousin," he said, jerking his head toward a grave behind him. Once-white picket fencing made a small enclosure around two Barbie dolls sitting side by side in front of a plain headstone. Time had not been kind to the Barbies, whose faces had been baked colorless by the sun.

"She was young, huh?"

"Two-year-old. Died in the storm."

There was a sort of cultural divide in New Orleans between people who had lived in the city during Katrina and people who hadn't. If you were in the latter group, the general rule was to shut up as much as possible whenever the topic came up.

"Shit. I'm sorry."

"House flooded up to the attic. We all got out, everybody fine 'cept the baby. She died."

"That's awful."

"Yeah." He wiped his brow and kept digging.

"If there was another shovel around, I'd give you a hand with that."

"Nah, man, I got it. Gives me some time to think, you know?"

"I feel you. I come here to think too."

"You got people buried here?"

Vik shook his head. "My family's back up north."

"Up north? Where at?"

"Oh. Uh, Jersey, mostly. Some in Connecticut. New York."

"New York City?"

"Some, yeah."

"You from there?"

"I went to school there."

"I never been to New York. Sometimes wished I could go."

"You're not missing out on much."

"Nah?"

"New Orleans is better."

"How come?"

Because of people like you, he might have said a few years ago. *Because of places like this, because the dead talk and the living listen and people here have been letting les bon temps rouler for three hundred years, because shit is* real, *here.* "Real." A younger Vik would have found poetry in this picture, a dirty young man digging a grave for his grandmother alone. But pathos didn't feel so romantic these days.

"It's warmer," he said.

The young man squinted at Vik with a hard-to-read expression. "Too hot, you ask me."

"Yeah," Vik said. "Too hot."

"'Cept today. Today it's too cold."

Crunch. The shovel hit the dirt.

"Have a good day, man," Vik said, nodding as he turned to go.

"Aright."

Home was just a couple of blocks away. Vik crossed the street, passing the bus that ran all the way up Canal from the Quarter here to its last stop, "Cemeteries," the word scrolling in orange letters above its grubby windshield. Someday, Vik liked to tell himself, he'd write a book or a play or an essay about New Orleans and title it *A Bus Called Cemeteries.* He'd be the next Tennessee Williams, pounding out his opus not from some little apartment in the Quarter surrounded by derelicts and debutantes but here in this big quiet house, alone, overlooking the dead. Or maybe he wouldn't. He'd never actually written much of anything.

Vik made himself another cup of coffee and sat out on his porch. He was reading a book about Storyville, New Orleans' notorious turn-of-the-century red light district, hoping to add some new material to his tour. But he couldn't concentrate. His head was throbbing, and he kept licking his lips. Something was bugging him; it had been bugging him all morning, and the fact that he was out of adderall wasn't helping. He'd hoped that his walk in the cemeteries would make the feeling go away, that by spending some time around death, that great equalizer, he'd be less bothered. But it hadn't worked.

Vik took a drag from his vape and opened Facebook again, went to Jordan's page. There it was, the link to the New York Times write-up. *"Jordan Heath: meet the bright young mind behind TekTonic, the startup that's taking VR by storm."*

They'd been best friends in college, both brilliant and funny and crazy. Vik and Jordan had been the leaders of their friend group, and Vik had been the one to come up with the name they called themselves, the "Dirty Dilettantes." The Dilettantes worked hard and played hard, and it was anyone's guess as to what great things they would accomplish with their lives. The professors loved them, upperclassmen loved them, girls loved them. By the end of freshman year, they ran the place. By the time they were seniors, they were practically gods.

The summer after graduation, Vik and Jordan had taken a road trip to New Orleans. Neither of them had been before, and it seemed like the right thing to do that summer, in those last precious days before Real Life officially began. That trip seemed so long ago now, back when Katrina was still a stinging open wound, back when Frenchmen Street had been cool, back when you could buy a shotgun house in the Bywater for a hundred grand. In those days, young people were flooding into the city as fast as the waters of the levee breach could recede, "rediscovering" this great blighted Southern gem and determined to make it something it hadn't been—couldn't have been—before. Vik realized now, of course, how ridiculous these aspirations had been, these delusions of importance. New Orleans is what New Orleans is and always has been and always will be and is not changed in the slightest by a couple twenty-two-year-olds with liberal arts degrees who show up thinking they're the first ones to have discovered a grubby creative mecca full of untapped potential. But Vik hadn't known that then. All he'd known was that this place was magic.

"Let's stay," he'd said to Jordan one night. They had been wandering down Dumaine Street in the Quarter and had been invited up to a party on someone's balcony, some stranger who'd seen them passing by. "Only in New Orleans," they'd been grinning to each other all week, strutting the streets with their Pat O'Brien's hurricanes and sharing smug looks as if to say that nobody else in the country knew how to live, and that by walking up and down Bourbon a few times they'd figured it out. It was at this party—which he was sure now had been thrown by some vacation-renters, not locals—that Vik, with a fistful of off-season Mardi Gras beads around his neck, had realized how much he dreaded going back to New York. There he would have to be an adult, get a job, have a life. And here, it seemed you could postpone adulthood indefinitely.

"What?" Jordan had asked, grimacing at the shot of Jägermeister he'd just taken.

"I mean it. What if we just didn't go back?"

"At all?

"At all."

"Like, live here?"

"Yeah."

"You're not serious."

"I am, man. Goddammit, let's stay in New Orleans."

And they'd done it. Rented a house in the Marigny for $500 a month, sent their parents to pick up and mail the rest of their shit from their apartment in New York, taken jobs as barbacks at a dive bar in the Quarter.

Jordan had lasted a year. One summer, one fall, one Mardi Gras. "I gotta go home," he'd said, drunk on a Tuesday night, sitting at the kitchen table as Vik painted his nails. It was a habit he'd picked up from one of the male bartenders, whom Vik had realized he had a crush on. Unconventional as he was, he wasn't sure he'd ever have acknowledged his bisexuality back in New York.

"Where do you think we are?" Vik had said, cleaning up his edges with a q-tip. "You are home, stupid."

"No, I mean…back. To New York."

"To visit?"

"No, man. I can't do this anymore. I have to get back to real life." He'd accidentally knocked over a beer bottle, sending it clattering to the floor, and Vik remembered getting mad, his voice rising.

"What's not real about this? It's New Orleans, this is as goddamn real as it gets."

"Dude, stop yelling. You yell too much."

"I'm serious. Why the fuck would you ever want to be anywhere but here?"

"We're drunk on a *Tuesday*."

"*You're* drunk. I can handle my booze."

Which was true. Vik had always been able to drink in moderation, but looking back on it, Jordan had been drinking every day, four or five or six beers a night, always with a shot or two of tequila as well. He'd probably saved himself from a lifetime of alcoholism by leaving when he did. He'd gone back up North and gotten into Virtual Reality or whatever it was, and now he had this startup, this startup that was supposedly "taking the VR world by storm." *I guess New Orleans was too real for you*, Vik remembered thinking bitterly when he'd first read about it. *You'd rather make a fake world than live in this one.*

Jordan was in town, and Vik was going to see him that night.

"Hey man," he'd texted yesterday. *"I'm in NOLA with a bunch of my coworkers! Sorry for the late notice, you free tomorrow night by chance?"*

"Working, actually. But do you wanna come on my ghost tour? I can get you tickets."

"Hahaha cool man, sure!"

And so, Jordan and some of his people would be taking Vik's tour tonight. He'd been sort of keyed up about it all morning, excited but nervous. It had been years since he'd seen Jordan, certainly not since before he'd made it big. He wondered if their rapport would still be there, if they'd still get along. He wished he had adderall.

Vik picked up the book again and slammed it down a few minutes later. He still couldn't concentrate, why the hell hadn't Ralphie hooked him up yet! He'd been promising for days but kept forgetting to bring it to work. Vik pulled out his phone and texted him, asking if he could come pick some up. He was up to eighty mil a day now: one forty mg pill in the morning crushed into his coffee, one swallowed with a beer before work. Without it, he felt bored, sluggish, directionless. Sofia was the only one who knew, and lately, she'd been giving him shit.

"What do you need to concentrate on?" Sofia had asked him. "You don't even do anything."

He went back into the house, storming across the carpeted living room to his dark bedroom. It was still there on the nightstand, the fake prescription the guy in Kenner had written him. His pinky twitched. Walgreens wasn't far, and the people who worked there were all zombies anyway, they wouldn't notice, they wouldn't care. Right?

His phone rang. Sofia.

"What."

"Hey, cutie."

"*What.*"

"Do you have to be so rude when you answer the phone?"

"I'm in the middle of something."

"Oh. Sorry."

"Christ, Sofia, get on with it."

"I was just wondering if you wanted to get lunch."

"I'm not hungry."

"Okay. Talk to you later, then."

Vik felt his agitation turning into something else, that familiar itch. "Wait," he said.

"Yeah?"

"Come over."

"Now?"

"Yeah. Now."

Fifteen minutes later, an Uber pulled up and Sofia came up the porch steps, smiling. He pulled her inside and put his mouth against hers before she could speak. The stiffness of shock in her body quickly gave way to soft pliancy. They didn't even make it to the bed but did it right there against the living room wall. Sofia fucked more enthusiastically than any girl he'd ever been with.

Afterward, he pulled his jeans on and went back out onto the porch to vape. Sofia followed, leaning naked against the door frame.

"That was really nice," she said.

He glanced at her over his shoulder and blew a cloud of vape mist at her. "Put something on, the neighbors will see."

Sofia jerked her head across the quiet street to the cemetery. "Your only neighbors are dead people."

"Still. It's tacky."

"My body is tacky?"

"No, your body is great," he sighed. "But civilized people don't walk around naked in front of the whole goddamn street, okay?"

"Okay, jeez."

"Just put something on."

She went back in. When she returned, she was wearing the tee he'd had on earlier, an old Muse tour shirt.

"*Your* clothes, not mine," he said. She'd been taking his t-shirts lately, wearing them home, stashing them. He'd told her to stop, but she kept acting all coquettish about it, like stealing his shit was cute. She behaved like such a teenager. He had to remind himself that she'd actually been a teenager just a few years ago. There were definitely downsides to getting that FYA, "fresh young ass," as James called it.

"But—"

"I'm serious, take it off."

"God, you're so mean!" She yanked the t-shirt off and threw it on the floor then turned her back to him.

"Oh, are you throwing a tantrum now?"

"Don't talk to me like I'm a child."

"Then stop acting like one."

"I'm leaving."

"Fine."

Her eyes filled with tears as she pulled her own clothes on. "So, I guess a booty call was all you wanted, then."

"Oh, did you not enjoy it? Because I seem to recall—*three times*, in fact—"

She ran down the porch steps and turned the corner.

"Goddammit," he muttered. He went back in and sank into the couch.

Female attention had always come easy to Vik, but not like this. Girls in New York were all sharp edges and witty banter, and dating there had felt like a contest, the winner being whoever could appear the least interested for the longest time. It had never been like that with Sofia. She was sweet and genuine and fun, never played games, and had a heart of fucking gold. People weren't like that up North, and Vik knew that if any of his old friends ever met her, they wouldn't understand the appeal. Frankly, they would think she was a bit of a dumpster fire, with her bright blue hair, cheap hoop earrings, mouthful of crooked teeth that said *mom and dad couldn't afford braces*...she even had a tramp stamp, a tacky little Tinkerbell above her buttcrack. It all aroused in Vik a mixture of attraction and revulsion. It was sexy to be with someone so raw, so real. But he knew he could do better. He flinched a little every time someone referred to her as his girlfriend. No, she wasn't, she was just the girl he was fucking, had been fucking for a year, the girl he'd accidentally said "I love you" to a couple nights before because some well-dressed guy had been interested in her and she was *his*, goddammit—shit. He had to extricate himself from this situation before it escalated.

Half an hour later, his phone buzzed. *"Sorry I freaked out. Sometimes I just feel like u don't like me."*

"It wasn't just a booty call," he responded. *"I wanted to hang out after."* That, of course, was a lie.

"Ur sweet," she said. *"See u at work."* And then a bunch of little emoji hearts, the sparkly one and the glowing one and the one with an arrow through it. Goddammit.

Vik drove to work early that night, restless without his adderall, and ended up wandering around the Lower Quarter for a little while before heading to Madame Livaudais'. He passed a series of bars on Lower Decatur, dropping in on bartenders he knew at the new hipster rave joint and the dive that had cheap steaks on Tuesdays, and then he made his way up toward the Fruit Loop, past an out-of-the-way gay bar where all the neighborhood queens had been drinking since 4 PM. "Come in here, baby!" one of them yelled from the sidewalk outside, a fat guy Vik recognized who sometimes dressed up like Ignatius J. Reilly. Without really meaning to, Vik went over to him. The man gave him a little peck on the cheek, and they made half a minute of small talk and then Vik excused himself into the cramped little bar, where two equally overweight old gays were crooning over a woman's little terrier dog and a man with very bad skin was sitting alone drinking Natty Light. Vik sat and ordered a beer and a shot of bourbon.

A drag queen walked in, soaking drunk. She was about 6 foot 5 and 250 pounds and was teetering in too-small stilettos, her swollen feet and ankles spilling out their tops. To Vik's alarm, she crashed down upon the bar stool next to him. "Johnny, Johnny Johnny Johnny Johnny Johnny," she crooned at him, tracing a line down his cheek with a broken nail.

"Woah, now. I'm not Johnny."

"Oh, sure you are, sugar butt. You're all Johnny, now come on and give mama a kiss."

Her breath was rank in his ear, and Vik recoiled. The bartender came over.

"Bob, come on. You can't be in here harassing the customers like this."

"Bob!" she shouted gutterally. "I am not Bob. I am *Swannie*."

"Whoever you are, you gotta get out. You can't do this no more, hear?"

"It's so hurtful," she was muttering. "All of you, so hurtful." She laid her head down gently on the bar fake-weeping, and a few seconds later, started snoring.

"Sorry about that, man. She's so big, there ain't much I can do," the bartender said, and went back to his business. Vik took a bitter swallow of beer. Ten years ago, he would have been delighted by this encounter: how strange, how genuine, how *New Orleans*! But now...he studied the drag queen's sleeping face, trying not to smell her breath. Her wig was askance, her makeup was clotted with sweat, and she had a five-o'clock shadow. Genuine, sure. This shit was as genuine as it got. But what does genuine get you? Drinking yourself into decrepitude with nothing to show for it, surrounded by misfits. He threw away the rest of his beer and left.

Angela and Ralphie were on the street when he got to work.

"Good evening," Angela said brightly as he approached. He ignored her and made a beeline for Ralphie.

"Hey, buddy!" Ralphie enthused. The man was like a goddamn teletubby. Vik gritted his teeth and pulled him aside.

"I texted you earlier. You didn't respond."

"Oh, yeah, sorry about that. I was writing, didn't look at my phone for a few hours."

"So did you bring it?"

"Sorry, bud, I forgot."

"Again? What good are you!" Vik barked. Ralphie looked taken aback, and Vik didn't feel like apologizing. He turned away and took a drag from his vape.

Angela came over. "You know, those things may be just as deleterious to your health as tobacco products. They haven't been around long enough for scientists to fully understand the long-term effects, but you might want to air on the side of caution."

Vik curled the fingers of his left hand in an O shape and held them up to Angela. "Number of fucks I give."

"Clever," she smiled.

"I can't do this," he muttered to himself, and walked away. Where was Jordan? Vik had told him to arrive early, he had six other people with him, for chrissakes. Vik checked his phone.

"Hey, we're looking for parking."

Looking for parking, in the French Quarter, on a Friday night, ten minutes before the tour was supposed to start? Fucking idiocy. Vik growled to himself and texted Jordan that they'd just have to find his group after the tour had started. *"In the alley by the Cathedral,"* he said. *"I'll be there until about 8:15."*

At the very end of Vik's first story, Jordan and his group strolled up. They didn't look like they'd made any particular effort to arrive quickly, and they were all in annoying business-casual clothes, some of the women wearing stilettos.

Jordan approached Vik after the story as he led the group away. "Hey, man, glad we found you." Jordan slapped Vik on the back. He'd grown a beard, which made him look older, and was wearing an expensive-looking bomber jacket.

Most of the eagerness Vik had felt about seeing his old friend had been replaced with annoyance. "Another couple minutes and you would have missed us."

"Yeah, sorry about that. We were having dinner with some clients, got a bit behind schedule."

"So, how you been?" Vik asked as they walked.

"Oh, man, so good! Life is just a whirlwind right now. We're actually doing a three-week conference circuit right now, sort of a media blitz thing. So that's been, y'know. Wow."

"Congrats."

"Thanks. It's not as glamorous as it sounds," Jordan laughed. "You do get tired of room service after a while. Anyway, how are you?"

"Pretty good, pretty good."

"Had no idea you were still doing the tour thing."

"Yep. It's fun, I mean, I like to think of it as a kind of street theatre—"

"Sure, totally. Fun little gig. So, what else you got going on?"

"Oh. Um…you know, I do a lot of research, some writing here and there..."

"Uh huh. By the way, Vik, this is my fiancée, Jennifer," Jordan said, gesturing to the woman next to him. She was gorgeous and tall, sleek blond hair pulled back into a ponytail, and there was a diamond the size of a golf ball on her left hand.

"Nice to meet you," she smiled. "So, you two were college roommates or something?"

Or something? Had Jordan told her nothing about him?

"Yeah, and remember I told you I lived here for a bit?" Jordan said.

"You did? In New Orleans?"

"Yeah, just for a year or so. That was Vik's idea," he said.

"Fun!"

"Didn't work out," Jordan laughed. "Not really my scene."

"Oh, I love it," Jennifer said, looking around at the dim facades of the houses as they walked. "Very charming."

"Yeah, but you wouldn't want to live here. Trust me."

"Why not?"

"I mean, look around. People just party; that's all they do. And the infrastructure sucks. I don't know how Vik's made it all these years," he laughed. Vik tried to smile.

They made small talk until the next stop, where Vik told a story about a Voodoo priest. He noticed that Jordan and one of his companions were at the back of the group having a quiet conversation, not paying attention. He tried to reel them back in, even worked in one of his and Jordan's old inside jokes, but his efforts went unnoticed. When he moved on to the next stop, Jordan's people remained at the back of the group, lagging behind the others. He heard one of the women in stilettos complaining about all the walking.

Some dumpy middle-aged women rushed up to the front, eager for Vik's company.

"So, how long have you lived in New Orleans?" one of them asked as he led the group down Dauphine.

"About ten years now," he grunted, not in the mood to make small talk.

"You're a *very* good storyteller," another chimed in.

"Thanks, I appreciate that."

"And cute too!"

"Hush, Carol," another scolded.

"Don't mind Carol," the first lady whispered in his ear, "she's a little drunk." It was clear from her too-close breath that this one was a little drunk as well. The whole middle-aged-women-gone-wild thing was as much a tourist trope as drunk bachelorette parties or herds of college frat bros, these gaggles of pasty ladies flying to New Orleans to escape their teenagers and desk jobs and limp-dicked husbands.

"So, is this your first time in New Orleans?" he asked them, forcing himself to make conversation for the sake of his tips. Every single night he asked the tourists these same stupid questions.

"Oh! Some of us. I was here a few times in my twenties, but that was a long time ago," one of them giggled.

"Welcome back." *Welcome to the greatest city in the world,* he always said at the beginning of his tours. What a joke.

The very last smudges of light were fading from the sky, and Vik could hear people in the group talking about the gas lanterns, a scenic detail which always seemed to capture tourists' fancy around this part of the walk. It happened every night without fail, the oohs and ahs as soon as they started to get into the darker streets of the lower Quarter, always with comments about the lanterns. Something about those little flickering flames took people back to the horse-and-carriage days of the 1700s, or across the ocean to some small town in Spain, or into a scene from a horror movie—whatever place in their imagination they longed for most, the dim, greasy light of the French Quarter's gas lanterns got them there. He envied them.

He turned down Dumaine and pointed out Madame John's Legacy, one of the oldest buildings in the Quarter, then walked down Chartres to the Convent and briefly talked about the Casket Girls. Jordan and his gang continued to carry on among themselves, and Vik started to really get pissed off. He'd gotten them all free tickets, for chrissakes, and it's not like his tour was boring; it was objectively very interesting, goddammit, judging by the fact that everyone else's attention was glued to him. He decided he'd say something to Jordan about it at the bar break.

But before they got to the next stop, Jordan jogged up from the back of the group to Vik's side. Vik was pleasantly surprised and figured maybe he'd apologize without Vik even having to say anything.

"Hey, bud," Jordan said. "This is fun stuff."

"Glad you think so."

"We're actually gonna take off, though—one of my team members isn't feeling too good."

Vik's heart skipped a beat and then sunk into a very dark, sour place.

"You're leaving? All of you?"

"Yeah, sorry, man. I'd love to catch up with you more before we take off, though; I'll shoot you a text if I get a spare second."

"Yeah, whatever," Vik muttered. Jordan looked a little taken aback, but Vik didn't care. Fuck him.

"Anyway, thanks for the tour. Take care, man." And the six of them turned away down St. Philip and left, laughing and talking. Didn't even tip.

At the bar break, Vik found Ralphie and vented to him.

"One of them 'wasn't feeling good?' Bull*shit*, she just had on fucking stilettos and didn't wanna walk. What a cunt."

"Yeah, people suck," Ralphie commiserated.

"And they *all* had to leave? All six of them? And no fucking tip!"

"Yeah. But you still have twenty-two left, though, right? I mean, people leave all the time, you shouldn't take it personally..."

"It's just..." Vik fumed. "Never mind."

Tonight was going to be an Axeman night, he decided darkly. It was his favorite story, his *pièce de résistance*, and he didn't always tell it; conditions had to be right. But tonight, they were. The group wasn't too drunk (he didn't do the story for drunks; it was pearls before swine), they were all adults (he'd made a little girl cry once and had gotten in trouble), and he was very, very riled up. An angry Axeman is the best Axeman.

As he rounded up the group at the end of the break, the middle-aged women all jostled for his attention. *"Do you live around here?"* they asked. *"Where are you from?" "Where did you learn all this?" "Do you have a girlfriend?"* Vik gallantly obliged all their inquiries, flirted a little, asked them about themselves. He liked the attention. Deserved the attention, he thought angrily.

After the bar break, he rushed through a couple more stories then took the group down the block to a dark little parking lot tucked behind a carriageway. This was his Axeman spot. It was surprisingly quiet back here, and the light from the street rapidly fell away as you walked under the low overhang. There were low titters from the group—the darkness always excited them.

"Folks, we are standing now in a part of town that would have been known in the early twentieth century as Little Palermo. In the late 1800s, Italian immigrants began to flood into the city of New Orleans, settling here on these blocks between Jackson Square and the river. And it was in this neighborhood that a series of grisly murders was committed, in which the victims were found in their own beds, all slaughtered by axes left at the scene.

"May 23, 1918. Mr. and Mrs. Joseph Maggio, Italian grocers, are found murdered in their home on Upperline and Magnolia Streets. Their heads have been bashed in with an axe, and their necks have been slit with a straight razor. The cut on Mrs. Maggio's neck is in fact so deep that her head nearly falls off her shoulders when they move the body." Grimaces from the group. "A small panel has been chiseled out of the back door, where the murderer seems to have gained entry, and it's clear that the axe belongs to the Maggios themselves, seemingly plucked from their very toolshed. The bloody straight razor found in the yard next door belongs to Andrew Maggio, the brother of the deceased, but his alibi leads the police to dismiss him as a suspect. Furthermore, he describes seeing an unknown man lurking near the scene of the crime prior to the murders.

"One month later: June 27, 1918. Louis Besumer, another Italian grocer, has been bludgeoned with an axe in the apartment where he lives behind his store. His mistress, Harriet Lowe, has been struck too, and a delivery driver finds them both bleeding from the head. They survive the attacks, but neither is able to give a clear account of what happened and who attacked them other than that the perpetrator was a dark young man who fled *as if he had wings*. Upon discovering letters in German, Russian, and Yiddish in Besumer's things, police suspect he is a spy, wrapped up in war espionage...but nothing comes of this theory. Harriet Lowe dies several months later due to complications from her wounds.

"August 5th. Twenty-eight years old and pregnant, Anna Schneider is found with her scalp cut open, completely covered in blood. She survives and gives birth several days later. August 10th, elderly Joseph Romano is found by his nieces with severe head trauma. He dies two days later. Police find a small panel of his door chiseled away and discover a bloody axe in the backyard."

A light breeze blew through the dark lot, rustling a piece of newspaper on the ground. Vik could tell by their reactions that the group was tense, nervous. He moved closer to them, lowering his voice.

"The murders and attacks continue for the next several months, all around New Orleans. All the victims are attacked in their own homes, at night, with an axe, and at each crime scene, the assailant seems to have gained entry by way of a small panel chiseled out of the back door. But these holes were not big enough for an adult human to fit through, nor were they positioned close enough to the door handle to serve as a means to unlock it.

"Police are at a total loss. They even begin to speculate that this murderer, the 'Axeman,' as he had come to be called, was not human. Then, on March 14, 1919, comes a surprising revelation. The Axeman sends a letter to the *Times-Picayune*, which is published for the entire city to read.

"Esteemed Mortal of New Orleans: They have never caught me, and they never will. They have never seen me, for I am invisible, even as the ether that surrounds your earth. I am not a human being, but a spirit and a demon from the

hottest hell. I am what you Orleanians and your foolish police call the Axeman. When I see fit, I shall come and claim other victims. I alone know whom they shall be. I shall leave no clue except my bloody axe, besmeared with blood and brains of he whom I have sent below to keep me company."

He knew the whole thing by heart. Most guides just spoke the first few lines or paraphrased it. But Vik made a production of the letter, delivering every word just as it had been written. He played the part of the Axeman with sinister grace, commanding the group's attention, dexterously manipulating their emotions with the littlest changes in his inflection, the slightest facial expressions. He got to the third paragraph.

"Undoubtedly, you Orleanians think of me as a most horrible murderer, which I am, but I could be much worse if I wanted to. If I wished, I could pay a visit to your city every night. At will, I could slay thousands of your best citizens (and the worst), for I am in close relationship with the Angel of Death. Now, to be exact, at 12:15 (earthly time) next Tuesday night, I am going to pass over New Orleans. In my infinite mercy, I am going to make a little proposition to you people. Here it is:"

Their eyes widened, and the whole group leaned forward just slightly. He had done it. Vik had achieved critical mass, that moment when 100% of the group is 100% invested, when cheap entertainment is elevated into theatre. The crowd was engrossed, their drinks forgotten in their hands, their faces frozen with fascination and just a little fear. What a rush it gave him. In moments like these, Vik wasn't a tour guide but a true storyteller, tapping into that eternal, divine human tradition stretching all the way back to the ancient Greeks, to Sophocles and Aeschylus and Homer.

"I am very fond of jazz music, and I swear by all the devils in the nether regions that every person shall be spared in whose home a jazz band is in full swing at the time I have just mentioned. If everyone has a jazz band going, well, then, so much the better for you people. One thing is certain, and that is that some of your people who do not jazz it out on that specific Tuesday night (if there be any) will get the axe." He delivered this last line with a sinister grin, then let it slip away with a carefree shrug.

"Well, as I am cold and crave the warmth of my native Tartarus, and it is about time I leave your earthly home, I will cease my discourse. Hoping that thou wilt publish this, that it may go well with thee, I have been, am, and will be the worst spirit that ever existed either in fact or realm of fancy. Signed...the Axeman."

He took a pause. Someone dropped a beer cup. This happened, sometimes, when they were really invested; they seemed to just lose control of their motor functions. The sound startled the rest of the group, and then they all giggled. Vik waited for them to quiet down and continued.

"And when Tuesday night came, you can bet that no home in New Orleans was without jazz music. The finest jazz bands took up residence in the wealthiest homes, while at the poorer homes, anyone who had ever played a note took up scrounged, battered instruments and did their best. A local musician, Joseph Davilla, wrote and began selling copies of sheet music he called 'The Axeman's Jazz.' No home was without jazz that night, and no one died.

"To this day, the case remains unsolved. The most likely suspect is a man named Joseph Momfre, a mafia blackmailer who was shot to death by the Widow Pepitone shortly after the last murder, presumably because she had some information implicating him in her husband's death. There's also a theory that the Axeman was none other than Jack the Ripper, fled across the ocean some thirty years after his killings in London. And some held onto the idea that he was, as he said, some sort of supernatural being. After all, many of the victims described their attacker as a shadowy figure, unnaturally light on his feet. This is New Orleans, after all. Stranger things have happened.

"Or perhaps, my friends, the Axeman was just an ordinary man...an ordinary man who got fed up with being ordinary. Maybe he was a painter, or a musician, or a writer with great aspirations that just never materialized. Or maybe he was just a barkeep or a store clerk, someone completely plain, doomed to a totally unremarkable life, never to be noticed. And isn't that what we all want, somewhere deep down, to be noticed? To be talked about, remembered, revered…*feared*? What elation must the Axeman have felt, seeing thousands upon thousands of faces buried in that newspaper on March 14, reading *his* words, finally paying him the attention he always craved. And how must he have soared that night as everyone in the city huddled around a jazz band, knowing that he'd made them do it, that he'd managed to leap off the pages of his own life and into the annals of history. Power. Influence. Fame. We all dream of getting our fifteen minutes in the spotlight…and look how many the Axeman got. One hundred years later, and here we are, still talking about him. And after all, the deaths of a few grocers…well. That's a small price to pay for immortality."

He took a dramatic pause. "Ladies and gentlemen, my name is Vik, and this has been the Tour of Lost Souls!"

"That was *amazing*," one of the middle-aged women said as he stood around after the tour, collecting tips. "You're such a great storyteller." The one named Carol pushed to the front, tripping over herself. "Look at this!" she said, shoving her arm in his face. "Goosebumps!"

"Can we get a picture with you?" another asked, and Vik gathered them around him, their doughy middles warm under his fingertips. Afterward, two of them handed him twenty dollar bills and they all wanted hugs.

He said goodbye, sending them off with waves and smiles, and began to walk back to the Rat. What a sweet bunch. He really had done a perfect Axeman, not a word flubbed, every sentence perfectly timed. There really was a lot of work that had gone into his tour, and he'd spent years perfecting that story in particular. First, the structure: beginning, middle, end, foreshadowing, thematic elements. Words next, all carefully chosen for the picture they painted, descriptive but not so high-falutin' that the more uneducated tourists couldn't follow. Tone: a balance of casual and dramatic, funny and serious. From there, he added gesture, body language, perfected his beats and timing. Every aspect of the story was so well-executed at this point that he'd begun fine-tuning his very facial expressions, letting his face drop from a confused furrow to a teasing smirk at certain moments, narrowing and widening his eyes. Vik was damn proud of what he'd done with the Axeman.

And then he passed Angela. She was at the Convent, wearing her stupid veiled hat and floor-length velvet dress, waving her parasol around as she waxed grandiloquent about the Casket Girls.

Jesus, Vik thought, *Is that what I look like on tour?* The whole thing was so tacky. A couple passed behind the group, and he could see them snickering quietly at Angela's theatrics. She didn't notice; she was lost in the sound of her own voice, just like Vik had been a few minutes prior. His cheeks flushed hot with embarrassment. Jordan and his stupid coworkers were probably in some swanky bar in the business district at that very moment, making fun of him. *"So that guy was your friend?"* one of them was asking Jordan. *"Yeah, but he used to be cooler. Had a lot of promise, back in college,"* Jordan answered as he stirred his $18 sazerac. *"Anyway, thanks for sticking out half of that cheesy tour with me. I felt like I ought to at least throw the guy a bone."* Whatever good mood Vik had been in was ruined.

"How was your tour?" James asked as Vik settled down at the table with him. They were the only ones in the courtyard.

"Not great."

"Why, what happened?"

"I don't wanna talk about it."

"Hmm."

Vik shrugged.

"You know, you're a bit…aloof…these days."

"Yeah, I guess."

"Everything okay?"

Vik shrugged again.

"Chin up. Just four days till Mardi Gras!"

"Eh. Fuck Mardi Gras."

James gasped. "'*Fuck Mardi Gras?*'"

"I dunno. I'm just not feeling it this year."

"It's chaos and debauchery and exhibitionism for twenty-four hours straight. It's literally the best day of the year!"

"Yeah, but it's always the *same*. Get dressed up, take drugs, wander around, go home."

James was looking at him with great alarm. "And that doesn't sound fun to you anymore?"

"Nothing sounds fun to me anymore."

"Goodness gracious."

Vik sighed into his beer. "I used to believe in this place."

"Uh oh. Are you and New Orleans having a fight?"

"I guess. Not a fight, really. More like…an estrangement."

"Oh, c'mon. I know tips are shit right now, but don't let the tourists get you down."

"It's not the tourists. It's us. Me, you, any of us, what are we even doing? This place is falling apart, and it's taking us with it."

"That's not true."

"It is!" he hissed. "Look at Poppy and Jeremy, that's us in twenty years."

James made a face. "Yeesh. I hope I'm not still giving tours at that age."

"What the hell else do you think you'll be doing?"

"Alright," James said. "Enough. Come on." He went around the table to Vik and pulled him up.

"What are you—get off me."

"We're going to Bourbon Street."

"What? Why? That is the last place I'd like to be right now."

"Yes. We're going to Bourbon, and we're gonna get a shark attack."

"A shark attack? Absolutely not."

"What's the alternative, going to the bars on St. Bernard and dancing to boring house music with a bunch of gutterpunks and their smelly B.O.? Maybe we should like, make Bourbon Street cool again."

"That's impossible. Bourbon Street is the all-caps-*worst*."

"Or maybe we're just jaded, and it's actually lovely. Come on, let's go; it'll be cute."

"Fine," Vik sighed. "But you're buying."

Around the corner on Bourbon, the guy dressed up in a sweat-stained hand grenade costume in front of Tropical Isle waved them right in. "God, it looks like somebody put Jimmy Buffet through a meat grinder and splattered him all over the walls," Vik said. The place was plastered floor to ceiling with beachy decor, surfboards, and fake coconuts and tiki-themed everything. There was a trio of bored-looking old white guys on stage playing reggae covers.

"Two shark attacks, please!" James said, sidling up to the bar.

"Coming right up," said the daisy-duked bartender. "Where y'all from?"

"Oh, here. We're just being really basic tonight."

"Aw, yeah? That's cool." The girl scooped up two cups of ice, poured three shots of clear booze in each, and topped them with a sludgy mix of what looked like pina colada.

"I don't even remember how they do this," Vik said, and James swatted at him. "Shhh. Just watch." The girl had two plastic sharks now and was pouring some sort of red liquid into their mouths. "Stay out of the water!" she yelled, then shoved a whistle in her mouth and began aggressively blowing it. She swam the plastic sharks through the air toward the cups and shoved them in, flooding the drinks with red and mashing the sharks up and down so the booze sloshed and spilled.

James began to clap. "Girl, that was so good! Amazing work, really authentic." He paid, and they went back into the street, sipping their sticky, sweet drinks.

Vik grimaced at the taste. "What *is* this, everclear and corn syrup?"

"Oh, just drink it. It's good for you."

They wandered up Bourbon, weaving in and out of the crowd of staggering drunks. James found some beads on the ground and threw them to some strippers on a balcony, and when one of them playfully showed them her tits, he made a show of gagging and looking away. "See, isn't this fun?" James shouted over the noise. The shark attack was really very boozy, and soon Vik found himself awash in pleasant waves of apathy.

"What next?" James asked.

"So, we're making a night of it, huh?"

"What else do you have going on?"

"Nothing, I guess."

"No plans with lil' bit?"

Vik shrugged.

"What, you had a fight?"

"Not really. I mean, kind of. I'm sure she's over it by now, though. She always gets over shit so fast. It's like I can do no wrong."

"It's the same thing with Landon. He's just so…*sweet*."

"You hate sweet."

"I kind of love sweet, actually. I kind of forgot sweet existed."

"I figured you would have dumped him by now."

"Yeah, me too. I really…I dunno. I really like him, though."

"Do you loooove him?" Vik took a tug from his vape and blew out playfully at James, who frowned sourly and swatted the cloud away.

"Gross. You're such a neckbeard, I don't know why I try to have civilized conversations with you."

"So, what now? Back to the Rat?"

"No, let's do something *fun*. Frenchmen?"

"Frenchmen? Really?" Only tourists went to Frenchmen anymore.

"Oh, don't be such a snob. If we can amuse ourselves on Bourbon, we can amuse ourselves on Frenchmen."

On Frenchmen Street, they went into Bamboula's, a bar and music venue that Vik probably hadn't been in since he was twenty-four or twenty-five. A swing band was playing, three jazz musicians and a white girl in a retro dress crooning into the mic, trying to sound like Ella Fitzgerald.

"Jesus, this is cheesy," Vik muttered to James as they squeezed through the doorway bottleneck of tourists in crocs and Hawaiian shirts.

"Is it, though? Or is it amazing?"

"Definitely cheesy."

"Just shut up and drink your overpriced alcohol." They ordered beers and sat at the bar, watching middle-aged couples grin at the stage and tap their feet off-beat to the music.

"Aw. Ain't that nice?" James said. "Look how much they love it."

"Is it ragtime? Is it classical?" Vik said in an old-timey radio voice. "No, ladies and gentlemen, it is JAZZ, the hottest new musical sensation to emerge from that notorious Sodom of the South, New Or-leens! Put on your dancing shoes, folks, it's gonna be a hot time in the old town tonight!"

"Come on, baby, let's show these people how it's done." James gulped down the rest of his beer and indicated that Vik should do the same then pulled him onto the dance floor. They launched into the *step-step-rock-step* of partner swing dancing as the people at the tables around them watched, a little taken aback at the sight of two men—one covered in piercings and wearing all black—dancing like they were at a sock hop.

"Stop it, let me lead," Vik insisted as James tried to twirl him.

"Why should *you* get to lead?"

"Because I am *obviously* the more masculine of the two of us."

"More masculine? Excuse me, but just because you stick your dick in pussy sometimes—"

Vik tickled James' ribs aggressively. "Okay, okay!" he gasped. "You can lead, fine."

Eventually, they got the hang of it and began to move fluidly around the dance floor. "Come on, get up here!" James called out to a young couple who were sitting near the stage. Within a few minutes, other people had gotten up to join them, tentatively at first, then more enthusiastically. By the end of the second song, there were plenty of people on the dance floor, a couple biker guys with their saggy tattooed wives, a flailing threesome of tipsy college girls, a nicely-dressed middle-aged couple who kept their steps simple. "These silly fucks. It's like they didn't even know dancing was an option," Vik said.

"*Dancing is always an option in New Orleans, y'all!*" James shouted over the music, drunk. Vik wasn't very sober anymore either and found himself tripping over James' shoes a lot, but it didn't matter, everyone was laughing and dancing, and this was fun, it was actually fun. When the band struck up a more bluesy song, James and Vik began to slow dance, resting their heads on each other's shoulders.

"Do you think they think we're gay?" Vik asked.

"We *are* gay."

"I don't know how many times I have to tell you, I'm not gay. I am *bisexual*."

James clucked disapprovingly. "Oh, stop that. Bisexual's just a stop on the train to Gay Town."

"Stop erasing my identity, asshole."

"I'm sorry, did someone say something?" James said, looking around. "Is someone there? Hello?"

Vik shoved him, and James shoved him back, and they began to giggle. And then, settling into the slow dance again, Vik looked around at all the other dancing people in Bamboula's. He saw in their faces the uncomplicated joy that he remembered feeling the first time he'd ever set foot in the Quarter. That delight, that *awe*, at finding a place where music happens on the streets and you can take your beer to go, where the pretty colorful houses are better dressed than most people in your hometown, where you can be who you want and do what you wanna do, and no matter how wild you get, nobody will pay you any attention except to bet you they know where you got your shoes. Vik remembered a night like this, a night with Jordan spent drinking and dancing on Bourbon and Frenchmen, probably one of the first nights he'd spent in New Orleans. And here he was again. Looking at it from the wrong end of a decade.

He thought then of his tour group that evening, the middle-aged women who'd loved him so. They'd go home and post blurry pictures of him on social media and tell their friends about the tour and for months, maybe years, whenever they remembered their girls' trip to New Orleans, Vik and his story of the mysterious axe-wielding maniac would stick in their minds. They wouldn't recall the dates or names; in fact, most of the details of the tour would probably be blurred by alcohol or eclipsed by the other million shiny pieces of their trip to New Orleans, but they'd remember their engaging, devilish young tour guide and the way he'd made them feel. And maybe that was something.

The band took a break. "You guys are awesome," the bartender said when James and Vik went back to the bar. "You really got people moving."

"Oh, we're just attention whores. Can we get another round of PBRs?"

"On the house. Always nice to see locals in here." She slid their beers across the bar, and Vik gave her a few bucks from his tour tips. On the way out, James stuffed a five into the band's tip jar.

Outside, the cold air felt electric on Vik's sweaty skin. "This is *delicious*," he said.

"The PBR?"

"No, the *cold*. It's so cold! I love it."

"New Orleans isn't supposed to be cold."

"New Orleans isn't supposed to be anything. New Orleans is just, whatever."

"Well put."

"Hey don't tease me. Don't mock me."

"I'm not mocking you."

"You have to, you know, respect me. Respect what I say."

"R-E-S-P-E-C-T!" James belted into the night. "Hey, let's go to karaoke!"

"No, fuck that noise. Let's—let's go over there." Vik pointed toward the levee. "Let's go to the river."

"*Take me to the river*," James began to sing.

"Stop fucking singing."

"I can sing if I want! I have a beeeeautiful voice!"

Arm in arm, James and Vik crossed Esplanade and walked through a series of dark parking lots to the steps that climbed the levee. On the riverwalk, a homeless guy clutching an empty plastic Taaka bottle began to whine as they passed.

"Hey, mister, you got a dollar, tryna get something to eat, man, it's so cold out here and I'm real hungry..."

Vik handed the guy the rest of his beer, which he eagerly drank.

"See?" he said to James as they walked away. "I did a good deed."

"Pfft. That's not a good deed, that's...that's enabling. That's a cycle. Of alcoholism."

"*We're* a cycle of alcoholism."

"You always say you're not an alcoholic."

"I am not! Not by—not by New Orleans' standards. But anywhere else, man, we are *addicts*. The whole lot of us."

They sat on the rocks leading from the riverwalk down to the water's edge.

"Yeah," James said. "But better that than the alternative."

"What do you mean?"

"I mean, better to be addicted to booze than, like, money. Or some soul-crushing desk job. People get addicted to their work, you know. People get addicted to all kinds of fucked up shit."

"Cheers to that." Vik raised his hand, but there wasn't a cup in it. "Oh. Oops. I gave my drink away."

"Can't take it with you anyway."

"That's right. Can't fucking take it with you, *any* of it. Money, fame, your glowing fucking write-ups in the *New York Times*..."

"What glowing write-ups in the *New York Times*?"

"Oh. Nothing." He picked up a bottle cap from a crevice in the rocks and flicked it away, feeling suddenly gloomy.

"You have to tell me. You owe me."

"For what?"

"Getting your sad ass out of the Quarter fucking Rathskeller for one night."

"It's nothing."

"Pleeeease—"

"Alright, whatever. My best friend. He and all his stupid losers came on my tour tonight but left halfway through."

"No!" James gasped. "What a tit!"

"It's fine. He has better things to do," Vik said, grinding the toe of his boot into the rock in front of him. "He's really, you know, successful and all that. Starting this company, making money and shit, living the...living the dream."

"Hey, fuck that," James said. "What do you call what we're doing?"

"Wasting time."

"Not wasting time. Using it. Using it to the goddamn fullest."

A few moments passed.

"And *I'm* your best friend," James added, more quietly.

"Is that right?"

"You know it."

Vik put his arm around James' shoulders, and together they looked out across the river at Algiers Point.

"No reason you can't follow your dreams too, you know," James said.

Vik was quiet for a moment. "I don't think I have any."

"Well, do you like giving tours?"

"Yeah. I love giving tours."

"Then fucking give tours and be happy. There's enough miserable people in the world."

The moon was fat in the sky, yellowish over the sparkling bridge.

James started humming again, gradually finding the tune of that old Louis Armstrong standard, "*Do You Know What It Means to Miss New Orleans*."

Vik raised an eyebrow. "Seriously?"

"Well," James shrugged between verses. "Do you?"

"Do I what? Know what it means to miss New Or-leens?" Vik said, pronouncing it the way Satchmo did to make that oh-so-neat rhyme.

"Mmhmm. Do you?"

Vik shrugged. "I guess not. 'Cause I've never fucking left."

"Aren't you lucky, then?" James sighed, leaning his head on Vik's shoulder. "Aren't we both just so damn lucky?"

"Maybe."

James raised his beer. "To America's last true bohemia!"

Vik smiled.

"And to us," James said. "A couple of morbid faggots too smart for our own damn good."

"Ain't that the truth."

"You gotta quit with the fucking adderall, though, okay? You're more interesting without it."

Vik grunted.

"We're worried, you know. Both of us."

"Who?"

"You know who. And I hope you realize that no one's ever gonna care about you even close to as much as that silly girl does."

Vik missed Sofia, then, terribly. He would have to find her, after this, hold her close. Say all the things.

As he looked out at the river, a freighter came gliding by from around its sharp bend. Vik wondered where it was going, so silent and dark and huge in the night. In a few seconds, it was gone, and the river was calm, so calm Vik thought he could almost see his own reflection at its edge. James was singing again, more loudly now, his eyes closed. A hobo on the riverwalk above, maybe the one Vik had given his drink to earlier, started to sing along as Vik and James swayed together on the rocks.

When James finished the song, he turned to Vik and smiled through a haze of booze. Vik kissed his cheek.

It was 12:48 AM, and you could still hear jazz drifting up to the river from the streets.

CHAPTER 11

The Vampire of Royal Street

Blood. How quickly it sprang from a wound, heavy droplets bursting int streaks of red. Jeremy's fingers traced the blood's path, smearing it acros the skin, and put a finger to his lips to taste its bitter sweetness. Blood. Life.

An insistent knocking. "Hey, what are you doing in there? I really have to pee came Elijah's nasally little voice from the hall. Jeremy scowled and wiped his neck

"I'm shaving. I'll be done in a moment." He finished up, rinsed off, exam ined his reflection. His skin looked mushy and bloated in the late afternoon ligh from the bathroom window, fine creases lining his eyes and mouth. He bare his teeth and ran his tongue over his fangs, pressing the tip against their point until it hurt.

"I'm serious, man, I'm about to take a piss in the kitchen sink if I can't ge in there."

Jeremy yanked the door open, glowering down at Elijah as he strode pas him into the hall. The little man was wearing sunglasses and was naked except fc threadbare boxer shorts and the floor-length leather duster that he never took of

"Learn to control your bladder, Elijah."

"I told you, call me—"

"I'm not calling you His Dark Majesty."

"That's disrespectful," Elijah whined.

"And yet my conscience is clear."

Elijah shrieked as soon as he went into the bathroom. "Why is the shade up There's daylight in here!"

Jeremy rolled his eyes and went back into his bedchamber, peeling off hi black silk pajamas and preparing to dress for the evening. It was embarrassing frankly, being associated with the likes of Elijah Horowitz, all of five feet tw inches tall with his child-sized combat boots and that awful leather duster. H touted himself as a sanguine vampire but was really nothing but a glutton fc attention, bragging to tourists about how he drank blood and letting them ru their grubby fingers over the cheap acrylic novelties he called fangs. Jeremy were real, professionally filed three decades prior, the front teeth shortened an the canines sharpened into points.

The toilet flushed, and Elijah let out a long, noisy exhale of relief. Jeremy gritted his teeth and threw open the doors of his armoire, tossing a satin tunic and a pair of slim black trousers onto the bed. He had to find new living arrangements. He'd lived in this spacious second floor apartment at Barracks and Burgundy since the eighties, back when you didn't walk the streets of the Lower Quarter at night if you knew what was good for you and rent was a couple hundred dollars a month, but things had changed. The fat old Italian landlady who'd crossed herself and muttered darkly whenever she saw Jeremy but always baked him a lasagna at Christmas had died, and the company that now owned the building had raised the rent more than ten percent a year since the storm. It was climbing toward $2000 a month. Unable to manage on his own anymore, Jeremy had regretfully put out feelers for a roommate some months prior. Elijah, who worked at Madame Livaudais' Curiosity Shop, had lived with him since New Year's. It wasn't working out.

Jeremy dressed and sat at his vanity, dabbing his face with translucent powder and combing out his long hair, which was noticeably thinning. Streaks of silver had begun to appear in the last year, and he dyed it now, but the "Havana Brown" drugstore kit didn't do justice to his natural color, rich and dark with auburn undertones. Elijah had the long, beautiful hair Jeremy once did, but it was obvious that the fool took it for granted. His bottle of fruity dollar store shampoo sat crushed and gummy in the shower next to Jeremy's forty-dollar salon brand, and he didn't even own conditioner.

After dressing and completing his toilette, Jeremy went into the kitchen to prepare a meal. He opened the refrigerator to pull out ingredients for a salad, only to discover that one of Elijah's tupperware containers had leaked, and there was congealed blood coating his box of romaine.

"Elijah!" he bellowed. "Get in here!"

He heard the shower turn off.

"Now!"

A minute later, Elijah appeared, muttering "it's *His Dark Majesty*" irritably under his breath as he pulled on the leather duster over a threadbare pink towel. Jeremy held up the bloody salad container.

"Oh," Elijah said. "Sorry."

"Enough of this. You want to drink the blood of swine, get a mini-fridge. No more of this in here. No more!"

"It's not *pig's* blood, it's human! Someone gave me that!"

Jeremy started opening the containers of blood and dumping them into the sink.

"Hey, what the heck are you doing? That's my food, I need that!"

"What you need is a shred of self-respect. Now get out."

"You can't treat me like this, you know. My Clan Queen is going to hear about this."

"I said, get out!"

"Hmph." Elijah turned with a dramatic sweep of the duster and slammed his bedroom door.

Jeremy angrily chopped some carrots. Clan Queen. What a joke. This was how New Orleans vampires were conducting themselves these days, organizing themselves into "houses" and "clans" like teenage cliques, all with their own charters and initiation protocols and hierarchies. Elijah's clan even had a newsletter, a poorly-written two-page printout that appeared on the coffee table once a month, the articles all in some nearly-illegible gothic font.

None of that had existed in Jeremy's day. When he'd come to New Orleans in '83, cast out by a brutish father who thought he could beat the strangeness out of his son and a weak mother who believed prayer alone would fix both of them, he'd been utterly alone for almost a year. Coming to understand his own power and needs had been a slow, complex process, often painful and primarily undertaken alone. He'd had some help from guides, old mystics he'd managed to find through underground channels, but even that had taken great time and effort. No, Jeremy's journey in finding himself as a vampire had been almost entirely his own. This modern one-size-fits-all approach—buy some cheap dental caps, join a club, drink some blood, and call yourself a vampire—disgusted him.

He ate most of his salad and dumped the scraps into the garbage bin. Human food brought Jeremy little pleasure, and he didn't need it in the way he needed other forms of nourishment. He'd become vegan several years before, finding raw fruits and vegetables much easier to stomach than heavy meats and carbohydrates. The grease-soaked, flavor-saturated food of New Orleans disgusted him, it always had, and he did his best to prepare all his meals at home. Elijah, when he wasn't chugging blood until he threw up, was always eating cheeseburgers and chicken wings, flooding the apartment with such a nauseating smell that Jeremy often had to throw open the windows. He was thinking of instituting a "no food in the apartment" policy, though he had to admit this could be seen as a bit extreme.

Heavy metal music was now reverberating from Elijah's room, bass thudding in the walls and making the furniture vibrate. There were still two hours to pass before his tour, but Jeremy couldn't stand being at home with Elijah anymore. He'd just have to find something else to do. He pulled on his boots, swept his heavy wool overcoat off the rack, and headed down the dimly lit stairs.

There was a young woman sitting in the courtyard below, texting. Jeremy didn't recognize her—probably a guest of the people in the downstairs apartment, who mostly kept to themselves—but she was very attractive, with long dark hair and a slender frame. She was wearing a sweatshirt that had slipped off one shoulder, and her mouth was slightly open as she gazed at her phone screen, rapidly moving her thumbs. Jeremy stopped at the bottom of the stairs. The girl's energy was muted, difficult to get a read on, most likely because it was all being directed into the void of an electronic device. Jeremy hated cell phones for this reason; they sucked life force, scrambled energy.

He cleared his throat, and she looked up, giving him a curt smile. Ah, yes, there it was. He could sense her more clearly now, could read her aura: a subtle lavender, very pale in places, indicating a lack of self-knowledge. She was young, though, and that was to be expected.

"Hello," he said.

"Hi."

"My name's Jeremy. I live upstairs."

"Cool. Michelle and David are my aunt and uncle." Michelle and David, those must be the downstairs neighbors. He'd never bothered to learn their names.

"Good people."

"Yeah, they're great." She smiled again and went back to her phone. Their brief interaction had revealed the girl more clearly to Jeremy, the edges of her energy peeling back for him like the petals of a flower. How old was she, eighteen, nineteen? He could sense the easiness she felt at being that age, the feeling of immortality it brought her. It made him hungry. He went over to her and sat down.

"So. Have you gotten a chance to explore the French Quarter?"

"Uh, not really. I think we're going on a tour of the cemetery later, though."

"St. Louis Number 1?"

"I think so."

"And you're going during the day? Hmm. That's a shame."

"What do you mean?"

"It's better at night."

"I don't think you can go in at night. The brochure said it closes at 3 PM."

"Not to people like me."

She leaned forward in her seat, and the sweatshirt slipped farther down her shoulder. Yes, good. He was reeling her in. "Do you like, work there?"

"I do give tours, yes," he said.

"So, there *is* a nighttime tour of the cemetery?" The girl's innocence was frustrating. Alluring.

"Not officially. But if you were interested in a more private experience...I could take you in. After hours."

She raised her eyebrows. "Oh, yeah? That sounds cool. I'll have to ask Michelle and David if they'd be into it. What's your name again?"

"Not Michelle and David," he said quietly, letting a mysterious smile play on his lips. She glanced down at his fingertips, which were brushing the very edge of her knee. Her brow furrowed.

"Oh. Um—that's cool, I think we probably have plans tonight, actually. Frenchmen Street or something."

"Frenchmen Street," he laughed dismissively. "Wouldn't you rather see the real New Orleans?"

"I'm good." She stood. "Well, it was nice to meet you, thanks." And she pulled up her sweatshirt over her shoulder and went back into the apartment.

Jeremy's mouth twitched, and he resisted the urge to shove the patio table away from him as he stood. It shouldn't be this difficult. It had never been this difficult. Ten or fifteen years ago he'd been able to pluck them off the street and out of the bars without even trying—murmur a few quiet sentences, let a lock of hair tumble down in front of his face, and they were putty in his hands. Sometimes he had two or three or even four in a night, sometimes all at once, every shape and ethnicity and aesthetic, a vast rainbow of beautiful women. They had been there for the picking, ripe as fruit from the vine, and he'd gorged himself on them.

But in the last five years, things had begun to shift. Sometimes the hunt still yielded acceptable prizes, good-looking women in their thirties or forties who were bored or lonely or intoxicated, but the really good ones—the fresh, young, beautiful ones whose very skin could make you drunk, the ones who tasted like flowers and whose light never seemed to diminish, no matter how much you feasted—well. They didn't seem interested in Jeremy anymore.

It was no great mystery as to why. He'd seen it in the mirror, the thinning hair, the creases around his mouth and eyes, the neck beginning to sag with age. His body, which had always been effortlessly lithe and smooth and well-defined, was starting to thicken, to bulge around the middle. It made him hate the little food he consumed even more, and he'd begun fasting on certain days of the week, but whenever he did, dark circles appeared under his eyes, and his skin became sallow, which he hated. A vampire should be pale but not sickly. He'd been having trouble sleeping, too, for almost a year now, and the tincture Poppy had given him the week before hadn't done much to help. He had been experimenting on-and-off with prescription medication, which he didn't particularly like. When he took it, he awoke feeling disoriented and stuck, and Elijah told him he sleepwalked. But when he didn't, when he stayed up all night wandering the streets, he not only felt wretched the next day but looked it, too, his face haunted and sagging. More and more often, Jeremy's day-to-day appearance enraged him. And the hunger he felt deep in his bones became increasingly painful the longer he went without real nourishment.

There was a sudden tangy taste in Jeremy's mouth, and he realized he'd been biting his lip with one of his fangs. He was bleeding.

He licked the blood away and swept out of the courtyard, letting the gate groan closed until it slammed with a punctuated *clang*. Perhaps it was time to pay a visit to Poppy again. Her place was just a few blocks away, a tightly shuttered building nondescript among the ornate galleries and cheery Creole cottages surrounding it. He walked there briskly, pulling his overcoat close around him against the gray wind. The buzzer of Poppy's apartment building echoed blandly through the front hall when he rang it, and a minute or two later, he could hear her heavy footsteps on the stairs. The door swung outward toward him.

"Who is it? What ya want?" Poppy's frowning face appeared, her head wrapped up turban-style in a grubby scarf. Jeremy had known Poppy for years, and once upon a time, she had been beautiful. She'd had gorgeous black hair down to her low back, a full bust always spilling out the tops of tight corsets, and a playful magnetism that had drawn Jeremy in like so many others. But the decades had not treated Poppy well. Her body was swollen and doughy now, her joints and organs failing. But the real tragedy, as Jeremy saw it, was less the loss of her beauty than the loss of her spirit. The easy brightness of her aura had gone dull over the years, consumed by bitterness and loss.

Her frown softened a little when she saw it was him at the door. "Oh. Hey there, J. What ya need?"

He reached out to take her hand and kissed it. "Well, that depends. What do you have?"

"Come on," she sighed, beckoning him in, and he followed her slow-moving form up the dark stairs. She wheezed as she climbed, complaining about how she hated coming down to answer the door. "This fibromyalgia just gets worse by the day."

"I'm sorry to have disturbed you."

"Oh, you know I'm always happy to see you. It's just these other people, some of them, the young people, you know? Coming over here demanding this and that, no patience, no respect…"

"I know exactly what you mean."

The door of Poppy's apartment was ajar, and as soon as they went in, Jeremy was hit with a familiar whiff of unwashed laundry, cat litter, and drowsy nag champa. The first room was the bedroom, and Poppy tossed clothing and debris onto the unmade bed to clear a path for him, limping slightly as she went. In the cramped kitchen, Poppy went to a chair next to the stove and began to pet the black cat that was sitting there, licking its toes.

"Hello, Asmodeus," Jeremy said, knowing that greeting the cats was expected.

"Say hi to Uncle Jeremy," Poppy said as she scratched his ears, then sighed. "Asmodeus has been having some problems."

"What kind of problems?"

"Pissing on stuff. I need to get him over to Melissa."

"Melissa?"

"Pet psychic, there on Iberville. Do some chakra work on you, how about that, kitty?" she said, leaning down into the cat's face. It grumbled and dashed away. "Yeah, he's a little shit. But I love him."

Sitting, she took off her matted fuzzy slippers and began to rub her feet. They were pasty and bloated, and the yellow nails were in need of trimming. "Sorry, but my feet are just killing me. Need to go to one of those places on Canal, get one of those little Asian girls to give 'em a good rub."

"Just don't accidentally go to a brothel."

"Oh, is that what they are, those health spa places?"

"Some of them."

"You been to one?"

Jeremy wished he hadn't said anything. Once, last year, he'd been so desperate to feed that he had in fact visited one of the "health clubs" on Canal, climbed the piss-soaked alley stair to spend half an hour with a silent Korean woman who had tiny hands and terribly bad-smelling genitalia. It had been wrong, all wrong, and he'd left hungrier than when he'd arrived.

"So, what's up?" she asked when he didn't answer.

"It's my skin," he said quietly. "My hair. My body." He hated to say it, felt his cheeks burning. "I don't like how I look."

Poppy chuckled. "Yeah, you and me ain't so young as we once were, huh?"

Jeremy was briefly horrified by the fact that she had lumped them in together. Poppy was much older than he was, wasn't she? Ten years, surely...at least five...

She hauled herself to her feet. "I've got just the thing."

"You do?"

"I just made a nice batch of soap, it's sandalwood and oats, a little honey, really exfoliates. Keeps you moisturized too."

"I don't need soap."

She sighed. "Nobody ever wants the soap. I end up just giving it away."

"It's not about the..." he whispered. "It's about *attraction*."

"Ah," she said, scrutinizing him for a moment. "I see. Alright, fine. I can whip you up a little something."

"I'd appreciate it."

Poppy shuffled to a table at the side of the room. "Dark over here," she muttered. "Emmie, honey, I'm gonna borrow this for a sec, kay?" Poppy gently removed a candle from the altar nearby. Softly illuminated by a dozen others, the altar was cluttered with little toys, cards, and framed pictures of a smiling girl with Down's syndrome.

"She won't mind," Poppy said, carefully setting the candle at her workstation. "My baby girl always loved to watch me work."

"Yes, she did." Jeremy had never particularly enjoyed being around Emmie—she was loud and jarring, and far too friendly. But it was true that she'd been enamored of her mother's spell work, just as Poppy had been enamored of everything about her daughter. She'd been a good mother.

"I'm just going to put together a little gris-gris for you." She had taken out a mortar and pestle and was grinding herbs, shuffling around, and pulling things off the shelves. "This is something you can carry with you, you know, for confidence."

"You don't have anything that will make me...?"

"What, younger?" Poppy laughed dryly. "Well. There's lots of things I can get for you with dark work, you know, love, money, power. But youth, that's hard. Getting older, that's just what it is to be human." *But I'm not,* he wanted to say. "And don't tell me you're not," she clucked. "Vampire or not, you're carrying around a sack of dying flesh just like the rest of us."

Jeremy rose and went to her, watching her work in the dim light. She had a little piece of bone in her hand.

"Is that human?"

"Mmhmm."

"Where do you get it?"

"Over at Holt Cemetery. After it rains, there's usually some there on the ground, they just come up. Believe me, I've got my qualms about taking them, but at least I don't go bragging like that one girl."

"What girl?"

"Didn't you hear? Went bone-picking at Holt then got online talking about how she did it, how people could send her money, and she'd go get them some too. They arrested her."

The bone was dust now, crushed under her pestle.

"Why do you need bone for the gris-gris?"

"You kidding? You want to stay young, you gotta keep death right here." She patted her heart. "Close. You can't escape it unless you can embrace it." Poppy tipped the bone dust into the little sachet she was making. "There. Now it just needs something of yours, you know, sweat, tears, semen, whatever."

"Poppy," he purred playfully. "Are you suggesting what I think you are?"

She laughed. "Always the Casanova, aren't you? You and me? Once upon a time, maybe."

"Once upon a time." He smiled and pulled out a strand of his hair. "How about this?"

"That'll do." She stuffed it in with her pinky and drew the bag shut, held it out to him.

"Wear this on your right side, don't let anybody touch it but you."

"How much do I owe you?"

She waved him off. "Oh, come on."

"Thank you." He kissed Poppy on her sagging cheek. "You work tonight?"

"Yep. Doubt I can give a tour, though. Last one was awful."

Jeremy frowned. "What are you going to do, then? If tours aren't an option anymore?"

"I don't know," she sighed.

"You could go somewhere else. Do something else."

She shook her head. "I just…I can't, you know? Knowing she might still need me."

"She's gone, Poppy."

"Dead. Not gone."

"No, certainly not. Never from here," he said, laying a hand on his chest. "But the Quarter? Why would a nasty place like this want to keep a sweetheart like Emmie?"

"It's home."

"It's a toilet."

"If you hate it so much, why do *you* stay?" she asked, crossing her flabby arms.

"I've got no choice."

"Neither do I."

They stood there looking at each other stubbornly.

"You do have a choice."

"I'll leave when you do," Poppy said.

"Deal." They shook on it.

Poppy walked him out. When he was halfway down the stairs, she stuck her head out the apartment door. "Jeremy!" she called. He turned. "Here. Take some soap." He went back up and took the waxy bar from her outstretched palm. "Exfoliation," she smiled.

It was getting dark now, the bland white sky dimming into gray. These were Jeremy's favorite days, cold and overcast, though he didn't get many of them. The sun shone nearly every day in New Orleans unless it was raining, and sometimes it shone then too.

Jeremy walked the couple of blocks to the Rat, settled in, and ordered a glass of wine. The bartender, a big busty girl with an annoying laugh, knew better than to try and make conversation with him. She set his glass down with a nervous smile and moved away, and Jeremy sat and sipped, brooding. He remembered coming here before it was the Quarter Rat, back in the early nineties when it had been just another hole-in-the-wall dive bar staffed by junkies, none of whom lasted very long. They dropped like flies in those days, killed by overdoses and AIDS. Losing friends had just been a fact of life when Jeremy was younger. Everybody was on drugs, hard drugs, and the AIDS epidemic had hit the vampire community hard. Of course, blood drinking became completely taboo, and anyone caught doing it was exiled. But there was no way to stop the outbreak completely, the community was just too close. If you hadn't seen someone for a time, you became afraid to ask about them because the answer was almost always the same. But of course, it was a relief, in some ways, not to have to watch.

Jeremy hadn't had that luxury with Mortimer. One of his first vampire friends and a flaming homosexual, Mortimer had been key in teaching Jeremy—shy, painfully different, scrawny nineteen-year-old Jeremy—to accept himself. "Fly your freak flag high," he'd always said, voguing in his beautiful brocade cape and perfect Frank-n-Furter brows. He'd come to stay with Jeremy in his final months. Jeremy had watched him waste away, consumed by illness until he was a pockmarked skeleton, unable to walk, barely able to talk, his cape swallowing his wasted frame. Jeremy had sat with him for hours at a time in those final weeks, holding Mortimer's hand to his heart and letting him feed on his energy. He would have given Mortimer everything, all his life force, every bit of it, if he could have. Instead, he'd had to watch his aura slowly fade to black. And the one person who had always been the most immortal in Jeremy's eyes was taken away.

The petite blue-haired girl walked behind Jeremy through the bar to the courtyard. She was probably the most appealing of the lot, with beautiful, sad eyes and a sweet, crooked smile. At one point, he'd thought it had been the other, the girl with dreadlocks, but lately, she'd been looking haggard and wan. Her skin was always blotchy now, she never wore makeup anymore, and her skinny frame was too soft, too fleshy, not an ounce of muscle on it. Too many drugs, probably...that was usually how it went with the young ones. The other, the one who'd died, had been quite attractive, but she was just ash and bone now, wasn't she? The thought of her lovely body collapsing in on itself, putrefying, made him shudder. Jeremy pushed his empty wine glass away and went out to the street.

He lounged against the wall of the Curiosity Shop, watching the goings-on in the street as the other guides checked people in for the tour. He observed their little interactions with each other, reading their energy, probing their auras. The blue-haired one was in love with the loud one, that much was obvious, but it was a turbulent love, volatile and high-frequency, and their energy was alternately connecting and repelling, like magnets with continuously reversing polarity. It was fascinating; something Jeremy might like to play in, he mused. The gay one's aura was bright, though Jeremy had seen it cloudy on many occasions. There was a piece missing from it, a hole in his energy, and Jeremy didn't know why. Not that he cared.

And then there was the transsexual. Veda, he believed her name was. Her aura was truly like nothing Jeremy had ever seen. It was almost iridescent, shimmery, and subtle, made of dozens of colors that revealed themselves differently depending on what sort of energy you approached with. Sometimes the aura was stormy, flecked with electric sparks and dark colors so thickly pigmented they blotted out whatever was behind her, and sometimes it was as fluffy and pale as cotton candy, just the softest, gentlest haze. While most auras appeared as two-dimensional, thin halos or outlines surrounding the person's physical body, Veda's seemed to extend in all directions, undulating and shifting in size and shape like a living thing. He had seen it expand to cover most of a city block; he'd also seen it dwindle to almost nothing, contracting so thinly around her that it was almost invisible. Jeremy was fascinated with Veda's energy but also slightly repulsed. He got the feeling that whatever made her different also made her dangerous, and that her power—because clearly, she had a great deal of it, whether or not she had fully discovered it—was not compatible with his own. He wondered if she could see him the way he saw her. He suspected that she could.

"Eight o'clock," Graham called out. "Jeremy, Veda, Sofia, let's go."

"You're passing?" he heard the blue-haired girl ask the loud one.

"Yeah, I told you yesterday," he said, gesturing at the gay one. "We're gonna catch the end of Endymion."

"Should I pass too? I want to come."

"Well, someone's gotta take the tour. There's three groups; we can't all pass."

The girl frowned but didn't argue. "So…I guess I'll catch you afterward, then?"

"Yeah, maybe." He gave her a peck on the cheek, and she sighed, wandering up to the launch spot where Jeremy was waiting.

"Have a good tour," Jeremy said, letting a mysterious smile play on his lips. Her eyes widened momentarily.

"Oh. Thanks, you too."

Jeremy was always sent out first, being the most senior of all the guides. Without so much as glancing back at them, he led his group to the corner of Père Antoine Alley by the Blue Dog Gallery. This was His Spot, and any other tour guide who came within forty feet of him here lived to regret it. Jeremy sometimes pitied the newer ones, who often had to learn the hard way. He'd made a girl cry in front of her tour group once.

"Ladies and gentlemen, welcome to the French Quarter of New Orleans," he said in a whisper as they gathered around him. Jeremy always spoke under his breath on tours, so quietly that his groups sometimes had to strain to hear. It was better that way. It kept their attention, and it prevented other tour guides from overhearing and stealing his stories. He launched into his cold open.

"Take a look around, please." They did, unsure of what to look at, their eyes wandering up to the tops of the buildings and over to the slow-moving cars on Royal Street a few feet away. "Now picture yourselves standing in this spot three hundred years ago. It's September 1718, and a hurricane is raging."

"Hurricanes are kind of a trend here, huh?" a man in the group called out. Jeremy found the voice; it belonged to a balding white man wearing a t-shirt tucked into jeans around his beer belly. He seemed to be with his wife and two teenage children. Jeremy ignored him.

"The fledgling city of *Nouvelle Orleans*, just four months old, is in ruins.

You're watching the few hundred ramshackle hovels the French have put here get swept away by the wind, which will deposit them like piles of kindling in the surrounding swamp. Fast forward to 1727. You're smelling the stench of raw sewage running through the streets, hearing the *'en guardes!'* and *'touches!'* of dueling Frenchmen in the garden behind you, and if you take a look to your right, you'll see the construction of St. Louis Cathedral, nearly finished. 1769: the Cathedral has been completed, and the Spanish flag is flying high. It's the middle of the night, and just behind you a group of French priests are carrying the corpses of five men who've been hanging here in the alley, executed for treason. They've stolen the bodies, you see, in order to give them a proper burial, and they're singing the *Kyrie* as they go. Their voices will haunt this alley for centuries to come."

The balding man was miming a noose now and pretending to hang himself, as if Jeremy's story needed illustration. As he prodded his teenage children to look at him, Jeremy cast a cold glare in his direction, and the man grinned.

"It's 1788 now, Good Friday. The city is in flames. Fire rages through the street to your left, all those cypress wood houses burning up in an instant. You won't hear the church bells ringing the city alarm because they've been muffled and tied for Good Friday. 1800. After that fire and then another, the city has been rebuilt by the Spanish, and you don't see those cypress wood buildings anymore. Instead, you see wrought iron, balconies and galleries all done in the Spanish style. 1825. *Nouvelle Orleans, Nuevo Orleans*...New Orleans. We're American now. These days you still hear *'Bonjour, Madame'* and *'Comment allez-vous?'* in the Quarter but not for long; wander over to the levee and you'll see dozens of steamboats going by, big beautiful wedding cakes on the river, bringing thousands upon thousands of opportunistic American businessmen into the city, and with them, the English language and the despised Protestant religion.

"1853, shh...do you hear that? Everything is dead quiet. The only sounds are the rattle of the death carts passing every afternoon, and the occasional boom of cannons over the river, trying to clear the air of yellow fever. It's not working. Two-hundred people are dying every day, and the street there to your left is piled high with their rotting corpses. There just aren't enough gravediggers to handle them all, and it's weeks before they can all be buried.

"Ten years later, 1863. Civil War has broken out, and New Orleans, a slave-owning Confederate city, has been captured by the Union. Maybe you hear some Union soldiers coming this way, making their rounds, and maybe you'll notice the windows above me are opening, as the indignant women of the city prepare to pour water on them and hit them over the heads with frying pans. You'll also notice that the streets aren't running with raw sewage anymore because the Union General who runs the city, a fellow the locals call 'Beast' Butler, is the first person in New Orleans history to take any real sanitary measures around here.

"It's 1900 now, and there are sailors flooding this way from the docks toward Storyville, our brand new red light district. They're all laughing and drinking and flipping through their 'Blue Books,' 25 cents a pop, which tell them the names and addresses of every woman working in that notorious haven of vice."

"Hey, where can I get one of those?" the annoying father interjected, chuckling.

"If we could save all questions for the end," Jeremy said with a scowl. His patience with this man was wearing *very* thin.

"1918. It's getting dark and everybody, especially the Italian grocers, are hurrying to get home and lock their doors. The city's in a panic because the Axeman still hasn't been caught. Rumor has it, he won't butcher anyone who's enjoying jazz tonight, and so all the musicians around town are getting ready to settle in and start playing. Ah—" he said, as a clarinetist down the street played a long, high note; it was nice when the timing worked out like this. "You can hear them warming up now." The crowd tittered and grinned, their eyes alight with excitement.

"And that's only the first two hundred years. All of that, all of that and more, transpiring right here in this very spot where we're standing. This spot—this corner—has witnessed three hundred years of death. Three hundred years of debauchery, three hundred years of disease, three hundred years of disorder. But you know what else this spot has witnessed in all that time? Exultation. Curiosity. A unique culture influenced by France, Spain, the Caribbean, and Latin America. And an indomitable human spirit unparalleled anywhere else in the United States of America, if you want my opinion, and I promise you do. My name is Jeremy, and I'll be your storyteller tonight."

Applause. He took a bow. "Let's get started," he said, turning sharply down the alley to lead them away.

"Storyville, huh?" The insufferable middle-aged man had somehow appeared at Jeremy's side, his sunglasses bouncing off his chest on a strap. "So, is that where the House of the Rising Sun was?"

Jeremy looked at him. He was the epitome of middle America mediocrity, indistinguishable from all the other hundreds of thousands of bland, aging white men across the country.

"You know, the song?" The man began to sing. *"There issss a houuuuse in*

New Or-leeeeens—"

"I've heard the song. And to answer your question, it wasn't a real place."

"Are you sure? A guy I knew came to visit New Or-leens and said he saw it, maybe over there in Storyville where you were talking about—"

"Storyville doesn't exist anymore; it was shut down in 1917. And 'The House of the Rising Sun' was adapted from a folk ballad that originated in England in the sixteenth century."

"Well, how about that! Learn something new every day. Honey, the House of the Rising Sun was in England," he said, turning to his wife who was walking a few paces behind.

"England?" Jeremy heard her say. "Then how come the song says New Or-leens?"

Jeremy rolled his eyes and sped up, but the man kept pace. "So how long have you been doing this?"

Suffering fools like you? "Two decades or so."

"Wow. And they still make you wear that get-up?"

Jeremy felt his cheeks go hot. He didn't answer.

"The little vampire teeth, that's a nice touch, though. Amanda, what do you say I get some of those? Wear them to work, give Gene a good scare? Maybe then I could get that promotion."

"Shut up, dad," one of the teenagers teased. *Yes, please. Shut up.*

"So how much will a pair of those run you, those little caps?"

"They're not caps."

"Oh, haha, of course. Because you're a real vampire."

"They are my teeth," he said quietly. "And if you doubt their veracity, I'll be happy to take you around the corner and demonstrate."

The dad threw his hands up. "Woah! Alright, no more lip from me!" He turned to his children and grinned. "Isn't this guy great? What's your name again?"

"Jeremy."

"I'm Bob. And this is my wife, Jess, and our two little hellspawn, Sean and Amanda."

"Dad…"

"I embarrass them."

You embarrass yourself.

The man continued to be a pain in the ass for the next several stories. He tickled his children's necks during the scary parts, interjected nonsense, and talked Jeremy's ear off on the walks between stops. At the bar break, Jeremy ducked around the corner to get away, but Bob managed to find him a few minutes later, double-fisting Voodoo daiquiris. Just looking at the purple sludge in those styrofoam cups made Jeremy feel nauseous; the Voodoo daiquiri was basically just frozen grape kool-aid mixed with so much booze and corn syrup that you'd get a sugar rush, brain freeze, and sudden onset tipsiness all at the same time.

"One for me, one for the wife," he said, laughing at the disdain on Jeremy's face. "Don't worry, I'm not that much of a drunk."

"I don't care what you are."

"That's the nice thing about New Or-leens, huh? You can really cut loose."

"Mmm."

"So, you from here?"

"More or less."

"Great city. Don't think I could live here, though." *Good. We don't want you to.*

He took a sip of his daiquiri. "But a great place to visit. The family's enjoying it."

Jeremy said nothing, hoping his silence would drive the man away.

"You got kids?"

He shook his head.

"Married?"

"No."

"Well, I'm sure the right one's out there for you somewhere. You'll find her."

"I'm not actually looking."

"Not looking? You don't want somebody to settle down with, take care of you in your old age and all that?"

Jeremy stared at the man as coldly he could manage without being downright malevolent.

"Hey, I'm just saying. I mean, who doesn't love the bachelor lifestyle and all that, but when you get to be our age...you have to start thinking about these things. Who's going to be by your side when things start to go downhill?"

Our age?

"It's time to get back to the tour."

Jeremy strode away across the street to where the rest of the group were gathering, and Bob hurried after him, trying not to spill his daiquiris. "We're loving the tour, by the way. Really fun stuff."

The rest of the evening went slightly better, with fewer interjections from the horrible man. The other tour guests, Jeremy noticed, were generally acceptable people, all interested and well-behaved. Some of them, he was sure, had specifically requested that he be their guide.

Jeremy's last stop was at the corner of Ursulines and Royal, at the shadowy house there on the corner. It was two stories tall, red brick, with tall windows and an elaborate wrought-iron balcony, fat ferns hanging from its upper levels. The house had looked the same as long as Jeremy could remember, though it had changed hands several times, different furniture appearing from time to time through the gaps in the drapes.

"Ladies and gentlemen, gather close," he said quietly. They edged to the front of the curb, glancing with interest between Jeremy and the house across the street.

"Our last story begins not in New Orleans, but in Paris, in the 1700s, in the Court of King Louis the Fifteenth. The King surrounds himself with the most prominent men of the age: nobles, artists, the *crème de la crème* of society, both in France and abroad. He hosts grand balls, feasts and fêtes, and always in attendance is one of the King's most popular courtiers, the *Comte de Saint Germain*. The Comte—the Count, we'll call him—is a fascinating figure. He is a tall man, quite distinctive-looking, with an unmistakably leftward-slanting nose. He's incredibly well-versed in art, literature, even the sciences; he plays multiple instruments, speaks multiple languages; he can converse intelligently on topics from astronomy to philosophy to alchemy. The Count is also incredibly wealthy, so wealthy, in fact, that he carries loose rubies in the pockets of his coat. No one knows his exact origins, but he is rumored to be the son of Francis II Rákóczi, the Prince of Transylvania."

Titters from the group. They always loved the bit about Transylvania, the simpletons.

"The Count St. Germain is, in fact, a bit of a celebrity in European court life. Those who know the Count long to renew the fascinating conversations they've all had with him, and those who have never met him are eager to. Yes, if you're a nobleman in Europe in the mid 1700s, the Count St. Germain is the one you want at your table. Yet although the Count graces the dinners of many dukes and even kings, he is never seen to eat even a morsel. Instead, he carries constantly in his hand a glass of deep red wine, from which he often sips."

More knowing titters. How clever they all thought they were, for picking up on these ridiculously obvious clues.

"After a time, however, the Count St. Germain grows tired of court life. He moves to a quiet part of Germany, where it is reported that he dies. However, many people around Europe claim to have seen him years after his supposed death."

"New Orleans, 1902. A man named Jacques St. Germain moves to the Crescent City, to this home. He claims to be a descendent of the popular Count, to whom he bears a striking resemblance, with the same leftward slanting nose. Like his ancestor, he enjoys high society, attends all the social affairs, and drinks plenty of wine. However, he never eats in public, claiming to adhere to a strict—and secret—diet.

"Jacques is a ladies man and is always in the company of one woman or another. He loves women, enjoys them...one could even say, he craves them. One evening, Jacques brings a beautiful young lady here to his dwelling. She is amazed at the opulence of the home, the beautiful curios and antiques everywhere, the plush rugs and delicate heirlooms. He invites her several times to his bedchamber, but she refuses, continuing to wander the house and admiring its beauty. On the second floor, she is entranced by a beautiful marble mantlepiece. Transfixed, mesmerized, she feels compelled to put her cheek on it, to feel its cold smoothness—and when she does, suddenly Jacques is behind her, having moved more swiftly across the room from the stair than any human should be able to. His arms are entwined around her body, and she feels a sudden hotness on her neck, an intoxicating pain, and she realizes that this man must be drinking her blood.

"She gives in for a moment, submitting to his caress, losing herself as he drains her life force. But then she comes to her senses. She wrestles away from him, dashes across the room and leaps from the second-floor window to the street below. If you'll look, you'll see the window is still bricked over. A common practice in the old days: you'd seal a window where evil got out, to make sure it didn't get back in. The woman breaks her leg in the fall and loses consciousness, and she is brought to Charity Hospital. She dies that night, but not before telling the police what Jacques did to her.

"But by the time the police arrive at Royal Street to ask the gentleman some questions, Jacques has vanished. When they go into the house to investigate, they notice the odd placement of the home's rugs—never centered in a room, often at strange angles—and they lift these rugs to reveal bloodstains of various ages and sizes. In the kitchen, they find no food or utensils, but there is a well-stocked wine rack. Upon examination, they find that these bottles are filled not with wine, but..."

Jeremy opened his palms to the group, inviting their answer. "Blood," they murmured. He nodded.

"And so, of course, it was decided that Jacques St. Germain was a vampire. But what makes a vampire? Is it immortality? A craving for human blood?

"No, my friends. You see, a true vampire is much more complex than that. He is the manifestation of that age-old tension between social mores and human longing, that ever-present need to flout convention in favor of the taboo, to turn away from the goodness of light in order to seek the thrills of darkness. From a literary perspective, the vampire has always been a metaphor for the things we find it hard to talk about: for humanity's relationship with death, which both attracts and repels us, and for human sexuality, which is both the lowest and highest of human pursuits. Sex makes us animals, but sex also elevates us to the divine; sex is death, and yet sex is eternal life.

"The Vampire is all of these contradictions wrapped together into one beautiful, dangerous, compelling package: someone more connected to the divine energies, that eternal tension between life and death. And more than anything else, the defining trait of a vampire is his need for human energy. He does not produce enough of his own, and so he must take it from others—through blood, perhaps, or in a more subtle way. There are many ways in which human beings create and release energy, and a vampire need not necessarily shed blood or cause harm to capture it. If a vampire's victim is willing, this exchange of energy—this divine gift—can be fulfilling for both parties." He always smiled mysteriously at this line and made eyes at any attractive women on the tour. Tonight, there were none.

"So. Perhaps Jacques St. Germain invited this woman to his home with no intention of drinking her blood. Perhaps he wanted to share her life force in a different way, a way that could have brought pleasure and exultation to them both. And perhaps it was only when she refused his invitation that he felt compelled to feed more forcefully. A vampire's need is real, and it is strong. And woe be to the mortal who stands in his way.

"Jacques St. Germain was never seen or heard from again after that night. Not officially, anyway." Jeremy leaned in close and did the creepy thing with his eyes that always got the group aflutter. "But on several occasions in the last fifty years, people around the French Quarter have reported meeting a man with a leftward-slanting nose, usually in some dark alley or other, who wears all black even in the heat of summer and moves just a little more quickly than a human should be able to. You see, the French Quarter still abounds with vampires. And you never know when you might meet one. Ladies and gentlemen…thank you, and goodnight."

He collected their tips, made the pleasantries that were expected of him. The middle-aged father handed him a five-dollar bill, presenting it with great pomp.

"You earned this. We had a lot of fun."

"Bless your heart," said Jeremy, using the syrupy-sweet pleasantry understood by Southerners to mean "fuck you." The man was oblivious.

"So how do we get to Cafe du Monde?"

Jeremy gave them directions, yearning for the moment the interaction would end. Finally, they left, wandering slowly down Ursulines like a group of lost ducks. He watched them go, vitriol coursing through him, hating the man and his family and everything they represented. Jeremy knew he was a joke to them, nothing more than a bit of entertainment between an overpriced seafood dinner and an hour or two on Frenchmen Street pretending to appreciate jazz. Their auras were beige, and their energy was dull, and he wished they would die, all of them, die and leave him alone in his dark, rare city. But then he wouldn't be able to make a living, would he? He needed their money, the ugliest of all needs, and he hated them for it.

Jeremy considered going directly home. But there was a restlessness in him that he knew would drive him mad alone in his chambers, and so he decided to wander the streets of the Quarter. He walked aimlessly, down Dumaine and then Chartres, overhearing bits of insipid conversation outside the bars. How pointless humanity was. Just simple sacks of flesh, all of them, driven by the same two or three desires wrapped in needlessly complicated packages. Food, sex, meaning. It's all any of them wanted, but how difficult it was to acknowledge, how difficult to see past all the other nonsense they'd been told had to matter. They came all the way to New Orleans to do just that, poisoning themselves with liquor until the pretense all fell away and they could see their true hunger. Feed themselves.

He was in Jackson Square now, empty of the buskers and fortune tellers who sprouted like pimples from its flagstones during the day. It was cold, and clouds were passing swiftly through the night sky. Jeremy felt a buzzing to his right, a slight magnetic pull in the direction of Père Antoine alley. Down at the end of it, near Royal Street where he always started his tour, he saw another tour group huddled. He made his way quietly toward them, wondering what the pull could be, and looked at his pocket-watch: 10:05. The tour was going late, past the 10:00 cut-off imposed by the city. As he drew nearer, he realized the group belonged to the blue-haired girl.

"*Michie,*" she was murmuring in a decent French accent, her sad eyes pleading. "*I do not know what else to do except beg. I swear I will not ask you for anything else, as long as I live—*"

Ah, yes. "Michie and Julie." It had been ages since Jeremy had told this story—he'd never quite been able to deliver it correctly—but clearly this wasn't a problem for the blue-haired girl. She was lost in it, her energy churning with real longing and pathos. It was intoxicating to witness, and he knew her group could feel it too. They were as swept up in the story as she was, their auras all shifting slightly toward the same hue. Jeremy hadn't seen this phenomenon often; there had to be a true converging of psyches, a deep group experience that leveled everyone's different energetic wavelengths into the same frequency. He'd seen it happen on Mardi Gras day, and every so often within his own tour groups. But never in another guide's. He was impressed.

"And that's the end of the tour!" she exclaimed at the end of the story, breaking the spell. The group applauded, and she beamed at them as they handed her their tips. Jeremy watched for the exact moment that she noticed him there, the flicker of surprise across her face. He stepped toward her after the last of the group had gone.

"Not bad," he said quietly.

"You were watching?"

"Just the end."

"It's my favorite story."

"I can tell. A little correction, though—if you don't mind."

"Oh, not at all."

"Michie?"

"Yeah?"

"That wasn't his name. *Michie* is a shortening of the word *Monsieur*."

"Like a pet name?"

"Something like that."

"What was his real name?"

"We don't know."

"Okay, cool, that's good to know. Thanks." He could tell she was a little apprehensive and didn't understand why he was talking to her. Her nervous energy made him hungry.

"Sofia, is it?"

"Yeah."

"Would you like to have a drink with me, Sofia? I have a few other pointers I could share with you."

Her big brown eyes widened. "Sure, that would be great. I'm always trying to get better."

"Let's go."

"Now?"

"Do you have somewhere else to be?"

"I guess not."

"Follow me, then."

He walked her to a bar on St. Philip, where he knew there wouldn't be any other tour guides hanging around. "What would you like?" he asked when they had settled in.

"What are you having?"

"Wine. Red."

"I'll have a glass too, then."

He looked at her silently for a moment, toying with her discomfort. "So," he said finally. "How long have you been working for Spirits of Yore now?"

"Um, six months or so?"

"And you're enjoying it?"

"Yeah, yeah. I was a waitress before but this is way better."

"You have talent."

"You think so?"

He looked her up and down. She was wearing knee-high black boots with a tight black skirt and a purple peacoat, her slender neck bound by a tight lacy choker. The effect was very appealing.

"You're a good storyteller. You've got the charisma…the style…I've noticed you."

"I didn't think you even knew who I was."

"You're hard to miss with that blue hair." He reached out and tucked a strand behind her ear.

"Oh, yeah. It changes color a lot." She blushed and took a sip of her wine. "So, you said you had some pointers and stuff?"

"Just a few things, if you'd like to hear them."

"Yeah, definitely."

He made up some advice about the best order for the stories, suggested a different tip line, pointed out a few historical inaccuracies in her Julie story. It was nothing important, really, though she listened eagerly. She drank her wine quickly, swallowing it in rapid little gulps, and Jeremy could feel her nervousness slipping away. He ordered her another glass.

"You must know, like, everything about the Quarter," she said. "Doing this as long as you have."

"I've seen some things, yes."

"How old are you, anyway?" she asked.

There was a number, and he knew the number, though he tried to keep it sequestered in the remotest part of his consciousness.

"Three hundred or so," he said, smirking playfully. She laughed.

"Three hundred, huh? So, you're the same age as New Orleans."

"Yes, that's right."

"Are you a real vampire?" she giggled.

He smiled mysteriously. "I'm enjoying your company," he said, too quietly for her to hear. This was how he had always done it: draw them in with his deep, chocolatey whispers, make them strain to hear. "What?" she asked, leaning in close.

"I said, I'm enjoying your company," he repeated, his lips inches from her ear.

"Oh. Um. Thanks. Me too."

"You're very beautiful."

"Thanks."

"And so young. There's so much you haven't experienced."

"Like what?"

"Like New Orleans."

"I grew up here.

"I mean, the *real* New Orleans. The New Orleans that only comes alive at night."

"What do you mean?"

"Let's go to the cemetery."

"What?"

"You heard me. I know a way in."

The girl smiled. "Some other time, maybe. I should probably get going."

"Don't go," he said, more bluntly than he meant to.

"Nah, I should. It's getting late. I'm gonna pee and then head out." She got up and made her way to the back of the bar.

What a waste of time this had turned out to be. Jeremy stood and pulled on his coat, looking around at the near-empty bar and glowering at the few people in it.

He shoved his hands into the pockets of his coat, feeling a square lump under his right hand—Poppy's soap, of course. He rolled his eyes. There was something in the other pocket too, though, a tiny, hard nugget. When he pulled it out, he realized it was half a little oval pill. He peered at it in his palm, trying to make out its letters. *AMB*. Yes, the other night, he'd taken a walk and brought the pill with him, swallowed half of it over by river so that by the time he got back to the apartment, the medicine would already be stroking his neurons into submission. And it had worked; his surroundings had gone soft and meaningless in no more than twenty minutes, and he didn't even remember his head hitting the pillow that night.

He took his coat off and sat back down, wrapping his pinky around the stem of the girl's wine glass and pulling it an inch or two closer to him. He crushed the pill against his thumbnail and brushed the dust in.

Sofia returned from the restroom, tightening the sash of her coat like she was ready to leave. "Have you been here before?" he asked, trying to get the conversation going again.

"This bar? No. Usually I just hang out at the Quarter Rat with everybody else."

"It's nice to have a change of scenery every once in a while, isn't it?"

"Oh, definitely. This was nice. Thanks so much for your advice about the tour."

He gestured at her glass. "You didn't finish your wine."

"Oh. Yeah, guess I didn't." She drank down its dregs. He watched her face, but she gave no indication that she noticed anything wrong with it.

"Would you like another?"

"No, that's okay."

"But surely, you'll stay while I finish mine."

"Oh," she said, her face flashing with embarrassment. "Sure, of course." She sat, and he watched her closely as they made small talk for another few minutes. After a little while, her attention began to drift, and she put her head in her hands.

"Are you alright?" Jeremy asked.

"Yeah—I'm just feeling kind of weird."

"Drank too much?"

"I mean, I only had two glasses of wine, but I guess I didn't eat dinner..."

"Poor thing," he purred.

"I need to go home," she said, tripping a little as she got off the stool.

"You shouldn't drive if you're feeling tipsy."

"I have my bike."

"That's even more dangerous. You could get hurt."

"Let me call Vik, then." She began to slowly rummage in her bag for her phone.

"Here," he said, pulling out his flip phone. "Use mine."

She took it, and he watched as she painstakingly punched in the number and hit the call button. She didn't notice that the phone had no signal. The thing rarely worked indoors.

"He's not—it's not working."

"He's not answering? He must be busy."

"He's—he went to the parade with James..."

"Hmmm. Probably can't hear his phone ring, then."

"He always ignores me."

"I can't imagine why. You're the most perfect creature I've ever seen," Jeremy whispered in her ear.

She pulled away. "I feel so weird. I gotta...go home."

"I'll drive you."

"You will?"

"Of course." Jeremy tossed some money on the bar and helped Sofia out to the curb. They began to walk, and he slipped his arm around her waist. She leaned on him, unsteady, dragging her feet.

"I don't know why I feel so weird," she muttered. He pulled her more tightly to him, and she quieted, her eyes slowly opening and closing as they made their way up to Rampart Street.

"Your car is close?" she said after a minute.

He didn't have a car. "Yes. But first we're going to take a little detour."

"De...detour? Where?"

"There's something I want to show you."

A few blocks later, they arrived at the gates of St. Louis Cemetery #1, its high white walls stretching away down the block in either direction. Jeremy took out his tools and picked the lock, looking over his shoulder for police or security guards. But the street behind them was empty, and the gate opened easily. He took Sofia's shoulders and steered her inside.

Tombs rose up around them, their ghostly white shapes barely visible in the darkness. There was no light in the cemetery, and Jeremy could hardly see the girl next to him. But he could feel her presence, her warm energy pulsating in the dark, sleepiness and innocence and confusion saturating her aura.

"I don't think we should be in here," she slurred.

"I told you, I have something to show you."

"I want to go home."

"Soon, *cherie*. Come this way." He took her by the hand and led her through a maze of tombs toward the back of the cemetery, his fingers brushing the gris-gris dangling at his side as they walked.

"It's so dark," Sofia said.

"Shhh. You'll wake the dead."

"Where are we going?"

He hadn't done this in a while. He hoped he would be able to find it. But sure enough, there in the middle-back near a crumbling section of wall vaults, the tomb he was looking for materialized. It was a standard-sized family vault, but the marble faceplate was broken in several pieces and lay at the foot of the tomb, waiting for a repair that had never been done.

"Look," he said to Sofia.

"Look at what?"

"There." He gestured to the marble plate on the ground.

"I can't read it."

Jeremy lit a match and knelt to illuminate it.

"*J. Trosclair,*" she read, fluently pronouncing the French. "*Née 1718, décédés 1746.*"

"Good."

"Who is it?"

He leaned in and nuzzled her hair, whispered softly in her ear. "Me."

"What?"

"Born 1718. Three hundred years ago."

"And so you—you died? And became a vampire." She spoke slowly, dreamily.

"Yes, my love," he hissed, delicately cupping her face in his hand.

"And those are...real?" She reached out tentatively to touch his fangs.

"Go ahead." She put her thumb up to one of their points and he bit down. She gasped as a tiny bubble of blood sprang from its tip.

"You really drink blood?" she said, her energy suddenly saturated with fear.

"No, *cherie*," he said gently. "I'm not that kind of vampire."

"What kind, then?"

"A tantric vampire," he whispered, pulling her close. It wasn't often that he said the words aloud.

"What does that mean?"

Her energy was electric, almost hot to the touch, drowsy with the drug but charged with fear and sex. Jeremy buried his face in her neck, kissing her, running his tongue along the top of her choker, gathering a handful of her skirt in his fist. He hadn't fed in weeks, and he was terribly hungry, perhaps hungrier than he'd ever been.

"It means I need you," he moaned, drinking in her scent, his hands exploring her body, her little waist, her wide hips.

"No," she was saying, trying to push him away. "No."

"Just give in, my angel. Let me taste you."

"No!" She continued to fight, more lucidly now.

"You have no idea the things I can show you—"

"Get off me!" she slurred, yelling.

Jeremy was getting angry now, why hadn't it worked, the thing with the tomb had *always* worked, he shouldn't even *need* the Ambien, who did this stuck-up little bitch think she was—he pulled her skirt up, grabbed a handful of her ass, reached down to unbutton his pants—and then he felt a sharp pain, a sudden hot burst in his neck. He let go of the girl for a moment, and she was running, disappearing, gone around a corner. He put his hand to his neck and felt blood there.

The whore had bitten him with that mouthful of mangled teeth. And there was no chance of catching up with her now, not in the dark, not in this maze.

Jeremy turned to J. Trosclair and kicked at his tomb. Who had he been? A nobody, surely. Alive for thirty short years and then extinguished, dead and buried like every other person who'd ever lived and every person who ever would.

He yanked the gris-gris from his belt and cast it onto the ground, grinding it into the dirt with his boot. Poppy's words rang in his mind. *You can't escape it unless you can embrace it.*

It was a long, cold walk home.

Elijah was in the living room when he returned to the apartment, reading a magazine with his booted feet up on the coffee table.

"I swear to God, the next time you put your feet on my antiques..." Jeremy growled. Elijah took his feet down. "Hey, man, what happened to you?" he asked, noticing Jeremy's hand on his neck. "You're bleeding."

Jeremy went to his bedchamber and slammed the door. It was dark, and there was a chilly breeze coming in from the window he'd left open. He closed it and touched a match to the wicks of a candelabra on his vanity, the little flames springing to life twofold in the reflection of the mirror. Jeremy sat and looked at himself, at the blood trickling down the sagging skin of his neck. His hair was stringy, his chin mushy and soft, his eyes ringed in fine, dark lines. It was the reflection of a man he didn't know. A reflection he wasn't even supposed to have.

Jeremy picked up the candelabra and heaved it at the mirror. The room went dark with the sound of breaking glass.

CHAPTER 12

The Other Side

Tonight's post-tour tableau: Poppy, alone at a hi-top table, drinking. Ruby and Ralphie at one of the other hi-tops, talking. And me, of course, over here in the corner, unnoticed by everyone.

The equilibrium is disrupted when Veda comes rushing in from the street through the bar, face pale, eyes wide. She looks frightened. Ruby and Ralphie are too engrossed in their conversation to notice, but Poppy beckons her over.

"You alright? What's the matter?"

Veda, looking relieved to have somewhere to go, sits across from Poppy. She's still practically hyperventilating.

"Come on, breathe," Poppy says, reaching out to take Veda's hand. "Deep breaths in, out. There ya go. Come on, girl, just breathe. You okay?"

Veda gulps and nods as she calms down a little. "I'm sorry."

"Don't be sorry, we all go through shit. What happened?"

"I just get really freaked out on tour sometimes," she says quietly.

"How come? Somebody do something to you, a heckler? You gotta learn to just ignore that stuff, you—"

Veda shakes her head. "It's not that."

"What, then?"

"I see them."

"Who?"

Veda's voiced wavered. "The people in the stories."

Poppy's brow furrows. "You see them? Like, actually see them?"

"Like Leah, the girl at the LaLaurie Mansion. Every night she—falls, and—and the—the slaves, and—I've tried helping them move on, but they don't want to go, they can't go, not with us bringing people there every night, talking about them, making a spectacle of their deaths, you know, and they're *angry*, some of them are so angry—"

"Shh, shh," Poppy says. "Slow down. Breathe."

Veda's close to tears. "I don't know if I can do it anymore. Every single night..."

"Do they talk to you?" Poppy asks.

"Sometimes."

Poppy leans forward and takes Veda's hands.

"That's it. That's your gift. The Knight of Cups, remember?"

"It doesn't feel like a gift," she says. "It feels like a curse."

"It's a gift. If I could...if I had your power," Poppy says.

"You don't want it."

"Of course I do!" Poppy cries, and Veda looks up at her with alarm.

"I'm sorry."

Veda studies Poppy's face. "There's someone you want to talk to, isn't there?" she says. "Someone dead."

Poppy looks away. "I can't reach her. I can never reach her, ever, not in seventeen years," she says, and the way she says it is so small, so vulnerable, that I'm sure she's never told this to anyone else.

"You've tried?"

"Almost every day. Scrivening, tarot, spells...none of it works."

"Well...some spirits are just harder to reach than others."

They're quiet for a few moments, and my attention wanders to Ralphie and Ruby over at the table closest to the door. They're talking quietly, maybe more quietly than I should be able to hear, but I can pick it up anyway. Lately, I seem to know everything that's going on in this bar without even trying.

"I guess I've never really told you what happened," Ruby is saying. "Veda knows, but that's it."

"I mean, I had some guesses...did he cheat on you?"

She takes a deep breath and shakes her head. "Way worse than that."

"Oh shit..."

"It happened last October. It was like six AM, and there was this pounding on the door. It was fucking scary, I mean, we both sat up in bed, I thought it was a break-in or something. So, he went to open it, and I stayed in bed, but then there were all these voices yelling, 'Is there anyone else in the house, get in here, hurry up and get in here!' so I ran in there, and there were like four guys at the door, and they had guns. Big guns, you know, like big semi-automatics, pointed at us. And all their clothes said 'FBI.'"

Ralphie whistles long and low.

"Have you ever had a gun pointed at you?" she asks.

He shakes his head, and I can tell he's picturing it in vivid detail, putting himself at the scene.

"It's fucking scary. You automatically put your hands up; it's like an instinct,

I guess from watching movies or whatever. So, they handcuffed both of us and took us outside to the sidewalk, and we just stood there for like twenty minutes while they went in the house. And I'm like racking my brain, you know, what did I *do*, why are we in trouble? And the only thing I could think of was Brian knew how to use the deep web, and he'd bought some acid on there. It was in a band-aid container in the bathroom; I was sure they'd find it and we'd both go to jail."

"Wait—I thought Brian didn't do drugs? Didn't he always give you shit just for smoking weed?"

"Uh, spoiler alert, Brian's a terrible person and a huge fucking hypocrite. Anyway. After a little while, they took him to the backyard to ask him questions, and they took me up to the porch and sat me down. And finally took my handcuffs off, thank God. Being handcuffed is not fun."

"I bet."

"And this FBI agent had someone go inside and get a blanket, and he put it over my shoulders. It was cold, you know, and I was just in my sleep shorts and a t-shirt, and I was barefoot…and he sat down and looked at me. And asked me if I knew what child porn was."

"Jesus Christ!" Ralphie exclaims, standing suddenly. "*Child porn?*"

"And I was so relieved, you know, because then I knew it had all been a big mistake, just a mix-up, because Brian would never…"

By the way her shoulders are moving, I'm pretty sure Ruby is crying. "Hey, hey," Ralphie says, and reaches out to touch her arm.

"They took his computer to search it. Then they left."

"They didn't arrest him?"

She shakes her head. "No, they didn't find anything right away because he had deleted it. They only knew his IP address had accessed it or something."

"So wait, did he…I mean, did he do it?"

"Yep. Confessed to all of it," she says. "He said he started back when we were still in college. Stumbled across it or something and then got addicted."

Ralphie's mouth is hanging open as he sits again. "Jesus! Did he ever… touch a kid?"

"No. Swore up and down he didn't. But of course, there's no way to know for sure."

"Christ."

"I didn't know how to leave him, you know? He was basically my first boyfriend, and I thought I should try to…try to stay with him. He was in so much pain, and I still loved him, and he was really remorseful at first, really really sorry. Started going to therapy and all that. But then…" Ruby wipes her nose. "Then he changed. He couldn't handle it, stopped taking responsibility."

"What do you mean?"

"After like a month, he started getting really mad at me for being upset. He said it was preventing him from healing."

"Preventing *him* from healing?"

She nods. "And then eventually he started blaming me. He said I drove him to it."

"What the fuck?"

"He said I didn't have sex with him enough."

Ralphie stands again. "This fuckin' guy! Where is he? I'll fuckin'—"

Ruby shrugs. "It's pointless, I'm telling you. There's no justice in this world."

"And he didn't go to jail?"

"Nope. They never prosecuted him. He covered his tracks well enough that they couldn't find enough evidence, I guess. Gave his computer back a few months later, and he just moved on with his life. No consequences."

"Well, I mean, he lost you. That's kind of a big one."

"He doesn't care."

"I'm sure he does."

"He doesn't care about *anything*, he's a sociopath, but me—I mean, I lost six fucking years of my life!"

"But at least you're not still with him! You had the courage to do it, to leave him—"

"Yeah," she says dully. "And look how fucking great I'm doing."

"You're doing fine," Ralphie says, unconvincingly.

"I thought if I just tried hard enough, I could be happy and not care and just move on, but…things are really bad." She starts to cry. "I got…I mean, someone..."

"Someone what?"

"Date raped me. The other night."

"What! Who? Oh my God!"

"I don't know who he was."

"Did you go to the police?"

Ruby shakes her head. "It wouldn't do any good. Men never get held accountable for the shit they do to women."

"Jesus."

"I feel like I'm just being punished, like the universe hates me or something…I wanna just give up."

"Please don't," Ralphie says. "Let me be there for you."

She sniffles and shrugs.

"I, uh..." he continues. "You know, it really kills me that me and Kat weren't talking before it happened. I would do anything to be able to go back and be a better friend."

"You *were* a good friend," Ruby says.

It's true, he was. I'll never forget how pale he got when he saw the cuts on my legs, and how hard he tried to keep smiling and cracking jokes even though he looked about ready to pass out. He was the only one of them who came to visit me at the hospital then, when I was on psych watch. To be fair, though, he may have been the only one who knew. It's not something I really broadcasted, these weird inner demons of mine. And after I got out of the hospital, I pretended like everything was fine.

I wish I hadn't. Turns out everyone else has them too.

"I miss her like fuckin' crazy. Sometimes I don't know how to even get through the day."

"Yeah."

"Can I ask you something?" Ralphie says.

"Sure."

"Why did you want to tell me all this?"

Ruby shrugs. "I guess because...because out of everyone I know, you're the only one who drunk-texts me in the middle of the night to tell me you care about me."

Ralphie smiles sweetly and looks down. "Yeah, well, y'know. I do."

Ruby reaches out and takes his hand, and they sit there like that for a minute, not saying anything.

I look back to Veda and Poppy.

Veda is shaking her head. "I don't know...it's not that easy. I can put out the invitation, but I never know who will respond."

"Here," Poppy says, reaching into her bag and pulling out an old worn Minnie Mouse doll. "Here, this was hers."

"It's just not that easy..."

"And when I do it, I think of things about her," Poppy says with urgency. "Y'know, things she liked or... she loved *101 Dalmatians*. And Spongebob. And her cat, Emmie loved cats, she had a kitten named Snowball, so maybe if you concentrate on those things, you can...y'know...maybe she'll come."

Veda looks like she's about to protest more but instead just sighs in resignation and closes her eyes. Her lips part. Slowly, over the next minute, her posture begins to change, and she sits up straighter than before, chest pushed slightly forward. Her breathing slows. Poppy watches all this intently, searching Veda's face. Soon, Veda's lips start to move, ever so slightly, as if she's whispering to someone. This goes on for a minute or two. Then the movement ceases, and she opens her eyes.

Poppy draws a sharp intake of breath, her eyes glued to Veda's face. Ralphie is watching too, eyeing them from the other table as he and Ruby talk.

"Was your daughter on the heavier side?" Veda asks.

"Yes," Poppy says eagerly. "Yes, she was a big girl."

"And did she have a…some sort of handicap?"

"Yes, yes, she had Down's, yes! Did she come to you? Did you see her?"

"I think so."

"Oh my God," Poppy says, tears springing to her eyes as she grabs Veda's hand. "Did she speak? What did she say?"

"She said she loves you very, very much."

"Oh, my baby girl. I love you too, I love you too," Poppy gushes. "Is she safe?"

"Very safe. And very comfortable."

"And does she understand that…that she's…you know?"

"Dead? Yes, she does."

"Does she understand that's the reason I can't…" Poppy starts to choke up. "...can't take care of her anymore?"

"Of course."

"Oh, thank Goddess. Thank Goddess. I just couldn't bear to think that…"

"In fact, she's not even in the spirit world. I had to call her from another plane of being entirely."

"So, she's not lingering here?"

"No," Veda says gently. "Not at all. She's right where she's supposed to be. She's happy."

There are fat tears running down Poppy's cheeks. "Did you tell her how much I love her?"

"She already knew. She said it's the one thing she could never, ever forget."

Poppy reaches across the table and pulls Veda into a tight hug. "You're an angel, Veda. An angel. Thank you, thank you, thank you," she splutters.

"I'm just glad I could help," Veda says.

Poppy wipes her eyes and stands. "I'd better get home," she says. "Snowball will want to know what you said about Emmie."

"Okay. Rest well," Veda says.

"You're an angel," Poppy says again, and squeezes Veda's shoulder on her way out of the courtyard.

And then she goes. I watch her leave, and for just a second—just a split second—I see her the way she must have looked twenty years ago. She was young once, beautiful and shiny-haired and lithe. I've never been able to picture it until now.

When she's gone, Ralphie looks meaningfully at Veda. "Wow," he says. "That was crazy."

"What?" Ruby asks. Her back was to them; she didn't see any of it.

"Um, Veda just talked to Poppy's dead daughter."

Veda blushes. "I—"

"Woah," Ruby says. "Seriously?"

Veda looks down.

"I mean, you did, didn't you? Can't you talk to ghosts or whatever?"

"Yes, I can."

"Holy shit," Ruby says.

"But I can't control who. I've never had that power."

"Ohhh," Ralphie says, slowly catching on. "You mean?"

"I had seen a picture," Veda says in a small voice.

"The one in her wallet, right?" Ruby asks, and Veda nods. "So, you were just…"

"I panicked, I just…she wanted my help so bad," Veda says desperately, apologetically.

"You did a good thing," Ruby says.

"You think so?"

"Yeah," Ralphie says. "You did."

"It's funny," Veda says. "Usually, it's the ghosts who need help moving on."

"We get it. Don't feel bad."

"Please don't tell anyone," Veda begs them.

"We won't. Scout's honor," Ralphie says, and holds up the Vulcan hand sign.

"Ralphie," Ruby laughs.

"What?"

"Never mind."

Ralphie smiles and looks between the two tired young women. "So. What now?"

"I dunno," Ruby says, rubbing her red eyes. "I'm exhausted."

"Yeah, you look like it. Maybe you should just go home and get some sleep."

"I can't."

"No?"

"I haven't slept more than a few hours a night since…God, I dunno. Probably last October."

"So, what do you do?"

"Wander around. Get drunk or take rolls. Sometimes when it's quiet like this, I just ride my bike for hours."

"That sounds lonely."

She shrugs. "Yeah. Sometimes."

"Why don't I stay up with you tonight?" Ralphie says.

"Yeah?"

He nods. "I've got nothing else to do. I'd probably just be at home having a dance party by myself."

"You have dance parties by yourself?"

"Oh, yeah. Turn out all the lights, blast some good music, get drunk..."

"That sounds fun."

"So, let's go have one now!"

"Seriously?"

"Why not? If we're gonna be up all night, we have time."

She smiles. "Yeah, I guess you're right. Let's go, then."

He stands, and she starts laughing.

"What? What is it?"

She's looking at his crotch. "What happened, Ralphie? Did you piss yourself?"

He looks down at a big dark blotch on his pants.

"Oh, right. That's beer."

"That looks like an *entire* beer."

"So, it's kind of a funny story..."

"Go on."

"So, you texted me, right? And asked me to meet you here."

"Yeah."

"And I was off tonight, so I was at a bar by my house. Well, I got your text, and I didn't want to waste any time, so I just sort of got a go-cup for my beer and started driving here."

"Yeah..."

"Well, on the way here, I got pulled over."

Ruby gasps.

"The cop's coming up to the car and I'm freaking out. I have a whole cup of beer in my hand. I don't know what to do, so I just toss it in the backseat."

"You *tossed* a full cup of beer into your backseat?"

"Yeah," Ralphie says, then shrugs. "And some of it spilled on me."

"Oh my God!" Ruby exclaims. "How are you sitting here right now, how did you not get a DUI?"

"Luck, I guess. The cop didn't notice anything. Turns out, he was just pulling me over for a broken taillight."

Ruby's jaw drops. "You lucky son of a bitch."

"Right?"

"You have to stop drinking and driving, Ralphie. You *have* to," Veda says from the other table.

"I know."

Ruby is getting fiery for the first time in a few days. "You should be ashamed of yourself. How could you?"

"Especially after—" Veda says.

He hangs his head. "—After what happened to Kat, I know. Believe me, I know."

"Promise you won't do it anymore," Ruby says to Ralphie.

"I promise."

"Swear it. Swear on Kat's grave."

And something comes into view, something that's been drifting around in the back of my mind for a while now, just out of reach of my consciousness. And now, all of a sudden, I come zooming up to it so fast I feel dizzy.

Ralphie looks at the ground for a few moments then back up at Ruby. "I swear it."

"I'm gonna hold you to that."

"Okay."

I'm glad someone will.

Ralphie takes a deep breath then smiles small and hopeful. "Still wanna have that dance party?"

"Yeah," Ruby sighs. "Okay."

"Good."

"But we're not gonna drink," she says sternly.

"At all?"

"No. No alcohol. We'll stop and get coffee instead."

"I don't like coffee. It tastes bad."

Ruby softens and rolls her eyes. "Oh Ralphie, you're such a manchild. How about hot chocolate, then?"

"I like hot chocolate!"

"Okay then. Veda, want to come?"

But before she can answer, there's a commotion. Someone's staggering through the door to the courtyard, and I realize it's Sofia, hair a mess, coat unbuttoned. She careens into a stool and collapses onto the table.

"Sofia? Jesus, what's going on?" Ruby says, going to her side. She's muttering incoherently.

"Is she okay?" Ralphie asks.

"I think she's really drunk or something. I've never seen her like this…"

"Something's wrong—I—I'm so tired," Sofia keeps muttering, the words falling unfinished out of her lolling mouth. She looks like she can barely stay awake.

"What happened?" Veda says, coming over.

"It's… he…"

I see Veda's face light up with alarm, and then she goes very pale. "Jeremy. Jeremy did something to her."

"Jeremy?" Ruby says. "What are you talking about?"

"He did this. I know it."

"Sofia, what happened?" Ruby asks again.

"Me…Jeremy…had a drink…"

"I dunno, guys, this doesn't seem like drunk to me," Ralphie says. "And I'm kind of an expert."

"He was…so nice…at first..."

Veda looks at Ruby, and I see the same scary thought flash across their faces. "Do you think…?" Ruby says.

"Think what?" Ralphie asks.

"He roofied her," Veda says darkly.

"No!" Ralphie exclaims. "I mean…you think? I know he's creepy and all, but…damn, he's not that kind of guy, is he?"

"I wouldn't put it past him."

"Sofia?" Ruby says, snapping her fingers in Sofia's face. "Hey, look at me. Did Jeremy hurt you?"

"We went…cemetery..."

"He took you to the cemetery?"

"He touched me…he tried...I bit him."

"Well, *that's* good!" Veda says.

"Ran away…"

"I think we need to get her to the hospital," Ruby says. "Ralphie, call an Uber."

"On it." He pulls out his phone.

Veda looks terrified. "I can't do hospitals."

"That's okay. We can take her," Ruby says.

"Vik…" Sofia murmurs.

"Do you have Vik's number?" Ruby asks Veda.

"I think so."

"Get ahold of him."

"Uber's two minutes away," Ralphie says.

"Okay. Let's get her out front." They scoop Sofia up, head lolling, feet dragging, and take her out of the courtyard.

Veda watches them go, looking upset, then starts digging through her bag. She pulls out a flip phone, scrolls through it, holds it up to her ear.

"Hi, this is Veda. Um, from work. Something bad happened to Sofia." She paces, a finger in her other ear. I get the feeling Veda doesn't use the phone much.

"Yeah, we think Jeremy did something to her. Like maybe tried to hurt her. Like maybe drugged her."

I can hear Vik swearing through the phone, demanding to know where she is.

"Um, the Quarter Rat. They're outside waiting for an Uber."

The line goes dead. Veda puts the phone away and takes a breath.

She notices me watching her.

"Hi," she says.

"Hi," I say.

"How did you know it was Jeremy?" I ask.

"Same way I know you're sitting there."

"Oh," I say, then pause. I'm afraid to ask it. "Do the others...not?"

But Veda doesn't answer because she's suddenly staring intently into the bar, looking distracted. I assume she hears someone coming in; probably Vik, maybe he was close by. But I see now that Veda's expression is more than just surprise. It's fear. She turns as if to dash past me into the bathroom, but a voice stops her.

"Is she here?"

Jeremy is there in the doorway. He looks awful, his hair falling in greasy strands in front of his face, his neck messy with clotted blood.

"What do you want?" Veda says, her voice wavering.

He takes a step forward. "I didn't want to hurt her. It wasn't supposed to happen like that."

"Don't come any closer."

"Is she here? I want to tell her I'm sorry. Please."

"Get away from me or I'll scream."

"Why are you afraid of me, Veda? I see you; you know I do. You're special, Veda. Just like me."

"You're not special. You're disgusting."

Jeremy's face gets very ugly and mean.

"Don't call me that." He's moving closer and closer to her, backing her up to the courtyard wall. "I didn't ask for this. I didn't ask to be like this!"

Veda screams, long and high-pitched. Jeremy, startled, lunges toward her. And then—it's all a blur; it happens so fast—someone is on top of Jeremy, tackling him, beating him down into the flagstones. Veda runs into the bathroom. I get a flash of Vik's furious face as he raises his fist to hit Jeremy again.

"You fucking piece of shit. What did you do to her? Did you rape her?"

"I tried."

Vik hits him again and again. They're both on the ground, Vik on top, but I realize Jeremy isn't hitting back. He's shielding his head from the blows, but he hasn't even tried to throw a punch at Vik. Some people from the bar have appeared in the doorway, and I hear one of them say something about calling the police.

Vik gets up, towering over Jeremy, who's on his hands and knees.

"Why don't you fight back, huh? Fight back! Coward!"

Jeremy lets a string of bloody saliva fall from his mouth. "You want to kill me, go ahead."

"What? I'm not gonna *kill* you," Vik spits. "You think I want to spend my life in prison over your sorry ass?"

"You don't know how lucky you are. To have..." Jeremy coughs up more blood, maybe a tooth. "...that girl. Sofia."

"Keep her name out of your fucking mouth."

"I've seen you. You take it for granted. Her, your looks, everything. But you'll be just like me someday."

"I'll never be like you."

Jeremy starts to laugh, his teeth pink and messy. "You will. Soon enough, I'll be dead, and you'll be me."

Blue lights are flashing from the street outside. Cops are always close in the Quarter. Staticky police-talk leaching from their shoulder radios, two officers heavy with guns and gear and handcuffs make their way back to the courtyard. Vik backs away from Jeremy as they approach, wiping blood from his knuckles onto his pants. Jeremy staggers to his feet.

"This man tried to rape my girlfriend," Vik says, pointing at him.

"Did you see what happened?" one of the cops, the female one, asks Veda, who's hovering in the doorway to the bathroom. "Who started the altercation?"

Veda, ashen-faced, doesn't answer.

"What's this about a rape?" the other asks.

"Her name is Sofia," Veda says, her voice barely more than a whisper. She points at Jeremy. "She said he tried to rape her. Our friends took her to the hospital."

"Know anything about this?" the cop asks Jeremy. He nods, then says quietly, "I committed a crime."

Vik raises an eyebrow, and the cops exchange a glance then go to Jeremy and handcuff him. "Alrighty then. Guess you're coming with us," one says.

"Do you know which hospital?" the other asks Veda, and she shakes her head.

The male cop mutters something into his radio, sounding tired. I wonder if cops ever don't sound tired. I'm starting to remember the ones who came for me now. They certainly did.

He takes Jeremy, limping, out to the street. I can see just a sliver of the squad car outside as he guides him into it.

"I'll need to ask you some questions," the other cop says to Vik.

"Can we go inside?" he asks, his voice unsteady. "I could really use a drink."

The cop shrugs and sighs and they go into the bar, leaving me alone in the courtyard.

And something feels terribly wrong. Something has felt wrong for weeks, months, but I couldn't put my finger on it until ten minutes ago. My mind is racing; I'm all keyed up…but there's no familiar *thump thump* in my chest, no tingly feeling of adrenaline in my blood, nothing. Why didn't I stand as they fought? Intervene, do something, say something?

Because I can't. I feel nothing. My body is just…nothing. Apart from the intermittent pain in my side, I've stopped feeling anything at all.

I look down. I see nothing but an empty chair and the dirty flagstones below, scattered with cigarette ash.

I suppose I'm not really here anymore.

CHAPTER 13

The Mistress of the Haunted House

For the birthday party, Veda was wearing a sheer black bodysuit, her pink shag coat, sparkly stripper heels, and her broken blue bug-eye sunglasses. For makeup, lots of glitter and some gold lipstick, and for accessories, a child's plastic purse and a tattered pink parasol she'd found in the trash on the abandoned lot down the street. She'd manifested the parasol; she could manifest anything. She just put the intention out into the universe, and whatever she needed would appear, usually on the street or in the trash, but sometimes in harder-to-find places.

It was a bright sunshiny morning, and the Dollhouse was full of people. That's what they called the shotgun house on St. Roch Avenue where they all lived, Veda and Albert and Razer on this side and Ricki and Agnes on the other. The house had been passed down through the queer and trans community for decades, and Veda had been invited to move in a few months ago. It was big and sloppy and wild, with old broken furniture hauled in from the curb and dirty dishes everywhere and a few chunks missing from the walls. It smelled like people and animals and sweat and food, and she loved it. Veda had painted the walls in her room twice since she'd arrived, first bubblegum pink and now lemon yellow, but she hadn't been very careful about it—no one was very careful about anything in the Dollhouse—and so the edges were sloppy, color spilling onto the floor and ceiling. After painting the walls, she'd started drawing on them and writing little bits of poetry around the door frames and tacking things up like magazine clippings and bits of fabric and some broken Christmas lights she'd found. She had an altar with candles and crystals and talismans, and a big rack where all of her clothes hung colorful and free, and a pile of notebooks and art supplies and do-dads and shoes and objects and dirty dishes and crusty laundry surrounding her bed. Veda's "nest," her housemates called it. She'd never had a whole room to herself before, and it still felt magical to be able to stretch out, make a mess, take up space.

Today was Veda's twentieth birthday, and she'd been going slow all morning, gazing at herself in the mirror a lot, picking up and looking at all her possessions, staring out the window. If anyone had asked her five years ago whether she'd live another year, let alone survive past eighteen, the answer would have been no. Survival had seemed impossible, then. But here she was. And it was going to be a good day.

"Veda, come out!" somebody called from the kitchen of the Dollhouse. All her housemates were gathered there, waiting for Veda to make her birthday appearance. She kissed herself in the mirror, leaving a gold pout on the glass, and fastened the straps of her sparkly platform heels. They were the wrong size, and she couldn't walk very fast in them, but they were too perfect not to wear. Veda's heart fluttered as she stood. Since it was a shotgun house, one room after another all in a line, Veda's bedroom led right into the kitchen. She opened the door a little and peeked through the crack until Razer caught sight of her and began to squeal. "Come out, come out!" they were all calling, and so Veda threw the door open and sashayed into the kitchen. They all began to clap.

"That outfit, oh my God!"

"You're wearing the stripper heels I gave you!"

"You look amazing. Happy birthday, my love," Razer said, and kissed her on the cheek. Razer always dressed so sleekly, usually in androgynous all black with crazy false lashes and metallic makeup. Veda was a little bit in love with Razer but in a platonic way. Sometimes they took baths together.

"Thanks," she said, blushing as she looked around at them all. Albert was there, out of bed for one of the first times since his top surgery; he still looked a little weak and cranky, as always, but he raised a hand in greeting. Agnes and Ricki were over by the stove cooking something, and Agnes' kid, Danse, was on the floor tugging at the neighborhood cat that sometimes came in. It was warm in the kitchen, stuffy with the smell of overripe fruit and their unwashed bodies and the bacon fat that had been coating their one frying pan since yesterday. There was lots of food on the table, a picked-over chicken and a bowl of strawberries and some greens that somebody had cooked. "You hungry?" Razer asked, waving away a cluster of flies that had settled on the chicken. "Or thirsty? Now that you're here, we can open the strawberry champagne."

"My favorite!"

"Alright, here we go," Agnes said, taking the bottle out of the fridge. She was tall and slender with beautiful long hair, completely confident in her body. She'd transitioned years ago. "Veda, want to do the honors?"

Veda grinned and nodded, holding the bottle away and squinting as she popped the cork. It zoomed up to the ceiling with a pop, and foam poured out of the bottle. She pressed it to her lips and sucked the foam away as everyone laughed and clapped.

"Want a cup?" Ricki said in their sweet little voice, handing Veda a teacup. The newest addition to the Dollhouse, Ricki was intersex. They had a muscular back, small breasts, stubble, and the highest, most melodic voice.

"I love your outfit," Veda said as she took the cup. Ricki was wearing a loincloth that they'd made out of some spare velour from Albert's curtains, with a shark's tooth necklace and a little fez hat.

"Oh, thanks," Ricki giggled self-consciously. Ricki was painfully shy, but of everybody in the Dollhouse, they were the one Veda felt the most connected to. Veda was native, Ricki was black, and they were both survivors. Of course, every queer person was a survivor, in one way or another.

"To our beautiful friend, Veda," Albert said, raising a teacup of champagne. "May this be the best year of your life."

"*All* your lives," Razer added. "Your whole existence. In this and every dimension."

"You deserve it, kiddo," Agnes purred in her deep voice. "You really do." Veda looked around at all of them—big Agnes and sticky, happy Danse, her friend Albert and her crush Razer and her angel Ricki. She felt tears in her eyes.

"What now?" Razer asked when they had finished the bottle of champagne. "A photoshoot?"

Everyone agreed that a photoshoot was an excellent idea, and they spent the next hour dressing up in Veda's clothes and striking poses against the lemon-yellow wall, all while Albert took photos with his cracked iPhone. Since it was Veda's birthday, the photoshoot was all about her. "Veda, try this on!" "Girl, strike a pose," "Yes, queen!" She felt high, intoxicated, as if she was floating up into the clouds and toward the sun.

And then Agnes tossed her a dress. It was a blue dress, frilly at the bottom, and when Veda caught it, she fell. The room around her vanished, and she was tumbling down into the terrible darkness she carried deep inside. She was five years old again, five years old in their shabby trailer on the res, surrounded by the smell of shit from the broken toilet and the empty cans of cat food that had been their breakfast and the cries of her baby brother in the laundry basket they used for a crib. And her mother and father were gone, at least she thought they were, and she was holding a dress, a blue dress, just like the one Agnes had just tossed her, a blue princess dress more beautiful than anything Veda had ever seen. She didn't remember where she'd gotten it—manifested it, maybe, pulled it out of another dimension just like the parasol last week—but she remembered holding it up to her naked body in front of the broken mirror that leaned against the wall in the trailer's one dark and sweaty bedroom, twirling around with it, watching the taffeta shimmer and shine against her brown skin and talking to herself. "Hello, Princess," she whispered. "Hello, Beautiful."

But her daddy wasn't gone after all. He was on the floor on the other side of the bed, in the lethargic half-sleep that Veda knew came after he used needles, and he'd woken up when he'd heard Veda talking to herself. He appeared behind her in the mirror, naked just like she was, the same dark body with all the same parts but bigger, scarier. He snatched the dress from her hands, and it tore.

"What the fuck are you doing, boy?"

"I don't know," she whispered.

"You want to be a girl, huh? You want to wear dresses?"

The baby started crying at the sound of their daddy's voice, and he growled shut up, kicking at the laundry basket.

"I just thought it was pretty."

"You thought it was pretty, huh?" he said, holding up the torn dress. "What's the matter with you? You don't want to be a boy?"

"I don't know," Veda whispered.

He grabbed Veda's penis. "You don't like having a cock?"

And then he began to touch his own, working it up and down until it got bigger and stood up. The next time he spoke was more softly.

"Maybe you just don't know how to use it right. Come here."

And he took Veda onto the bed and did it for the first time, the same thing he'd done for ten years after, the same thing he did to her brother when he got older, the same thing he sometimes let other men come into the trailer and do to both of them. Most of it was hazy, lost in the twilight of the drugs that her daddy usually gave her beforehand. Needles, the same ones he used in his own arms.

Her mother had beaten Veda with a frying pan when she'd told her.

"Your daddy isn't no kind of homo, you think you can lie like that, you think you can blame him for what you are?" *Whack.* Frying pan to the temple.

"You think I never seen you playing in my makeup, you freak? You better get straight and man up, hear me? I won't have no kind of pervert for a son." Whack. Frying pan to the collarbone, where Veda still had a scar. "You tell anybody else what you just told me, I'll kill you. Hear? I'll kill you."

Kill you. Kill you. Kill you. The words rang in Veda's ears, and the baby was crying again, she could see him, he was there across the room in the laundry basket by Albert's leg. She rushed over to it, desperate to rescue him, but when she got to the basket, it was empty and the crying stopped and there was a voice from behind her, her brother's voice, ten years old now, saying her name. "*Veda,*" he choked. He was the only one on the res that she'd ever told her real name to. "*Veda,*" he gasped again. She turned around and there he was, she could see him standing there in her room in the Dollhouse with his too-small underwear around his ankles, and he was crying, still mouthing her name but no sound was coming out, he couldn't breathe, and her mother's voice was still saying *Kill you, Kill you, Kill you* over and over, and her brother was clutching at his throat, he was having an asthma attack, and Veda was screaming, and her brother's face was turning red, redder, purple, the little gasps in his throat getting smaller and smaller, his eyes frantic, until there was no more sound and no more gasping, and his eyes went glassy, and he was gone.

When Veda came to, she was on the floor of her room with the blue dress on top of her and her friends gathered around her, all clamoring with concern.

"I'm okay." She sat up and threw the blue dress aside, searching the room for something to ground her. The pink parasol, there leaning against the door… her spider's web charm, woven by her elementary school teacher, hanging on the wall…her threadbare plushie moose, one of the few things she'd brought from South Dakota, right here on the bed next to her. *You're safe*, she whispered to her soul. You're safe. Soon, she was breathing normally again, her muscles relaxing, her heartbeat beginning to slow.

"I'm sorry."

"Don't apologize!"

"I just. I saw—never mind. I'm okay."

This happened sometimes. All of a sudden, without warning, the darkness would come rushing in, and she'd see things, feel things, her father's sweaty thighs in her face, or the smell of her mother's cigarettes mingling with the odor of burning flesh as she put them out on Veda's wrists, or the sound of her brother's asthma attacks. Lately, she'd been seeing his death. She hadn't been there when it happened, but she knew it was her father's fault, knew that it had happened after he'd done something bad to him. "You're faking," their parents had always told her baby brother when he struggled to breathe, and he'd never had medicine. The coroner had ruled it an accidental death.

Ricki helped Veda to the bed. "Hey." They sat, laying a hand on Veda's leg. "Don't let it in, okay? You just tell that bullshit to fuck right off."

Veda smiled; she'd never heard Ricki swear before.

"Why don't we give y'all some space?" Agnes said, and Veda nodded.

"It happens to me too, you know," Ricki said when the others had gone.

"Just out of nowhere. I'll see something or smell something, and suddenly, I'm back in the nightmare."

"What do you do?"

Ricki shrugged. "Just try to breathe. Tell myself it's over."

"Do they ever talk to you?"

"Who?"

"People from the past. People who have…died."

Ricki shook their head. "No. I don't have that gift."

Since she was young, Veda had heard and seen things that other people didn't. She must have been only six or seven the first time it happened, playing in the dirt outside the trailer when a fat boy with blue skin walked up from the bottom of the hill. His body flickered in and out, and sometimes it wasn't there at all. But she could hear his voice clearly.

"Where are the firemen?" he'd asked.

What firemen, she'd wondered, and he'd responded as though he'd heard her speak.

"My cousin said she was going to get the firemen to help me."

Why?

And then he'd flickered out completely. At morning assembly the next day, everyone was talking about how a sixth grader, Marvin Sokalexis, had been playing with his cousins at the pond behind the empty gas station when the ice had broken. *Drowned,* they whispered. *Dead.*

Ghosts came to Veda lots of times after that, though they rarely appeared the way Marvin had. Mostly they came in whispers or sensations, not in bodies. Often, she'd be minding her own business at home or at school or in the woods when all of a sudden, she became consumed by feelings that weren't her own: anger, or confusion, or the need to find something. She learned to invite communication with the entities the feelings belonged to and was usually able to send them on their way. But some were more stubborn than others. The spirit of her grandmother always came to her after her father did something bad to her, pleading in her ear. *"Forgive him,"* it begged. *"He's like you and he doesn't know what to do about it, he hates himself, it's not his fault…"* Veda did her best to ignore it. But sometimes the spirit took a visible form—a dark, shifting gloom with the face of her grandmother, whom she'd never met in life—and its whispers became angry rages, whipping circles around Veda like a tornado, screaming at her, until Veda was afraid the energy would rip a portal in the stuffy air of the trailer and drag her into some hell-dimension. The only way to escape from it was to run out onto the empty plains where it couldn't follow.

"People keep calling it a gift," Veda said.

"Isn't it?" Ricki asked. "Don't they...you know. Guide you?"

"Well...I guess so. Sometimes."

Although many of the ghosts were needy and stormy and dark, there was also a soft, kind whisper that Veda had heard many times over the years. Over time, Veda came to recognize it as the voice of her spirit guide, one of her ancestors, whose purpose was to guide and protect her. Sometimes it took a physical form, just the softest shimmer of light out of the corner of her eye, a presence like someone else was there in the room. "You are strong," it whispered, when she curled up against the wall in the bathroom stall at school, sure her legs would snap like matchsticks if she tried to stand. "You are sacred," it said, when she looked down at her body and cursed its wrongness, hitting herself, pinching her genitals. "You are innocent," it said, when the only way to live through the pain was to tell herself she deserved it. And it was the voice of her spirit guide that gave Veda her true name when she was thirteen.

But its most important message came one night when Veda had run into the woods after her father had taunted her with scissors, threatening to mutilate her, to "make her a girl like she wanted" and let her bleed to death in the snow. She was sixteen years old and wished she had never been born.

Why, Veda's soul had cried out as she curled up under a tree, her fingers and toes going numb in the ten-degree cold. *Why am I like this? What's wrong with me?*

And then, more plainly than she'd ever seen it before, her spirit guide appeared. It was much more than a hazy shimmer this time; it was a woman, tall as a mighty oak, her light bathing the wintery forest in a warm glow. Her hair was long, tumbling all the way down to the forest floor where it became a rushing river, and her body was a kaleidoscope of stars.

"You are Two-Spirit," the voice said.

Two-Spirit?

"Two-Spirit, the one who is both and neither. You are exalted."

No one has ever exalted me. They hate me. They want me to die.

"You are Two-Spirit," the voice said again, and its face became that of a man. "You are sacred. And you will survive."

At the school library the next day, Veda did some research. Two-Spirit was a concept present in almost every tribe: a third gender, a sacred role recognized by the Elders. And yet, in her sixteen years on the res, Veda had never heard the words uttered. After school, she snuck out to the baseball field and cried under the bleachers, both with grief at having been denied her identity all these years and joy at the discovery that she *did* have a place in the world. Two-Spirit, the one who is both and neither. Ceremonially exalted. Spiritually key.

When she was eighteen, on the day after graduation when she opened her eyes and realized that it was over, that she'd done it, that she'd gotten the piece of paper that proved to the world she was worth something, the light appeared again and the voice of her spirit guide whispered: "Go."

Where? she'd asked it.

And her guide had spoken two words, the name of a place that Veda had barely heard of. So, she'd gone to her special place in the woods and dug up her life savings, packed a bag, and hitchhiked to Pierre to buy a bus ticket. Forty-one hours after leaving the station, the bus came down over a high rise, and the city of New Orleans appeared, wavering in the June heat. And Veda had cried at the sight of it. Not because she'd eaten nothing but one Big Mac and one bag of chips in the last two days, not because her back ached and her eyes burned with exhaustion or because she was almost two-thousand miles away from the only place she'd ever been, but because the voice of her spirit guide whispered to her again as the bus hurtled down the highway toward New Orleans. It said just one word. *Home.*

Veda stretched out on the worn sheets of her bed, which were sprinkled with glitter and dirt and crumbs of makeup and food. "They do guide me," she said. "Sometimes. But most of the time, they just want something."

Ricki lay down beside her, folding their hands demurely below their head like an angel. "That sounds exhausting."

"It is. Especially at my job."

"They bother you at your job?"

"Yeah, sometimes. I want to quit."

"Why don't you?"

"Because they need me. They don't have anyone else."

Veda changed three more times that day, finally settling on some lace curtains she'd pinned together into a dress, her furry pink coat, glittery sneakers, and Ricki's fez. She felt anxious about going to work, given what had happened the night before. The entire time Veda had known the man Jeremy, his energy had worried her; he was a tantric vampire, and in Veda's experience, the line between tantric vampires and sexual predators could wane very, very thin. Last night, Jeremy had crossed that line, from what Veda understood, and then threatened her in the bar. She was still shaken up.

Ruby was there in the street when Veda arrived. Veda rushed over, and they hugged.

"How are you?" Veda asked.

"Tired. We were at the hospital all night."

"How's Sofia?"

"She's okay now, home resting. The drugs are pretty much out of her system."

"So, it was roofies?"

"Ambien. You were right. That fucking *creep.*"

"But he didn't actually—you know?"

"No, she got away."

"Thank Goddess."

"Yeah. She got lucky."

Ruby was hurt, very hurt, deep in her body. And not just because of what had happened to Sofia—there was something worse. Veda could tell.

She reached out to put a hand on Ruby's arm. "Are you okay? Did something happen to you?"

Ruby swallowed and nodded. "A few days ago, yeah."

"Do you want to talk about it?"

"After work, maybe."

"Okay."

A chilly breeze blew down the street, scattering the cigarette butts and bits of trash at their feet. "Brr. Wanna huddle?"

"Yeah." They turned away from the wind and leaned into each other. And as they stood together, shoulders touching softly, Veda wondered if there was any woman in the world who hadn't been hurt by a man.

Veda's tour was different from the others. First, she led her group down St. Peter Street past the Cathedral to Jackson Square, where she told them about the Natchez Priestess who was publicly burned at the stake there in 1730. She'd heard other guides talk about Bienville, the founder of New Orleans, as a man who'd been friendly with the natives: "He learned their language," they said. "He let them tattoo him." Veda set the record straight, describing how the French settlers had abused the Natchez tribes, displacing, and in some cases, enslaving them. The public execution of the Priestess had been punishment for the tribe's attempts to defend itself. Veda hadn't found the Priestess in any history books but had heard her voice the very first time she visited Jackson Square. She was an angry spirit, but Veda felt her grow calmer and calmer with each night's telling of the story. Tonight's group was nice. It was smallish, only about fifteen or sixteen people, and none of them were drunk.

The worst tour Veda had ever given was to a group that was mostly high school boys and their dads, all of them hammered, the dads obviously supplying alcohol for the teenagers. "Any questions?" Veda had asked after the first stop.

"Yeah," one of the teenagers called out. "Are you really a girl?"

The other boys tittered malevolently. Panic rose in Veda's throat, the kind of panic she hadn't really had to deal with since high school. She waited for the boy's father—or anybody, literally anybody in the group—to say something, to scold him, but it didn't happen.

And so, she said yes.

"But you're like, actually a boy, right?"

"Let's get to our next stop."

"No, I wanna know too," one of the dads had called out drunkenly. "Which is it? Are those little titties real?" She turned and started walking, her cheeks burning.

"You really think it's a dude?" she'd heard one of the boys whisper to another as they walked. "Aw man, I'm gonna throw up."

"What, you thought he was cute or something?"

"No."

"Yes, you did."

"Shut up."

And soon they were all taunting the kid, chanting *"Kevin's a faggot, Kevin's a faggot."* Veda could feel the darkness closing in from all sides, and so she took the group directly to the bar even though it wasn't technically time for the break. After sending them in, she'd called Graham and asked if she could kick the group off the tour.

"It's how many people?"

"Like ten."

"That's a lot of refunds...I'm sorry, Veda, I think you just gotta suffer through it."

She'd hid behind the empty patio bar at Lafitte's and cried. And then Kat—sweet, strong Kat, Veda's first friend at Spirits of Yore—had found her there and knelt beside her, listened while she explained what had happened.

"I just don't know how I can keep going," she'd cried. Kat's brow had furrowed, and she'd looked away for a moment then stood.

"You don't have to. I'll take it from here."

"What?"

"I'm just killing time waiting for Ralphie anyway. I'll tell them I'm their new tour guide, finish it out for you."

"Won't the group be upset?"

"Upset? They won't even notice. A bunch of drunks like that, two pretty girls like us…they won't even be able to tell the difference." And she'd kissed Veda on the cheek and gone out into the street to round up the group.

Veda missed Kat terribly. Seeing her lingering at the Quarter Rat wasn't the same as having a real friend in her life.

Luckily, there were no mean people or drunks in Veda's group tonight. She chatted with some of them at the bar break, a lesbian couple from Portland who were loving the "feminist spin" of the tour and a goth teen girl who was there with her dad. She had lots of questions, mostly about witchcraft, and Veda told her about her favorite spot in the Quarter to buy crystals and get her cards read.

"What's your Instagram?" the girl asked. "Can I add you?"

When she wandered off to take pictures of the bar with her polaroid, her kindly and slightly self-conscious-looking dad leaned over to Veda and smiled.

"Thanks. She's really into this stuff; she's loving it."

"I'm glad. She seems cool."

"Oh, she is. Great kid. It was her idea to come here, y'know, to New Orleans. She kept her grades up this year, so we're taking this little trip."

"Just the two of you?"

"Yeah, her mom had to work. Sort of a daddy-daughter thing."

Veda smiled. "It's really awesome of you to do that for her."

The girl hurried back, waving a polaroid. "Hey Dad, check it out!" she exclaimed. "I think I got an orb in this pic!"

The man peered over his glasses at his daughter's picture, making encouraging sounds, and Veda felt a complicated pang in her heart. She did her best to chase it away.

After the bar break, a little ball of dread always began to form in Veda's chest, growing bigger and tighter with every story until they arrived at the LaLaurie Mansion. Veda hated telling this story, hated it so much that she always put it off until the very end, and she would have cut it from her tour completely if it weren't the one story the guides were all required to tell.

She always started to feel queasy when the square gray mansion came into view on Royal Street, its three stories jutting up sharp above the shorter buildings, murky orange clouds drifting behind its dark facade. It was the corner house on the block, the dozen or more windows on each side gazing out on Royal and Governor Nicholls like all-seeing eyes. Veda never walked on the same side of the street as the horrible house, but even from twenty or thirty feet away, she could feel the waves of sinister energy that rolled off it like mist. She did her best not to look at it as they passed, pretending not to notice the evil that lurked there. But it liked her, and wanted her, and couldn't stand being ignored for long.

She parked her group across the street from the house's carriageway on Governor Nicholls Street. "Everybody, please take a look behind me at this big gray building behind me. This is the LaLaurie Mansion, one of the most famous haunted places in New Orleans; in fact, this house often makes it onto top-ten lists of haunted places throughout the country and even throughout the world. Has anyone here seen *American Horror Story*?" Some hands shot up; the third season, set in New Orleans, had made this story famous. "Okay, so this is Kathy Bates' character we're talking about." The group nodded eagerly, grinning. They were always so excited to hear this horrible story. It made Veda tired.

"Born Delphine McCarty, she came from one of the wealthiest families in town and was married three times—both of her first two husbands 'died under mysterious circumstances,' and both left her everything. It was with her third husband, a doctor named Louis LaLaurie, that she bought and moved into this house in 1831. Their wealth combined made them the richest, most powerful people in town, and they loved to entertain.

"But pretty early on in their time here, rumors started to circulate about the LaLauries, rumors that they were abusing their slaves. Now, I think we'll all agree that enslaving people in the first place is just about the most abusive thing you can do. But according to the people of New Orleans at the time, the LaLauries are taking things a bit too far—Madame LaLaurie, in particular. The rumors began because of one particular incident.

"As the legend goes, Madame LaLaurie is upstairs in her dressing room getting ready for a party. And with her, she has a little girl. An enslaved child, about eight years old, named Leah. Leah is brushing Madame's hair when she comes across a tangle...and rather than gently combing through the tangle, she *rips* through it. This little mistake sends Madame into a rage. She starts screaming at the little girl and grabs her bullwhip off her vanity then starts whipping the girl full force. Now, a bullwhip could kill a grown man, and in those days, it often did. But Leah is quick—she runs out of the room, onto the gallery." Veda watched the people in her group as their eyes rose to the wraparound gallery on the second floor of the house behind her. They wouldn't see it.

"But Madame chases her. Still screaming, still lashing out with the whip... the chase goes on for a few seconds until the little girl, Leah, goes over the gallery railing and tumbles down to the street below."

The hairs on the back of Veda's neck stood up as it came. A howl, a bloodcurdling shriek, in the high-pitched voice of a child. Veda never wanted to turn around, but she always did, and there was the girl, suspended in the air, her malnourished body frozen mid-fall with her limbs flung out around her. Her mouth was twisted in a terrified scream, and the whites of her eyes glowed in the dark. They always stared directly into Veda's own.

The group saw nothing. Veda swallowed, her heart pounding, and turned back to them to continue.

"But when the girl falls, Madame LaLaurie doesn't gasp. She doesn't look over the edge or call for help. She just shrugs, turns on her heel, and goes back into her dressing room where she simply calls for someone else to come and finish her hair. Later, it comes to light that Leah died in the fall; she broke her neck. And people find out. But does anyone confront the LaLauries about it? Does anyone do anything, or investigate? Of course not." *Of course not,* Veda thought, remembering her teachers, her coaches, her own grandparents. "They all turned a blind eye."

"Well. Time goes on. A few more years pass until April 10th, 1834. But on that day, something happens. A fire breaks out in the kitchen." Veda pointed to the little garage on the other side of the courtyard where the detached service wing had been.

"People start to gather out here where you are, wanting to see what's going on. And a man in the crowd realizes that the slave quarters are right above the kitchen, where the fire started—but there are no enslaved people out here safely on the street. He's concerned about that and actually finds Louis LaLaurie and confronts him about it, but Louis basically tells him to mind his own business.

"He doesn't mind his own business. In fact, he's a total gossip," Veda said, and she saw the goth girl smile. "He actually gets together a group of men who agree to go in, *secretly*, against the LaLaurie's wishes, to see if anyone needs help.

"They begin by going into the kitchen, where the fire started. The fire has been put out by now, but in the ashes...they find something very disturbing." The image broke Veda's heart every time she described it, and she thanked the Creator that she'd never had to see it the way she saw the girl fall.

"They find an eighty-five-year-old woman, enslaved, who has been chained to the stove. Her wrists are raw and bloody from the shackles, she's badly burned, and she has nearly lost her mind from being chained here. It's clear she's been shackled like this for months, maybe years, doing all the family's cooking. Well, the firefighters are horrified. *What's going on here?* they ask her. She's near death, but she manages to tell them one thing. She says that she set the fire herself. Because, earlier in the day, she had 'angered Madame.' And she says she'd rather die in a fire…than be taken upstairs."

Fear shook her voice. They'd think it was acting; it wasn't.

"The woman dies before they can learn anything else. So, they decide to investigate. They go upstairs–to a little attic room above the kitchen."

Soon it would begin. Veda wanted to run.

"The first thing they are met with is the stench of rotting flesh. They light their lanterns, they look around…and they realize that what they have found above the LaLauries' kitchen can only be described as a torture chamber. It's full of the mutilated, mangled bodies of about seven or eight people…some dead, some still alive, all of them enslaved. The first person they go to is a young woman. When they get to her, they realize that her legs and her arms have been cut clean off. Her mouth has been sewn shut, and one long strip of skin has been peeled from around her torso in the shape of a spiral. They say all these injuries combined make this poor young woman look like a human caterpillar."

The teenage girl was holding onto her dad's arm, her mouth hanging open in fascination and horror. Veda wished she could be like her: an ordinary girl, just hearing a story. But she'd never be an ordinary girl. And it would never be just a story.

Veda went on to describe the other victims in the torture chamber, the man whose nose had been cut off, his face crawling with maggots, a hole drilled in his skull in order to stir his brains. The beautiful young woman covered in small, deep cuts whose blood Madame had drained every night then smeared herself with as an antidote to aging. The teenage girl, every bone in her legs and arms shattered, shoved into a little box where her limbs had set at sickening angles.

And as Veda spoke, so did they.

At first it was faint, just soft cries from the little room above the garage behind her where the torture chamber had been. But quickly, very quickly, the sounds became louder, more desperate, more complex. Soon, Veda could hear the grinding of metal against bone as the man's skull collapsed under Madame's hand drill, and the whimpers of the beautiful young woman as she faded in and out of consciousness, her blood seeping into Madame's cup, and the uneven thuds of twisted limbs on wooden planks as the firefighters lifted the girl from the box and found she could only move by dragging herself across the floor, crab-like. *Help us,* their spirits cried. *Do something. We've been ignored for so long.*

Veda struggled to continue, barely able to hear her own voice over the noise. "The men didn't know what to do but bring the victims out. And so they did, on makeshift stretchers, down through the torture chamber, through the kitchen, out here to the street."

"Where all the people still are," the goth girl whispered.

"Yes. Where an entire block of onlookers is still gathered, loitering after the fire. And then suddenly, all of these mutilated, mangled people are brought out right past them."

And as always, there they were. Just out of the corner of her eye, Veda could see their ravaged bodies, a line of them going down the sidewalk under the dark overhang of the gallery behind her, reaching through time to her, pleading. Veda focused all of her attention directly ahead, concentrating on the details of the faces in her group. That man's receding hairline. The woman's glasses, that red lipstick… their eyes. Living eyes, human eyes. They gave her the bravery to continue.

"It doesn't take people in the crowd long to figure out what's going on. They've all heard the rumors; they know *something* isn't right in that house. But up until now, of course, they could turn a blind eye…not anymore. Torture, murder? People are very upset. And before long, this crowd becomes an angry mob. Word spreads, the mob gets bigger, but the LaLauries have locked themselves in the house, and they're not coming out. And people out here are angry! They're throwing rocks, they're lighting torches, but nothing happens. An hour passes…an hour and a half…two hours. Finally, after two hours, these carriage doors burst open"—Veda pointed to the arched doorway on the house behind her without looking because they were still there, the victims, crying, calling out to her for help—"and out comes a horse-drawn carriage containing Delphine and Louis LaLaurie, heading top-speed toward Lake Pontchartrain. The crowd follows, but they're not as fast, and the carriage gets away. The LaLauries take a boat across the lake, travel to New York City, and get on a ship bound for France, where Delphine lives out the rest of her days and dies fifteen years later of natural causes. She was never put on trial, and she was never brought to justice for what happened here."

A moment. A pause.

"Is it haunted?" the teenage girl asked. *Don't you hear them?* Veda wanted to plead. *Don't you see them, don't you feel them, why is it only ME, why am I the one they want something from, why, why—*

"Yes, of course." She told them about the imprints of human forms that always appeared on the beds, the sound of chains being dragged through the ceilings, the scent of a sickening floral perfume—Madame's—that sometimes drifted through the ballroom. Silly anecdotes. All the while, the spirits screamed at her. *Help us. Do something. Make them see.*

I'm trying, she pleaded with them psychically. *I tell your story every night, but it's not enough; it's never enough. What do you want?*

Veda took a few more questions, thanked the group for coming, and ended the tour. Everyone was very nice, thanking her, promising to leave good reviews. The dad and his daughter were the last to go. He gave Veda a twenty folded up thin, so she wouldn't see what it was, but she knew. Tour guides know the feel of every bill.

"That was so awesome. You're amazing," the girl said. "Here." And she handed Veda a polaroid, still murky and undeveloped. "I just took this. It's of you, telling your story."

Veda's heart surged. "Thank you. I can't wait to see it! Can I give you a hug?" She put the photo into her bag, and they embraced. And as they did, the spirits in the street faded away, their voices dwindling to whispers and then to nothing as Veda felt the girl's heartbeat against her own, steady and strong, and smelled the healthy scent of her thick, freshly-dyed black hair. She was everything a sixteen-year-old girl should be. Veda didn't ever want to let go.

"You're awesome," the girl said, smiling as the hug ended. She took her dad by the arm and away they went, chatting about the tour. Veda watched them turn the corner and disappear.

It was just her now, her and the shadowy house, alone on the quiet street. Usually, there were other guides around when she finished her tour, but tonight there was no one. Feeling brave, she turned to face the house and looked at it closely, her eyes searching every gray brick, every window. It wasn't so bad, was it? Just an object, a pile of stone. It couldn't hurt her. Only the living could hurt her, real living people, and the people who wanted to hurt her were thousands of miles away. She never had to see any of them again. She was safe now, safe in New Orleans among people who loved her, so many kind people who saw her and liked her and would keep her safe from harm; the nightmare was over; she was—

Thud. Crack.

Veda turned sharply. There, not three feet away, lay little Leah again, her body broken in the street. The girl's collarbone jutted out from her skin at a right angle, her neck lolling back so that her head nearly touched her spine. She was staring at Veda upside down, blood bubbling out of her mouth. Veda had never seen her so close, and she screamed, jumping back.

Why—the girl gasped, straining through the snapped bones in her neck and the blood in her throat. Veda tried to step backward, but the girl's hand clamped down on her ankle.

Why didn't you—

Let me go, Veda shouted at her, but Leah's spindly little fingers held tight.

Why didn't you save me? she choked.

With all her psychic might, Veda pushed the spirit away. The fingers released her ankle as the girl's form rushed upward, exploding into the darkness with a whooshing scream. But her voice remained, echoing, growing lower and more sinister. *Why didn't you save me?* it cried. *Why didn't you save me? Why didn't you save me?* Veda turned to run, her heart pounding, desperate to get away from the house. She could feel the tendrils of its dark energy licking at her, pulling at her, threatening to suck her in, but she was faster, she was stronger, she could outrun it, *Why didn't you save me?* the voice was screaming now in a distorted baritone, *Why didn't you save me? Why didn't you save me?*

She was almost to the corner, almost out of sight of the mansion, when suddenly, she stopped. Because the voice changed. It was quiet now, just a whisper, just a plaintive little plea in her ear. It was the voice of her brother. *Why didn't you save me?*

Veda turned back to the LaLaurie Mansion. Inside one of the first-floor windows, a curtain rustled. And behind the glass, her brother's face appeared, shadowy and dim in the empty, dark house. He was mouthing the words that she could hear inside her ear. There was no more "why didn't you" now. Just *Save me.*

Save me. Save me, he pleaded. *Save me, Veda.*

Without thinking, she ran to him, into the eerie veil around the house that she'd avoided for all these months, toward its darkness and its ghosts and the deep, deep evil that had settled there centuries ago. She had to get to her brother. She reached the window. Their faces were inches apart, separated only by the pane of glass.

Save me, he said again.

I can't.

Why not?

It's too late. You're gone.

He looked sadly into her eyes. It's your birthday.

Yes.

You've lived twice as long as I did.

I know.

Why do you get to live, when I had to die?

I don't know.

Her brother put his hand up to the glass, and Veda reached out to lay her palm against his own.

You should die too, he said.

As soon as she touched the mansion, her brother's face behind the glass changed. His mouth spread into a wicked grin, growing bigger and bigger and bigger until it swallowed his face and a new face emerged from the inside-out skin, Veda's father's, his Adam's apple bobbing up and down as he panted obscenely. Veda tried to pull her hand away from the window, but it was stuck there, wet and sticky and burning, and her father was pulling her through the glass into the mansion, but now it wasn't her father at all, the face was shifting again, and his Adam's apple was multiplying into a strand of fat pearls, and the figure was a woman now, growing taller and taller with a thin, cruel mouth and pale, empty shark eyes. Madame LaLaurie, her fingernails digging into Veda's wrist like claws, pulling her into the black void of the mansion. *You will pay for what you did,* she said, looming over Veda, swallowing her with those big, empty eyes. The street was gone, and Veda was somewhere very dark and alone, and then she felt it, a burning pain in her belly button, skin being ripped off in a spiral up her torso. She screamed, but a needle was puncturing her lips, sewing them up, silencing her. She felt her legs break, her arms break, her skull split under the weight of a drill. The pain was unbearable; she couldn't survive it; the weight of what had been done here was simply too heavy, and it was crushing her, killing her, pressing her into nothingness. Veda had been wrong to think she could survive. Today was the day of her birth, and it would also be the day of her death. Her brother was right; she didn't deserve to live.

And then there was warmth. A living hand on her back, the breath of a human being, the voice of a woman.

"Veda! Veda, are you alright?"

Veda opened her eyes. She was lying on the sidewalk. And there was Angela, the tour guide, kneeling next to her.

"What happened? Did you faint?"

"I have to get away from here," she choked. "This house is so bad."

"I believe it. This place has bad juju to the maximum." Angela helped Veda to her feet and guided her down the street half a block, out of sight of the mansion. They sat on a stoop. Veda's heart was pounding. She tried to breathe.

"I've often had bad experiences there myself," Angela was saying. "You know, a lot of tour guides don't like to walk on the same side of the street as the LaLaurie Mansion, and I do see why. I actually once had a tour guest faint after touching its wall. It was a hot day, mind you, but nevertheless, I don't trust the place."

Veda began to cry.

"Oh!" Angela exclaimed, seeming to suddenly remember that Veda was there.

"Every night," she sobbed.

"Every night what?"

"Every night I watch her die."

"Who?"

"The girl! The little girl. Leah."

"Oh, goodness...so you're a medium, then?"

"I guess," Veda shrugged through the tears. "I always see them. Lots of them."

"I'm so sorry," Angela said. "That must be very draining."

"It is. I hate it, I *hate* it, they won't leave me alone, they—"

"Just take a deep breath. Here, breathe with me." Veda followed Angela's slow, steady breaths until she began to feel calmer.

"Thank you."

"No worries, dear."

Veda wiped the hot tears off her face, and her hand came away stained with the thick blue eyeliner she'd put on before work.

"You, my dear lady, have smudged all your makeup."

"Yeah, I figured."

"Let's get that fixed, shall we?" Angela got her purse and pulled out a sleek tube of mascara, some sort of compact that looked like a pincushion, an eye-shadow palette, and a handful of lipsticks, lining it all up neatly on the step below them. It was all much nicer makeup than anything Veda had ever owned; she didn't even recognize some of the brand names.

"Let's start with a clean slate," Angela said, and took out a little packet of moist towelettes. She gently wiped the tears and makeup and dirt off Veda's face. "There you go. You have such beautiful skin...so soft and radiant, no blemish-es…take care of it, promise? There's a nice Vitamin C serum I can recommend if you remind me." Veda nodded. Angela had picked up the foundation now and was dabbing it on. Next came eyeshadow, mascara, blush. Veda sat patiently as she worked, observing the look of deep concentration on Angela's face just inch-es from her own, studying the woman's perfect lipstick and eyeshadow and con-touring. She talked as she worked, describing every step, every product. Veda had never learned how to do any of this.

When she was finished, Angela pulled a little folding mirror out of her bag and held it up. Veda's fingers drifted up to touch her face, her mouth opening slightly. Her lips were full and red, her cheeks radiant, her lashes beautiful and dark and long. She looked like a princess. A goddess. A woman.

"It's beautiful."

"*You're* beautiful. But I'm glad you like it. I consider myself something of a make-up maven; I actually have a blog. If you'd like, I could give you a tutorial sometime."

"You would do that for me?"

"Of course! I'd like nothing more."

"Thank you. Thank you for helping me."

"That's what friends are for."

A friend! Veda's heart leapt. She imagined going to Angela's house, having dinner, trying on clothes, learning to do makeup. She'd never dreamed that someone so confident and put-together would want to be her friend. She wanted to cry again, tears of gratitude this time, and her eyes began to well.

"Don't you do it!" Angela warned teasingly. "Don't you dare cry, not after I just gave you that amazing smokey eye!"

Veda laughed and swallowed and nodded.

"Do you need help getting home?"

"No, I'm okay. I think I'm actually going to go back to the bar for a little while. Ruby's waiting for me."

"Alright. Be safe."

"Thank you. For helping me."

"More than happy to. Truly."

Angela gave her a hug and went on her way, and Veda sat on the stoop for a few more minutes. Then she stood, smoothing her curtain dress, picking her bag up from the sidewalk. Something fell out, and she realized it was that polaroid, the picture the girl from the tour had given her, fully developed now. Veda picked it up and looked at it.

There she was, standing in the street in front of the LaLaurie Mansion. She was gesturing big with her arms, her face open and expressive, and her outfit looked amazing. In the background, there were no ghosts. No spirits, no dead children in the street, no tortured slaves. Just Veda. She remembered the girl's words as she'd handed her the picture.

It's of you, telling your story.

CHAPTER 14

The Singing Rain

Max lived in "the box." St. Charles to the river, Napoleon to Canal: durin Carnival season, everything within those bounds was closed in by th parade routes. If a person were going from somewhere inside the box to some where outside of the box during a parade, he'd have to cross the route on foo between the floats, up to somewhere he could catch a bus or a cab or an "Uber which is what the kids seemed to be calling hired cars these days. Max didn drive. He normally took the Tchoupitoulas bus to work, caught it at Louisian and got off at Canal and Magazine then walked the rest of the way; about a hour's trip, all told. But the Tchoupitoulas bus didn't run during parades, an tonight was a parade night. The last parade night of the season, in fact. Toda was Lundi Gras. Rex and Zulu would be the last big ones in the morning, Mar Gras day, and then it would all be over.

Tonight, Max would cross the St. Charles route, walk up to Freret street, an catch the bus there. This would be a longer trip than usual, and he'd need to giv himself plenty of time. He didn't move very quickly anymore.

"Seamus. Here boy," he whistled from the table, and his old, half-blind Iris Setter came trotting in from wherever he'd been napping to lick up the remair of Max's Hungry Man frozen meatloaf and peas. His tongue pushed the pape tray across the floor and under the couch to where he couldn't reach it, and h gave Max a sad look.

"That's enough for you anyway. That stuff will kill a human being, I'm no keen to learn what it'll do to a dog."

Seamus followed Max around the house as he got his things together, clip ping his tour guide license to his shirt, sitting down to lace his heavy boot When he went to the rack for his overcoat, the dog sank down with his chin o the floor between his outstretched paws, sighing.

"I'll be back in a jiffy, don't you worry." Seamus didn't like it when Max le and gave him a forlorn look.

"I will. I promised her, and I'm promising you. I'm not going anywher except work and back."

Seamus looked away.

Max stepped out on his small stoop into the chill of the sinking sun. The cold temperature didn't feel so bad during the day when it was sunny, and he'd taken the dog for a long, slow stroll at Audubon Park earlier in the afternoon. But tonight would be unpleasant. It had been cold for weeks now, and after the sun went down, he could never seem to get warm. There wasn't enough meat on his bones these days. He did his best to eat the microwave dinners, for Molly's sake, but it wasn't enough. *You'd better fatten up,* he imagined her teasing. *Better fatten up or you'll fall down and break a hip like some old fogey.*

He raised a hand in greeting to his neighbor, a plump little white woman with three kids, who was just getting home from work.

"How's it going, Mr. Montgomery?" she smiled when she saw him. He'd told her to call him Max, but young people could be so stubborn about etiquette.

"I'm doing just fine, Miss Jenna, and yourself?"

"Oh, y'know. Mardi Gras break, the kids are keeping me busy!"

"Are you all going to the parades tonight?"

She opened the door to her house, and warm light spilled out onto the stoop. Max could hear the children's voices inside, eager for their mother's arrival. "Yes sir, just as soon as I can get the monsters fed. How about you?"

"I'm sure I'll see a bit of it on my way to work here in a minute."

"Hope you catch some beads!"

The warm light and little voices disappeared as she stepped in and closed the door. Max descended the two shallow steps of the stoop and began his slow walk up the street.

It had been Molly's idea to buy the little house on Annunciation. They'd lived in Gentilly for decades, raised the kids there in a roomy four-bedroom house, but after the storm, Molly decided they ought to move. Max had put up a fuss at first, but she'd convinced him. "You were born in Gentilly, why would you want to die there?" She'd suggested they downsize to a little one-bedroom in the Irish Channel, a compact neighborhood under the Garden District with few trees but "plenty of charm," he remembered the real estate agent saying. Molly was Irish, and she'd liked the idea of living somewhere settled by her people, where they'd all crammed together in these little houses in the 1800s to cook and clean and wash for the proper whites in the big mansions up on St. Charles. Molly had liked to fuss about the plight of the Irish in American society and all the discrimination her ancestors had endured. "But were they slaves?" was always Max's gentle dig in return, to which Molly would roll her eyes and grumble that yes, fine, he won that particular contest of suffering.

The last glow of sunset faded as he made his way up Harmony Street, watching for the treacherous patch of sidewalk that had taken him to the ground a week prior when there'd been ice. Ice in New Orleans, unheard of. "Gives new meaning to the phrase, 'When hell freezes over,'" he'd been saying on his tours. When he'd fallen, he'd wondered if he'd sprained his ankle. *Go to the hospital,* he'd imagined Molly urging him. *Don't be a proud fool.* And he had, just to make her happy. But his ankle had been fine; that was how it always went with him, wasn't it? Max could barely remember a time in his life that he'd been sick or injured. And Moll was the same, always strong as a horse, almost never sick. "Just a little pneumonia," the doctor had said. "She'll be fine in a few days."

Max found the treacherous spot, a square of sidewalk that had cracked down the middle and caved in, a martyr of New Orleans' punishing cycles of wet heat and wet cold. He stepped over it.

On the other side of Magazine, the dark streets were busier, and Max became one of dozens of people all trickling toward the parade route. There were college kids and parents pulling toddlers in wagons and folks closer to Max's age carrying camp chairs, all of them laughing and making merry as the sounds of the parade grew closer in the dark. There was music from up ahead, too faint yet to make out anything but a heavy drum beat, and the intermittent roar of the crowd as each float went by. Up on St. Charles in the distance, you could see the flashing lights against the darkening sky, the towering shadows of the floats, the big crowds of people gathered there. He'd made this same walk up to the route with Molly many times before. She'd loved living in the box, close to the action. "Just a few steps from Mardi Gras for the rest of our lives. Isn't that nice, Mackie?" And he'd agreed that yes, it was.

He reached St. Charles. The parade was in full swing, and the streets were packed, the crowds stretching as far as the eye could see down the Avenue in both directions. He stepped through a mess of beer cans and food debris and dirty, uncaught beads to the back of the crowd, where the people who weren't so interested in the parade were gathered drinking and talking. Most of them were young people, folks in their late twenties who'd been in New Orleans more than a few years and didn't care much about catching beads and throws anymore but still wanted to be close to it all. In front of them were the ladders, hand-painted and built up with seats on top for the small children, their happy little legs dangling as their parents caught throws for them. Ahead of the ladders, the general crowd: college kids, families, tourists, thousands and thousands and thousands of them packing St. Charles for three miles straight. And up in the very front were the old people, settled into the camp chairs their children and grandchildren had set out for them there early in the day. They'd seen decades of Mardi Gras, the same year after year after year. But they still sat here for five, six, seven hours at a time on parade days, just watching the floats go by. It startled Max to think that he was their age. He'd never been one to sit during parades and neither had Molly. She'd always dressed up in wigs and hats and behaved just like the youngsters, waving wildly at the people on the floats, demanding beads, calling out "Throw me something, mister!" And they always had. No one could ignore Moll.

A float rolled by, soaring three levels high down the Avenue, and the crowd surged forward toward it. There was no way Max would be able to cross to the other side of St. Charles, at least not until the end of this parade and before the start of the next. Luckily, he'd allowed himself plenty of time and didn't have to be in the French Quarter for another hour and fifteen minutes.

The float was followed by a marching band, dozens of high school children in neat lines swinging trombones and trumpets and saxophones back and forth, the biggest boys behind the tubas and the littlest ones rat-tat-tatting on the snare drums in their too-baggy uniforms. Their chaperones and teachers walked up ahead with flashlights and whistles, aggressively pushing the crowd back to make room. They always looked so serious, the children in the marching bands, eyes straight ahead, toes tapping to the beat. Toward the end of the route, they'd begin to get sluggish, lagging in their steps, letting their instruments sag at their sides between parts, but on this section of St. Charles, their act was sharp as a tack. Max's son, Terence, had been in his high school's marching band decades ago. It had been highly competitive, and the uniforms had cost a fortune. But it was all worth it on a night like this when you got to watch your son march down the parade route with one of the Super Krewes, forehead beaded with sweat, playing that horn with every ounce of effort he could muster. Terence was up North, now, in Detroit. Max hadn't seen him since the funeral.

Another float approached, this one in the shape of a dragon. Its scales were a rainbow of colors; it had wings lined with lights, and its teeth were as long as Max's arm. *What a spectacle,* he marveled. It really was amazing, the care that went into building these things. He watched a little boy and his sister jostle for position as the float rolled by, jumping up and down and shouting as the throws rained down, teddy bears and beads and glowsticks. The little girl caught a light-up sword, and her brother tried to grab it from her, resulting in a skirmish that wasn't resolved until an older teenager came and took the sword and whacked them both over the head with it then gave it to a toddler in someone's lap nearby. The siblings were angry now, yelling and fussing at each other, but it would all be resolved in a few minutes' time when another float came along and showered them both with all kinds of new throws.

Max remembered these moments well. Piling everybody in the station wagon, driving around for half an hour looking for parking anywhere within a mile of the route, finally arriving among the noisy, shoulder-to-shoulder crowd dragging a cooler and chairs and a couple of whiny kids behind you, wondering why the hell you didn't live someplace like Cleveland where you wouldn't be expected to go through this every weekend for a month straight. But then of course, you'd crack open a beer, and the kids would start to laugh and toss a football with somebody else's kids, and you'd feel that electric anticipation in the air and finally the floats would start to roll by, so big and vibrant against the dusky sky, and everyone would cheer, and the kids would run up to every float waving and hollering, and you'd drink and chat with strangers, quick becoming friends, and catch beads without even meaning to, so that by the time it was all over, the pile of them around your neck would feel almost as heavy as the sleepy children in your arms, but it wasn't so bad, you had a nice buzz going, and the car didn't feel so far away after all, and your beautiful bride was there at your side laughing, and you didn't have to be at work the next day even though it would be just an ordinary Tuesday everywhere else, and you were actually glad, so glad, so goddamn drop-down-on-your-knees-and-give-thanks glad, that you did not, in fact, live in Cleveland.

The dragon float rolled off into the distance under a canopy of live oaks, nearly brushing their branches. Next came the flambeaux, a group of sweaty men all toting poles with fire at the top, the flames flickering hot and bright against the metal backsplashes. The men grinned as they held up their torch rigs, still managing to dance and spin and strut as they sweated under seventy pounds of kerosene, their faces and necks wrapped in bandanas to protect them from the fumes and the fuel drips. Max's uncle and cousin had both been flambeaux men, carrying on a tradition that had begun with slaves and free men of color in the 1850s when carrying torches to light the route was the only way that black people were allowed to participate in the parades. Uncle Toby and cousin Keith had taken their jobs as flambeaux men seriously, always strict about safety and protective of tradition, and Uncle Toby used to tell stories of the strike in '46 when the Krewe of Momus refused to up their wage. After one unpleasant Mardi Gras in the dark, the Krewe had acquiesced, and the rate had been raised to four dollars per man per parade, plus tips from the crowd.

Max pulled a dollar out of his wallet and handed it to the nearest flambeaux man then lit a cigarette. He had carried flambeaux himself a couple times in the sixties before he got involved with the Panthers. He remembered a conversation about it with Malik Rahim on a stoop in the St. Thomas Projects. "Why should you be walking in the street, lighting the way for white men in floats you're not allowed to ride on, huh?" Malik had asked him, cool as a cucumber in his leather jacket and black beret. Max had made the same point to his uncle and cousin, but they weren't interested in such logic. In fact, they hadn't talked to him much at all after Max started running around with Malik. Despite the fact that all the Panthers were really doing in New Orleans at the time was feeding breakfast to children in the Housing Projects and printing flyers about social change, much of the black community weren't happy about the resulting police presence in the projects, and Max began to drift away from his family. The fact that he returned from the Peace Corps a few years later with a white girl on his arm certainly didn't improve things.

Another marching band, then a majorette corps of young girls sashaying their hips and twirling batons, then another float. Its riders were faceless in their blank white masks, all of them identical with just dark holes for their eyes and mouths. Max had been afraid of them as a boy because the masks looked like KKK hoods. For a time, he'd refused to get close to the floats, afraid one of the riders would reach down and take him away to murder him like the boy Emmett Till from the papers. His grandfather had shown him the picture of the corpse in the *Louisiana Weekly*, and young Max had been afraid of all white people for months after that. "They not gonna do anything to ya," his grandma had told him during one of those first parades, urging him to go up alongside the white children and catch some beads. He'd refused. The only parade he'd liked in those days was Zulu, an all-black Krewe that decorated coconuts for throws, and as a boy, he'd had a whole shelf of them in his room. What had happened to all those coconuts, he wondered. Probably lost in Katrina with all his other boyhood things at his mama's home.

When folks on his tour learned he'd lived in New Orleans all his life, they almost always asked him about the storm. Max's story wasn't too different from anybody else's. His family had all gotten out before it hit—everyone except his cousin Keith, who'd been a nurse at Charity Hospital at the time. He'd saved lives and made it to safety with them all in Atlanta a few days later,but had sworn never to live in New Orleans again, washed his hands of it. Not that you could blame him. His house—same as Max and Molly's, same as everybody's in Gentilly—had eight feet of water in it. There had been a couple of months that Max felt like throwing in the towel too, suggested moving somewhere up North closer to the kids. Molly, as always, had won the argument. "If it's a choice between starting over somewhere new and strange or starting over somewhere we love, I choose the latter."

"We're getting old, Moll." They'd been near retirement age when the storm had hit.

"Oh, baloney, Mackie. We've got all the time in the world."

His fingers found their way to Molly's wedding ring on the chain around his neck. He didn't let himself feel anything but the metal under his fingertips.

The parade was finally over, police cars rolling slowly by with their lights flashing as kids darted out into the now-empty street to scavenge the throws that had accumulated there. Max squeezed his way through the crowd and crossed to the other side of St. Charles. It was another eight blocks to the bus stop, and the air felt chilly away from all the people. The bus came on time, imagine that, and he climbed on. A young lady offered her seat to him, which always felt surprising, and he declined. He didn't *feel* old, but then again, maybe no one ever does. Surely, no one ever feels old enough that death makes any kind of sense.

The bus arrived at North Rampart and Canal at 7:10 PM, and Max made the last leg of his journey, the nine-block walk to St. Peter Street. He was the first one there.

Over the next ten minutes, the other tour guides began to arrive outside the Curiosity Shop. Good kids, all of them. People talked about how the younger generations were so entitled, so narcissistic, but Max didn't see it. As far as he could tell, they struggled in the same ways young people always had: to make an impact, to find meaning, to define themselves. He wanted to tell them that it never got any easier. You wake up one day and you're seventy years old, and you still haven't figured any of it out, not really. And if you're lucky enough to find one thing—one person—that does make sense, chances are they'll go away someday, and you'll be left as lost and adrift as you were in your twenties, except this time, you're missing a part of yourself that you didn't even have back then.

"Hey, Max, take sales for a minute?" Graham said. "I gotta pee."

"Sure thing, captain." Max took the stack of money and the tickets and sat on Graham's stool. James was standing next to him with the credit card machine. There was no one in line.

"Evening, James," Max said with a nod.

"Hi, Max," James said, adjusting his yellow scarf and blowing on his hands. It was getting chillier by the hour. "Oh, hey, can I get your opinion on something?"

"Shoot."

"You might be a good person to ask about this...you've got more style than everyone else around here put together," he said dryly. Max chuckled. Why James liked the way he dressed, he had no idea.

James pulled up a shopping website on his phone and showed Max a picture of a leather jacket. "Okay, so here's the first one," he said. "I'm trying to decide between this one, and this one." With a swipe of his thumb, he pulled up a different jacket, this one a sleek bomber-style in what looked like waxed canvas.

"They're both pretty cool," Max said. "I'm more keen on the leather, though. Nothing more classic than a black leather jacket."

"Yeah," James said. "Yeah, you're right."

"Not exactly your style, though, is it? I've never seen you wear leather."

"Oh, it's not for me. It's for my—this guy I'm seeing."

"That's a nice gesture," Max smiled. "Let me see it again?" James held up the phone again, and Max noticed the price next to the jacket.

"Two hundred bucks!" he exclaimed. "Holy mackerel."

"I've been saving up," James said. "He got me this vintage camera for Valentine's Day, I wanted to...you know. Do something nice."

"Then do something nice. You don't need to *buy* something nice."

"But that's like...what people do."

Max smiled. "Doesn't have to be. Molly never wanted jewelry or anything like that. Hand-picked flowers and love letters, that's all I ever gave her. All she ever wanted."

"That's cute."

"Just tell him how you feel. And mean it."

James sighed. "I don't know how."

"And so, you're gonna spend two hundred dollars just to avoid doing something you're nervous about?" Max shook his head. "Life's too short to be playing games, son. Sometimes you just gotta lay it all out there."

"Yikes."

"Why yikes?"

"Lay it all out there? That's terrifying!"

"Ain't nothing worth doing in life that isn't just a little bit scary."

James put his phone back into his pocket and sighed, looking pensive.

Graham was back and took the money and tickets from Max. "Thanks, buddy. Appreciate it."

"I think I'll wet my whistle," Max said, winking at them both and went into the bar. The bartender, Leela, poured him a coke.

"How's it going tonight, Max?"

"Oh, hanging in there. How about yourself?"

"Just bracing myself for tomorrow. It'll be my first Mardi Gras as a bartender."

"Ah, you'll kill it. I know you will."

"Maybe," she said. "Hopefully, I don't kill myself or somebody else first!" She threw back her head and laughed. "Maybe I'll see you, though, you gonna be in the Quarter?"

"Oh, I don't know. Haven't made any plans yet."

"Well, I hope to see you!"

"We'll see how I'm feeling. Now if you'll excuse me, I'm off to the smoking section."

He took his coke back out into the street, away from the others, and lit a cigarette. The tour group was lining up on the sidewalk, and there were lots of people going by, laughing, shouting, drinking. It felt good to be in the Quarter. He'd started giving tours after they retired six years ago, just for fun, but Max wasn't sure if he could have survived the last year without this job. Making the commute downtown, having to pull himself together enough to tell stories to strangers—it kept him functioning. And he knew Molly would be proud.

"Max!" Ralphie exclaimed, appearing at his side.

"Well, hey there, stranger."

"I have something for you." Ralphie reached into his backpack and pulled out a stack of pages, grinning.

"Can it be?" Max said.

"Yep. Finished it yesterday."

Max peered at the title. "*Calzone's Folly.*"

"It's Cal-zone-ay. Like in Italian."

"Can't wait to read it," Max said, tucking the manuscript inside his coat.

"It's stupid. I only finished it because you kept telling me to."

"I'm sure it's brilliant," Max smiled. Ralphie was such a good kid. Max had tried his hand at writing too, once upon a time, even had the first draft of a novel sitting in a desk drawer to this day. He hoped Ralphie wouldn't give up as easily as he had.

"By the way, what are you doing for Mardi Gras tomorrow?" Ralphie asked.

"Oh, I don't know. I just have to take things minute by minute these days, hadn't really gotten that far."

"You've got to come down for Krewe du Tour!"

"Pardon?" Ralphie always spoke so fast, it was hard for Max to keep up.

"Krewe du Tour! I told you about it last week, remember?"

"You'll have to refresh my memory."

"It's a tradition we've had for the last few years. We dress up as our favorite New Orleans ghosts and do a little second line to the river. Or, well, it doesn't have to be a ghost. A historical figure, whatever. Just someone from a story you love."

"Well, how about that." Sounded like a neat idea.

"I'm serious, you've gotta come. 11:00, after Rex and Zulu."

"I don't know. Maybe."

The others had caught wind of the conversation and had all joined in, urging. "Come on, Max, we wanna see you!" Ruby said.

"I'll do my best," he smiled. Why they all wanted anything to do with a sad old man like him, he didn't know. But their enthusiasm was touching.

Ralphie pulled him aside. "And we're, uh…we're gonna say goodbye. To Kat."

"Max, James, time to go," Graham called before Max could respond, gesturing to the launch spot down the street where the groups were waiting.

"And that's my cue to exit," Max said, giving Ralphie a two-finger wave.

"Have a good tour, Max," James said as they neared the front of the waiting mass of people.

"Oh, I will. My girl's looking out for me," he said, patting her ring under his shirt.

"See you tomorrow? Krewe du Tour, 11:00."

"I might be a bit fagged out, but I'll do my best."

"Cool."

"James," Max called out as he took his place at the front of the group. "Be safe out there tonight." He worried about these kids, running around the Quarter at all hours of the night like they did. Especially after what had happened to the girl, Kat. Broke his heart.

James smiled. "Yes sir."

"Don't do anything I wouldn't do. And if you do, don't get caught," he winked.

"Ladies and gentlemen here for the Tour of Lost Souls," Graham was shouting, as he always did at 8:00 sharp. "I'm going to introduce you to the first tour guide being sent out tonight—everybody say, 'Hello, Max!'"

"Hello, Max," they all called out. Max flicked his cigarette to the curb and kissed Molly's ring. "Let's do this," he whispered.

He gathered the group around him in Pirate's Alley, where he always began the tour. "Good evening, ladies and gentlemen." His voice was already husky from fifty-five years of smoking, but he dialed it up a notch for the tour. If "haggard old man" was how the world saw Max these days, why not use it to his advantage? "I'd like to welcome you to the Tour of Lost Souls, and to New Orleans. This city is, of course, the birthplace of jazz, one of the oldest cities in the

Southern United States, and the most European city in America; they call us the Big Easy, the Crescent City, the City that Care Forgot. New Orleans is also considered one of the most haunted cities in the country. And tonight, I would like to share with you some of the dark, disturbing, and bloody events in our city's past that have earned us this reputation. Are y'all ready to begin?"

The group cheered.

"I was born in New Orleans, up there in Gentilly under the lake, just after everybody had come home from the war. Believe it or not, New Orleans was very important to the war effort—right here in the city was where Andrew Higgins designed and manufactured the Higgins Boats, very important in the war; those were the boats used on D-Day if you didn't know. My daddy actually worked in the factory there, for a time. But I digress. In the fifties and sixties, I grew up hearing scary stories from my mama and aunties. They'd tell me about the Rougarou, the swamp werewolf, that would snatch me up in its jaws if I stayed out too late after dark—what the Rougarou would be doing in Gentilly, I couldn't tell you, but that story sure kept me in line until I was old enough to know better. The Witch of the Irish Bayou, that was another one. They said I better be careful and treat all my sweethearts right because every gal in New Orleans was on a first-name basis with that witch, and she'd give them a potion that would make my pecker fall off if I misbehaved. Well, I managed to get around that one. I just went and got myself a nice girl from Philly, where they don't have swamp witches." The group laughed.

"But my favorite story was always Michie and Julie. When I was a little boy, I'd curl up on the bed by my mama and ask her to tell me about that cold, cold night way back in the 1830s. We didn't come to the Quarters much in those days, but she always painted the picture so well as she described this house, right across the garden behind me, and the dark roof with its little white attic windows."

This was a good story, especially on cold nights. First, he told them about *plaçage*, the system that allowed wealthy white men to date free women of color despite the ban on interracial marriage. "Did it work the other way too? Black men and white women?" he sometimes got asked, and he always wanted to laugh at the absurdity of the question. "No, it sure did not," he told them. *Are you kidding? You think they would have tolerated black men getting with white women in the 1800s? Hell, they practically burned us at the stake for doing it in the 1970s.*

And then he told the story of the white man, Michie, and his *placée*, Julie. He spoke of their epic love, her desperation to be married, his refusal for fear of social repercussions. Every time he'd heard the story as little boy, Max remembered hoping against hope that this time it would be different, that somehow it would have a happy ending—that she'd tell him she was pregnant, that she'd bring a blanket to the roof, that he wouldn't get so drunk at the party—and even sometimes as he told it, Max found himself wishing this same absurd wish, hoping that things would turn out differently. But they never did. As always, Michie ordered Julie to prove her love by waiting for him on the roof; as always, Julie froze to death in the night. But so what? Even if she'd lived, even if they'd married and raised a family together and lived decades and decades happily side by side…in the end, one of them would still pass before the other. And wouldn't that hurt more than if they had never had any of it to begin with?

He was nearing the end of the story. "He takes her body to the morgue, and when they do an autopsy, they learn something very sad…can anyone guess?" They always did. *Pregnant*, they murmured.

He nodded. "And so Michie learns that not only has he killed the love of his life, he has also killed his child. And I don't suppose that's something a man can really come back from. He retreats into himself, retreats into his house, and waits for death. Because without her, life is not worth living. Michie becomes an alcoholic and drinks himself to death in three short months."

Molly's ring hung heavy on his chest. And how many months had it been now? Eleven? He'd stopped counting the days; she wouldn't want him to.

"That was really your favorite story as a kid?" a pretty young lady asked him after he'd finished and they were walking. "The tragic romance?"

"What can I say?" he winked. "I reckon I'm a bit of a romantic, always have been."

"That's sweet. Ben here is a bit of a softie too; I think I saw a little tear in his eye..."

"Hey!" The handsome young man she was holding hands with gave her a playful shove.

"Where y'all from?" Max asked.

"Boston."

"Cold up there."

"Yes, it is."

"Cold down here too these days, though," Max said. "I've been wearing this big ol' coat nearly every day lately."

The young man, who was in just a light jacket and dungarees, shrugged. "Feels pretty good to us. It's like seven degrees back home right now."

"Holy mackerel."

"Yeah, I hate it. I'm trying to convince him to move somewhere warm."

"Well, why don't you come give New Orleans a shot? We can always use more good people down here."

"I mentioned that to him yesterday, actually! It's our first time here, and we're just in love..." she looked at her beau and squeezed his arm.

"Hey, come on, Max doesn't want to hear all that sappy stuff," the young man teased.

"I didn't mean with each other, dummy."

"You're not in love with me?" he gasped in mock shock. "This changes everything!"

"Oh, stop. Sorry," she said to Max. "He's a bit of a ham." The young man gave her a peck on the cheek.

Max took them to the Sultan's Palace next, then the Andrew Jackson Hotel, then the LaLaurie Mansion. That one was long and took a lot out of him, and he was always relieved to get to the bar after and rest his feet.

"Go on in and get yourselves a hurricane, use the restroom, meet back out here in ten minutes. If you need me, I'll be sitting in there by the fireplace, my dogs are barking."

Lafitte's was warm and dim, and he settled in at a table by the fire. They didn't often light it, only on very cold nights, and the fact that it had been lit almost every night for two weeks straight said something about the kind of winter New Orleans was having. Max took off his old leather gloves and laid them across the brick mantel to warm up, breathed on his stiff fingers as he glanced around the bar. It was very crowded. The most famous bar in New Orleans on the night before Mardi Gras, how could it not be? Max remembered coming to Lafitte's as a kid, just fifteen or sixteen years old, on the few occasions that he and his buddies had made it down to the Quarters. In fact, Lafitte's must have been one of the first bars he brought Molly to when she was new in town and eager to see the city. He remembered that night well. She'd never been a drinker before moving to New Orleans, whereas Max had been shotgunning Dixie beers since he was no older than twelve or thirteen, and she'd tripped all over him as they danced to the jukebox, three sheets to the wind on hurricanes.

"Aren't Irish people supposed to be able to hold their liquor?" he'd teased.

"You tell me," she'd slurred. "Aren't colored people supposed to be good dancers?" Always a wit like a hot poker, that one, even drunk. At the end of the night, she'd been so loaded that Max had to sling her over his shoulder and carry her to the bus stop, fireman style.

The next day she'd been horribly embarrassed. "Am I still your girl?" she'd mumbled from behind big Jackie O sunglasses when they met for coffee at Cafe du Monde.

"Baby, you could dance a jig in your underpants in front of the Queen of England and you'd still be my girl." And they'd taken a stroll through the Quarters up to Basin Street where the old canal used to be, and he'd pointed through the gates of St. Louis Cemetery #1 to all the old, crumbling tombs inside. "You'll be my girl until we both end up in there."

"Just toss me in now," she'd groaned. "Death sounds pretty good compared to this hangover."

Max was startled by a hand on his shoulder.

"Hey man, do you want a drink?" It was the young fellow Max had been talking to earlier, his sweetheart at his side.

"Do I want one? Surely. But I'd be cruisin' for a bruisin' if the boss found out I was drinking on the job," he winked.

"We won't tell!"

"That's very kind of you, but I have to decline," he said. Truth was, he was so pitifully scrawny these days that one drink would really do a number on him. "What do you think of that stuff?" he asked, gesturing to the girl's purple daiquiri.

"Tastes like grape kool-aid," she grimaced, and Max chuckled.

"I guess I can't complain, though. I'm amazed we were even able to get anything with how crowded it is in here."

"Oh, come on," the young man said, touching the small of her back. "Just look at you. Any bartender with eyes is gonna make sure you get served." She blushed.

"Anyway," she said. "We just wanted to let you know how much we're enjoying this. The ghost tour was like the number one thing I wanted to do in New Orleans."

"Besides Mardi Gras," the man added.

"Well, yeah. Besides Mardi Gras. But that's different!"

"So, do you have to give tours tomorrow?"

Max shook his head. "No sir. Mardi Gras day is the one day of the year that Spirits of Yore goes dark."

"Big plans? Gonna come down to Bourbon Street?"

"Honestly, I don't rightly know yet. We'll see how I feel."

Max looked at his watch. "We'd better get back out there," he said, and hauled himself to his feet, his joints creaking audibly. *Mercy,* he thought to himself, *I'm a walking cliché.*

The wind outside had picked up, and Max pulled his gloves on, thankful for the warmth they'd absorbed from the fireplace. He spoke about the bar's history and Jean Lafitte's exploits, briefly described Lafitte's role in the Battle of New Orleans and told a little ghost story about a young man who wanted to be a pirate. Not too much longer now, just a few more stops on the tour. He told a story on Dumaine then took a right on Chartres to talk about the Convent.

Chartres was always a pretty gloomy street, quieter than the rest of the Quarter, and on cold nights, it felt particularly desolate. The slender little trees near the Convent were shivering in the wind, their branches bare. In springtime, they'd bloom quickly; you'd wake up one morning in late March, and the whole city would be green again. Then there would be a couple months of beautiful, sunny seventy-five-degree days, but come June, the weather would start to get uncomfortable. It would get worse and worse until August, when the city was so boiling hot that you'd try to remember how chilly these February nights had felt and end up convincing yourself that it must have all been a figment of your imagination, and then somehow September would manage to be even hotter, and you'd decide that not only had you imagined last year's winter, but surely, this year the cooler weather wouldn't come at all. The heat and humidity would just keep squatting over the city like a fat man with clammy thighs, and you'd boil in it forever, stuck in this horrible, hot swamp of a city until the ocean washed it away.

But tonight, the cold wind whipping at his cheeks and his toes going stiff in his boots, that all sounded heavenly to Max. *I just want to get warm,* he thought, the sentence playing over and over in his mind while he told the story. *I just want to get warm.*

After the Convent, he led the group through Jackson Square to Père Antoine alley on the opposite side of the Cathedral from where they'd started. "Ladies and gentlemen, this is the last stop of the tour. Our tale begins in 1762, when King Louis decided that he was done with this failed colony and sold Louisiana to cousin Carlos, the king of Spain. Well, Carlos sent a new governor here, a fellow named Ulloa. He was a nice enough cat. Shy, quiet, and he liked to read. Well, when he arrived here in *La Nouvelle Orleans*, he announced that we were under Spanish rule and that from then on, he'd be in charge. And that would all have been well and good except for one little overlooked detail—see, nobody from France had bothered sending word ahead of time. No one in New Orleans had any idea that this transfer of power had occurred, and we weren't happy about it.

"Well. We reacted to this bad news more or less the way New Orleanians have always reacted to bad news: we got drunk." Smiles and chuckles from the group. "Thirteen of the city's most important bigwigs got together at a bar, they got loaded, and they got angry. So angry, in fact, that they decided to start an uprising against the new Spanish government. Well, the next day, sober, they decided that this plan of theirs was…still a top-notch idea!" The crowd laughed. "And so, these thirteen men took up arms against the new Spanish governor and his army. Folks…do you think those thirteen men won the fight?" People shook their heads and murmured no, as always.

"You sure wouldn't think so, would you? But they did. Those fellows won!

In fact, not even a drop of blood was shed. Because that governor who I mentioned—remember him? Shy, quiet, liked to read? Well, he didn't fit in too well here in New Orleans. Didn't like it here, in fact. And he took this uprising as an opportunity to just get on his ship and leave, go all the way back home to Spain. And we celebrated, thinking we'd won, thinking we'd be French again. But Spain wasn't ready to give up. No, Spain decided to send somebody a little bit tougher to deal with New Orleans. This cat's name was *Don Alejandro*...O'Reilly." That one always got a big laugh. "That's right, he was Irish. But he had moved to Spain at a young age, and he was their top guy. In fact, very early in his military career, he earned himself the nickname *Bloody* O'Reilly. So Bloody O'Reilly was sent here to New Orleans, our new Spanish governor. And the first thing he did was get the names of those thirteen rebels. And he invited them to dinner! Isn't that nice? And they accepted his invitation. Couldn't tell you why...well, actually, I reckon I can tell you why. New Orleanians don't ever turn down free food," he smiled. "So, they all went to dinner with him, had a lovely meal...and afterward, he had them all arrested. Later, these fellows were all put on trial for treason. Now, eight of them were just exiled. To Cuba. But five of them, the ringleaders... well, they were sentenced to death. These five men were taken over by the old Mint building and executed by firing squad.

"But even after the execution, O'Reilly wasn't finished teaching us our lesson. He brought those corpses here, to Père Antoine Alley, where we're standing. Then he strung those corpses up between these two buildings"—Max pointed to the wall of the Cathedral on one side of them and the Presbytère on the other—"and left them, hanging on display for the whole city to see. Now, this is New Orleans we're talking about...New Orleans in the summer." The group began to groan and wrinkle their noses. "That's right. And it wasn't long before there was very little left of these bodies. They started dripping. Melting. Skin sliding right off the bone, falling down here to the ground below. Everyone in New Orleans was horrified, especially Père Antoine, the city's most beloved priest. He begged Bloody O'Reilly to let him take the bodies down, so they could at least have a proper burial. But O'Reilly refused. And then he posted a group of Spanish guards here in the alley so nobody could interfere.

"And so, the bodies hung. For days, for weeks. The stench became so bad that folks stopped going to mass here at the Cathedral. But of course, nothing could be done...until a hurricane hit. And the Spanish guards, well, they were new in town. Never seen a hurricane. So, they fled, left their posts. And that is when Père Antoine leapt into action. He gathered some of the other French priests and they rushed here to the alley in the middle of the night through the hurricane. They took down what was left of the bodies, wrapped them in burial shrouds, and carried these corpses, in their bare arms, through the French Quarter. Through the driving rain, through the howling wind, until finally… finally, they were able to lay these men to rest. To give them the proper burial they deserved, there in our first graveyard, St. Peter Cemetery.

"And as the priests were carrying these dead men…burying these dead men…Père Antoine was leading them in song. They were singing the *Kyrie*, a Catholic liturgy." He pronounced the word as it was said in Greek—*keer-ee-ay.* "'*Kyrie eleison*,' they sang in Greek. *Kyrie eleison*, which meant, Lord have mercy.

"And that, my friends," he said with gravity, "brings us to our final haunting of the evening. You see, if you are here in this alley on a cold, wet night…you may hear something. And it's very faint. So faint, in fact, you'll hardly be able to tell if it's real or just in your mind. It's the sound of voices singing." He sang the kyrie for the group then, just those two Greek words, the notes trembling up and then down again in his smoke-ravaged throat. The song brought peaceful half-smiles to some of the faces in the group.

"This is the oldest reported haunting in New Orleans history. So old, in fact, that we locals have a name for it: we call it the *Singing Rain*. And it's not frightening. Père Antoine and his priests aren't going to bother you, they aren't going to interact with you; in fact, they're probably not aware of the living. They're just here, stuck in time, carrying out their task…perhaps one of the most important tasks of all. Mourning the dead.

"We all die. That's just what it is to be human, isn't it? And death is different for everyone; some of us depart before our time, some leave unfinished business, and some, I'm sure, are happy to go. What all the dead have in common, though, is what they leave behind. They leave us. The living. And it's our job to figure out how to make sense of their departure.

"I've told you many stories this evening. Stories of angry ghosts, lost ghosts, even playful ghosts. And listen, folks…it's not my job to tell you whether or not to believe in the supernatural. That's a very personal thing for each of us. But whether or not you believe in ghosts, or hauntings, I hope you can agree that these stories have value. Because what are ghost stories, really, but a way for the living to make sense of death?

"And maybe we never can make sense of death, not really. It's more or less the one great mystery. But we can do what those priests did, here in this very spot, hundreds of years ago. We can do right by the dead. We can keep their memory alive. We can walk through the hurricane...and we can sing. Thank you all, and goodnight."

Max never asked for tips, but people usually gave them. "Have you ever heard it? The Singing Rain?" a woman asked, pressing a bill into his hand.

Max shook his head. "Can't say that I have."

He must have looked sad when he said it because the woman smiled encouragingly and touched his shoulder. "I bet someday you will. When the conditions are right."

"Maybe," he smiled.

The young man from earlier handed Max a twenty.

"Why, I don't know if I deserve that!"

"You do. Trust me."

Max didn't see the young lady. "Where's your girl?" he asked.

"Dashed off to find a bathroom. Bladder the size of a peanut."

"Well, it was very nice to meet both of y'all. Hope you have a nice Mardi Gras tomorrow."

"Oh, we will," the man said, grinning. "I, uh..." he leaned in close. "I'm actually gonna propose."

Max's right knee suddenly went weak, and he stumbled back a step or two, catching himself on the fence of the garden behind him.

"Woah, you okay?"

"Fine, just fine. These old joints, you know."

"I was thinking of doing it right there in Jackson Square tomorrow. The proposal. What do you think?"

"I reckon that's a real nice idea. Best of luck to you both," Max said.

The man reached out to shake his hand. "Thank you. Really. For making this such a memorable night."

"I hope y'all have many, many more."

The fellow waved and smiled and went off to find his girl. The alley was empty now, except for some young scalawag at the opposite end taking a piss against the Presbytère. Max took a step, tentatively testing the knee that had just gone bad. It was weak, but he could manage. He headed back down the alley toward Royal Street, limping slightly, and checked his watch. It was 10:04, and the last bus left Rampart and Canal at 10:19. Eleven blocks. He wasn't going to think about anything but getting to his bus.

Royal was alive with music and people, the buskers still going strong. Max made his way across the street, dodging pedicabs, taking care not to put too much weight on his right leg. The wind picked up again, and he pulled the collar of his coat up around his neck. The temperature must have dropped ten degrees in the last two hours. Max hated the cold, always had. "My sweet Southern boy," Molly had always called him. Mercy, how he'd despised that first winter after Katrina, which they'd spent with their youngest son in Chicago. Those ten-degree nights, with the wind whipping off the lake…no matter how many layers a man put on, he could never seem to get warm. Yet these last few weeks, Max had been as miserable as he'd ever been in the short time he'd spent up North. The house wasn't insulated, and the hot water heater hadn't been working properly, and he was so thin now, so terribly underweight, that the wet, shivery cold seeped right through his coat and settled in his bones. But no one else seemed to notice it, all these young lads in t-shirts and girls in short skirts and high heels, warmed by alcohol, distracted by each other's company. He envied them.

Max turned to cross Bourbon and immediately regretted it. He became swept up in a wave of people, thousands of them, all packed together shoulder to shoulder. There was music coming from every direction, a brass band blaring on the corner, and reggae spilling out the doors of Tropical Isle, and rap and jazz and all the rest of it, and everyone had a drink, and everyone was shouting, and there were beads everywhere, draped around necks and over balconies and in big piles on the concrete, half-drowned in the puddles of greasy gutter water and whatever fluorescent liquor they put in hand grenades. The bodies around him were warm, and the glow of the neon signs made everything bright, and everyone was drunk and costumed and happy. Bourbon Street on Lundi Gras: the center of the universe. To all of these thousands of people, there was no such thing as cold, or pain, or loneliness. In two hours, it would be Mardi Gras, the best day of the year, and all that mattered was music and food and booze and *laissez les bon temps rouler*.

Tomorrow. Mardi Gras. The best day of the year.

How many Fat Tuesdays would this be now? They'd almost never missed it; Molly had insisted on that. Sure, Max loved Mardi Gras, but when a fellow grows up with something, he takes it for granted, at least to some degree. But for Molly, Mardi Gras was pure magic. Max tried to catalogue all their Mardi Gras in his mind, an impossible task, but a few stood out. Last year had been the grandson's first, when the King of Zulu had pointed right at the boy and tossed him a coconut…and how could anyone forget the Mardi Gras a few years prior, the one they all called "Soggy Gras," when Molly had dressed them both in her mother's old fur coats and insisted they go out anyway? Their first Mardi Gras back after the storm was a good one, when she'd been so delighted at living so close to the route that they dragged folding chairs out to watch every parade, even the ones no one gave a hoot about, just because they could. And Mardi Gras '96, that had been the one during the audit, when they'd fought the whole time. '93, their first Fat Tuesday as empty nesters, when both the kids were finally out of the house, and they'd blown a week's paycheck on cocaine—what a bender that had been. A few years prior, around that time, maybe '87, Molly had eaten some bad shrimp and had been stuck at home the whole day, but she'd insisted Max go out without her. He had, but only for a couple hours, and then they'd spent the rest of the day in bed watching *Mork and Mindy* reruns. The kids were young in the early eighties, all those years just blurred together... of course, '79 was the year Mardi Gras had been canceled because of the police strike, and that year they'd left the kids with Max's parents, gotten in the car and driven to Galveston, Texas for no reason at all. Turned out Galveston had a little Mardi Gras of its own, and they'd watched the modest floats go by and slurped down daiquiris until they were too drunk to drive home and slept in the car in the parking lot of a Piggly Wiggly. And '75 they hadn't caught much of because Terence had been just a couple weeks old.

And Mardi Gras 1973. Their first together. Max had just brought Molly home with him from the Peace Corps, this loud and stubborn and sweet white girl from Philadelphia, to meet his family and see his city. They'd only been in town a few weeks when Mardi Gras came, and she'd had a million questions. "Why are all the men in blackface when they're already black?" she'd asked at Zulu. "Where do all the beads come from?" "Where do all the beads go?" "What's in a hurricane?" "Do I really have to show my tatas?" Over the course of the day, though, the questions subsided, and the most sublime grin crept onto her face, growing bigger and sweeter and brighter by the hour until she was blowing kisses at every person she met in the street and pulling Max aside to dance with every passing band. They'd gone to the river and sat there for a while throwing flowers into it, and she'd told him that she wanted every day to be Mardi Gras. And he'd looked at her, with her crooked bangs and freckly nose and that big, sweet smile on her face and thought to himself that every day he spent with her felt like Mardi Gras. And that he wanted every day to feel like that for the rest of his life.

They'd gone back to Jackson Square, and she'd asked if he wanted another beer, and he'd said, "Yes, after this."

And she'd said, "After what?"

And he'd got down on one knee and asked her to marry him.

Someone bumped into Max, and he felt his right knee go soft again. He stumbled, sinking down onto the pavement in the middle of Bourbon Street. Pain shot through his hip.

"Hey man, you okay?" A young fellow in baggy pants pulled him to his feet.

"I think so. Must have just tripped a little."

"Yeah, brother, it's crazy out here. Can you walk okay?"

"I'll be fine. Thank you for your kindness."

"No problem." And the man hurried back to his friends up ahead.

It was difficult to walk now, his hip was bursting with pain, and he could barely put weight on the leg. He needed to get off Bourbon Street, away from the crowds, but there were people pushing in on all sides, and he couldn't seem to manage to make his way to the other side of the street. He stopped to lean against a gallery pole. What if he'd broken something, he wondered. What if he'd broken his hip like the frail old man he was; what if he couldn't give tours anymore; how would he survive? He'd be trapped alone in his little house with his sad dog, time stretching out empty ahead of him, nothing to look forward to but the visits from his kids once or twice a year. He'd be alone and useless, his body falling apart, and eventually his mind would fall apart too, and at least then maybe he'd be able to forget the loneliness, the despair, the absolutely crushing emptiness of being in a world where she wasn't.

His watch said 10:16. There was no way he'd make the bus.

One hour and forty-four minutes until Mardi Gras. Mardi Gras, the best day of the year. His first Mardi Gras without her.

He reached for Molly's ring around his neck. It wasn't there.

His hands scrambled into his pockets, into his coat, searching. The ring was gone, the chain and all.

Max gave up.

He couldn't cross Bourbon; he wouldn't make his bus; he was just walking now, back the way he came down St. Ann, blinded by tears. His hip hurt terribly, and he was limping, and it was cold away from Bourbon Street, the wind shooting right down the street, cutting into him, and it had begun to rain a little, heavy cold drops falling sporadically to the pavement. He felt one hit the back of his neck and shuddered. Rapidly, the rain picked up, soaking his wool coat and his newsboy cap. He shivered, feeling the dampness in his very bones. And he knew he would never be warm again, ever, even if summer did come.

Max realized that he was walking toward the river. Maybe he'd go there, look out at it, that big dark wet expanse under the twinkling lights of the bridge. The biggest river in the country, it was, one of the biggest in the world. He'd look at it, watch it go by, maybe even go down to its banks and touch it, that slick, murky water, millions of gallons of it under the palm of his hand. Maybe he'd slip his hand under. How heavy all those millions of gallons of water must be. How warm. And how dark and calm and quiet it must be, down there under the weight of all that water. You wouldn't hear the sounds of the French Quarter, of Mardi Gras, under the river. Midnight would never come, and Mardi Gras would never happen, and in fact, no more days would happen at all, the hundreds or thousands of days that stretched out meaningless ahead; they'd all be extinguished under the Mississippi's warm weight.

Max turned down Père Antoine alley, bracing against the rain. He'd lost his umbrella, misplaced it somewhere, but this was the kind of sideways rain that didn't care whether you had an umbrella or not. The uneven gray flagstones were soaked, and the one lamppost seemed to have gone out, leaving the alley darker than usual. The usual loitering restaurant employees and tourists making their way from Bourbon to the Square were gone, driven away by the rain, and Max was alone in the alley's corridor. He walked past the garden, past the open arms of Jesus' shadow on the wall, past the back of the Cathedral where the choir was singing inside. Just a few more steps to Jackson Square, then a few more steps to the levee, then a few more steps into the dark waters of the Mississippi, and he'd be warm and whole again.

Our sons, she'd say. *The grandkids. Seamus.* But he didn't want to hear it. In the last eleven months, he'd sometimes tricked himself into thinking that she was whispering to him, watching over him, there with him somehow. But the dead can't communicate with the living, can they? She wasn't whispering; she wasn't watching; she wasn't anywhere. He'd lost her ring, that was the only sign he needed. The voices of the choir crescendoed. It was time.

Time.

Max looked at his watch. It was 10:30 PM. On Lundi Gras.

The choir does not practice at 10:30 PM on Lundi Gras.

Max stopped and looked up at the side of the Cathedral looming over the alley, its windows dark. There was most certainly no one inside.

Lightning flashed, and a shape on the ground caught Max's eye. There at his feet lay Molly's ring on its chain.

The sweet, haunting notes of the Kyrie rose and fell and faded into the rain.

CHAPTER 15

The River

On Mardi Gras morning, everyone gets up early. Zulu rolls at eight AM, so you've got to be up in Central City around nine if you want to catch it, and then Rex starts at ten. Although, most people I know prefer to start Mardi Gras in the Marigny with the Krewe of Saint Anne. It's a walking parade, thousands of locals in these amazing, outlandish, elaborate costumes, and you want to be there on the street in front of Mimi's bar by eight or nine at the latest, so you can see everybody and get your cocktail and take your pictures before they pass around the big bowl of dry red beans and rice, and everyone takes a handful, and then you all throw it into the air together to make your Mardi Gras blessing, and the parade's slow procession gets started.

Either way, it's a little while before people start to make it into the Quarter. I'm here at the Quarter Rat, sitting in the courtyard, waiting. I can't believe it's Mardi Gras already. It seems like just a few months since I was here getting into costume for the last Krewe du Tour, taking shots with James and Vik and listening to Poppy grouse and waiting on Ruby, who's always late for everything. But that's always how Mardi Gras happens, isn't it? It's over and you mourn and whine and feel like it'll be ages till the next one, but once you get through summer, it all goes pretty fast, the cool fall weather and the holidays and then bam, Rouses has towers of king cakes again and WWOZ is playing "Carnival Time" ten times a day.

The clock above the bar inside says 10:45. There are already some tourists in there, starting to take over our little pub like they always do on Mardi Gras day. We're only half a block from Bourbon, after all, and they usually find their way here when they decide they'd like a drink that isn't neon-colored. But as of this minute, the courtyard is empty except for me and Vik. He's wearing a vest and a newsboy cap and has an axe, which sits on the table next to him, and he's got a bandage on his right hand.

Sofia comes into the courtyard. I barely recognize her at first; her hair isn't blue anymore, it's black, all trussed up in a pretty updo. It takes me a second to realize she's wearing a wig. Vik stands, and she looks surprised to see him.

"Wow. You look great," he says.

Sofia crosses her arms. "Thanks."

"I, uh…I've missed you the last couple days," Vik says.

"Yeah."

"I thought I'd hear more from you. You didn't even text."

"Didn't want to bother you."

"I could have…you know...helped."

"I didn't really think you'd want to."

"Jesus," he says, rubbing his forehead. "It's like that now, huh?"

"It's like what it's always been like," she shrugs.

"You think I don't care about what happened to you? I beat him up, for chrissakes, nearly got arrested!"

"No one asked you to do that."

"What, then? What do you want from me?"

"I feel like I've always made that pretty clear."

"I have *tried*, okay? To be what you want."

"No, you haven't. You never have."

"Yes, I—" he begins to argue, then takes a breath. "Look. Enough with the mind games. Just be straight with me."

"Okay."

"So…are you…I mean, what is this, are you breaking up with me?"

She looks him dead in the eye. "Oh. Were we dating?"

Angela's voice precedes her, that perfect diction ringing bell-like into the courtyard a couple seconds before she bustles in carrying a stack of aluminum trays. She's wearing a simple period-style dress, floor length with a flared waist and severe collar, and as she gets closer, I realize she's wearing very light foundation so that her skin appears even paler than usual. There's a scarf around her neck and a dab of blood at the corner of her mouth, and I can't see her teeth, but I'd bet you anything she's wearing vampire fangs. Veda, I realize, is behind her, carrying a tote bag full of utensils and plates. She's in a plain, short blue dress with big buttons, and she has her hair braided in pigtails. It's the simplest thing I've ever seen her wear—the one day you're supposed to wear a costume, and Veda dresses like an ordinary person. Sort of funny, actually.

"Good morning!" Angela says cheerily. Vik glowers and goes back into the bar. "Happy Mardi Gras!"

Sofia goes over to them, smiling. "Happy Mardi Gras. You made food?"

"We did! Fried okra, gumbo, a little salad. And of course, my famous blueberry mascarpone king cake."

"Yum, wow!" Sofia exclaims. "So, you must be a Casket Girl," she says. "Love it." She turns to Veda. "And you are?"

"Oh. Um. Leah? From the LaLaurie story."

"Aw, that's cute."

"I never got to be a little girl," she says. "Thought maybe it would be nice."

"Can you believe how warm it is?" Sofia says, looking up at the slice of bright blue sky above the courtyard.

"Simply gorgeous." Angela says. "I was certain we'd have a cold one this year, the way the weather's been these last few weeks."

"Same!"

"You look fantastic, by the way." Sofia's also in some sort of period get-up, a long blue taffeta dress with white gloves and a big cameo brooch.

"Thanks! It's actually just my mom's old prom dress from like the eighties, but Ruby did some stuff to it. Added the tulle underneath so that it flares out, see?"

"Very nice work," Angela says, examining the dress. "It really does achieve something like a Victorian look! And you are…?"

"Julie," Sofia says. "I mean, I wasn't going to put on blackface or anything, but Ralphie said to dress as our favorite character."

There's a big commotion as James comes in. He's wearing a turban, a floor length belly dancer skirt, and a white tank top, and he's got some blond girl in tow.

"Haaaaappy Mardi Gras," James says grandly, and upon closer examination, I realize it's not a girl at all but the boy, Landon, the one James has been seeing, wearing a cheap wig. Everything he's wearing is Mardi Gras colors: a green-, purple-, and gold-feathered boa, a pile of beads as thick as my arm, and a green-, purple-, and gold-striped polo, the kind you always see the basic frat boys uptown wearing. James has quite a lot of beads on too, and they're clearly both already pretty tipsy.

"Wow," Sofia says. "Y'all went to the parades this morning, huh?"

"It's baby's first Mardi Gras!" James says, hauling the beads off his neck and dumping them on the table.

"Yep! My very first one," Landon beams. "We got this, and this, and this…" he's pulling throws out of a bag and plopping them on the table. "Some lady at Zulu tried to take the boa I caught, but I got it back."

"Where's Vik?" James asks. "Isn't he with you?"

"He went into the bar," Sofia says.

"James, Landon, have some food!" Angela says. "We made it all this morning."

"Mmm, don't mind if I do." James scoops a little gumbo into a cup and starts eating. "Wow. You made this?"

"You like it?"

"Yeah, really good."

"Thank you! I do pride myself on my cooking. And Veda did a wonderful job with the okra!"

"So, you're a Casket Girl," James says to Angela, his mouth full. "And who are you, Madame LaLaurie?" he asks Sofia.

"No!" she gasps. "Madame LaLaurie was old and ugly."

"—she was actually very beautiful, according to many sources," Angela interjects.

"I'm Julie, obviously."

James raises an eyebrow. "But Julie was black..."

"So?"

"That's like, cultural appropriation."

"Well, what are you, the Sultan? You don't look very Arabic to me."

"Mardi Graaaaas!" Landon hollers out of nowhere.

"Sorry, he's a bit drunk," James says in a mock whisper.

Landon shoves him lightly. "Hey! So are you!"

"*That is a bold-faced lie*! I have never had a drink in my life," James says as he takes a dainty sip of his gin and tonic. Landon starts to tickle him, and James shrieks, then they start smooching.

Vik comes back from the bar with a fresh drink and picks up his axe.

"Girl, *there* you are," James says.

I'm watching Vik watch Sofia. She's avoiding eye contact.

"Look at all our throws!" Landon gestures to the giant pile on the table.

"So, where's everyone else?" Angela asks.

"Yeah. Is Max coming?" Sofia says.

"Unclear," James shrugs. "He told me he might be 'too fagged out;' I tried not to take it personally."

"Actually," Angela announces, "I'm sure that expression has nothing to do with the homophobic usage of the word, 'fagged out' was a common term in—"

"Hey, speak of the devil," Vik says.

Max is here, and he has a dog with him, a big Irish setter with graying fur.

"You made it!" Sofia exclaims. Everyone's genuinely happy to see him, patting him on the back and hugging him.

"I'm just glad it's warmed up," Max says, shaking his head. "I couldn't take one more cold day."

"Who's this guy?" Sofia asks, kneeling to pet the dog.

"That's my buddy, Seamus."

"What a good boy!"

"He's a bit long in the tooth. But he's never been out on Mardi Gras, I thought he might enjoy it."

"Great costume," Angela says. "Père Antoine?"

Max winks. "You guessed it." He's in a long white robe with a heavy cross around his neck.

"Where'd you get the robe?" Vik asks.

"It was Molly's. She was in the church choir for a time."

"Fits you well."

"Well. I'm losing weight these days."

"Let's fatten you up, then!" Angela says, and hands him a plate of food.

"Holy mackerel," Max says. "Where'd all this come from?"

"Veda and I cooked. Have as much as you want."

"Hey, Max, have you met my boyfriend?" James asks. "This is Landon."

Vik's eyebrows climb up his forehead so high it's comical. "Nice to meet you," Max says, shaking Landon's hand.

"You too, sir," he smiles. "I'm gonna grab another drink, anybody want anything?" A few people request beers, and he gets up and goes in.

"I'm glad you made it," James says to Max.

"It was touch and go for a little while there," Max says. "Wasn't sure I would. But here I am."

"Good," James smiles. "I also, uh, wanted to thank you."

"Thank me?"

"What you said last night. You're right. Life's too short to play games."

Max squeezes his shoulder. "I'm glad for you, son. Now if you'll excuse me, I just walked a very long way, and I need to pay a visit to the little boys' room."

As soon as Max is gone, Vik swoops over and gets up in James' face.

"Your '*boyfriend*?'"

"Yeah. I asked him this morning."

"You asked *him*?"

"Yeah."

"To be your boyfriend."

"Yeah, so what? Calm your tits."

"That's just…unexpected."

"We've been hooking up for months. I really like him…it's not a big deal."

"Okay. Whatever you say."

"Are you like, *offended*?"

"No. Just surprised."

"So, what's going on with you and Sofia? She's not hanging all over you like usual."

"I dunno," Vik says quietly.

"You don't know?"

"We haven't hung out in a couple days. Ever since the thing with Jeremy."

"Oh, right. What a creep."

"She's been acting weird ever since. I think she's upset with me."

"Dramaaaa."

Vik gets annoyed. "It's not...I mean, it's different this time. She's never acted like this before."

Ruby has just made a grand entrance and is now sweeping over to Vik and James in her long dress, interrupting. Landon comes back with more beer.

"Hello, my darlings," Ruby says, giving each of them a long hug. "Am I late?"

"You're literally always late," says James.

I expect Ruby to snap at him, make some witty comeback, but she just smiles. "Love you too," she says.

Vik raises an eyebrow. "Well, aren't *you* in a good mood."

"It's Mardi Gras! And I'm here with my friends, and you're all so beautiful, and oh my God, the *weather*. Can you believe how gorgeous it is?"

"Yeah, it's nice," James agrees. "I was afraid I'd have to wear something over my domestic tranquility garment, but now I get to show off my arms."

"Domestic tranquility garment? That's a wife beat—oh," Ruby says. "I get it. Cute."

"I'm nothing if not politically correct," he drawls.

Sofia comes over to join them. "Isn't Ruby's costume great?"

"Yeah, Ruby, what is that?" asks Landon.

"I'm the swamp witch," she says, and does a little twirl. The dress she's wearing is made of a dozen different kinds of fabric, a scrappy patchwork of purple and silver and green, tattered but beautiful. She's woven Spanish moss through her glittery dreadlocks, and she's wearing a shawl that looks like it's made of old fishing net.

"Not bad," James said. "So, tell me, swamp witch, do you have any...potions today?"

"No, just weed," she says.

"Seriously? No acid, no coke?"

She shrugs. "I'm kind of taking a head break."

"Well, *that's* disappointing. For me, I mean."

Veda's attention wanders as they chat. I catch her eye from the corner of the room, and she gives me a tiny little wave.

A few minutes later Poppy comes in. She's not wearing a costume, but she's dressed differently than usual. She's wearing a long white skirt and a shirt with dalmatians on it.

"Poppy," Max smiles, and gives her a hug.

"Max! Glad you made it, old man."

"Same to you."

"No costume?" Angela asks.

"I'm not wearing black," Poppy says. "Ain't that enough?"

"That's true, I suppose I've only ever seen you in black."

"Well, not anymore! I just went through my closet, got rid of all that."

"Got rid of your black clothes? Why?" Sofia asks, coming over.

"'Cause I don't need 'em. 'Cause I don't work for Spirits of Yore anymore," Poppy grins.

"You're kidding," Max says.

"No shit. Handed in my notice yesterday."

Everyone makes a commotion. "Feels good," she says. "Twenty-four years giving tours. But it's finally time to move on."

"What's next?" Angela asks.

"I think I might get out of here, actually."

"Leave New Orleans?"

"There's some mountains out there, been calling my name for a long time now."

"I'm so happy for you," Veda smiles, and gives her a big hug.

"Will you come back and visit?" Sofia asks.

"Not a chance," Poppy smirks, and they all laugh.

The courtyard is so different in the daytime. The bricks of the walls are pale in the light, the wooden tables more worn-out than you realize under the evening sconces. And the sky above the courtyard walls doesn't feel like a ceiling the way it does at night. Instead, it's like a window. The top has been lifted from our little world, and you can see all the way up to the clouds.

The eating and chatting and laughing continues. After a few minutes, Vik goes to Poppy and takes her aside.

"Have you heard anything about Jeremy?" he asks quietly.

"He got out yesterday. Someone musta posted his bail, Elijah probably."

"Did you see him?"

She nods. "He came to my place."

"And you talked to him?"

"You gotta understand, me and Jeremy have been friends for twenty, thirty years. Figured I at least owed him a conversation."

"What did he say?"

"He was in rough shape. Looked like he hadn't slept since it happened."

"Good."

"He was sorry, though. Real sorry. Said that wasn't the kind of man he wanted to be."

"I spoke to the boss. He's been fired."

"Yeah, he knows. Listen—is Sofia gonna press charges?"

"You bet your ass she will."

Poppy sighs. "He won't survive in jail, you know. There's no way."

"So? Why should I care."

"I'm not asking you to care. Just stating a fact."

"He lives in the Quarter, right? If she doesn't press charges, she'll have to see him. There's no way she'll never run into him."

"I don't know about that."

"What do you mean?"

Poppy shakes her head. "When he came to see me, he said something about getting out of here. Ready to be done."

"Really?"

"Yeah. He's been in New Orleans since he was just a kid, though, never could manage to belong anywhere else...I dunno where else he thinks he could go."

"Yeah, well. Not my problem."

And then Ralphie shows up, wearing a cheap pirate hat. The last of us to arrive.

"Young man, it is 11:25!" James shouts at him. "Where have you been?"

"Sorry, sorry."

"Who are you, 'Gene' Lafitte?" Vik asks.

"You mean *Jean* Lafitte?" Angela says.

"Yeah, but this idiot couldn't pronounce it right until about a month ago. Isn't that right, Ralphie?" Vik says, more aggressively than necessary. Ralphie blushes, and Sofia shoots Vik a glare.

"What can I say, I'm a bear of very little brains," Ralphie says.

"Oh, I think you've got plenty," Max says. "Maybe more than most."

Ralphie's face lights up when he sees him. "Max! Buddy, you made it!" He throws his arms around Max, nearly knocking him off his feet, and the old man smiles.

"Wouldn't miss it. Hope it's alright that I brought my dog."

"Well, hey there, doggo!" Ralphie says, patting Seamus on the head. "Anyway. I'm here. Krewe du Tour, let's do this!"

"Now, how does this work, exactly?" Max asks.

"Oh, it's pretty low key, honestly," James says. "We just sort of get drinks and walk to the river and yell made-up facts at people along the way."

"It was on this spot in 1831 that Andrew Jackson invented jazz!" Ruby yells.

"Jean Lafitte single handedly put out the Great Fire of 1788 with a bucket of Napoleon's tears," Vik deadpans, and everyone laughs.

"You get the idea."

"Is it time?" Sofia asks. "Is everybody here?"

"Yep. Everybody except Kat," Ruby sighs.

I rise at the sound of my name.

I didn't know I could do that.

"I've got her," Ralphie says, digging in his pocket. He pulls out a little glass jar, just a few inches wide and an inch or two tall. "That's why I'm late, actually. I left it at home, had to go back."

"Who let *you* be in charge of the ashes, for God's sake?" Vik ribs, again a little too aggressively.

"Simmer down," James scolds him.

Ralphie makes a sad little laughing sound. "I may be a hot mess or whatever you call me. But I'm not gonna lose my best friend."

There's a quiet moment.

"Well, jeez, let's all just be a little more awkward about it, shall we?" James says. "Come on, y'all, it's Mardi Gras, let's go if we're going!" And soon, they're all laughing and talking and straightening their costumes and gathering up their things. James gives Landon a little peck on the lips and tells him he'll catch up with him after. Most of them go into the bar for another round to go, and Leela gives them all little air hugs across the bar and blows them kisses and tells them to come back when they're done.

They leave the bar.

And somehow, I follow.

The street is an explosion of noise and color. There's music coming from every direction, a brass band up on Royal and all kinds of cacophony emanating from Bourbon, and it's just packed out here, tons of people wandering and drinking and celebrating. Around here, just half a block from Bourbon, most of them are tourists. They're sunburned and drunk, and they're not really in costume, although some of them have cheap masks, and of course, they're all wearing beads. They have their hurricanes and hand grenades and "Big Ass Beers," and they're all shouting and hollering and showing their tits to each other; tourists are the only people I've ever seen do that. It's not actually a thing, contrary to popular belief.

James is at the head of the pack. He's yelling, "Happy Mardi Gras! Tip your tour guides, you cheap motherfuckers!" and Vik is shouting something too, probably fake history. We have to go pretty slow in order to stay together; there are people and obstacles everywhere. Ruby and Sofia are toward the back of the group, having a quiet conversation. Well, it isn't actually quiet; they're speaking at full volume, but under the din of everything else, it's about as audible as a whisper. I walk behind them.

"So, what's going on? Things seem weird between you and Vik," Ruby says.

"Yeah, I dunno."

"I heard he beat up Jeremy."

"Yeah."

"Wow. Wish I could have seen that."

"I don't. What did it accomplish? Stupid macho shit…what I need is someone to just..." she sighs. "*Be* there for me. And he never is."

"Are you gonna break up with him?"

"I don't know. How do you break up with someone you're in love with?"

"Well, in my case, you wait till they fuck up so royally that you have no choice."

Veda falls back from where she was walking with Max and joins them.

"Hey, y'all."

"Hey, girl! You look so cute."

"Thanks. I feel cute," she smiles. "Hey, I was wondering… are you free a week from today?"

"Probably," Sofia shrugs. "Why?" Ruby asks.

"I've decided to have a funeral for my parents."

"A funeral? But…they're not dead, are they?"

"No, not physically. But I need to lay the past to rest. Say a real goodbye, you know?"

"That's a good idea."

"Can we have a funeral for Brian too?" Ruby asks.

"Of course," Veda says.

Sofia rolls her eyes. "And Vik."

"All of them," Veda smiles. "All the people our hearts have been holding too tightly. We'll take them to the river and scatter them to the wind."

Veda slips her hand into Ruby's, and Ruby takes Sofia's, and the three young women walk hand in hand down St. Peter Street.

We take a left on Royal, which is even more crowded. There's a cart roll going by, one of these big mobile DJ stations hooked up to giant speakers, and people just follow it around, dancing. There are people up on the balconies, people crowding the streets and sidewalks, and they're going by me in what feels like slow motion, so slowly that I can't focus on any of them properly, can't hear what they're saying, and I feel like I'm in the way, but no one asks me to move; I'm just standing there in the middle of Royal Street watching it all happen around me. The sky is brilliant blue, and the sun is bright, and it's probably very warm, though I can't feel it. I close my eyes, and for a moment, I'm gone. There is nothing.

And when I open my eyes again, I'm not on Royal Street anymore; I've caught up with my friends; they're in the alley now, Père Antoine alley behind the Cathedral, still heading toward the river. It's so strange to be here in the daytime. I've been in the alley after sunset on tours a thousand times, telling the Singing Rain or Julie or talking about the duels in the garden, but I can probably count on two hands the number of times I've walked these gray stones under the sun. I see Max's white robe up ahead, his uneven gait a little more pronounced than usual, and hurry to catch up.

He's walking next to Ralphie, whose pirate hat is askew. I want to straighten it for him; it's an almost unconscious habit, the way I've always tidied Ralphie, fussed over him. Tucking in his pockets, smoothing his shirt collars, sometimes even bending down in the street at work to tie his shoes. He always acted like it annoyed him, but I don't know. It's human contact. And we all need that, don't we? I wish I could do it for him now.

Max pulls a rolled-up stack of papers out of his bag.

"Got to read this last night," he smiles.

"My story! You did?"

"Sorry it got a little wet. Got stuck in the rain after my tour."

"What did you think?" Ralphie asks eagerly.

"Smart stuff. I think you've got a very unique voice," Max says.

"You mean it?"

"I do."

"Thanks," Ralphie says. "I dunno. Sometimes I just...I wonder if it's *too* unique."

"What do you mean?"

"I mean, my brain just...I'm just different, you know? My writing's different. What are the chances I'll ever get published, probably pretty low."

"It's not about getting published."

"It's not?"

"Nah. I've got a novel sitting in a desk drawer, never did anything with it."

"You're a writer too? Max! Why didn't you tell me?"

Max waves him off. "Dunno if I'd call myself a writer. But I started that thing, and I finished it, and when I go, it's a little piece of me I'll leave behind. My own little shard of mirror held up to the world."

"Can I read it?"

"Maybe someday," Max smiles. "When I die, how 'bout?"

"Die? Woah there, buddy, you'd better not be planning on doing that anytime soon."

"Hate to tell you this, but it's bound to happen eventually," Max says. "I'll try not to go too soon, though."

"Promise me," Ralphie says, his blue eyes brilliant in the sun.

The Cathedral casts a shadow on them as they walk by it, and Max glances up at its high walls. "I promise," he says. "It's not my time. Not just yet."

Max puts a hand on Ralphie's shoulder, and I see his other hand leave his side and wander to his chest. I know he's holding Molly's ring.

Vik pokes his head around the corner of the alley from up ahead in Jackson Square. "People! Stay together! It's madness out here!"

We emerge into the Square, and sure enough, it's madness. Hundreds of people, an overwhelming scene of revelry. Over to our left is a drum circle, ten or twelve people with big djembes and bongos, hammering out a rowdy, fast-paced percussion that makes your feet ache to stomp. There are dozens of people gathered around and among the drummers dancing, some of them grinning and laughing, some so lost in the beat that their eyes are closed and their mouths are open, and they look like they're about to depart this plane of reality entirely.

Two Mardi Gras Indians go by in their elaborate handmade regalia, enormous, beautiful pink and blue and yellow suits made of feathers and beads and jewels that make them look like giant birds of paradise and take a whole year to make. On every day of the year besides Mardi Gras and St. Joseph's Day, these are just ordinary guys from New Orleans' working-class neighborhoods, fathers and sons who work in muffler shops and grocery stores and post offices. But today, they're royalty. They promenade proudly throughout the city in their hundred-pound suits, sending their spy boys ahead to scope out other tribes, and when the rival Big Chiefs meet, there's grand theatrics, a competition over whose suit is the prettiest. It's a tradition that's been passed on for generations in the black community, dating all the way back to the 1700s when the enslaved fled the city for the bayous, where they befriended Native Americans and began to adopt their customs. Three hundred years of history in every feather, every bead.

And on the other side of us, there's a brass band, a different one than we saw on Royal, horns blaring, sweat beading the musicians' brows, and there are people dancing over there too. And I'm thinking about how there was no such thing as jazz before New Orleans; it all started here, just a few blocks away in Congo Square where the enslaved gathered on Sundays to sing and dance and extend a big hearty *Fuck You* to capitalism and white supremacy and all the other awful defining obsessions of this country that bought New Orleans in 1803, but which never really owned us, no, just as the French never fully did, just as the Spanish never fully did. There's something else in us, maybe you can trace it to Latin America or the Caribbean or maybe not, maybe you can't define it at all. The divine? The diabolical? I don't know what to call it. But there's magic here. In Jackson Square on Mardi Gras day, it's undeniable.

We're walking up the side of the park now, under the Pontalba apartments. I look back at Ralphie, who's dawdling behind, acting out some little play in his head, and up at Angela in her costume, her heels tidily clicking as she explains something to Sofia. Ruby's got a big grin on her face, and Veda is sort of skipping and humming, and Vik is yelling a story at James, swinging his axe wildly in the air in front of him. I'm so terribly fond of all of them. I don't think I realized how much until now.

We're crossing Decatur now. And as we get closer to the river, the crowd begins to change. The hordes of bead-wearing tourists thin out, and you can tell that the people around are predominantly locals now because of what they're wearing. The costumes have got to be one of the best parts of Mardi Gras. There's a guy near me in a white tutu, a white corset, and a papier mache rabbit mask, and he's holding hands with a guy in a rhinestone vest with a big purple storm painted on his face, slashed through by a white lightning bolt. This woman over here is wearing what looks like a whole cow skull on her head, with a tailcoat covered in shells and glittery gold cowboy boots ringed in gold fringe. Someone is wearing a suit made of balloons with a harlequin mask, that guy over there is somehow entirely covered in sunflowers, and there are hundreds more, an almost shoulder-to-shoulder crowd of people making their way in this direction from the Marigny where the Krewe of Saint Anne began this morning. None of them are fall-down drunk like the tourists on Bourbon. Locals know that there are generally two proper approaches to Mardi Gras Day: pace yourself very carefully if you're drinking, or just forgo alcohol altogether and take a lot of drugs instead. As I look at the faces around me, I notice several people with dilated pupils and big smiles, sailing through the day on their psychedelic ships.

And then we crest the levee, and there it is, wide and magnificent under the bright blue sky, the Mississippi River. There's something about the river, a sort of tacit understanding we all have of it. You go to the river to know yourself. And if you go to the river with someone else, you end up knowing them too. Standing here, situated between a three-hundred-year-old city and its reason for being here, a body of water two thousand miles long and the same number of years old, the things that aren't key to human existence tend to fall away. How many times have I come here, I wonder, with Ralphie or Ruby or Veda, just to sit and look at the water and talk?

There are hundreds of people at the river today. They're climbing up and down the rocks in their costumes and wigs, stretching out on the little strips of grass along the Riverwalk, napping, drinking, playing instruments, laughing.

And then I see him. There, just fifteen or twenty feet away, sitting on a rock not far from the water. It's Jeremy. He looks different, somehow, though I'm pretty sure he's wearing the same clothes he was in the last time I saw him. Maybe it's the stubble. He's staring out at the river, and as the group approaches, he turns slowly to look at them.

I expect a scene. Ruby or Vik will rush over, I'm sure, yell at him, chase him off. But they don't. In fact, they don't even seem to notice him. Sofia's oblivious, Poppy too, all of them, they just climb down the rocks a stone's throw from where he's sitting. How is it possible that they don't see him? I watch him watch them.

"Let's get closer to the water," Ralphie says, and they make their way down to the very edge of the river, settling in on the rocks there.

"Well," Vik says when they're all gathered close. "First things first." He takes a flask out of his pocket and passes it around. James takes a swig, Poppy too, even Angela. But Ralphie declines.

"You're saying no to whiskey?" James says.

"Yeah, I'm not drinking."

Vik raises an eyebrow. "You're not drinking."

"Nope. I need to dry up for a bit."

The flask gets to Ruby, and she waves it away as well. "You too?" James asks with alarm.

"Yeah. Me and Ralphie decided we aren't gonna drink for a while."

"A period following Mardi Gras in which one gives up one's vices? What a novel idea," Vik says.

"Actually, it's not a novel idea at all. It's called Lent," Angela says as earnestly as humanly possible, and James does a spit-take.

Then Ralphie gets out the jar and everyone goes quiet.

"So, uh…this is Kat," he says after a moment. "A little bit of her, anyway."

I'm watching them from the top of the rocks. Veda turns over her shoulder and looks at me. She smiles.

"I guess we should…say something?" James says.

Max nods. "We should tell her story."

"Tell her story?" Ralphie asks.

"Yeah," Ruby says. "Yeah, I mean, isn't that what we're good at?"

"On April 10th, 1834," Vik begins, and everyone laughs. That's the date of the LaLaurie fire, a date every tour guide knows by heart. "Oh wait, I'm thinking of something else. When was Kat born, anybody know her birthday?"

"November eleventh," Ralphie says. "Not sure what year, though."

"That's fine. Just go with it."

"Okay, so on November eleventh, 1990-something," Ralphie continues, "A baby named Kat Irving was born in Shreveport. A town she described as 'the toilet of Louisiana,' and begged us never to go there."

"Don't worry, girl, I won't," James says, raising his eyes to heaven.

"Anyway, her mom died when she was born, so she was raised by her dad."

"Holy shit, really? I didn't know that," Vik says.

"Yep. Single dad. They had a weird relationship, though. He was crazy."

"Like, cuckoo crazy?" Sofia asks.

"Yeah. She was pretty sure he was mentally ill."

"Yikes," James says. Yikes is right.

"She was an only child, right?" Ruby asks.

"Mmhmm. And kind of a weirdo, always got bullied by her classmates."

"Weren't we all…" Angela says.

"I remember she said people always thought she was a freak, and by high school, she just gave up trying to be anything else."

"Didn't she deal drugs?" Vik asks.

"Yep," Ralphie says. "Started when her dad was in jail."

"Her dad went to jail?"

"For a minute," Ruby says. "She was in foster care or something."

"Almost went to juvie, at one point," Ralphie adds. "And when her dad got out of jail, he was even worse than before."

I had a boyfriend, then. My dad told me, "Whenever you look into his eyes, you'll really be looking into mine."

"She moved out, right? When she was like seventeen?"

"Yeah," Ralphie nods. "She didn't want to live with him anymore, but she didn't want to go back to foster care, so she just sort of ended up on the streets for six months."

"Shit, really?" Sofia asks. "I thought she went to college."

"She did," Vik says. "Southeastern. Just for a couple years, though."

"Oh, I thought about applying there," Sofia says.

"Why don't you?" Max asks.

"I'm too old."

"Well, how about I apply with you, then, and we'll both go. I always wanted a degree in the Classics."

"Max," she giggles.

"Come on, we'll live in the dorms," he smiles. "Go to keggers."

"Stay on topic, people," Vik barks.

"Right," Ralphie says. "So, yeah, Kat went to college, but she dropped out after like two and a half years."

That's right. Went to school just long enough to bog myself down in debt for the first decade or so of my adult life. Not that a degree would have done much for me anyway. Philosophy? Yeah, right. Instead, I met a boy and decided to follow him to New Orleans. My dad, who couldn't decide whether I was the cause of all his problems or his only hope for a meaningful human relationship, tried to stop me by telling me he had cancer. Later, I found out that was a lie. I didn't really speak to him after that, told him I was done. Which was hard because I loved him. You never stop loving your dad, no matter how shitty a person he is.

"How'd she get here?" Max asks. "Anyone know?"

"Came down with some gutterpunk, I think." Poppy says.

That's a good word for him. The guy, Billy, was a drifter—one of these trust-fund kids who ride the rails from city to city, lounging around obstructing sidewalks with their beat-up instruments and unneutered dogs, thinking they're terribly wise and brave. It didn't take me long to figure out Billy wasn't anything but unshowered.

"They broke up pretty quick," Ruby says. "But she stayed in New Orleans."

"So, when did she start giving tours?" Sofia asks.

"Around the same time I did," James says. "We trained together."

"Wait, Sofia, did you not know her?" Veda asks.

"Barely. I started just a couple weeks before…you know. She was nice to me, though."

"She was always nice to the noobs," Ruby says.

Veda smiles. "Yeah, she was awesome. She finished my tour for me one time when these people were being jerks."

I remember that; those guys were assholes. They laughed at her and harassed her with a bunch of transphobic bullshit, and I found her at the bar break in the Lafitte's courtyard, sobbing. The fact that people will treat someone that way, for no reason at all...I remember how angry I was.

"It was the nicest thing anyone had ever done for me," Veda adds, more quietly.

Ralphie smiles. "Yeah, she used to keep the orange envelopes from parking tickets and stick them on my windshield but put nice little notes in them. Stuff like, *Have a great day*, or, *You are loved*."

I didn't think he knew who was leaving those.

"How about this," Poppy says. "Were y'all around the night she tackled that fellow on the street? Remember that?"

"What? What happened?" Sofia asks.

"Ooh! I was there," Ruby says. "Kat was sitting outside the shop selling tickets, counting out somebody's change, and that homeless dude—with the headgear and the dog, you know the one—grabbed a bunch of bills right out of her hand."

James gasps. "I don't remember that!"

"Oh, yeah," Vik says. "You haven't heard this? She gets up and sprints right after him, all the way to Bourbon, and tackles him to the ground. Gets the cash back, comes back down the street all covered in gutter water, gives a tour twenty minutes later."

I'm not sure why everyone acts like this is such a big deal.

"I mean, let's be real," James says. "Kat was kinda crazy."

"James! You can't talk that way about the dead," Sofia gasps.

James shrugs. "Why not? We've all got our quirks or whatever; she was no different."

"And moody," Ralphie adds. "Don't forget moody."

"And she could hold a damn grudge. She didn't talk to me for a month one time because I made a joke she didn't like," Vik says.

Ralphie laughs. "Yeah, Kat was never one to let go, was she? I swear she kept a catalogue in her head of every dumb thing I ever said."

"Oh, she had dirt on all of us," James says. "She definitely told me off a few times for not being a good enough person."

I have no idea what he's talking about. I certainly never told James off for anything except refusing to let himself be loved and for being a dick to Ralphie.

Well. Maybe he's got a point.

"I always liked that about Kat," Angela says. "She held people to a high standard."

Poppy grunts. "Too high of a standard, you ask me. She could never seem to accept that people are just…people. And people are gonna disappoint you. You can't fix 'em."

"I think she figured that out, toward the end," Ralphie says quietly, fidgeting with the jar. "About me, anyway."

"Ralphie, stop," Ruby says. "Kat loved you."

"Poppy's right, though," James says. "I mean, the last few months… didn't she seem…?"

"Quiet?" Max says.

"Yeah."

"Especially after she came back from that trip last winter."

"That wasn't a trip," Ralphie says, looking up at them. "She was in the hospital."

"What?"

"Yeah. On psych watch. Big cuts all over her legs. It was horrible."

"Oh my God."

"Kat was—she did that to herself?" Vik asks. Ralphie nods.

"Never would have guessed," Max says, looking stricken.

Never would have guessed what? That I hated myself? That I was probably a little bit fucking crazy, courtesy of my dad's wacky genes? Yes, Max, one night I drank way too much and felt that dark veil settling around me and just couldn't do it anymore, couldn't look out at a world where everything was ash, and so I sliced up my ankles. Why? To feel something? Cliché, but yes, maybe that's it. Or maybe that's not it, no, maybe I was already feeling something. Feeling a big something. Pain, anger, despair, so much of it and so hideous that I couldn't look at it, couldn't think about it, couldn't talk about it, and the only way to not go crazy with the magnitude of it was to direct it all into a simpler kind of pain. Hot, wet, tangible redness. Because a bleeding body is so much easier to tend to than a broken soul.

"Poor kid," Poppy mutters. "I had no idea."

"You never really know what people are going through," Sofia says. Ruby squeezes her hand.

"But she got through it," Ralphie says. "I mean, she was really good and brave and...she got through it. She was okay."

Yeah. I came home from the hospital, lied to most of them about where I'd been, moved on with my life. The wounds scabbed over, became scars. That was all the evidence Ralphie needed. But I wasn't okay, not really, not before or after or since. I don't think I ever have been.

They're all quiet for a moment.

"We should finish the story," Veda says. "To the end."

"What else is there to say?" Vik says. "Kat was cool; she was our friend. She gave tours for three years. And then...shit."

They're getting to it now. The part that none of them want to say.

"And then, one day," Poppy says. "Last year."

"September third."

"On September third, Kat was telling her story, y'know, as we do. On Dauphine, talking about old St. Peter Cemetery," James says.

Ralphie nods. "And she's got her group on the sidewalk, and she's standing in the street."

"Because that's what tour guides do, we stand in the street," Vik says. "We've always stood in the goddamn street; it's a city regulation. Group on the sidewalk, guide in the street."

"And then some asshole—"

"Some *drunk* asshole—"

"Going forty miles an hour down Dauphine—"

They're all quiet. Ralphie's crying, Ruby too, even James. Shit. Lots of them.

"And it wouldn't have been so bad except that she only has one lung," Veda says.

"Remember how she used to brag? I'm the loudest tour guide in town, and I've only got one lung!" Ruby says. And I was.

"And her lung got punctured by her broken rib...and she couldn't breathe."

It comes back quickly. Mostly just the noise—there's pain, yes, a pain in my side that I still feel sometimes, even now, but the sounds are what stick. Blaring music, the high-pitched screech of brakes, a thud, a scream, people shouting, blood thudding hot in my head until everything else was drowned out. Voices fading in and out, cops, my group, the driver—"an accident," he said. I heard him wailing about it.

He was drunk. He didn't mean to hit me. Just an accident. A meaningless twist of fate.

"That piece of crap," Poppy spits. "Speeding through the Quarters like that, of course someone's gonna get hurt."

But I'm remembering something else now. Something more than the terrible sound and the pain in my side. It's coming back, jagged images, memories of thoughts—

Max shakes his head. "I'm a pacifist. But drunk drivers...I've got no sympathy whatsoever for someone who makes a choice to get in a car like that and ends up taking a life. Even accidentally."

But it wasn't accidental. No, it wasn't accidental, I'm remembering. *I'm remembering.*

I'm remembering that I heard him coming.

Here's the thing: when you've been giving tours for years, you're well aware of everything going on around you, even when by all appearances, every iota of your focus is on your story and your group. They don't realize it, but I'm always tuned into every possible distraction, every variable on my makeshift stage. I know how many people are walking behind me across the street, whether or not there's another group down the block that will need to pass behind us soon, and always—*always*—when a car is coming. Sometimes, if one passes behind me a little too fast or a little too close, the group gasps, maybe a mom in front makes a motion to reach out for me, pull me to safety. But I always know exactly how close each car is and exactly how much I need to move to avoid being hit. Even without looking, I know. I'll take a step forward, or two steps, or none at all, whatever's necessary. It's second nature to a tour guide. Ask any of us.

On that night, though. September third of last year, I guess it was. I heard the car coming. I knew it was coming. And I didn't step forward, out of the way.

I stepped back.

The memory hits me so hard I think I'd gasp if I still had breath.

I can't explain it, really. My group was nice that night. It was a Sunday, I think, and Sunday nights are usually pretty tame. I didn't set out that night with the intention of not waking up the next morning. So why, then? Why this sudden decision to move my body just an inch or two in the wrong direction?

You hear a lot about the instinct of self-preservation. But I'm pretty sure there's another instinct in all of us too, a competing one. An impulse of self-destruction, this dark little urge to burn it all down. Why else would we poison ourselves with alcohol night after night? Why else would we make the same shitty mistakes over and over when we know what the outcome will be? And why else—what other *possible* explanation could there be—would we insist on living in a city below sea level, knowing that someday the oceans will swallow us?

The void called to me my entire life. And I guess that night, I just decided to answer. Stepped over that line between life and death, and...*poof.*

"I think it's time, son," Max says to Ralphie.

They all have tears on their faces now, this little group of costumed people huddled on the rocks. We're still surrounded by hundreds of revelers, the cart roll has made it up this way and there's an *untz, untz, untz* bass line thumping from its speakers, there are shouts and laughter and a kaleidoscope of colors, everyone in costume, everything glittery, but they don't notice anymore. Their attention is focused on the little jar in Ralphie's hand, the lid he's so carefully unscrewing. *Don't spill it,* I'm thinking, and I know they're all thinking the same thing because that's totally the kind of thing Ralphie would do. But they hold their tongues, and he gets the top off, and he's sitting very still.

"You were my best friend," Ralphie says. "I love you." He turns the jar sideways, and there's a momentary shimmer in the air above the river. "Goodbye."

"Goodbye, Kat," Angela says. "Thank you for letting us be a part of your story."

"To Kat," Vik says, raising his beer. "May you live forever in tour guide lore."

"To Kat," they echo.

I notice Jeremy watching from his spot down the rocks. They don't see him, but he raises a hand too.

And as the ash drifts away on the breeze and into the river, a weight is lifted. The pain in my side goes away, and the fog clears, the fog that's been in my head for how long now? Six months, seven? Is that how long I've been sitting in the Rat, waiting for them to notice me?

They all sit there for a while longer. Then, quietly, Veda stands and comes climbing up the rocks, dainty in her little blue dress and Mary Janes. She gets up to where I am and stands next to me. We're both looking out at the river and the bright blue sky.

"They love you," she says.

"I love them too."

"Did you like the story we told about you?"

I think about it. "It wasn't really a story," I say. "Just a collection of experiences."

"Isn't that all a story is?"

"I guess so." I pause. "Did I really mean so much to them?"

She nods.

I don't have a body, or a face, or a mouth, but I know Veda can feel my smile.

She smiles back. "You can go now. If you like."

"Thank you."

The rest of them are climbing up the rocks now too. Krewe du Tour usually ends after the journey to the river, and everyone goes their separate ways, off to meet up with other friends or away to parties or just out into the great humid yonder to keep dancing and drinking and reveling. It seems that's what's happening today too. They're hugging each other, saying their goodbyes. Max's dog is wagging his tail, and Ruby has her hand on Ralphie's shoulder, and James just said something that made Poppy laugh. "Can we talk later?" I hear Vik ask Sofia, but her back is turned to me, and her response is unclear.

In twos and threes, they go away. First, James and Vik, leading the exodus down the levee. Max and Poppy, the dog between them. Then Ralphie with Ruby and Sofia, who walk arm in arm. Veda and Angela are the last to go. Veda looks over her shoulder at me, blows me a kiss, and is gone.

I turn and realize that Jeremy's still alone on the rocks, watching. His gaze wanders over to me. I'm not sure, exactly, but when his eyes meet mine, I think the corners of his mouth inch upward into a smile.

By the time I turn back, the others are gone, lost in the crowd. I am free, I suppose, to go where I like.

And so I leave the river. I go down the stairs, across the streetcar tracks, then back up to the promenade overlooking Decatur Street. It's a breathtaking view of the Quarter, with Cafe du Monde down to the right, and the mule buggies all lined up across the street so picturesque in front of Jackson Square, and St. Louis Cathedral there beyond, facing me, its spires stabbing triumphantly into the blue sky. I can see thousands of people from where I'm standing, surging through the streets, making the whole city vibrate with life. And I think of a story I used to tell.

Once upon a time in the French Quarter, there was a very happy woman. And she was married to a very happy man. They were so happy, you see, because they were terribly, beautifully in love. Their future stretched out bright before them, and every day, their love grew more and more.

But, as anyone who's taken a French Quarter ghost tour knows, it isn't always easy to stay alive in New Orleans. And one summer, when the annual yellow fever epidemic came, the husband got sick. Though he was just thirty-five years old, young and strong, he lasted barely three days before succumbing to the terrible scourge. As you can imagine, his poor widow was devastated. She dressed from head to toe in black, wept constantly, and every afternoon, she went to visit her husband's tomb, just to sit by it, to lay flowers on it, to mourn and reminisce. But one afternoon, it was very warm, and she hadn't slept well the night before, and so sitting by her husband's tomb, she fell asleep. She slept very deeply, for several hours, in fact. And then, at dusk, she was awakened by a hand on her cheek.

And when she opened her eyes, who should she see sitting in front of her? *Him.* Her husband, rosy-cheeked and smiling, handsome as the day they'd met. And he wasn't an apparition, no, he was real flesh-and-blood, kneeling there next to the open door of his tomb. The widow cried out with joy and threw her arms around his neck.

"My love," she said. "I've missed you so!"

"I've missed you as well, my darling," he smiled, and kissed her on the forehead.

And then, looking around the cemetery, the woman realized that she and her husband weren't alone. Outside the other tombs sat dozens of other people, all with the same youthful glow, talking and laughing beside the tombs.

"Who are they?" she asked her husband, wide-eyed.

"Why, these are my friends," he said pleasantly. "These are the dead."

"They look so happy."

"They are."

And then the woman heard a terrible noise. It was a loud, rattling, rushing sound, and it was only when she looked out the gates of the cemetery that she realized where it was coming from. There, outside on the street, was a vast crowd, shoving and pushing in the streets. But this was like no crowd she had ever seen. This crowd was composed not of men, women, and children, but *skeletons.* Dry, brittle skeletons, a giant mob of them, rushing past the gates at great speed, heads turned to look everywhere but the direction they were going. And the horrible rattling was the sound of these skeletons bumping and shoving each other, so hard and so carelessly that little pieces of bone were constantly falling off and clattering to the ground where they were trampled to dust. Horrified, the woman turned to her husband and asked if he saw.

He laughed. "Of course I see them."

"Who are they?"

"They, my dear, are the living."

"But they're all skeletons!"

"Well, yes," he shrugged. "You see, my love, that's how the living appear to us. Rushing by, day after day, so anxious to get to wherever they're going that they smash themselves and each other to bits without realizing it. And where are they racing to?" he said, gesturing around at the rows of tombs, the city of the dead. "Here."

"How terrible!" the woman exclaimed.

"Not for me," smiled her husband. "Because now, my race is run. And having finally gotten where I'm going, I'm more content than ever before."

They sat together for hours, the husband and wife, catching up, reminiscing, enjoying each other's company. But finally, as the night drew to a close, he told her it was time to say goodbye. "But only for now," he reassured her. "So go and rejoin the race, my love. But walk, don't run. Enjoy the time you have left. Because when you come back here—and I promise, you will—we'll have an eternity to make up for that short time apart." And as dawn's first light broke over the cemetery wall, the man leaned over to kiss his wife one last time, and then he was gone, disappearing with the night. The woman rose, slipped out of the cemetery gates, and returned to the world of the living, back to her life, determined not to waste a moment of it.

It is such a precious thing, after all.

That story was my favorite. I'd do it at St. Ann and Dauphine, where St. Peter Cemetery used to be, at the very end of my tour. I go through it in my mind now, word by word, every sentence polished by repetition like water over a stone. But I'm realizing that there's something my favorite ghost story leaves out.

Because I've been watching the parade of skeletons, watching them ever so carefully from my dark little corner in the tour guide bar now that I have no race of my own to run. And yes, they do rush around terribly, and yes, little pieces of them do get knocked off and clatter to the ground. But most of the time, they diligently pick those pieces up again, and try to put them back in the right places. And sometimes they hold out their precious shards to others, whose own have shattered into dust.

Mardi Gras ends at midnight. Of course, it doesn't really, nothing truly ends in New Orleans, especially a party. But at midnight, the mounted police will ride through the streets and make a big commotion and tell everyone to go away, and ultimately, they will, maybe not till three or four in the morning, but they'll get tired eventually. And tomorrow or the next day, the tourists will drag themselves out to the airport with their suitcases full of beads and pralines and chicory coffee and go home. And for weeks, months, hell, probably the rest of their lives, whenever they're stuck in traffic or struggling to warm up under cold gray skies or sitting alone in their cubicles, watching their lives tick by, they'll dream of their time in New Orleans. That week they spent drinking in the streets and making friends with strangers and having shiny objects thrown at them and listening to ghost stories and living. Just living. And today, on Fat Tuesday, celebrating living like only a dying city can.

But for the locals, well. That's a different story. We don't stay out until three or four AM or even midnight on Mardi Gras because it's been Carnival Season since January, and we've already been partying for six weeks straight. We turn in at 4:00 in the afternoon, maybe five or six if it's really a good one. We don't need to make quite as much of a fuss about it because for us, Mardi Gras isn't so huge a departure from daily life. Bourbon Street is always just half a block away, and we'll get into costume again for Jazz Fest and Halloween and Thanksgiving and just any night that we feel like it, honestly, and Ruby usually has drugs if you want them, and the drinks at the Rat are always half off for tour guides, and all it really takes to turn a bad day around is a good two hours telling ghost stories to strangers. And just living—sloppily, desperately, zero fucks given—it's not something we need a holiday to do. It's all we were really good at to begin with.

I look down at the vast throng of humanity on the streets below me. As the shape of the Mardi Gras mass shifts and moves and undulates, masks and costumes and bodies and hearts marking time and space, I can feel it for the first time ever. The pulse, the one universal heartbeat. But I'm not part of that heartbeat now. Not anymore. I can see it clearly now for the first time in all these months. There are two worlds, theirs and mine, the something of life and the nothing of death. I made a decision, and I crossed that line. I can't go back.

You can go now, Veda told me. It's time. I can feel it, the desire to depart, a pulling sensation deep in my core. I close my eyes, and there is nothing. I am not here; I am not anywhere. This is what I always felt beckoning me from the other side, this mode of being that isn't being at all: no thoughts, no suffering, no chaos, no pain. There, I'm sure, I will be comfortable. There I will find rest.

But I can't do it.

I open my eyes again. Because now there is another sensation, a different kind of tug, more insistent, and it's taking me down the stairs to street level, across Decatur, back to the crowd in Jackson Square. I move dreamlike through the rowdy living bodies, taking in the sound and color. It's been so long since I've been outside.

And I'm feeling something else now, something I haven't felt since that Sunday night when I stepped backward and ended my life. It takes me a moment to put my finger on what it is, this strange and pleasant sensation. It's warmth. I am feeling warmth. Not the warmth of the sun, but the warmth of these bodies all around me. I can't touch them, exactly, but the same way they say you feel cold if you put your hand through a ghost, I seem to feel warm when I get close to the living.

Because here in the French Quarter, the two worlds aren't quite so separate after all, are they? The line between life and death is more of a blurry smudge here, and maybe it's because all these tour guides spend so much time talking about dead people, or maybe it's because once New Orleans gets ahold of your soul, it never lets go, or maybe it's just the damn humidity, creating some sort of atmospheric barrier that prevents ascension or damnation. But there's a coexistence. The living are on the streets, and the dead are in the ground below and the air above, and I, Kat Irving, am still here.

And I will stay. I will walk the streets of the French Quarter, I will smell the vomit on Bourbon Street and hear the Cathedral bells ring on Mardi Gras day, I will be here with Julie and the Sultan and the Casket Girls and the rest of them, till the end of it, till the gulf rises and the levees break and New Orleans sinks into the sea. I will sit with my friends in the Quarter Rat as they age with this living, dying city, and as they tell stories of ghosts, I will tell stories of them.

Three hundred years of history. And now I have become it.

THE END

ACKNOWLEDGEMENTS

My deepest gratitude to Lance and everyone at April Gloaming for taking a chance on this strange little cast of characters and sending them forth into the world. Not every author finds a home for their debut novel, and I am thrilled to be working with such a top-notch press.

Special thanks to my Patreon supporters, who so generously helped me through tough pandemic times and continue to believe in my work: Alix Briggs, James Brown, Rebecca Gehman, Beth Grobman, Rachel Kamischke, Rachel Konchinsky-Pate, David Littlejohn, Michelle Littlejohn, Al Luna, Megen Nardo Smith, Janine Repka, Scott Smith, and Terry Sullivan. Your support means the world. Thank you to my beta readers for your time and feedback: Sarah Akers, Katherine Cartusciello, Linnea Gregg, Sarah Harburg-Petrich, Connie Immerzeel Newton, and others. And thank you to my friend and mentor, Michael Bourne, for teaching me the ins and outs of the industry and always pushing me to become a better writer.

I am very grateful for my job at Haunted History Tours, without which this book wouldn't exist. To all the beautiful and strange people I have sat by the river with over the years—Randy, Starr, Gabe, Trent, Lucy, Kyle, Jack, Drew, Rose, Claire, Sarahbelle, and all the rest—thank you for your friendship and inspiration.

Most of all, thank you to my family. To Duwan and Greg for your love and support, and to my mom and Andy for always believing in me so fiercely. To Ian, for being my biggest fan, best friend, and deepest love.

Finally: New Orleans, thank you for your magic. This one's for you.

❦

PHOTO BY LOUIS MAISTROS

ARIADNE BLAYDE is a New Orleans-based fiction writer and playwright. Her play "The Other Room" won the VSA Playwright Discovery Award and has been produced hundreds of times around the world, and her fiction has been shortlisted by the Tennessee Williams Festival, the Saints and Sinners Festival, and more. Her short stories have been published in Parhelion Literary Magazine, the Fountain Magazine, and various anthologies; her story "Shinichi's Tricycle" won the 2020 Quantum Shorts Competition's People's Choice Award.

Ariadne moonlights as a ghost tour guide and jazz singer in the French Quarter.

www.ariadneblayde.com